Sweet TEMPTATION

ALEXANDRA MOODY

Developmental Editing by Pete Thompson
Proofreading & Copy-editing by Kelly Hartigan (XterraWeb)
editing.xterraweb.com

ISBN: 9798366975209

CHAPTER ONE

I thought I knew what heartbreak was. I'd experienced the hurt and betrayal of a relationship ending in disaster once before, so I was familiar with the empty feeling that came from my chest being torn open and my heart ripped out. Somehow though, this time felt worse. I'd foolishly trusted Noah with my slowly healing heart only for him to take a hammer to the cracks, shattering the fragile pieces until they were nothing more than specks of dust.

I let out a long sigh as I stared up at the night sky. It was dark and completely clear tonight, and the stars were so bright it almost felt like they were mocking me from above. Why couldn't I be a star? They were perfect and untouchable, and they never had to deal with pain or sorrow.

A low chuckle came from beside me, and I glanced over to find Wes had turned his head and was watching me rather than the sky. It was just the two of us. We were resting on the hood of his car in the middle of a field. He had found me crying alone in the courtyard after Noah broke up with me and had whisked me away. He hadn't pressured me to explain why I was so upset. He just listened to me when I said I wanted to leave the ball and get as far away from the school as possible.

I'd had no idea where Wes was planning to take me. I hadn't really cared. I would have happily gone anywhere to get away from the school, but the quiet field he had chosen was the perfect place. The long grasses rustled pleasantly in the breeze, and though we were only a ten-minute trip from Weybridge Academy, it felt like we were a million miles from civilization. It was peaceful out here and, until now, Wes had stayed silent, giving me space to work through whatever it was he thought I was going through.

"Is something funny?" I asked, tugging his suit jacket in closer around me as the evening air danced across my skin. Wes had to be cold without his jacket, but he had refused to take it back when I'd offered it to him. I didn't have the energy to argue.

"You're scowling at the stars like they've done something to piss you off."

"Yeah, well, maybe they have." I threw another scowl up at the sky. "It feels like they are rubbing their happy, sparkling butts in my face."

"I didn't know stars had butts."

"Oh, they do," I replied, rolling to my side so I could look directly at Wes. "They're big balls of gas, after all. And we all know where gas comes from…"

Wes laughed, and I somehow managed a small grin in response. It quickly fell from my lips though. How could I smile after everything that had happened tonight?

"So, Matthew LaFleur is your father," Wes said.

Now that we'd broken the silence, Wes was probably eager to start asking questions. I wasn't surprised this was the first one he ventured, having seen the stunned look on his face when Matthew had introduced himself at the ball earlier.

I slowly nodded in reply. "He is." I hoped my short response was enough to deter Wes from digging any deeper. I wasn't particularly interested in talking about my father, but I had to admit it was damn sight better than lying here thinking about Noah.

"Why didn't you tell anyone?" Wes's voice was soft, and I knew he wasn't annoyed about being kept in the dark. It seemed he was just trying to understand.

"It's not like I was keeping it a secret. It's just that I barely know the man, and I never thought to bring it up. He doesn't feel like my dad, so why would I say anything?"

"That makes sense," Wes said, but his head was tilted as though he was still considering my response.

"What?"

"I was just thinking a lot of people at school will be surprised. You'll probably find them all clambering to be your friend now that you're a LaFleur."

"I'm not a LaFleur." My response was immediate, and my defensive tone caught me off guard. I took a quick, calming breath before I tried to explain. "Just because Matthew LaFleur is my father, it doesn't mean I'm a LaFleur," I said more gently. "Surely the kids at school won't care who he is?"

"A lot of them might. Your father has a lot of success and influence in our world."

That was just it. This was Wes's world, not mine. And I didn't care one bit how much influence someone's parents had. In my view, a person's worth came from their actions, not their DNA. Apparently, I was in the minority when it came to that opinion though. At least, around here I was.

"This isn't my world," I muttered.

Wes frowned and nodded, as though he was thinking of a different way to get his point across.

"All I'm saying is that The LaFleur Corporation is just as big and well-known as Hastings Laboratories. And look at how people around here treat Noah. The fact that Matthew LaFleur is involved with Weybridge Academy now won't go unnoticed by the kids or the parents."

"As long as *I* can go back to being unnoticed, then I don't care."

Wes smiled at me but shook his head slightly. I guess that meant I was out of luck.

"Most people at Weybridge would have been shouting from the rooftops on their first day if they had a parent as rich and influential as your dad," he continued. "I mean, Veronica never would have targeted you the way she did or teased you about your mom's business if she'd known who your dad was."

The fact it was normal, expected even, to brag about how rich and influential your parents were in order to make friends at Weybridge only made me more certain I would never really belong there. A wave of guilt washed over me at Wes's words though. While I never had any intention of publicly promoting my messy family history and newly discovered father, I shouldn't have hidden the truth about my mom and my life back in Rapid Bay. She's the parent I should have been proudly bragging about on my first day at school.

"I doubt it would have made a difference to Veronica," I said. "She's been trying to take me down one way or another since the moment Noah first looked my way. If she wasn't teasing me about being a charity case, she would have done something else."

"Yeah, maybe."

"I guess I won't have to worry about her so much now. She's got what she wanted." The empty cavity in my chest seemed to ache as I uttered the words. I could only imagine how happy Veronica would be when she heard the news about Noah and me.

Wes hesitated but, sensing I might be getting closer to revealing the source of my tears, he continued. "Do you want to talk about what happened tonight?"

"Not really." I glanced away from him, struggling to stop the tears from welling in my eyes again. Just the thought of Noah had me turning into a pathetic mess, and I didn't want Wes to see me that way. But as the silence between us grew once more, I wondered if it would really be so bad to talk to Wes about what happened. He was going to find out eventually, and I hated trying to keep these feelings all bottled up inside of me. If there was one thing my first heartbreak with Levi had taught me, it was that sometimes sharing the burden with someone else lessened the load. My mom wasn't here to help me this time, so maybe it would be good to open up to Wes.

I let out a breath and the words tumbled from my lips. "Noah broke up with me."

"What?" From the shock lighting Wes's eyes, it was clear this wasn't what he expected. "Why?"

"Because his grandfather asked him to."

Wes's mouth dropped open, and it took him a moment to recover from his surprise. "You're kidding."

"I wish I was."

He was quiet for a moment before he continued. "Do you have any idea why his grandfather would want that?"

"I think it's because of Matthew. There was definitely some hostility between my father and Noah's grandfather, and I got the feeling this wasn't the first time they'd clashed. William Hastings told Noah to end things with me, so he did."

Wes shook his head. "I get that they run competing companies, but that's ridiculous. Why do you think they don't get along?"

I hesitated. Noah had been seething when he discovered Matthew was my father. He was convinced Matthew was the reason behind his family's ruin—whatever that meant. He had stormed off without giving me a proper explanation. All I knew was that, whatever the rift, it was enough for Noah to break up with me, no questions asked.

"I'm not sure," I said. "Our breakup was hardly a discussion."

"I'm sorry, that really sucks."

"Tell me about it."

Wes shook his head again and sat up, bracing his arms against his legs. "I kind of want to pummel Noah's face right now."

"Easy there, tiger." I gave him a soft smile and sat up beside him. I felt somewhat better sitting upright so I didn't have to keep looking up at the mocking night sky.

"I'm serious. Who breaks up with a girl because his grandfather asked him to?"

"Noah, apparently." The more I thought about it, the more heated I began to feel. Noah had dumped me and not even given me a good reason why. Did he really think he could just walk away from our relationship, leaving me heartbroken, and expect me to just accept that? I deserved better. I deserved answers.

My phone lit up, the screen almost blinding in the darkness of the field. It was another message from Cress asking where I was. The ball had finished an hour ago, and everyone had moved on to the after-party at Luther's house.

Wes's phone brightened at almost the same time, and he let out a deep sigh. "Sawyer's hounding me."

"Yeah, I've got Cress harassing me too." I bit my lip as I considered her text. "Do you think we should go to Luther's party?"

"We don't have to," Wes said. "I'll happily stay here all night if that's what you want."

I took a moment to think it over. I was so glad Wes had brought me here. It was exactly the escape I'd needed after everything that had happened at the ball. I don't know what I would have done if he hadn't shown up. I'd probably have still been crying in a heap outside the ballroom doors as the guests started to trickle out at the end of the evening.

I didn't know if I could face the party, especially if Noah was there. I felt like I'd only just managed to get control of my emotions amid the soothing calm that currently surrounded us. I was worried seeing Noah again so soon would only bring the pain, shock, and anger rushing back to the surface.

But, lying here staring up at the stars only had my mind replaying the events of the evening, recalling Noah's shock when he found out who my father was. The anger in his grandfather's eyes when he glared at Matthew and then at me. Most of all, I couldn't stop picturing the look of resigned certainty on Noah's face as he told me we could never be together.

No matter how many times I went over his words and his reasons in my head, I couldn't understand or believe what had happened. Gazing up at the stars certainly wasn't going to give me the clarity or closure I needed. As much as it terrified me to admit, Noah was the only person who could provide that.

"We should go," I said.

"Really?"

"Yeah." I slid from the hood of the car and landed lightly on the ground. The grass was cool and wet beneath my bare feet. I was probably getting mud along the hem of my white dress, but I didn't really care.

"You're sure?"

"Not really, but at the very least, it might distract me." I did my best to sound convincing, but even I wasn't sure I meant what I said.

"Okay. After-party it is then." Wes jumped off the car and went to open the door for me.

I paused before I climbed into the passenger seat and reached out to lightly touch his hand. "Thanks for rescuing me tonight, Wes. I don't know what I would have done if you hadn't been there."

"You didn't need rescuing. You just needed a getaway driver, and I was happy to help." He smiled. "If anything, you kind of rescued me tonight too."

I frowned as I tried to understand why he'd think that. Then I remembered his girlfriend had ditched him at the last minute.

"I'm not sure being your date to the ball counts as rescuing you," I said. "But I am sorry Sarah didn't come tonight."

Wes shrugged. "Things haven't been all that great between us. I guess she didn't see the point in coming if she had something better to do."

I put my arms around Wes and gave him a tight hug. "It's her loss." He slowly wrapped his arms around me in response. He didn't hug me too tightly, but I felt secure and warm, all the same. Wes gave really good hugs, and I felt like perhaps he needed one as much as I did right now.

The hug went on for a few seconds too long, and the two of us seemed to realize it at the same time. We awkwardly stepped back, refusing to meet each other's gaze.

"So, after-party?" he said.

"After-party," I quickly agreed.

I still didn't sound convincing, but I jumped in the car before Wes could point that out. My heart couldn't take another beating, and it felt dangerous to leave the safety of this random field where I felt somewhat protected. But, how much worse could this night really get? How much more of my heart was there left to break? Maybe if I stopped staring up at the stars and went looking for the answers I so desperately needed, I might be able to start putting it back together again.

CHAPTER TWO

The after-party was well and truly underway by the time Wes and I arrived. It was in the same clearing in the woods where Luther had held his last party, and tonight there were huge white lanterns strung between the trees that surrounded the wide-open space, and a live band was blasting out a tune on the other side of the dancing crowd.

Most of the students had changed out of their formal wear, but Wes and I were still dressed in our outfits from the ball. Wes was in his shiny black tuxedo, and I was in my flowing white dress. I hesitated at the edge of the clearing as I watched everyone dancing and having fun. I didn't know if I could pretend I was okay when I so clearly was not. It felt like everyone here would be able to see my heartbreak as plainly as if it were written in permanent marker across my face.

Wes gave my hand a tight squeeze. "Let's go get some drinks."

"Uh, sure." I still wasn't certain if I wanted to stay at the party, but if I was, a little liquid courage was probably going to be necessary.

His hand dropped from mine as he started into the party, but

I didn't move to follow him right away. Instead, I paused as I watched him disappear into the crowd. The small amount of confidence I'd had in my reasons for coming here was slipping away. I'd thought it might offer a brief distraction and maybe I'd be able to talk to Noah and ask him why all this had happened. The latter was enough to make me shrink back into the safety of the trees. Now that I was here, Noah was the last person I wanted to see.

I lurched forward as someone knocked their shoulder into mine, and I stumbled as I tried to stay on my feet. Thankfully, I managed to avoid falling to the ground and making my dress any dirtier than it already was.

"Oops, I didn't see you there, Charity." I recognized Veronica's high-pitched voice immediately. Her words were met with cackling laughter from her friends. "Although, I guess we can't call you that now we know you're actually Isobel *LaFleur.*"

How did she know already? Maybe she'd seen us dancing together. If Matthew was as well-known as Wes had suggested, our dance might have been enough to alert the entire school.

As I righted myself, I turned to face Veronica. The scrap of clothing she was wearing was barely long enough to cover her underwear. She had to be freezing. Not many girls would have been brave enough to wear a dress like that, but she had the build of a model and could pretty much wear anything. Even now I could see several guys drooling as they watched her. It didn't matter how hot she was though; her looks could never wipe away the viciousness that was always present in her eyes. They were a little hazy tonight. Probably from one too many drinks.

"Imagine my shock when your father introduced himself to my parents tonight and I overheard him talking about *you,*" she continued. "But don't think that changes anything. Just because your daddy happens to have money doesn't mean you're one of us. Once a charity case, always a charity case. We all know you don't belong in this school."

It was hard to argue with that. Ever since I'd arrived at Weybridge Academy, I'd felt out of place. I'd never be one of them, and I didn't want to be. Certainly not if it meant becoming anything like Veronica. It seemed Wes had underestimated her. Finding out who my father was hadn't dampened her vendetta against me. It seemed to have reignited it.

"This only serves to prove what a fraud you really are," she continued. "First you lie about your mother because you're embarrassed by her. Next you lie about your father."

She lifted her hand and tapped her fingers on her cheek, an exaggerated look of thoughtfulness covering her face. "But why would you lie about such a thing?" she wondered out loud. "Perhaps you were trying to keep Noah from finding out. Understandable, given the history between your two families. Still, I don't think he'll be very happy to hear he was being manipulated again."

My breath caught in my throat. Was Veronica talking about the feud Noah had mentioned? What did she know about it all? I felt the desperate urge to ask her, but Veronica was the last person I wanted answers from, and I refused to admit my ignorance to her. Instead, I gritted my teeth. "I didn't manipulate anyone."

She glanced down at her nails, ignoring my response as she inspected her manicure like she was suddenly bored by the whole conversation. "Anyway, I'm sure it won't be long before Noah learns the truth and breaks up with you. Then everything will return to the way it *should* be."

My eyes widened with surprise. She didn't already know Noah had broken up with me? How was that even possible? She had to have seen him when he'd returned to the ball. If she didn't know the truth, I was hardly about to enlighten her. I couldn't bear to witness the satisfaction I knew would light up her cruel features.

"Are you done, Veronica?" I asked.

She lifted her eyes to meet mine, slowly lowering her hand back to her side. "It depends. Are you done lying to everyone?"

The girls surrounding her all shared knowing smiles. They were all looking at me like they'd won. And I had to wonder if they had. Would everyone else at school share their opinion? Was I about to be outcast yet again simply because I hadn't shared private details about my family?

"There you are!" Anna gasped, looping her arm through mine. I hadn't seen her coming, but I couldn't have been happier she was here. I didn't tend to shy away from confrontations with Veronica, but I was feeling too broken to handle her right now. "We've been waiting for you to get here."

Anna was grinning at me, but when she turned and saw Veronica standing across from us, her nose scrunched like she'd just been hit by a foul smell. "Geez, Veronica, did your dress shrink in the wash or something? Seriously, you've got to leave *some* mystery for the guys."

Veronica didn't look even slightly bothered by Anna's comment. "At least my clothes are clean." Her eyes dipped to the mud staining the bottom of my white dress. "I guess you can take a peasant out of the village, but you can't turn her into a princess."

She didn't give us an opportunity to respond as she turned on her heel and disappeared into the crowd with her friends trailing behind her. Anna growled and started after her, but I grabbed her arm, pulling her back.

"She's not worth it."

Anna let out a slow breath and nodded. "You're right. We'll go get drinks and let karma deal with Veronica." She lifted her head to the sky. "Karma, if you're listening, I'm pretty sure I saw some poison ivy on the path here tonight. If you could help Veronica trip into it, I'd really appreciate that." She grinned as she turned to me. "Just think, she's got all that exposed skin…"

I shook my head at my friend. "That's brutal, even for you."

"Eh, she deserves it."

Anna took my hand and pulled me into the party. We wound our way through the crowd of dancing students to the other side of the forest clearing. There was a long drinks table set up near the makeshift dance floor, where Cress and Sawyer laughed as they drank shots.

Wes was there too, holding two bottles of beer. He turned as we approached and smiled as he offered me one of the bottles. "I was just coming back to find you. You like beer, right?"

"This is great, thanks." I took the beer, but I didn't take a sip. My stomach was swirling uneasily and I wasn't sure if beer was going to help. Ever since my run-in with Veronica, a wave of nerves had hit me, and I felt kind of sick.

"You're here!" Cress squealed, gathering me in a hug as she found me standing behind her. She was smiling so brightly, but the smile fell from her lips when she took a good look at me. "You look upset. Why do you look upset?"

I swallowed the lump that formed in my throat. I thought I was holding myself together quite well, considering. But Cress somehow seemed to sense something was off. I didn't know what to say, and it felt especially hard when my friends were all looking at me, waiting expectantly. I didn't think I could utter the words without breaking down, and that was the last thing I needed right now. All I wanted was to forget. So, I stole the shot glass out of Cress's hand and knocked it back.

The liquor burned as it made its way down my throat, and I scrunched my eyes as I shuddered. I wasn't a big fan of tequila, and I chased the shot with a sip of my beer.

When I opened my eyes again, I caught Cress wincing. "That bad, huh?" she asked.

"It must be something terrible," Sawyer added. "She didn't even have salt or lime with her shot."

"I don't want to talk about it," I said. "At least, not right now. Let's just focus on having fun."

Nobody pushed me to explain, and Sawyer happily handed me another shot. "Well, if you want fun, you're going to need another one of these."

I took the drink without complaint before dragging the girls onto the dance floor. If they had been worried about me before, they would only be more concerned now. I was absolutely terrible at dancing and normally did anything I could to avoid being dragged onto the dance floor. But tonight, dancing was the perfect escape. All I cared about was numbing the pain that radiated through me and fogging my brain so I could stop thinking about the boy who broke my heart.

I danced with the girls for song after song. And for a little while, I was able to forget why I was so damn miserable. But the pain never totally went away. My body grew tired, and my blood started to cool. The alcohol no longer ran hot through my veins, and the ache in my heart returned with a vengeance.

When it grew too much to bear, I left the girls on the dance floor in search of another drink. I wandered through the dancing crowd to the drinks table but hesitated when I reached it. As much as I wanted to numb the pain once more, I wasn't sure alcohol was the answer.

"You okay there, newbie?" I looked up at Luther standing beside me. My body stiffened. Where Luther was, Noah wasn't usually too far behind.

"I'm fine. Just searching for a drink." I gave him a tight smile, trying to hide the tension I was feeling.

"You don't look like you're fine," he said. "Then again, neither does Noah."

I tried to ignore the way my heart leaped and then plummeted at his mention of Noah. "Oh, I didn't realize he was here."

Despite the resolve I'd felt when I'd told Wes we should come to the party, I'd been doing my best not to look for Noah tonight. It wasn't easy, and I still found myself glancing at people on the dance floor or by the drinks table. My heart would skip a beat when I thought I saw him, but so far, there was no real sign of him.

"He's not here," Luther replied. "He refused to come tonight and went back to his room after the ball finished."

I wasn't sure whether to feel relieved by this or not. I'd been feeling sick to my stomach all night at the thought of seeing Noah, but there was still a desire to confront him growing inside me. Another part of me just desperately missed him.

"What happened between you two tonight?" he asked. "Because Noah was like a zombie all evening. You should have seen the way he flinched when I mentioned you. He refused to talk to me at the ball. He said it wasn't the time, but I know something happened."

I reached down and plucked the first drink my hand came across out of the ice bucket. I didn't intend on drinking it. I just wanted a reason to leave. "I've got to go. I'm sure you can talk to him about it."

I turned away, but Luther reached out and lightly grabbed my arm, stopping me. "Noah really likes you, Isobel. I've never seen him like this about anyone, or anything. I know it was probably a lot to see Veronica on his arm tonight, but he really wanted to be there with you."

I spun back to face Luther. "Veronica is the least of our problems," I replied. "You should talk to your friend."

His eyes widened with surprise, and he opened his mouth to question me, but then he stopped, a look of confusion and concern crossing his features. Like Veronica, Luther didn't seem to know Noah had broken up with me. I was also assuming he didn't yet know about Matthew. Perhaps I had a few more hours to savor before the whole school knew about both.

"Enjoy your party, Luther." I shook his arm off and walked away.

I briefly considered opening the drink in my hand but then placed it down on the nearest table. I was tired, and the party wasn't helping to distract me from Noah anymore. Now that I knew he wasn't here, the small part of me that had considered confronting him was also done with the party. All I wanted was to go to bed, so I hunted down the girls to let them know I was leaving.

They were coming off the dance floor when I found them with Sawyer and Wes following closely behind. I wondered if Cress could sense the pain I'd endured tonight because, as soon as I said I was planning to leave, she wrapped an arm around my shoulder.

"Okay, let's get you home then," she said.

I gave her a sad smile and nodded. Anna wrapped her arm around the other side of me, and the boys led the way as we headed back through the crowd and started down the track back to the house.

The twins quickly pulled ahead of us as we followed the lanterns that dimly lit the way. I suspected the guys were giving me some privacy to talk with the girls. As Wes gripped his brother in a playful headlock, I had to wonder where they found the energy after a night on the dance floor. Then again, simply breathing felt like hard work to me right now.

"Do you feel up to telling us what happened tonight?" Cress asked, as the noise of the party turned to a muffled beat. She said it gently, and I knew she'd leave me alone if I didn't feel ready to talk about it.

I blew out a breath as I considered my friends. My heart actually contracted in pain when I thought about Noah and the things he'd said to me. It seemed silly because I'd only known him a few weeks, but somehow, he'd managed to embed himself deeply into my heart in that short time. His rejection hurt far more than it should have.

As I looked at the two girls, I remembered Cress was Noah's cousin. What if she rejected me because of who my dad was too? The thought was enough to steal the breath from my chest, and I struggled to get it back.

Cress's eyes widened, and she rubbed a hand down my back as I started to hyperventilate. I couldn't lose both Cress and Noah in the same night. And what if I lost Anna as a friend too? There was no way I could survive another day at this school without my friends by my side.

"Isobel, it's okay," Cress said.

"Take deep breaths," Anna added.

They shared a concerned look as I tried to calm myself down. I was freaking out, but I did as Anna suggested and took some deep breaths in and slowly blew them out. I really didn't think the drinks I'd had were helping the situation. I'd been blissfully numb for a while there, but now every emotion felt darker and so much worse. Tequila was not a good friend. She was all false promises and bailed on you when you needed her the most. Tequila was a bit of a bitch.

"You don't have to tell us if you don't want," Cress said as I started breathing calmly again.

"No, I want to tell you guys." I knew they'd find out one way or another, and I'd never meant to keep my father's identity a secret. I exhaled before I began. "Noah broke things off with me tonight."

The two girls gasped.

"Why on earth would Noah break up with you?" Cress asked. "He's crazy about you."

"My father was at the ball tonight. When Noah's grandfather found out who he was, he demanded Noah break up with me."

"What?" Anna scoffed. "Why does it matter who your father is?"

"Apparently there's a feud between our families…"

"Well, that's just ridiculous," Anna replied. "What kind of medieval shit is he trying to pull? Who even says feud these days?"

I shrugged. I was as dumbfounded as she was.

Cress had stayed quiet. There was a look of confusion in her eyes, and I could see she was trying to piece it all together.

"You've never really spoken about your father," she finally said. "Never told us who he is."

"Only because I don't have a relationship with the guy," I explained. "He left my mom before I was born. Even *I* didn't know who he was until a few weeks ago. I wasn't intentionally keeping it from anyone. I just don't particularly like him or want anything to do with him." Although, after everything he'd revealed to me tonight, I had to wonder if my feelings toward him were starting to shift.

Cress nodded, and I could see she believed me. At least she hadn't jumped to the conclusion I'd been deliberately lying like Noah had.

"Isobel, I'm just trying to understand… Who is your father?" Cress continued.

My body tensed at her question. This was the moment of truth. The time when I would find out if I was about to lose both Noah and my friends all in one night.

"My father is Matthew LaFleur."

After Noah's reaction, I expected some kind of explosion from the two of them. To see looks of disgust or to see them shying away. Cress appeared thoughtful though, and Anna gave me a completely blank look.

"Who?" Anna shrugged. She seemed so blasé about the whole thing I might have laughed with relief if I wasn't still terrified to hear Cress's response.

Cress didn't immediately react and took her time as she

considered my revelation. "Matthew LaFleur as in The LaFleur Corporation?" she asked.

"That's the one."

She bit her lower lip and glanced at Anna who still looked clueless.

"What?" I asked. "What am I missing?"

"Don't look at me," Anna said. "Never heard of the guy."

Cress slowly returned to meet my anxious gaze. "The LaFleur and the Hastings families are business rivals," she said. "I remember my parents used to talk about it a lot when I was younger. There was always some new drama between the companies as one tried to one-up, or screw over, the other. From what I understand, they've been at each other's throats for decades."

"This seemed like more than just a business rivalry," I said.

"You might be right," she agreed. "You know my family doesn't have much to do with the Hastings family anymore, so I don't know much about it. But I do remember overhearing one conversation..."

"What?" I felt myself edging slightly closer to Cress as she hesitated. She wasn't scowling at me like her cousin had, and there wasn't anger in her eyes. If anything, she just seemed thoughtful.

"Well, it was years ago, but I remember once when I heard my mom and dad talking about it all. My dad said that Mr. LaFleur would do anything he could to destroy William Hastings. Something about the way he said *anything* stuck with me, I guess." She paused again when she saw the look of concern in my eyes. "They were just gossiping though. And it was so long ago. I'm sure your father isn't like that."

She was trying to reassure me, but my stomach plunged. If her parents were gossiping about my family wanting to destroy Noah's, then surely there had to be some element of truth to that.

I felt like I was going to be sick. Was my father the villain in all of this? And what did that make me?

"Seriously," Cress emphasized. "William Hastings is not a nice man. Even if your dad did want to destroy him, I don't think anyone would blame him..."

It still wasn't what I needed to hear, and it left me terrified my friends would want nothing to do with me. Even if they didn't hold a personal grudge against Matthew, maybe they would worry that I was just like him. That this apple hadn't fallen far from the proverbial tree.

It took me a moment to build up the courage before I asked, "Does this change anything for you guys?" My heart was in my throat as I looked at my friends. "Now that you know who my father is?"

Cress gathered me in a hug straightaway. "I would never think differently about you because of who your father is. Never."

Anna quickly joined in on the huddle. "Your dad could be the devil, and I'd still have no doubt about the fact you're the sweetest person ever. None of us are like our parents, and Noah's an idiot if he thinks different."

Tears gathered in my eyes as the two girls held me tight. I didn't know how much I needed this reassurance until now. I loved these girls so much.

"Uh, is this hug a girl-only thing, or are boys welcome to join the sandwich?" one of the twins called out to us from up ahead. Given the cheeky tone in his voice, it definitely had to be Sawyer. I'd thought he was too busy messing around with his brother to notice us, but the boy seemed to have a sixth sense that alerted him whenever there was an emotional moment that needed ruining.

Anna and Cress laughed as they drew back from the hug.

"Sawyer, learn to read the room!" Anna shouted at him.

He simply shrugged, his face lighting in a cheeky smile in reply. "Hey, you don't get what you want in life unless you ask."

"Oh, well, in that case. Sawyer, can you disappear?" Anna fired back.

Even I couldn't hold in my laughter.

Tonight might have been a disaster for my love life, but it only made me appreciate my friends more than ever. And I had a feeling I was going to need them if I wanted to survive the rest of the school year.

CHAPTER THREE

"Wake up!"

I groaned as Anna chirped the words into my ear. My head was throbbing, my mouth felt furry and dry, and my stomach turned uneasily. I'd never had a hangover before, but I was pretty sure I was experiencing one now. It was enough to put me off alcohol for life.

As much as my body hurt though, the most visceral pain was the one in my heart. I didn't want to be that girl. You know the one—the girl that fell hard and fast and then struggled to get over a guy. That was exactly how I felt right now. Like I would never fill the void Noah had left in my chest when he broke up with me.

I wasn't ready to face reality just yet, and the thought of opening my eyes made me bury my head under my pillow.

Before I could smother myself, the pillow was unceremoniously ripped away from me.

"Anna," I groaned.

"Isobel," she replied, mimicking my tone.

I slowly blinked my eyes open so I could scowl up at her. She was already dressed for the day but not in her normal casual Sunday attire. Instead, she was wearing a floral summer dress. It wasn't low-cut, and it actually fell below her knees, so I had to wonder if I was still dreaming.

"What are you wearing?"

Her bright face turned stormy as she glanced down at her dress. "Ugh, don't remind me. Cress lent it to me. I didn't have anything appropriate to wear, and she insisted I'd probably get detention if I wore my regular getup."

I stole my pillow back out of her hands and hugged it to my chest. "Appropriate for what?"

"Please tell me you know about the garden party today."

"Uh…"

"Seriously?" She shook her head. "Well, I guess you know now. Every year, the principal hosts a garden party the morning after the ball because a lot of the parents and alumni are still in town. It's always torture, but seniors are expected to go."

I let out a sigh and slowly eased myself up. My head spun at the subtle movement, and I knew I was in for a rough day. "We don't *have* to go though, right?" My head wanted nothing more than to return to the pillow it just left.

Anna shared an understanding smile with me. "Just show your face, and then you can come back here and bury yourself under the covers again. Cress has gone to get us coffees, so hopefully that will help."

I'd probably need a whole lot more than coffee to get through today, but it certainly wouldn't hurt.

Anna's expression softened slightly before she continued. "How do you feel today?"

I knew she was asking about Noah rather than my hangover, and my heart clenched painfully at the thought of him. My pounding head might be bad, but it didn't compare to how hard it was to think about last night.

"It feels like it didn't really happen," I said. "Like I experienced some terrible nightmare." I shook my head. "I don't want to think about it."

"Well, if there's one benefit to being dragged to an early-morning garden party, it's that you'll hopefully be distracted."

Unless, of course, Noah was there. Despite my warring feelings about whether I wanted to see him again, I'd decided it was a blessing I hadn't bumped into him at the after-party last night. The thought of seeing him again today caused all the same uncertainty to flow through me once again.

"So, jump in the shower," Anna said. "Cress will be back with coffee soon, and then we need to get going."

I understood why Cress had gone to get the coffees and left Anna to wake me up. Anna didn't look like she'd take no for an answer, and I didn't have it in me to try to convince her otherwise.

I let out a sigh and nodded. "Okay, fine. I'll be quick."

"That's my girl."

There were so many reasons for me not to go to the event, but as I got out of bed, I began to think of one that might make it worthwhile: Matthew might be there.

It was the first time I'd ever found myself actually wanting to see my father, but we had a lot to discuss. Before Noah had brought my entire evening crashing down, my father had opened up to me about his past relationship with my mom. After thinking he'd wanted nothing to do with me my whole life, I now knew he hadn't known I even existed. His parents had prevented news of my birth from getting to him and tried to pay off my mom.

Despite the shock, I believed my father, and it left me unsure how to feel about him. That uncertainty had only escalated later in the night when Cress shared what she knew about the decades of rivalry between my father's family and Noah's. How my father would supposedly stop at nothing to destroy William.

I'd only just met my father, but he didn't seem like the kind of person who would try to *destroy* another person. I had no idea if Matthew would be attending the garden party, but I had so many unanswered questions after last night I knew I needed to speak with him.

When I entered the bathroom, I was surprised by just how bad I looked. I knew I felt like crap, but my skin was pale, my eyes were puffy, and my curls looked limp and sad. Even my eyes were a duller shade of blue this morning. I had hoped a shower would help, but once I was done, I still looked like hell. I tamed my hair as best I could and even put a little makeup on, but it didn't seem to make much difference.

I emerged from the bathroom to find Cress had returned and was waiting for me, coffee in hand. She was wearing a similar style of dress to Anna, but hers was cornflower blue, making her reddish-brown hair pop. She smiled as she offered a coffee to me. "How are you feeling?"

"Like death warmed up," I replied. "Thanks for getting us coffee."

"It's no problem. I figured we could all use the caffeine boost after last night."

"Definitely." I took a deep swig of the drink, relishing the feeling of it warming me from the inside.

"Here, put this on," Anna said, passing me a dress that looked similar to her own. "Of course, it came from your magical closet that has every outfit a girl could ever need."

I took the dress, somewhat relieved I didn't have to try to figure out an outfit for myself. I had no idea what to wear to a garden party, and with the way I felt right now, there was every chance, if I was allowed to dress myself, I'd be leaving the room in sweats.

I slipped into the closet to quickly change. If my closet had been stocked with a perfect dress for the party, then maybe Matthew did know about the event and would be attending.

"Perfect," Cress said as I stepped back into the bedroom. She had to be lying because I felt far from perfect. I looked like a zombie dressed up in an unconvincing disguise.

"We should probably go," Anna said. "We're already running late."

I clutched my coffee cup tightly and followed Anna and Cress from the room. We weren't the only ones running late, and there were lots of other girls out in the halls and on the quad rushing to get to the event.

The garden party was held at the principal's cottage on the school campus, but when I saw the gorgeous stone house the principal lived in, I thought cottage was a little bit of an understatement. It looked like something out of a fairy tale. Vines almost completely coated the façade, and a wide array of bright and perfumed flowers bloomed in the front garden as though the house had been stolen right out of a picture book.

The soft sound of a string ensemble could be heard as we made our way out to the lawn behind the cottage, but it was hard to hear the melody given the chatter and laughter that overpowered the music. It sounded like the party had drawn quite the crowd, and I wasn't sure if I was mentally prepared to deal with so many people this morning. Hopefully, Anna and Cress would handle most of the socializing. I certainly didn't feel up to small talk or putting on a happy face.

A marquee was set up on the lawn with round tables covered in white linen dotted beneath the canopy. The area was already packed with students, parents, and teachers. Everyone was dressed far more casually than they had been for the ball with the women mostly in bright, modest dresses, similar to the one I wore, while the men tended toward slacks and button-up shirts.

As waitstaff weaved their way around the area with trays of canapés and drinks held high above their heads, I scanned the scene closely for signs of my father. I couldn't see Matthew among the crowd, and I felt a wave of relief when there was no sign of Noah or his grandfather either.

I quietly followed the girls as we went to grab seats at one of the tables. They were all laid out beautifully with fine china teacups and towers of sandwiches and appetizers in the center of the table. I was glad my friends didn't want to walk about and socialize with the adults. I could think of nothing worse right now. I gratefully sank in my seat and started to nibble on the end of a sandwich.

Anna and Cress were chatting, but I wasn't really concentrating on what they said. I was too focused on trying to make sure I could stomach my sandwich. Even the small bites I was taking didn't seem to sit well and swirled uneasily inside me. I wasn't sure if it was my hangover, the chance of seeing Noah, or potentially confronting my dad for answers that had me so queasy. It was probably a combination of the three.

"Hey, Isobel."

I swallowed the small piece of sandwich I was chewing and glanced up as Lily came to sit next to me. "Hey, Lily. How was your night?"

"It was pretty uneventful," she said. "I only made a quick appearance at the ball before I went to bed. I'm really not a fan of this weekend. It's all about schmoozing, and I'm absolutely terrible at it."

"Me too," I agreed.

"How about you? How was your night?"

"I've had better," I quietly replied. "Noah and I broke up."

Lily's eyes went wide with surprise. "Seriously?"

I nodded.

"Shit, I'm really sorry, Isobel."

"Thanks." I shared a sad smile with her. "It sucks, but there's nothing I can do about it. It's not like we were dating long."

"That doesn't mean it doesn't hurt," she replied. "I just can't believe he broke up with you. It was obvious how much he liked you."

"Not enough, apparently. He ended things because his family is business rivals of my dad."

Her mouth opened and closed several times like she was

searching for something to say. Eventually, she settled on shaking her head. "I definitely didn't expect *that* to be the reason," she said. "I swear, I'm never going to understand these people."

I couldn't have agreed with her more. Lily's confusion mirrored my own so closely, and I wondered if it was because, like me, she wasn't from this world of wealth and social climbing.

"Yeah, I don't get it either. I didn't have much choice in the matter though."

Lily reached out and grasped my hand, giving it a firm squeeze. "Well, it's his loss. He's an idiot."

"A complete idiot," Anna said, chiming in. "It's lucky I haven't seen him here today. I swear, I'm going to tear into that boy so hard when I get the chance he's going to wish he didn't have ears."

"Please don't do that," I said. I couldn't imagine how embarrassing it would be.

"What? He deserves it. I know everyone at this school thinks he walks on water, but that doesn't mean he can treat one of my besties like crap." She suddenly glanced at Cress. "Sorry, Cress, I know he's your cousin, so maybe pretend you've got earmuffs on."

"No need, I'm annoyed too," Cress said. "Noah completely messed up on this one. Screw the Hastings family. Isobel is worth a million of them."

"A billion," Anna added.

"A million billion," Cress said, making us laugh.

My cheeks flushed as I looked at my friends. They always had my back, no matter what, and I felt like I didn't deserve them.

Cress turned to me. "So, after all the drama last night, is your dad coming today?"

"He didn't say." I shrugged. "He always seems incredibly busy though, so it's far more likely he's already left town." I considered sending him a text to find out, but I didn't feel all that comfortable contacting him. The message would likely only get as far as Caldwell anyway.

"Did your parents end up coming last night?" I asked Cress. I'd bailed on the ball too early to know whether they'd shown up.

"No." She sighed. "I would have liked to see them too. I suppose I'll have to try and get them to come to the Halloween carnival next month."

"There's a carnival?" I sat up slightly straighter in my chair. I normally loved Halloween, but I was usually working at the café, so I wasn't able to really enjoy it.

"Oh yeah, it's the best," Lily said. "The local town hosts Halloween Fest every year. It's set up on this creepy farm, and people from all over the area come to it."

"The money raised from the carnival goes to charity," Anna added. "So, the school makes sure all the clubs get involved and help out. As you can imagine, the academy brings in some pretty hefty donations, so the town is always happy to have us."

"It's a blast," Cress agreed. "*Way* better than some stuffy garden party." She lowered her voice as she said the last part, like she didn't want to be caught badmouthing the principal's event.

Someone cleared their voice behind us, and as we all looked back, we saw my English teacher, Mr. Wagner, standing all too close and frowning in our direction.

"Ladies," he said before continuing on his way.

As soon as we were out of earshot, we all burst into laughter. I had a feeling Mr. Wagner agreed with Cress.

I'd been dreading the garden party this morning, but it wasn't half as bad as I'd expected when I got to sit in the corner chatting with my friends in the sunshine. We relaxed and talked and drank plenty of water as an hour or two went by. No one seemed to care I was hungover, and I thankfully didn't see Noah. I even sent a text message to my father. I decided to keep it light to give myself the best chance of getting a response, so I asked how the rest of his evening had been and whether he was coming this morning. Hopefully he, or Caldwell, would reply before the party ended. But either way, I actually found I was enjoying myself. It was just the kind of Sunday morning I needed after a traumatic Saturday night.

When Anna started trying to rank which of our teachers were the hottest, I decided it was a good time to excuse myself and find the bathroom. There was a long line for the one in the cottage, but I overheard one of the girls mention people were also using the bathrooms in a school building close by. I had to leave the party to reach them, but I wasn't against the idea of a short walk to stretch my legs.

I cut around the side of the house and was walking alongside the hedge that followed the perimeter of the property when I heard voices on the other side of it.

"I expected better from you," a woman said. "Your father and I have been here two days, and the boy has barely looked your way."

"I can't help it if he's not interested in me, Mother."

I froze as I recognized Veronica's voice.

"Clearly, you're not trying hard enough," her mother replied. "Where is he this morning?"

"I don't know. I'm sure he's around. Noah tends to do as he pleases."

"With that kind of attitude, you'll never catch his attention."

"I don't know what you expect from me. He has a girlfriend."

"*You* should be his girlfriend," her mother scoffed. "And you will be. You just need to get this *other* girl out of the picture."

"Yes, Mother."

"Now, we should get back to the party. There are still many people I need to speak with. I'm yet to see that intriguing man we met yesterday—Mr. LaFleur."

Veronica's mother practically purred Matthew's name. Perhaps Wes was right. Maybe the news about my secret father would be a big deal at Weybridge.

"And you must introduce me to his daughter," Veronica's mother continued. "I'm sure she will be an excellent friend for you to have."

Veronica didn't answer, but I could practically hear the steam coming out of her ears. The irony of Mrs. Cordeaux unknowingly wanting her daughter to be friends with the so-called *other* girl probably wasn't helping.

I heard movement on the other side of the hedge and quickly kept walking so I wouldn't be caught eavesdropping. I certainly didn't want to meet Veronica's mother, especially seeing as I was the girl who had, in her mind, prevented her daughter from obtaining the prestigious boyfriend she apparently needed so urgently. Veronica was calculating and mean, but it seemed like she'd inherited the traits from her mom, and I was surprised by just how strongly Veronica was being pushed toward Noah. For a moment, *just a moment*, I almost felt sorry for her.

I quickly used the bathroom before returning to the party, but as I was following the path back down the side of the house toward the marquee, I saw Veronica standing with her mother at the end of the path. It seemed they hadn't got far before Mrs. Cordeaux had bumped into someone she needed to chat with. She was laughing away with two other women while Veronica did her best to feign interest and force out smiles at the right moments. I hesitated as I watched them. I didn't want to have to speak to either one of them, but they were standing right in the middle of the path. I also didn't want to overhear another conversation that might make me feel any more sympathy toward Weybridge's evil queen.

Just as I was contemplating turning around and walking back the way I'd come, a hand wrapped around my arm, and I gasped as I was tugged from the path and into the bushes. My heart was racing from the shock, but it started to gallop like a bolted horse when I looked up into Noah's eyes.

"Noah," I gasped. "What are you doing?" He was still holding my arm, sending sparks flying across my skin, and I roughly shook him off. Despite everything he'd done last night, my body still yearned for him.

He was dressed smartly with a deep navy jacket over a crisp white shirt, but his blue tie hung loose around his neck as though he had been just as reluctant and rushed as I was this morning. His hair was a mess, like he'd only recently gotten out of bed, and there were dark bags drooping under his eyes. He looked as bad as I felt.

"I needed to talk to you." Despite the drained look on his face, his green eyes still bore into mine. Their sparkle was missing, replaced by an emotion I couldn't quite put my finger on. Pain, longing, anger. It could have been a mix of all three.

"So, you pulled me into the bushes?" The sounds of the party were muffled in the background, and we were completely shielded from view by the low-lying branches of the trees and shrubs surrounding us.

"I can't be seen with you," he said. "Especially when my grandfather's here."

"So, don't be seen with me then," I replied. "I'm going back to the party."

He reached out and grasped my arm again. "Don't."

His voice was low and rough, and that one word sent a ripple of emotion pulsing through me. His word was a desperate tug, pulling me toward him with more power than if he'd yanked me with his hands. I closed my eyes for a second and breathed in as I tried to forget just how much I still wanted Noah. How even now, every part of my body hummed with energy, like his presence was the battery keeping me alive.

It felt impossible to deny my feelings for him. To pretend I wasn't hurt. That I didn't still care. My emotions were at war within me, but I couldn't give in to any of them. Not if I didn't want to completely fall to pieces. I tried to burrow my feelings away, but it felt a little like trying to squeeze them into a box that was far too small. The lid wouldn't fit on properly, and the contents simply spilled out.

Somehow, I managed to calm myself enough, and when I opened my eyes, I had some hope my expression didn't display the turmoil that raged inside. I looked down at his hand, which still lightly gripped my arm, and he quickly let go as though he suddenly regretted touching me.

"Look," he stuttered. "I just wanted to say I'm sorry."

I let out a humorless laugh. "You pulled me into the bushes to apologize for breaking my heart?"

"You're not the only one whose heart was broken last night."

"I find that hard to believe. You chose to abandon our relationship the moment things got slightly difficult."

"*Slightly* difficult?" Anger flashed in his eyes, briefly overwhelming the other emotions I'd seen swirling there. "Things between us are more than slightly difficult. And I had no choice."

"Well, I seem to remember it differently. I didn't do anything wrong. I didn't do anything other than have the wrong family. And you *were* given a choice. I watched you decide, and you chose to cast me aside."

I'd been hurt and confused by our breakup, and the pain still radiated deep in my chest, but right now, my anguish and desire for answers was quashed by my overwhelming sense of anger. "Is this some kind of game you like to play? You reel girls in, make them fall for you, only to turn around and ditch them when you discover being with them might be more complicated than you anticipated?"

"I wasn't playing any game."

"You could have fooled me." I was breathing quickly, and my heart was racing. I hated this boy so much in this moment. I hated him for making me fall for him. I hated him for making me believe things could be different. But mostly, I hated him because, as he stared at me with those deep green eyes, I still wanted him.

It was so messed up.

"Look, just because we can't be together doesn't mean I don't still have feelings for you," Noah said. "That I'm not going to spend every second of this torturous year thinking about you." His eyes dipped to look at my lips, and I forgot how to breathe.

The space between us suddenly felt smaller as though we had unconsciously stepped closer together. We were too close now, and the air between us felt electric, like every breath I took was charged with furious desire. How could you hate someone— despise them to the depths of your soul—and still want nothing more than to kiss them?

Noah seemed just as torn. He was scowling darkly at me, but there was a hunger in his gaze that struck me low in my stomach.

"If you want me that badly, then what's stopping you?"

"You don't understand."

"Then talk to me," I pleaded. "Explain it to me, please."

I paused for a moment, pushing my anger and frustration down just beneath the surface. Although it still bubbled there, I wanted to offer him a chance to give me the answers I needed. The answers I deserved. But he wasn't looking me in the eyes, and he had the same hopeless expression he'd worn last night right before he turned his back on me.

"I have explained, Isobel," he whispered. "We just can't be together. It's impossible."

My heart sank. I'd thought it was already at rock bottom, but apparently it could still plummet further. He wasn't even going to try to help me understand? He was refusing, just like he'd refused to fight for us last night.

"Okay then, why don't I explain it to you, Noah," I started. "I thought you were different. But I can see now you're just like the rest of the rich assholes that go to this school—the ones you despise so much because all they see when they look at you is your last name.

"I would never judge someone based on the actions of their family. And I would never abandon someone I cared about because someone else asked me to. I might not know the intricate details of what happened between our families, but I sure as hell know I'm not to blame. And no matter what happened, it will never change the fact that you didn't care enough about me to see beyond it."

"Isobel…" His voice implored me. It was filled with anguish. "If I could be with you, I would."

"You can't say that to me."

"I know."

"You made it very clear we don't have a future, Noah."

"I know."

He was still standing so close, and he was looking at me like he wanted to be closer still. He couldn't tell me we'd never be together and still look at me that way. It wasn't fair. I needed to leave before I forgot the words coming out of his mouth didn't match the raw emotion in his eyes.

"Maybe you're right. There's no way we can be together. Not after this." I shoved him back and quickly escaped the bushes before he could befuddle my mind any further with his proximity. A cool breeze seemed to drive his scent from my nostrils as I stepped onto the path, and I was able to think more clearly again.

Screw this garden party. Screw waiting around to see if Matthew might show up. And screw Noah Hastings. I started walking away from the cottage in the direction of the dormitories. I hadn't been given the answers I was looking for, but I might have just taken a big step toward finding that closure.

CHAPTER FOUR

I woke early on Monday morning. I'd had a rough night, struggling to sleep as I'd been plagued by thoughts of Noah. I was still in so much pain after our breakup, but my body betrayed me because I still wanted him despite everything that had happened.

I was exhausted, and I considered rolling over to try to get back to sleep again. The thought was tempting, but given how active my mind was, I knew it would be useless. Whenever I closed my eyes, I saw Noah and the way he had looked at my lips yesterday. I didn't want to lay here and torture myself thinking about him.

I groggily pushed myself up and smiled when I saw Anna and Cress both asleep in Cress's bed. They'd escaped from the garden party not long after me and taken it upon themselves to distract me from the breakup for the rest of the day. We spent all of Sunday afternoon watching movies and eating ice cream, and we'd stayed up late into the night painting our nails and applying face masks. Anna had ended up crashing here, and it warmed my heart to know that, despite everything that happened with Noah, I still had some pretty amazing friends at this school.

I reached over to my bedside table and picked up my phone. There was a notification splayed across the lock screen. I had a message, and although the contact name said Caldwell, it was from my father. Judging by the timestamp on the message, he had sent it the day before. I must have missed it while spending time with the girls.

> Hello, Isobel, I hope you're well. Please accept my sincerest apologies for my absence at the principal's garden party today. I had to get back to New York for urgent business this morning, and I'm afraid it will keep me here for a couple of weeks. I know we still have a lot to catch up on, and I promise we will do just that as soon as I can get back to Weybridge.

> In the meantime, if you need anything at all, please feel free to reach out. Matthew.

It was hard not to be disappointed. It felt like he was avoiding me just when I needed to talk to him most. I was completely in the dark about what had happened between him and the Hastings family. It must have been pretty bad considering Noah had to break up with me. I was also still wrestling with how to feel about my father after hearing the history of his relationship with my mom. Now was just about the worst time for him to disappear to New York for a couple of weeks.

I considered calling him right back but then thought better of it. It was too early in the morning, and I needed to try to clear my head as much as possible before I spoke to him. I slowly eased myself from bed, trying my best to be quiet, and changed into my running gear. I was tiptoeing to the door when I heard movement, and I glanced over to find Cress propped up in bed.

"Where are you going?" she whispered.

"For a run."

"Now?" She struggled to keep the disbelief from her eyes.

"You know I like to run in the mornings."

"But it's not even light out."

I rolled my eyes. "The sun will be rising any minute. I'll see you when I get back."

She shook her head, muttering something about how crazy I was before burrowing back under her blanket. I felt a twinge of jealousy but knew I wasn't going to feel any better if I went back to bed. I left the room before I could reconsider. The last thing I felt like doing was exercising, but I desperately needed the peace I always felt when jogging.

The morning was crisp, and my skin prickled from the cool air as I emerged from the dorm. The sky was overcast with darker clouds gathering across the horizon. I was somewhat grateful I couldn't see the sun rising to greet the new day. I didn't need its happy face mocking me today.

I set out at a brisk walk, hoping to warm up my limbs before I started jogging. I'd barely made it across the quad when my phone started to ring. The sound made me jump as it broke through the silent morning air and my chest tightened as I wondered whether it could be my father. I hadn't replied to his message from the day before so perhaps he had decided to reach out directly. My shoulders relaxed when I checked the screen and saw it was my mom.

"Hey, Mom," I answered, slowing my steps so I could focus on the call.

"Oh great, you're up," she said, sounding far more chipper than I felt. "I was hoping to catch you before school started for the day."

"You know it doesn't start for a couple more hours, right?" This was early, even for her.

"Yes, but I know you rarely sleep past sunrise, and I'm starting work early today because I've got to spend time later training the new waitress."

"Ah." I couldn't help feeling guilty when she mentioned my replacement at the café. The new girl had been working there for a little while now, but Norma had said she'd been struggling, so maybe she was in need of a little extra training. I felt bad because my mom had more than enough to worry about already. It should be me helping her with the café. But I was never going to convince her to let me ditch school and come home no matter how hard I tried.

"So, how was it?" Mom asked, her voice filled with anticipation.

I knew she was talking about the ball, and it took all of my self-control not to give in to the emotions battling their way to the surface as I recalled the evening's events once again.

"Noah and I broke up," I said.

"What?" Confusion colored my mom's tone. "I can't believe it. He was so clearly lovestruck by you."

"Well, whatever he felt for me mustn't have been strong enough because we're over."

"But why?"

"Apparently there's some bad blood between Matthew and Noah's families, and Noah's grandfather told him to break it off with me."

"And he did it?"

"Yeah." I was really struggling to keep from crying now. I'd managed not to shed a single tear yesterday, but speaking with my mom made it all suddenly feel real.

"What happened between their families?"

"They're business rivals, I guess. I've been wanting to talk to Matthew about it, but I haven't seen him since the ball. Whatever the issue, it was enough for Noah to just cast me aside. I guess you did warn me."

"Oh, Isobel. I'm so sorry. I really thought he was different. I wish I could be there to give you a big hug."

"Me too," I said. "But I'm about to do the next best thing. I'm going to go for a run to clear my head."

"That sounds like a good idea," Mom replied. "You always feel better about things after running."

"Yeah."

The other end of the line went silent for a few seconds before my mother spoke again. "Have you had a chance to talk to your dad about anything else?" I knew she was referring to Matthew's side of the story about their past relationship.

"Yeah, we spoke at the ball."

"And..."

"He told me that his parents stopped him from finding out about me. He only learned I existed after his dad died and he found your letter."

We both fell silent again. No matter how many times I recalled what my father had told me at the ball, it always seemed to take a few moments to digest.

"How do you feel?" Mom finally broke the silence. "I know it's a lot to take in."

"Well, I believe him, if that's what you mean," I replied. "I feel like he really does want to get to know me."

"He does." My mom's voice cracked as she spoke, and she took a couple of deep breaths.

"Mom, are you okay?"

"Yes, yes." She sniffed, clearly holding back tears. "I just... I just feel so bad that you're going through all this on your own. Everything with your father and now Noah. I should be there to help you through it."

"It's okay, Mom," I reassured her. "I'm okay. You've got to look after the café. My replacement isn't going to train herself."

I heard her splutter out a laugh on the other end of the line. "I guess that's true," she said, though her voice was still rough with emotion. It had been sounding a little scratchy the whole conversation, so I wondered if she was coming down with a cold.

"I just want you to know how proud I am of you," she continued. "I know there's a lot going on, but you're going to come through all of this stronger than ever."

"Thanks, Mom."

"And I'll do my best to come and visit you as soon as I can."

"Okay." I smiled. "I'll hold you to that."

Silence fell over the phone call once again. Neither of us wanted to hang up, but I wasn't sure what else there was to say. I needed to get running, and my mom needed to get to work

"I'll let you get back to it, Mom." I finally said. "Plus, it's cold out here, so I better start running.

"Okay," she agreed. "But call me anytime. I love you, Iz."

"I love you too, Mom."

I hung up the phone and took a moment to gather myself. Hearing my mom's voice made me feel better, but the moment the phone call ended, I felt the gaping void of her absence. She'd been the one to get me through my last breakup, and I knew it was going to be a battle trying to get over Noah without her hugs, optimism, and pecan pie to keep me going.

I had no choice in the matter though. Mom was back in Rapid Bay and I was here at Weybridge. I was just going to have to muddle through this breakup on my own—as hard as that might be.

As I set out on my jog, I considered heading into the forest that surrounded the school. The idea of disappearing among the trees was quite appealing to me right now. But as I neared the worn dirt path that led into the trees, I decided not to take it. The woods reminded me too much of Noah. We'd had our first proper conversation there—yes, I'd wanted to kill him at the time, but looking back, I knew I'd misjudged him then.

It almost brought a smile to my face, thinking of how he'd gotten so thoroughly under my skin, but I started to scowl instead. Noah being under my skin was the whole problem. He was like a splinter I couldn't get rid of, wedged so firm and deep within me that I suffered from an almost constant ache.

I turned from the forest, determined to leave thoughts of Noah back in the woods where we met. Instead of following the trail through the trees, I chose to follow the path that bordered the lake. The water was completely still this morning and mirrored the dark clouds gathering above. The rumble of thunder thrummed across the horizon, and its soft growl whispered a promise of rain. I probably should have turned back, but I didn't care whether I got wet or not. Not when the alternative was sitting back in my room with my thoughts.

My runs were normally calming and therapeutic, but today I couldn't seem to find any rhythm. Every breath I took was painful, and my body felt far heavier than normal. I kept waiting to feel the peaceful bliss I usually experienced once my legs found a steady beat, but my mind refused to focus on the repetitive thud of my feet against the ground. All I could think about was how much everything hurt. Both my body and my heart were in agony. I pushed myself to run harder, hoping the physical strain might distract me from the pain I felt inside. It was no use though, and even once I was practically sprinting, it only seemed to be making everything worse.

I finally gave up, slowed my steps, and stared out at the lake. A cold breeze had started to pick up as the clouds above grew even more ominous, creating ripples that shattered the usually glassy surface of the water. My breath was ragged, and I put my hands on my knees, bowing my head as I tried to keep myself from heaving. I scrunched my eyes shut as I waited for my breaths to stop coming so quickly. No matter how fast I ran, I was never going to lessen the pain I felt inside.

I stood there for several minutes as my breathing slowly came under control. I was sweating like crazy, and my head was throbbing from exhaustion. This morning's run had to be one of the worst ideas I'd ever come up with.

When I finally caught my breath, I turned and slowly started jogging back the way I'd come. The chill in the air gave me goose bumps, and the increasing wind whipped across the lake. Just when I thought I might be finally finding a steady rhythm, my focus was broken by the sound of pounding footsteps coming up behind me.

I didn't look over my shoulder. Whoever was running behind me was moving fast, and I knew they would overtake me in a matter of moments. When they didn't come tearing past me and fell into step at my side instead, I glanced across the path to see who it was.

My racing heart tripped as I found Noah running alongside me. Of course, it was him. I couldn't escape him even when I tried. I'd followed this route to make certain I wouldn't see him, but fate had other ideas.

He didn't look my way. He kept his focus straight ahead, and his feet slapped against the ground in perfect unison with my own. I had no idea what he was doing. Why didn't he overtake me? Why didn't he turn and run the other way? Why, oh why, did he have to run just inches from me? My body buzzed at his proximity, and I had to believe he was doing this to torment me.

I was so tempted to stop. Either to shout at him or to let him carry on without me. My legs refused to cease moving though. They appeared to have a mind of their own, as if they wanted to help give me the space I so desperately needed from him.

As my irritation at Noah's presence grew, my speed increased and my breaths came in quicker. Before long, I was again sprinting as fast as my legs would carry me. Noah kept pace easily at my side, which only angered me more. He was tormenting me on purpose. He had to be. And I didn't want any part of it.

Just when I felt my legs couldn't move any quicker, I slammed to a halt. Noah stopped just after me. Thunder rumbled from somewhere in the distance, almost as if the sky was warning me to stay clear of him. Noah's eyes were pained and heated, and I wondered if he was as tortured by my presence as I was by his. Did he enjoy the pain?

"I told you to stop messing with me," I growled at him. "I don't want to play this game anymore."

"I'm not messing with you."

"How is this"—I waved between us—"not messing with me? Is this some kind of payback for who my father is? Are you trying to torture me?"

"I'm not. I…" He huffed out a hard breath and paced away from me before he turned and quickly closed the distance between us once more. "Can't you see how much I'm struggling with this? How hard it is to stay away from you? You may think I'm torturing you, but I can assure you I'm the one who's tortured."

Mere inches separated us, and those inches were only getting smaller with the rapid rise and fall of our puffing chests. We were both breathless from running so fast, but I thought maybe my emotions were just as much to blame for the way I was panting. Fire and lust surged through me as I stared into his green eyes. They were lit with so much desire, and I could see he wanted me just as much as I wanted him. That he wished for nothing more than to eviscerate the small gap between us.

It would be so easy to reach out to him. To pretend for just one moment he wasn't Noah and I wasn't Isobel and our families didn't exist. That we were simply two people who desperately wanted one another.

Would it really be so bad to give in to the temptation? To kiss him one more time, like my body so desperately wanted. Like I desperately needed. Noah must have been considering the same question because the longing in his eyes was mixed with obvious indecision.

"Maybe it doesn't have to be this way," he murmured.

"And how would it be?" I whispered.

He reached out to touch me, but his fingers stopped just

before they caressed my face. They hovered there a moment before they dropped to his side, and his gaze turned more serious. "I can't go against my grandfather, but what if he didn't know..."

I swallowed a heavy lump that had formed in my throat. I thought I knew what he was suggesting, but I needed him to be clear. "What are you saying, Noah?"

"I'm saying what if we stayed together, but in secret?"

"Noah—"

"It could work," he said. "No one would have to know. We might not be able to sit together in class or in the cafeteria, but we could go for morning runs and watch the sun rise before anyone wakes up. We'll spend our weekends down at the old boathouse or disappear completely and fly to Rapid Bay so we can lay together on the beach."

I clenched my eyes shut as the images he was conjuring up overwhelmed me. It sounded like bliss. Just Noah and me, shutting out the world so we could be together, just the two of us. I wanted to be with Noah so badly, but was I willing to have him no matter the cost? Deep down, I knew his dream would actually be a nightmare. My life would turn into a lie, just so I could be with him. I'd already made the mistake of hiding parts of myself, as though I was ashamed of who I was, and I couldn't do that again. The stupid part was, even if I did what he was asking, I wouldn't have all of him. I'd only get the fragments of a relationship he threw my way behind closed doors. I deserved so much better than that.

"It could work," he repeated. "As long as my grandfather doesn't find out."

I opened my eyes to look at him again. "You want me to be your dirty little secret?"

"I just want you." He moved closer to me as he spoke. His hands gripped my waist, and he pulled me against him. I pressed my hands on his firm chest to stop us from colliding, but we were just a hairbreadth from each other as he looked down at me. "I know this isn't fair, but I can't imagine my future without you."

I shook my head and lowered my gaze from his. "Can you really see a future with someone you have to hide?"

"Yes." He sounded so sure of himself as he gripped me tighter, but I didn't share an ounce of his certainty. "It wouldn't be forever. I—"

"I'm not going to be with you that way," I said, lifting my head to lock eyes with him once more.

"Isobel..." His gaze pleaded with me to reconsider.

"No. We're either together or we're not. I deserve better than some half-assed secret relationship."

He suddenly loosened his grip on my waist, and the distance between us seemed to grow, like the conviction in my words had struck him in the chest and forced him to take a step back. Ever so slowly, his shoulders sagged and his arms fell back at his side.

"Please, Isobel," he murmured. "I'll do anything to make this work."

"Anything?" I challenged him. "Can you tell me what happened between your grandfather and my father?"

His lips tensed into a firm line as he glanced away. I guessed that was all the answer I was going to get.

"Is it really so bad my father is Matthew LaFleur? Can't you get your grandfather to reconsider?" I asked.

"Yes. It's that bad." He sounded completely defeated. "And no, I can't do that."

"I can't try to fix things if I don't know the problem..."

"It doesn't matter what happened. There's no fixing things." His reply was abrupt. He seemed to be pulling further away now, and a look of hopelessness had fallen over him. The desire and longing I'd thought we'd shared was nowhere to be seen. He'd finally found his restraint.

"Right." I took another step back. "Then won't do anything to make this work, will you?"

"Isobel..."

I shook my head. He clearly didn't want to talk about why his family despised my father so much, but he couldn't just expect me to accept that. To just let it lie when he continued to tease me with his presence. I certainly wasn't going to give him a free pass to keep that up by agreeing to a secret relationship.

"Just stop messing with me, and leave me alone, Noah."

I took off running again, and this time he didn't come after me. I could feel his eyes on me, but I didn't look back. I wasn't sure what game Noah was trying to play, but I wanted no part of it.

There was still so much pain in my heart from our breakup, but the more I saw Noah, the angrier I was becoming. Every time he got close to me, he played with my emotions, reminding me how much I wanted him but also how what we had was gone forever. And now he had offered to have a relationship with me in secret. He wanted me enough to keep seeing me on the side but not enough to stand up to his grandfather and fight for me.

I was starting to prefer the anger over the sadness. Sadness only made me feel helpless, but my anger gave me a sense of power. It urged me to keep moving. To run harder and faster and put Noah so far behind me he became nothing more than a distant memory.

CHAPTER FIVE

Anna was gone by the time I returned to my room, but Cress was still in bed lightly snoring. She was absolutely terrible at getting up in the mornings. I knew if I didn't try to wake her there was a chance she'd snooze her alarm past breakfast, so I went over and gave her a nudge.

"Cress," I whispered, gently shaking her arm. "You have to get up."

"No," she groaned into her pillow. She was generally a pretty positive person, but only after her morning coffee.

"We've got to go to breakfast soon," I said. "And I need to jump in the shower."

"But it's so warm and cozy in here." Her voice was muffled by her pillow. "Please tell me it's hot outside."

"It's hot outside."

"Really?" She sounded surprised, and one of her eyes finally opened to glance up at me.

"No, not really."

Her eye scrunched shut again. "You're supposed to lie about the weather until I'm out of bed."

"I'll remember for next time."

She groaned but finally started to push herself upright.

Happy to see she seemed awake, I made my way into the bathroom and jumped in the shower. I was sweaty and gross from my run, and I worried about the fact Noah had just been so close to me when I looked like this. I threw my head under the cascading water and ran my hands through my hair trying to wash away any further thoughts of him.

Again, I'd failed to get any explanation out of him. I wasn't sure if understanding the feud between our families would change anything, but I felt like I had a right to some answers. My life had been upended. My heart broken. Telling me the reason why seemed the least Noah could do.

When I emerged from the bathroom, Cress was thankfully still awake.

"Something came for you while you were in the shower," she said, nodding at my bed.

I looked where she was indicating and found a small package waiting there for me. "What is it?"

"Beats me." She shrugged and walked past me into the bathroom, closing the door behind her.

I slowly approached the box, completely uncertain what could be inside or who it could be from. It was small and square, and the packaging was simple and white, giving no clue what it contained. I hoped it wasn't some sort of apology gift from Noah. If it was, it might be about to get thrown from the window.

There was a short note on top of the box that read: "I believe you will find this useful. Matthew."

Although it wasn't from Noah, my confusion didn't ease. My father was sending me gifts now? After everything he'd revealed on the weekend, I wasn't sure how to feel about it. A week ago, I might have felt the urge to throw his gift out the window too, but now I wasn't so sure.

I slowly opened the lid on the box and gasped when I saw a set of car keys inside. He bought me a car. *A car?* What on earth was he thinking? Cars were expensive, and given the Mercedes logo on the keyring, I had to assume this one was no exception. I knew it was probably pocket change to my father, but I didn't want to accept something so lavish from him.

I immediately took my phone out and did the one thing I thought I'd never voluntarily do: I called Matthew.

His butler, Caldwell, answered after several rings. "LaFleur residence." He sounded like even more of a pompous ass on the phone. The guy really needed to loosen up a little.

"Hey, Caldwell, it's Isobel. Isobel Grace. Uh, is my father around?" I wasn't sure why I sounded so awkward. It was probably because I'd never called this number before. I still couldn't believe I was actively seeking my father out.

"Hello, Miss Isobel. I'll see if he's available to talk. One moment, please."

The line went quiet as I was put on hold. A jittery kind of nervousness pulsed through my veins, and I paced back and forth in my room as I waited for him to answer. I barely knew my father, and I didn't know the first thing about how to have a conversation with the guy—especially when we had so much more to talk about than just the new car.

Just as I was starting to think about hanging up, my father's voice sounded on the other end of the line. "Isobel, this is a nice surprise." Matthew sounded genuinely happy I'd called, but I wasn't planning for pleasant small talk.

"You bought me a car?"

"Ah, it finally came," he replied. "It was supposed to be with you on your first day at school, but there was a delay. I'm glad it arrived."

He'd obviously missed the unimpressed tone to my voice. "You shouldn't have done that. I don't want you buying me expensive things."

"But you don't have a driver at school, so it's necessary to have you own form of transportation." He responded calmly, as though it was the most normal thing in the world

"We clearly have different definitions of what constitutes a necessity," I said. "I have friends who can drive me around. I really don't need one."

"I understand," he said. "The vehicle is bought and paid for now though, and it's in your name. It's up to you what you do with the car, but I would feel comfortable knowing you have it if you ever need it."

I let out a sigh. I had a feeling there was no way I was going to win this fight with Matthew. "It really is too much," I murmured.

"It's not even a fraction of the things I'd give you if you'd let me," he said. "I know I can't make up for lost time with expensive gifts, but it makes me feel slightly less useless if I can help provide for you now. Especially when I can see a need of yours I can fulfill."

I knew he was trying. That he wanted to build a relationship between us. Material things really didn't matter to me, but the fact he'd got me a car because he thought I might need it did make me feel slightly less annoyed. I couldn't bring myself to tell him I could barely drive. He clearly had no idea I'd refused to get behind the wheel of any car since I'd crashed my mom's one day after getting my license. I'd almost hit a dog that had darted across the road, and I swerved into a fire hydrant. By some miracle, I hadn't been hurt, but my mom's car never looked quite the same, and I'd completely lost all confidence in driving. Matthew's car was probably going to sit in the parking lot all year, but he didn't need to know that.

"Well, thank you for thinking of me," I said. "It was unnecessary but very kind."

"You're welcome," he replied.

I drew in a breath as I tried to gather the courage I needed for the next part of our conversation. I still had so many questions about why Noah's grandfather had reacted the way he did at the ball. What had happened between our families? I didn't think I was going to get the answers I needed from Noah, so Matthew was my only hope of getting any closure.

"There was something else I wanted to ask you," I said. "About Noah Hastings. You and his grandfather wanted us to end our relationship. You said that we could never work. What happened with you and the Hastings family?"

The other end of the line went silent, and I wondered if the call had somehow dropped out. "Matthew?"

"Sorry," he said. "I was just trying to gather my thoughts."

He went quiet again.

"And?"

"This isn't an easy conversation," he said. "Our family shares a troubled past with the Hastings. They are terrible people."

"Funny, that's what Noah said about your family."

Matthew let out a long sigh. "We're not without our flaws. But there are some things that can't be looked past."

"Can you tell me what happened?"

"I can tell you. But it's complicated. This is a conversation best had in person."

"Oh." My shoulders slumped in response. "Well, will you be back in town anytime soon?" His text this morning had indicated he wouldn't, but I hoped he'd relent and give me the explanation I wanted when he realized how long I'd have to wait.

"Not for a while," he said. "I've got a busy time with work at the moment, and I'm going to be in New York for the next couple of weeks."

I let out a sigh. "Surely you can tell me something?"

He went quiet for a moment, taking his time as he considered his response. "Only that the more distance you have from that family the better. They're dangerous, and I don't want you getting caught up with them."

"Dangerous how?"

"Just... Dangerous. I promise I'll explain in more detail as soon as I can."

"But I know Noah's not like that."

Matthew slowly exhaled, and I could tell he didn't agree with me.

"He's not," I insisted.

"I'd still like you to keep your distance," my father said. His voice was calm, but I felt like he was holding back. Maybe if he wasn't wary of my feelings, he would have given a more damning response. I got the impression he was struggling to stop himself from ordering me to never even look at Noah ever again. Matthew clearly had a very poor opinion of him.

A part of me wanted to argue with him. To try to convince him Noah wasn't anything like his grandfather. But what would be the point? Noah had made it clear he was done with me.

"Well, that won't be hard," I said. "He did what his grandfather asked and broke up with me."

"I'm sorry you're hurting," Matthew replied. "But I think once we've had a proper talk you'll understand why it has to be this way."

That proper talk was weeks away. Did he really expect me to sit here clueless for all that time? There had to be another way I could get the answers I needed. Clearly it wasn't going to happen on this phone call right now.

"Have you thought any more about the other things we talked about on Saturday night?" Matthew asked.

He must have been talking about the revelations he'd made as we'd danced at the ball. About how he'd never known I existed and how he wanted to build a relationship with me.

"A little," I admitted.

"Do you have any questions?" I could have sworn he sounded nervous.

"Not that I can think of right now, but we can talk some more about it all when you're back in town." If I was being honest, there were too many questions rolling around inside my head; I didn't know where to start. He was probably right about it being easier in person.

"I'd like that," he replied.

It felt strange to talk to Matthew like this. When I'd first met him, all he'd done was order me about. He still spoke with the same formality and rigidness, but I could clearly see he was making an effort to connect with me. Even though he hadn't told me what I needed to know, it still felt like we were communicating better. Mom had told me to give him a chance. Perhaps I needed to listen to her advice and give him the benefit of the doubt.

Cress emerged from the bathroom, and I knew I needed to bring the conversation to an end. "Well, I should probably go and get ready for school."

"Yes, and I have work to get back to." He paused. "Isobel?"

"Yeah?"

"Feel free to call at any time."

As I hung up the phone, I felt an unusual warm feeling in my chest. I hadn't totally hated that conversation with my father. He was always going to be far too posh for my liking, and I doubted he was ever going to be the kind of dad I went to whenever I needed a heart-to-heart, but despite the fact I was still in the dark about so much, it felt something like progress.

CHAPTER SIX

There was way too much attention on me as I made my way into the dining hall for breakfast. I'd caught a few people glancing in my direction and whispering about me in the quad on the way here. But that was nothing compared to the obvious curiosity I received as I walked by people's tables and they turned in their seats to watch me pass.

I kept my head down and tried to ignore the strange looks. Word must have finally got out about my breakup with Noah. The kids at Weybridge Academy were all obsessed with him and loved nothing more than to gossip, so I guessed I was the day's big news.

I should have thought about that before coming to breakfast on my own. Cress was running late today, but I really wished I'd waited for her. I did my best to ignore the attention as I headed for the buffet and began to load my plate with whatever I could find. I was hoping that the sooner I got my food and sat down the sooner people would find someone else to gossip about. At least I could be grateful Noah wasn't in the dining hall too.

"Hey, you're Isobel, right?"

I glanced up from my plate to look at the girl standing next to me in the line for the buffet. I recognized her from my chemistry class, but she'd never bothered to speak with me before. She was always too busy flirting with her lab mate or complaining loudly about whatever homework was set. I didn't think she even knew I existed.

"Uh, yeah..."

"I'm Mandy, and this is Trish." She nodded to the girl beside her who gave me a smile. "It's so crazy we haven't run into each other yet. How are you liking Weybridge?"

It seemed like a strange thing for her to say considering we'd been in the same class for weeks already.

"We should hang out some time," she continued.

"Definitely," Trish agreed.

"Uh..."

I was saved from having to answer as Anna appeared at my side.

"Everything okay here, Isobel?" she asked, linking her arm through mine.

"Oh, hey, Anna." Mandy didn't wait for me to reply. "We were just introducing ourselves to Isobel and welcoming her to Weybridge."

"How nice." Anna's voice was thick with sarcasm. "But you know she's been here for over a month now, right? What could possibly have sparked such a random act of kindness from you girls?"

The girls shared a look, and Trish scoffed. "What are you talking about?"

Anna didn't answer. She just raised her eyebrows and cocked her head at the pair as though she was waiting for Trish to answer her own question.

"Whatever, Anna." Mandy shrugged before focusing back on me. "Seriously, Isobel, if you ever want to hang out with me and my friends, you're always welcome. We have a lot of fun, and it would be nice to have someone like you in our group."

"Someone like me?"

She tittered a laugh and waved a hand at me. "Oh, you know what I mean."

I was about to tell her I actually didn't, but she kept talking before I had a chance. "It was nice to finally meet you, Isobel" she said, before turning and walking away with Trish close behind.

I glanced at Anna. "What was that all about?"

"Ugh." Anna rolled her eyes as she reached past me to grab an apple. "I think word about your dad finally got out. I heard some girls talking about it on the way here."

"They were only talking to me because of my *dad*?"

Anna nodded. "I'd say there's probably a ninety percent chance that's the reason. Sorry."

"Don't be sorry. I thought it was weird they were talking to me."

"They probably won't be the only ones," Anna said. "I'm sure you'll have plenty of 'networking opportunities' today."

"Sounds fun," I groaned.

"Oh yeah." Anna matched my lack of enthusiasm. "There's nothing better than people only talking to you because they want to use you."

"And I thought my biggest problem today was going to be people gossiping about me and Noah," I said as we made our way to our usual table.

"Actually, I haven't heard anyone talking about it." Anna shrugged.

"But I thought that was why I've been getting so much attention this morning."

"No, I'd say that's all thanks to Daddy Dearest," she explained. "A secret LaFleur heir in our midst is quite the scandal."

"Great," I muttered. I wasn't sure if that was better or worse than people gossiping about Noah and me. It was probably worse since apparently it also meant people like Trish and Mandy thought they needed to try to befriend me because of it. Was this what it was like for Noah? He was used to people talking to him with the sole objective of getting more closely connected to his family. I could see why he was so shut off because of it. I didn't want any fake offers of friendship either.

Cress arrived just as Anna and I sat down at our table. She looked a little winded and was still scooping her hair back in a ponytail. She'd clearly rushed to get here this morning.

"Sorry I'm running so late," she said.

"You're always running late." I smiled at her.

"Yeah, but I wanted to be here in case you saw Noah again for the first time. To support you." She landed in the seat beside me and stole a hashbrown off my plate.

My cheeks flushed because I knew it wouldn't be the first time I'd seen Noah since the ball. It wouldn't even be the second. I hadn't told Anna or Cress about either of those encounters though.

"Actually, you already missed the first time," I said.

"What?" Cress sat up a little straighter. "Did you see him already this morning?"

"And yesterday..."

"Wait you've seen him *twice?*"

I nodded.

"And..." Anna prompted.

"And it was a disaster. I ran into him at the garden party yesterday and then again on my run this morning. He refused to give me a proper explanation and said we needed to stay away from each other. But then he kept looking at me like he wanted to kiss me and suggested we stay together but keep it a secret."

"Seriously?" Cress asked.

"What did you do?" Anna added, her eyes wide.

"I walked away. I still have feelings for him, but I'm not going to kiss someone who broke my heart, and I'm definitely not agreeing to a secret relationship." Although, a part of me still wondered if that was the right choice. Maybe I'd acted too hastily. Surely getting some of Noah was better than nothing?

"That's good," Cress said. "I know how hard it must have been, but I think you made the right choice."

"Yeah, well, I hope he's going to keep his distance now. I'm not sure I can handle another one of these encounters."

"He needs to leave you alone," Anna huffed. "Why does he think he can try and kiss you? And I can't believe he asked you to be with him in secret. That's so unfair. He should be shouting his love for you from the roof of the school." She was getting so agitated I was worried she was about to jump up on the table and do some shouting of her own.

"Agreed," Cress nodded. "What was he thinking?"

"I'm not really sure he *is* thinking clearly right now," I murmured. "And, I mean, he didn't actually *try* to kiss me, but I felt like that was what he wanted." I shook my head. "You're right, though. He's not being fair, and it makes me so mad. I guess the small blessing is that when he makes me angry, I feel like I might one day be able to get over him."

"Yes, you should definitely focus on moving on," Cress agreed.

"What you need is a rebound," Anna said.

"Anna…" Cress hissed.

"What? Isobel needs to get over Noah, and rebounding is the quickest way. Not to mention it's fun too." She wiggled her eyebrows suggestively.

"I'm not sure that's such a great idea." I was completely with Cress on this one. I couldn't even picture kissing another guy, and the last thing I wanted at school this year was any more emotional entanglements.

"It's a great idea," Anna said. "I can start brainstorming candidates in class this morning."

"Please don't make a list for me," I groaned.

Anna waved my complaint away "You'll thank me later. Trust me."

I lowered my head onto the table and groaned again. Not only did I have to handle a broken heart, but now I had to deal with Anna throwing boys at me.

The sound of scraping chairs made me sit up again. The twins were taking a seat at our table and throwing curious looks in my direction.

"Don't tell me you've already given up on the day, Grace," Sawyer said.

"The day, the week, and maybe the year," I replied.

He looked sympathetic as he shook his head at me. "Don't let Noah get you down."

I shared a smile with him and nodded though following his advice was easier said than done.

"She won't be down for too long," Anna piped in. "I'm going to find her a rebound."

Sawyer started to grin and sat up a little straighter in his chair. "I know this is a very important assignment, so I volunteer as tribute."

Wes slapped a hand across the back of his brother's head. "Dude!"

"What?" Sawyer looked baffled. "I'm just being a good friend, and if making out with Isobel will make her feel better, I'm all in."

Wes cuffed him across the back of the head again and gave me an apologetic smile on behalf of his brother

"Thanks for the offer, Sawyer, but I'm not looking for a rebound—no matter what Anna thinks."

Sawyer let out a long dramatic sigh and shrugged. "Okay, well, the offer is always there if you need it."

"Uh, thanks." I thought he was joking, but he seemed completely serious. It was totally weird to offer to be my rebound, but I actually believed him when he said he was doing it because he wanted to be a good friend. Also, he seemed to have no problem kissing girls and it meaning nothing. He was probably a good rebound option if I wanted one—*and I didn't.*

"So, can we talk about something other than my miserable love life?" I said, hoping to change the topic before anyone else could make unhelpful suggestions for boys I should kiss.

"Uh, how about the new car you got?" Cress squealed. With everything that had happened this morning, I'd almost forgotten about the car.

"You got a new car?"

"What'd you get?"

"Can I drive it?"

Wes, Anna, and Sawyer all seemed to be talking at once. They were far more excited than I was about the car, and I worried I was going to sound ungrateful if I didn't match their enthusiasm.

"Yes, I got a new car. No idea what kind it is. And no, Sawyer, you can't drive it," I answered everyone in turn.

"You're no fun," Sawyer grumbled.

"How do you not know what it is?" Anna asked.

"My dad just got it for me, and I haven't seen it yet." I wasn't in a rush to go looking for it out in the parking lot. It wasn't like I planned to drive it.

They all started guessing what type of car it might be, but I stopped listening because Noah entered the cafeteria.

My heart leaped to my throat and lodged itself there, making it impossible to breathe. He usually looked so impossibly handsome, but this morning, he looked like hell—worse even than when I'd seen him on our run. The circles ringing his eyes seemed to have grown darker, and it made me wonder if he was suffering as much as I was with our breakup—not that I should be concerned by that. He'd made this decision for us. This was what he wanted. He shouldn't get an ounce of sympathy from me.

He didn't look my way as he walked over to his usual table. He didn't even try to sneak a glance. He seemed resolute to pretend I didn't exist, and as much as I didn't want that to hurt, it did. I'd gotten used to him sending me subtle smiles, to seeing his face light up whenever we were in the same room, and it was painful to know those stolen moments were gone forever.

As if it wasn't hard enough to see him again, I had to watch as Veronica went bounding over to him. Her whole face brightened as she started chatting to Noah, but he'd turned away so I couldn't see his response. He'd told me plenty of times he wasn't interested in Veronica, but it was hard to see him with her after they'd attended the ball together on Saturday night.

I felt a hand at my shoulder. Wes was waiting at my side. "Hey, I was wondering if you could help me with one of our econ problems before classes started for the day?"

"Oh, ah, sure." I shot him a grateful smile before turning to the others. "I'll catch you guys later."

I happily hurried from the dining hall and followed Wes outside. Although it hadn't rained on my run, there were still dark clouds overheard and the air was heavy with moisture. Wes sat down at one of the benches, and I took in a deep breath of the fresh morning air as I went to join him.

"Just so you know, I don't actually want you to help with the homework," he said. "It just looked like you really wanted to get out of there."

"Thanks," I murmured. "Seeing Noah was harder than I was expecting. I wasn't prepared for what it would feel like to be ignored by him."

"Noah's an idiot," he murmured.

"I know. It doesn't make it any easier though." I let out a long sigh. "I'm going to have to get used to seeing him every day, aren't I?"

"Probably," Wes agreed. "It will get easier though."

"Yeah, maybe." I hoped he was right. At least when Levi and I had broken up, I'd had the summer without him, and I didn't have to see him every day at school. I'd been devastated when we'd broken up, and yet, despite the fact Noah and I had barely dated, this felt so much worse. People always said time healed all wounds—but that didn't mean you weren't left with a deep scar.

CHAPTER SEVEN

Classes that morning were strange. Several students I'd never spoken to before came up to me to say hi, and even one of the teachers I passed greeted me as Miss LaFleur. He wasn't even my teacher. Wes had predicted this on Saturday night. He said people were going to view me differently now they knew who my father was. I couldn't understand why it made a difference. I was still the same person I'd been last week. It was crazy to think who your parents were could change people's whole perception of you.

The increased attention was only made harder when I still felt broken over Noah. I wanted to be curled up in a corner somewhere—not trading fake smiles with people I had no interest in getting to know.

While students I didn't know were suddenly interested in me, I assumed Noah's friends would start to ignore me now we were no longer together. But when I walked into math class, Luther didn't give me the opportunity to avoid them. I made my way toward a free desk at the front of the classroom, but Luther grabbed my arm and dragged me to the back of the room before I had a chance to pull out the chair.

"Sit, newbie," Luther said, nodding at the free chair and returning to his desk right by it.

I slowly lowered myself into the seat. "I thought you wouldn't want me to sit with you now Noah and I aren't together"

"You kidding, newbie? Math with you is practically the highlight of my week."

I glanced at Kaden, trying to determine if Luther was joking. Kaden just gave an easy shrug.

"So, you get your kicks out of disrupting my learning?" I asked, focusing on Luther once more. He tended to talk throughout every lesson, and it was a miracle I was managing to keep up with my math homework.

He gave me a bright smile. "I happen to think I make your learning more enjoyable. We all know you're top of the class."

"Except, I'm not. Even if I was, it would only be because I have to study my butt off outside of class."

"See?" he replied. "I'm a great influence."

I rolled my eyes at him but laughed. Luther was absolutely terrible to sit by in class, but I was secretly glad he still wanted to be friends.

As I sat with him and Kaden, I itched to ask them about how Noah was doing. Perhaps they had some small insight into the inner workings of his mind. I couldn't bring myself to ask though. Not when I was trying to put the past behind me. If my interaction with Noah this morning was anything to go by, he was struggling to cope as much as I was.

"There's going to be a party this Friday night at the boathouse," Luther said. "You should come."

"I don't think that's a good idea," I immediately replied. Surely Noah would object to me being there. Plus, I wasn't stupid enough to willingly go to a small, intimate party where I'd have no choice but to see him.

"It's a great idea," Luther replied. "Kaden and I both want to challenge you to a beer pong rematch."

I looked between the two of them. "So, you want to get me drunk?"

"I intend no such thing." Given the way Luther's eyes sparkled though, he was totally lying.

"I still think it's a bad idea."

Luther's expression dimmed, and he let out a sigh. "Look, Noah's got issues. I'm one of his best friends, but even I know he can be a total stubborn idiot sometimes."

"Whatever happened between you two, he'll come round," Kaden added.

I frowned as I looked between the two of them. "That's why you're still talking to me? Because you think he'll change his mind? Did he even tell you guys why he broke up with me?"

Luther shrugged. "He just said the two of you could never work because of your families, but I'm a firm believer that love always finds a way."

"And we're still talking to you because we like you," Kaden added with a soft smile.

"Yeah, you can't get rid of us that easily even if you are *a LaFleur*." Luther ruffled my hair with his hand, and I swatted it away with a smile.

It was kind of awkward talking about Noah with his friends, but I was somewhat glad we'd cleared the air, and that the boys still wanted to be friends with me despite my father's surname.

I didn't believe Noah would ever come around like the boys suggested. And I refused to devote even the smallest crumb of hope to the idea. Hope like that was dangerous, and I'd wasted far too much time hoping Levi would realize his mistake during my last breakup. No, my time was far better served focusing on moving on—no matter what Luther or Kaden said.

NOAH DIDN'T corner me again that week at school. Not like he had at the garden party or on our run. That didn't mean it was easy when I saw him. He didn't speak to me, and yet he was always around. Every meal he was in the dining hall, and it felt like I was constantly passing him in the corridors. Even in the class we shared, he continued to sit behind me. He made every minute of that class a living hell because all I could concentrate on was the feel of his eyes against the back of my neck.

I wanted to pretend he didn't exist. But Noah was almost impossible to ignore even when he didn't say a word. It was hardly surprising. Noah had always been difficult to turn a blind eye to even when we hadn't been dating.

Despite the obvious distance between us, no one else mentioned our breakup to me after I spoke with Luther and Kaden. I'd been so caught up in all the attention I'd received because of my father that it took me a while to realize that no one seemed to be gossiping about the fact Noah and I were over.

I'd told my friends and Noah had told his, but it seemed that was as far as the news had travelled. I did overhear a couple of girls speculating about it in the locker room after PE on Tuesday though.

"Do you think something's up with Noah and Isobel?" one girl said, drawing my attention.

"Yeah, Noah's always sending her those dreamy little smiles of his," another girl replied. "He didn't even talk to her in class today though, and no one's seen them together since the ball on Saturday night."

The girls were standing on the other side of the lockers, so I couldn't see who was speaking, and their voices weren't familiar.

"You'd think the fact she's a LaFleur would only cement the relationship," the first girl said.

"Really? I heard their families are like total rivals..."

I'd heard enough and quickly grabbed my bag and rushed from the room. It was one thing to know people were gossiping about you, but another thing entirely to have to overhear it.

Cress and Anna were waiting outside the locker room for me, and they frowned when they caught my expression.

"Everything okay?" Cress asked.

I shrugged. "Nothing I can't handle."

My friends had been so supportive of me since the breakup, and I really didn't want to off-load my problems on them again. I should have known people would start to theorize about Noah and I when we weren't being seen together. And it's not like the girls had said anything malicious. If anything, they'd simply stated the facts.

"You sure?" Anna asked.

"Positive."

Those two girls were just the beginning, and as the week wore on, I overheard more and more whispers from people wondering if Noah and I were still together. One girl was even brazen enough to ask me outright.

"What's the deal with you and Noah?" she said as I made my way to English on Thursday morning.

I cleared my throat. "Excuse me?"

"You and Noah. What's happening with you two?"

Her friends standing behind her started to giggle, and I folded my arms, clutching my laptop to my chest. The girl looked too young to be in my year, and I got the impression she was asking me just to impress her friends.

"Look, I don't know you, and my relationship is really none of your business." I wasn't trying to avoid the fact Noah and I were over; I just didn't particularly want to have to talk about it with some kid who was trying to be a smart-ass.

"So, does that mean you're broken up?" She continued to pry.

"It means I'm late to English." I walked off before the girl could hound me any further because she looked ready to fire more questions at me. Thankfully, I was right by the classroom, and I escaped inside before she could respond.

I was more than ready for this school week to be over, and I collapsed into the free chair beside Cress. "I swear, some people have zero boundaries in this place," I complained.

"Mmm." Cress murmured a sound of agreement though she didn't look up from her phone, so I wasn't sure she'd actually heard me. It looked like she was trying to draft a message, but whenever she wrote something, she deleted it right away.

"What's up?" I asked.

She let out a sigh and placed her phone down on the desk as she looked up at me. "I was supposed to go to a social committee meeting about the Halloween carnival this morning, but it was so damn early, and I arrived late. I swear, no one should ever have to arrive anywhere at 7:00 A.M. It's so uncivilized."

I frowned because it didn't explain why she seemed so bothered. It wasn't exactly unusual for Cress to arrive late to something. "Are you in trouble about it or something?"

"No." She sighed. "If only."

"So, why do you look so down?"

"Because they were assigning booths for each club to run at the carnival, and because I was late, all the good ones were taken."

"Shit."

"I know." She nodded. "Not only that, but the cheerleaders got the booth we wanted. The girls on my dance squad are going to be so disappointed."

"Surely, it's not that bad. What did you get stuck with?"

"The kissing booth." She gave such an exaggerated shudder I couldn't help but laugh.

"That sounds okay." I tried my best to sound convincing.

"Not when you realize that *anyone* can buy a token for a kiss. It's the worst booth in the fair..."

"Oh, yeah, that does suck." I was suddenly grateful I hadn't joined any clubs at school.

"Tell me about it," she said. "Quite a few of the girls on the squad have boyfriends too, so I think I'm going to struggle to find volunteers to man the booth."

"Well, there's always Anna. I'm sure she'd be more than happy to help you out."

"Yeah, I'm sure she will." Cress laughed, but her expression dimmed as she glanced down at her phone once more. "I'm trying to figure out how to break the news to the squad. Everyone is asking in the group chat what happened at the meeting."

I shrugged. "I'd just be honest. Tell them the cheerleaders stole your booth and that they're going to need to pucker up."

"I don't think that's going to make them feel any better about it."

I smiled as an idea came to me. "*Or*, you could tell them you got stuck with the stand but you're going to change it to a kiss *or scare* booth. When people come up for their turn, they don't know if they're getting a kiss or a scare from the girls."

"Oh, I like that," Cress said. "Definitely more fitting for Halloween. Maybe I'll create some kind of coin that can be flipped with kiss on one side and scare on the other so it's a game of chance."

"That would be so fun," I agreed. "You could also get some cute guys to volunteer so the girls wouldn't have to do all the kissing."

"Like who?"

"Well, a certain twin who loves kissing comes to mind."

Cress looked thoughtful. "Yeah, I'm sure I can rope Sawyer into it."

"I think it would be harder trying to keep him away."

Cress giggled, her familiar bright smile fully restored. "Okay, I think this might go down better with the team. I guess we'll just have to convince a few other guys to help us out."

She grew quiet as Veronica entered the room and took her usual seat in front of me. Veronica slowly turned to Cress and flashed her a fake smile. "Sorry the dance team missed out on the photo booth this morning. I know you girls were thinking about doing it, but I'm sure you can understand that I didn't have a choice. I was just doing what the cheer team wanted. They have all these ideas for different backdrops, and I'd hate to disappoint them."

Cress returned Veronica's smile with one that was just as empty. "Oh, I understand," she said. "But you don't need to worry, we're pretty excited to be doing the kissing booth."

"Seriously?" Veronica scoffed. "You can't actually want to kiss all the losers who are going to be lining up."

Cress shrugged. "We have a few ideas that might make it more fun."

Veronica lifted one eyebrow, as though she was having a hard time believing Cress, but she didn't respond. Instead, she turned her attention to me. "I haven't seen you and Noah together this week. Of course, everyone's wondering is there trouble in paradise already?"

I swallowed a heavy lump that rose in my throat. I'd heard the whispers, and to be honest, I had no idea how everyone at school hadn't already confirmed the truth. I didn't want to have to admit it to Veronica though. The gloating look in her eyes might just kill me.

"Because I heard a rumor you two were over, and since you've been looking so..." She paused as she considered her next word. "So *tired*, I had to wonder if it's true," Veronica continued. "Did Noah already get bored of slumming it with the help?"

"She's not the help," Cress growled.

Veronica's eyes flashed with vile pleasure. "Oh, so you'll deny she's a charity case but not that their relationship is over. Interesting..."

"I'm not sure why you'd even take interest in their relationship," Cress replied. "It's not like my cousin will ever be interested in you."

Veronica shrugged. "That's not what he was saying at the ball on Saturday night."

The teacher started the class, and Veronica gave us one last smug smile before she returned her attention to the front of the room. I felt frozen to the spot. I hadn't been able to utter a single word in my defense, and I hated that Cress had felt the need to fight my battle for me. I didn't want to give Veronica the pleasure of knowing Noah and I were finished, but pretending we weren't made me feel even worse. Was I really so pathetic I couldn't admit to people the relationship was over?

I must have been completely tuned out to what the teacher was saying because the class erupted into excited murmurs and I had no idea why. My eyes darted to Cress. "What did I miss?"

She was grinning widely as she faced me. "Were you really not listening?"

"I was distracted." I shot an annoyed look at the back of Veronica's head.

Cress gave me an understanding smile. "Mr. Wagner just announced we're going on a field trip for English."

"We are?"

"Yep." She punctuated the word with an enthused nod. "All the senior English classes are going to New York to see *Romeo and Juliet* next week."

"Seriously?" It was hard to contain my excitement. I'd always wanted to go to New York, and even my conversation with Veronica couldn't dampen the delight I felt that I was finally going to visit the city. Seeing the play would be fun too, but it was New York that had my heart racing with anticipation.

"Quiet down, everyone," Mr. Wagner said in a weak attempt to wrangle back control of the class. No one wanted to listen. He let out a heavy breath like he knew it was a lost cause and started scribbling on the whiteboard.

"This is going to be so much fun," Cress said as I faced her again. "I'm sure we'll get free time so I can show you all of my favorite haunts."

"That sounds great."

"It does, doesn't it? Oh," she gasped. "We should make a weekend of it and stay at my place."

"Do you think the school will let us do that?"

"I'm sure they'd be fine with it. Plenty of other kids are from the city and will probably do the same. So, what do you think?"

"I'll have to check with my mom first, but if she says yes, then obviously I'm in."

"Excellent." She grinned brightly and continued chatting happily as she came up with ideas for all the fun things we could do. It all sounded amazing and exactly what I needed to create some space away from Noah. This school felt too suffocating at the moment. His presence was near impossible to ignore. I often felt like I could feel him even when he wasn't in the room.

As Cress started planning out our time in the city, another thought came to mind. She wasn't the only person based in New York. Matthew was there for the next couple of weeks too. He was supposed to be too busy with work to come to Weybridge and answer all my questions, but that didn't mean I couldn't go to him.

The more I thought about it, the more I started to like the idea. I was never going to get over Noah when my thoughts were still so tangled and confused about the reason behind our breakup. Matthew could give me answers. Perhaps with this trip. I could also get some much-needed closure.

But, first, there was something else I was going to have to do if I wanted to get over Noah. I was never going to move on when everyone still thought we were together and constantly gossiping as they tried to figure out what was going on.

It was time I grew more proactive about our breakup, which meant I needed to put an end to the constant cycles of rumors. So, when class ended and everyone started to file out of the class-room, I touched Veronica's arm, stopping her before she walked through the door.

She rolled her eyes as she turned to me. "If it's taken you all lesson to find your tongue and come up with a retort for me, I don't want to hear it."

"No." I shook my head. "That's not it. I just thought you should know that you were right. Noah and I are over."

Veronica looked too stunned by my revelation to make fun of me. And even Cress, who knew the truth, appeared surprised I'd just admitted it to Veronica.

"So, he's all yours," I said before I pushed past her and left the room.

I didn't see the point in fighting over a guy when he wasn't mine anymore. I knew Veronica would tell the whole school the news. I just hoped any extra attention I received would be short-lived. Once everyone knew the truth, I'm sure they'd soon grow tired of the rumors and gossip.

As much as it hurt, it felt like a small weight had lifted from my shoulders. Saying the words out loud, that Noah and I were over, felt like a step in the right direction. I just had to hope I didn't stray from the path.

CHAPTER EIGHT

Word about my breakup with Noah got around quickly once Veronica found out. She hadn't wasted any time informing the whole school, and by Thursday lunchtime, it was all anyone could talk about.

I found I was actually relieved by the gossip. All week, it had felt like I was waiting for a bomb to detonate, and now that it had, I just needed to lie low until the initial shockwave blew over. Once the dust began to settle, I could slowly begin to pick up the pieces.

I decided it was best to skip Noah's soccer game on Thursday night. I wanted to keep my head down while everyone worked the news about Noah and I through their systems, and the last thing I felt like doing was watching Noah lead his team to glory while the whole school cheered him on.

Cress was bummed because missing the game meant I also missed her dance at halftime. I hated that I wasn't there to support her, especially when she'd been there for me all week, so I promised to make it up to her. I probably should have considered the offer more carefully because, as soon as Friday night rolled around, she insisted I went with her to the boathouse party.

I knew it was a terrible idea, but there was no way I could let Cress down again. And so, as soon as it grew dark, I found myself trailing after her and Anna to the old boatshed by the lake. As I stepped through the wide-open wooden doors, I took a deep breath in. Tonight, I had a chance to show I really was putting Noah behind me.

Still, I couldn't help doing a quick scan of the room for him as soon as I arrived. The place was packed with people, and I was all too relieved I didn't see him. I wasn't sure how he'd react to me being at the party. His friends had invited me, but I was almost certain they wouldn't have run it by him first.

"Come on, let's get drinks," Anna said, grabbing me by the hand and tugging me toward the fridge at the back of the room.

I'd vowed after last weekend that I never wanted to drink again, but I found myself reaching for the beer Anna offered. I was way too tense, and perhaps the drink might help me get through the party.

Anna and Cress seemed to have the same idea because they were both knocking back their drinks too.

"I still can't believe your dad bought you a new car and you're not going to drive it," Cress said.

"What do you mean you're not going to drive it!" Anna practically shouted.

"Don't listen to her," Cress said. "Anna likes cars more than she likes most people."

Anna ignored her. "You're really not going to drive it?"

"I'm not a very confident driver," I murmured.

"So, you're going to let your poor car rot in the parking lot all year?" Anna made it sound like I was committing some kind of cardinal sin.

"I crashed trying to avoid a dog that ran in the road the day after I passed my test," I said. "I've been too nervous to drive ever since."

"Accidents happen." Anna tried to reassure me. "I'm sure you're a great driver when dogs aren't running in front of the car. You just need to get your confidence back."

"And how do I do that?"

"I'll go with you. Like a driving lesson. I'm a great teacher." Anna waved a hand and flicked back her hair like she had already solved the problem.

"Uh, I'm not sure that's a good idea."

"What's the worst that can happen?"

"Well, we'd be driving, so a lot."

"Our school is in the middle of nowhere, and the chances we'll encounter a stray dog are minuscule," Anna argued. "Come on, please. If it's that bad, you can go back to ignoring your car for the rest of the year, and I won't mention it again."

I hesitated.

"Come on, *please?*"

"Okay, fine, but only because I know you'll keep bugging me all night if I don't agree."

"Yes!" She clapped her hands together excitedly. "This is going to be fun."

I didn't see how driving lessons could be fun for anyone, but she seemed genuinely excited about it.

Cress hadn't spoken since we'd started talking about driving lessons. She'd been staring off into the distance for most of our conversation, and as I followed her gaze, I could see why. Her eyes were fixed on Kaden who was chatting with a group of girls.

Anna also noticed where Cress's attention was because she started to squeal. "*Ohmygosh, Cress!* You're totally checking out Kaden!"

Cress blushed and glanced away. "I am not."

"You definitely are," Anna replied. "And I don't blame you. He's looking superhot tonight."

"I'm not checking him out."

"He does look pretty good," I agreed with a knowing smile.

Cress's cheeks only grew pinker.

"You've crushed on him forever," Anna said. "You should go for it. You are both single, after all."

"I don't think so." Cress was normally so bubbly and enthusiastic, but she lacked Anna's confidence when it came to chasing after guys. I hoped she wasn't waiting for Kaden to make the first move because he wasn't very forward either. They might spend their entire senior year sending each other furtive glances and nothing more.

"You don't have to make a move on him, but why don't you just go chat with him?" I asked her.

Cress lifted her drink and finished the bottle in one long swig. "Maybe later. I just saw some of the dance squad arrive so I should probably go say hey." She placed her empty bottle down on the table before rushing away from us.

Anna shook her head. "She's being a chicken."

"Not all of us have your confidence with guys, Anna."

"*Pshh*, I'm not confident. It's all about faking it till you make it. I've been faking it for such a long time now I forget my confidence isn't real."

I shook my head but smiled. I had to disagree with her. I thought Anna was one of the most confident people I'd ever met. If she was pretending, then I was very impressed because I was thoroughly convinced.

"Newbie, you came!" I turned to find Luther walking up behind me. "You ready for our beer pong rematch?"

I snorted. "Do I look like an idiot?"

He squinted as he looked me up and down. "Not particularly."

"Then the answer is no."

Luther shrugged and turned to Anna. "How about you, London?"

Anna folded her arms and glared at him. "How many times do I have to tell you I'm not from London? I'm from Oxford."

"Maybe one more time."

Anna rolled her eyes at him. "Go bother someone else, Luther. I'm not playing your little game with you either."

"Suit yourselves," he said before sauntering off to find another victim to play against.

"Is it just me, or does he get more annoying every time you see him?" Anna asked as she watched him leave.

I laughed. "No, it's not just you. His ability to annoy people is a true talent."

She shook her head before focusing on me again. "Speaking of talent, have you considered any of the guys on the rebound list I gave you?"

Anna had actually provided me with a full list of names earlier in the week. I hadn't looked at it because there was no way I was going to kiss a guy just to get over another one.

"A few of those guys are here tonight..." Anna raised her eyebrows and nudged me with her shoulder.

"I might need a few more drinks before I can seriously talk about rebounds." I hoped that would be enough to end the conversation. I was never going to consider that list. Not anytime soon, at least. I couldn't even look at other guys right now.

Someone loudly cleared their throat behind me, and I turned to find Noah standing there. When I realized how close he was, my stomach dropped, and the glare in his eyes did nothing to ease my nerves. He'd clearly heard us talking about rebounds, and he wasn't happy.

It felt like a thunderstorm had just entered the room and I was standing directly in its path. Noah was practically crackling with irritation, and his hands clenched at his sides. It was like he was having to restrain himself from throwing me over his shoulder and stealing me away from the party to stop any more talk of rebounds.

"Oh, hey, Noah," Anna said. Usually, her playful personality could defuse the tension in any situation, but now her tone was cold as she glared at Noah. He didn't respond. It was almost like he hadn't heard her at all.

"So, how many drinks will it take?" he asked. "You know, before you start working your way down Anna's list."

My cheeks heated in anger. "That's not your concern, Noah."

"Isn't it?"

"No, it's not. You made that perfectly clear when you broke up with me." He had no right to question me. He wouldn't even answer my questions about what happened between our families. He just made it plain and clear, time and again, that we would never be together—unless, of course, we kept it a secret from the whole world.

I met his glare with one of my own. I wanted nothing more than to be done with this conversation. Be done with him. I swallowed the remainder of my drink and shoved the empty bottle into his chest. "I guess that's one drink less now," I said before stalking past him.

Anna quickly rushed after me, her eyes filled with concern as we pushed through people and made our way to the other end of the room—as far from Noah as possible.

"Wow," she murmured.

"What?"

"I can't believe that just happened. You are my breakup idol," she said. "That was badass."

I shook my head. "It really wasn't. He just got to me. He keeps getting to me."

"Yeah, because he's clearly jealous. He doesn't want anyone else to have you."

"Well, that's not up to him."

"Totally." Anna shrugged. "But no one ever said boys were sane."

"Yeah, well, he's acting like an ass..."

Anna gave me a sad smile. "I'm sure he's just upset. Your breakup was hardly normal. It's not like you stopped liking each other, and it's never easy to see someone you care about moving on."

"You're sounding far too reasonable," I said. "I prefer to think he's an ass."

Anna laughed. "Well, he's that too, obviously." Anna's gaze flicked past me, and she started to frown. "Speaking of... It looks like one of the twins is already making a drunken ass of himself."

I turned to see one of the boys stumbling into a table. He had his back to us, so it was impossible to tell if it was Wes or Sawyer. It had to be Sawyer though. Wes was always very sensible when it came to alcohol, and messy drinking seemed to be one of Sawyer's favorite pastimes.

"Sawyer must have gone a little hard on his pregame," Anna said. She had come to the same conclusion as I had about which twin it was.

"One of us should really go help him."

"I guess." Anna didn't seem the least bit keen to deal with a drunken Sawyer. I didn't really blame her. He was a handful enough when sober.

"I'll go," I quickly offered. I was only too eager for a distraction after my run-in with Noah. "It's probably the least I can do after he so gallantly offered to be my rebound."

Anna laughed. "Yeah, he was totally selfless in that offer too."

"Totally," I agreed. "Wish me luck."

I grabbed a bottle of water and headed over to Sawyer. He was trying to chat with a girl I recognized from my English class, but I didn't know her name. His words were slurred, and he was swaying on his feet. He kept bumping into the table at his side, causing the glasses and bottles on it to shake dangerously. The party had barely started, so Anna was probably right in suggesting he'd had too much to drink before he arrived.

"Hey, Sawyer," I said as I approached. "Can you come outside with me for a sec?"

The girl shot me a grateful smile, and I got the distinct impression I'd come to her rescue. She darted away as he turned to me, and as soon as his sad eyes landed on mine, I realized my mistake.

"You're not Sawyer," I murmured.

"Not Sawyer," Wes slurred in reply.

His eyes were ringed red, and he looked like he'd been crying.

"Wes, you look like hell."

"I feel like hell," he agreed. "Sarah broke up with me."

"Oh no."

He nodded and let out a sigh as he stared down into the red cup he was holding. He went to take another sip out of it, but I gently removed it from his hand and placed it on the table. I could smell the vodka from here.

"I'm not sure you need to drink any more."

"You're probably right. I think I'd rather sleep." He started to stumble toward one of the sofas, but I grabbed hold of his arm and steered him in the direction of the exit.

"It might be a better idea if we find you an actual bed," I said.

He nodded and let me guide him out of the boathouse. Cress caught sight of us as we were about to leave and hurried over.

"What's wrong with Sawyer?" His reputation clearly preceded him as Cress made the same mistake.

"Not Sawyer. Wes," I confirmed, and her eyes widened with surprise. "Sarah broke up with him. I'm going to get him back to his dorm room. He just needs to sleep it off."

"Do you want a hand?"

I shook my head. "Nah, he seems pretty steady on his feet. I think I should be able to get him back in one piece. You stay and have fun."

"Are you sure?"

"I'm sure." I was somewhat relieved to leave the party. I hadn't wanted to go in the first place, and I didn't feel much like staying after seeing Noah. Every time he came close to me, I felt my resolve to get over him slowly breaking.

"Well, call me if you need some extra help."

"I will."

There was a chill in the air as we stepped out into the night, and I hoped it would help sober Wes up. I passed him the bottle of water I was holding. "Here, drink this."

He happily took the bottle and guzzled it down. Wes might have been slightly sloppy and sad, but at least he wasn't a difficult drunk. He stumbled along the path as we walked, and I was grateful he was able to stay on his feet without much support from me. He was way too big for me to carry him on my own.

"So, what happened with Sarah?" I asked as we followed the darkened path that wound around the lake back to school, leaving the soft lights of the boatshed behind us.

"Things haven't been great between us recently," he started. "We rarely see each other. She wants someone who's *there*. And I'm *here*. So, she dumped me."

The ache in my chest echoed the confused and anguished tone in his voice. I was far too familiar with the hurt he was enduring.

"Long distance must be hard," I murmured.

He nodded sadly, but was distracted as he stumbled over a divot in the path. I quickly reached out to steady him, and he grasped tightly onto my arms. As he looked up and into my eyes, his pain was so visceral and clear to see.

"Why wasn't I enough?" His voice was raw and filled with emotion.

"For the right girl, you will be," I replied. "No matter what hurdles or distance are put in your way."

He let out a hard breath and nodded. He slowly let go of my arms, and we continued back to school in silence.

My words to Wes played on repeat in my mind. If Noah was

the right guy for me, then nothing would have stopped us from being together.

Nothing.

By the time Wes and I reached the school buildings, he was struggling to walk straight, and I had to prop him up to stop him from stumbling into walls. We only had a short way to go before we arrived at the boys' dorm, but Wes was starting to lean on me more and more. He was big and heavy, and as I tried to keep him upright, I was worried we might not make it much farther.

When we somehow made it to the dorm, I had to keep shushing him as we made our way through the entrance, up the stairs, and along the hallways. He'd been so quiet for most of our walk back, but he suddenly seemed to have a lot to say. He was still slurring and had no control over the volume of his voice. He was obviously drunk.

"Sarah had the most beautiful hair," he mumbled. "It was like the night's sky."

"I know. You told me just before—"

"And her eyes. Did I tell you about her eyes?"

"Yes."

"They were so big and beautiful. I don't know if you know this about me, Isobel, but I'm an eyes guy. It's all about the eyes." His words were tumbling into one another, and it was difficult to make sense of most of what he said. "I wish I could have seen them one last time."

"Wes, you have to speak quietly, or you'll wake everyone up," I said. The last thing I wanted was to draw attention to us. If we were caught, there was no way Wes would be able to act sober enough to avoid getting in trouble.

He ignored me. "Do you think she's found someone else?"

"I'm sure she hasn't. From what you've told me about her, she doesn't sound like the kind of girl to cheat."

"I bet she has," he said. "She's so damn beautiful."

"You can't torture yourself with guessing," I replied. "You need to focus on mending your own heart."

"I wish it were that easy."

I wished the same thing too.

Somehow, Wes managed to direct me to his room without causing a scene. He'd done little to keep his voice down, so we'd gotten a few funny looks from other guys who were wandering the halls, but thankfully most just ignored us.

Wes fiddled with his swipe card, dropping it on the ground twice before he finally got the door to his room open. I helped him inside, turning on the light as I went.

There were two beds in the room. I knew Wes shared with Sawyer, but his brother was nowhere to be seen. I hadn't noticed him at the boathouse earlier, but he must have been there somewhere.

The two halves of the room were so different. One side was a total mess. The bed was unmade, and clothes were strewn across the floor. The other side was so neat it barely looked lived in. Of course, Wes stumbled over to the clean side of the room. It didn't take a genius to realize Sawyer was the slovenly one of the twins.

He collapsed down onto the bed in a heap and groaned as his head hit the pillow. I went into the bathroom and grabbed him a glass of water.

"I feel like crap," he moaned as I returned.

I sat on the bed next to him and gently rubbed his back. "I know. And you'll probably feel even worse tomorrow."

He turned his head and peered up at me. "That doesn't make me feel better."

I shrugged and gave him a smile. "I'm not here to baby you. But I am here to help. Drink this." He propped himself up, and I handed him the glass.

He only took a couple of sips before he lowered it from his lips. "I think I prefer the vodka better. At least it helps me forget."

"It's not exactly a healthy way to move on though, is it?"

Wes shrugged. "It's probably not much worse than the

rebound list Anna gave you."

I let out a sigh. "No, probably not. I'm not planning to use it though."

"Why not? There's nothing wrong with using unhealthy methods for moving on if it works. Do you think Anna would make me a list too?"

"You don't want a rebound list."

"Sure, I do. If it helps me forget Sarah ever existed, it sounds like a great idea."

"It sounds like a terrible idea."

"No, a terrible idea would be if we were each other's rebound..."

My heart leaped, and I swallowed to stop myself from reacting too obviously. I didn't think he was joking.

"You're right. That's a terrible idea."

He smiled. "Okay, so I better not ask to be on your list then?"

"Wes, you don't want that. You've just had too much to drink. Besides, we're already breakup buddies. We help each other get through breakups, which is a far more important job than a rebound."

"Breakup buddies," he repeated. "I like it." He smiled before his eyes became a little hazier. "I should probably get some sleep."

"That's a good idea. Do you need me to get you anything else before I go?"

He shook his head and started to melt back into his bed as his eyes slowly shut. "No, I'm good." He blinked his eyes open one last time as I stood to leave. "Thanks, Isobel. You're a really good friend."

I gave him a warm smile in response. "Have a good sleep, Wes."

I flicked the light off as I left the room. Poor Wes was going to feel absolutely terrible come tomorrow. I knew what it was like to wake up with a broken heart and a hangover, and I didn't envy him one bit.

CHAPTER NINE

When I woke in the morning, it was to a stream of text messages from Wes.

Wes: Thank you for helping me back last night.

Wes: I feel like total crap today, but I think I'd feel worse if you hadn't been there.

Wes: I have a bad feeling I was a terrible drunk. I'm sorry if I offended you at all!!! Forgive me?

I smiled and responded right away.

Me: Nothing to forgive. You were fine.

Me: You did offer to be my rebound though...

He didn't reply immediately, and I hopped in the shower while I waited. Cress was completely passed out in bed. She hadn't come home until late, so I didn't expect her to wake up any time soon. As soon as I was dressed, I checked my phone again and found a new message from Wes.

Wes: Wow, drunk me has game. Who would have thought?

I chuckled under my breath and started to type a reply, but another message from him arrived before I could hit send.

Wes: Seriously though, I'm sorry.

Me: You can stop apologizing. You were in pain and had too many drinks. I'm sure I was in a far worse state last weekend.

Wes: Yes, you did voluntarily dance.

Me: Please don't remind me.

Wes: I'll never speak of it again.

I smiled down at my phone, glad Wes was in good enough spirits that he could still joke around with me. I let out a sigh as I remembered why he was hurting. Why we both were. My encounter with Noah last night hadn't made me feel any better about our breakup. It was clear he was in pain over it—perhaps as much as I was. That only made me want answers more. Answers I was hoping to get from Matthew when I visited New York next week.

At least, that was the plan. First, I had to figure out if I could get my father to spare some time to meet with me while I was there. It was after 9 A.M., so it wasn't too early to give him a call. Now was as good a time as any.

I went into the bathroom and closed the door so I wouldn't wake Cress up before I dialed his number. It rang three times before there was an answer.

"LaFleur residence."

It was hard not to be disappointed. I'd been hoping to get

straight through to my father, but apparently that wasn't possible, even on a Saturday.

"Hey, Caldwell, it's Isobel.".

"Good morning, Miss Grace."

"Is my father around?"

"I'm afraid not. He's at the lab and will be unavailable all day."

I let out a sigh.

"Is there anything I can help you with?"

I was about to tell him no and hang up, but then I wondered if maybe he could be of some help. Caldwell probably knew my dad's schedule better than Matthew himself.

"Actually, yeah. I was wondering if my father has plans on Friday next week? I'm going to be in New York for a school field trip and was hoping to see him."

"I'm afraid Mr. LaFleur has meetings scheduled at his office all day on that Friday," Caldwell replied.

"Well, I was thinking of staying the weekend too. Has he got any time then..."

"While he's in New York, he plans to work every day, even the weekends," Caldwell replied. "His schedule is extremely tight at the moment, but I believe he's allotted some time to come to Weybridge the following weekend. Is that suitable for you?"

I let out another sigh. "Yeah, that's fine." Apparently, seeing my father was like trying to schedule an appointment with the doctor. You had to book it weeks in advance, and even then, it was near impossible to get in.

"I will inform Mr. LaFleur that you'll be in the city. If any time opens up, I'll be in contact."

I didn't hold out much hope. "Thanks, Caldwell."

I hung up the phone feeling defeated. I knew it was just one extra week of waiting to see my father, but the questions churning inside my gut were killing me. I wanted answers now. Not weeks from now. There wasn't even any guarantee my father would come back to Weybridge when he planned. He was always so busy, and there was every chance he'd get caught up with work and stay in New York.

A light knock sounded at the door as I exited the bathroom, and I turned to see Anna barreling into the room. She was all dressed for the day and looking wide-awake. It was like witnessing a miracle. I'd never seen Anna look so peppy first thing in the morning. Let alone on a weekend when she'd been out drinking the night before.

"Are you ready?" she asked me.

"For…"

"Your driving lesson, obviously."

I'd forgotten she'd offered to help me drive my new car. A part of me had hoped she'd been joking and would forget all about it.

"You're here first thing in the morning to teach me how to drive?"

"Yeah, I couldn't sleep. I have serious regrets over the guy I kissed last night, and I keep visualizing it every time I close my eyes."

"You kissed Angus again?"

"Ugh, I wish. Angus I could stomach."

I shook my head. "Who did you kiss then?"

"Please don't make me repeat their name. It only makes it more real." She scrunched up her face in disgust.

"Okay. We won't talk about the mystery kisser from last night." I didn't particularly want to talk about my night either. I'd practically fled the boathouse party after Noah confronted me about the rebound list, and then Wes had actually offered to be my rebound. Last night was certainly best forgotten.

"The mystery kisser. Ugh, now he has a villain nickname too." Anna shook her head. "But enough about him. Do you have your keys?"

I nodded and went to grab them off my desk. A nervous flutter took flight in my stomach as I grasped them in my hand.

Was I really ready to get behind the wheel of a car again? Probably not. The fact I was allowing a seventeen-year-old to guide me wasn't helping the nerves. Was this really a good idea? I didn't have a chance to answer the question. Anna grabbed my arm and dragged me from the room.

"Don't look so nervous," she said. "You'll be a racecar driver by the afternoon."

She sounded confident, but I didn't share her faith. I had a feeling I was destined to be more of a slow, steady, and super-cautious driver rather than one who tested the speed limits.

When we got to the parking lot, Anna looked at me in expectation. "So..." she prompted. "Which baby's yours?"

I pointed my keys at the vehicle, and it lit up when I hit the unlock button.

"*Nice*," Anna gushed as she started toward my new car. "You have good taste."

"Thanks, but I didn't choose it. My dad did."

"Well, he did really well. I've always wanted to drive a G-Class." She was still admiring it and nodding her approval.

I spent some time considering the car—if you could call it that. It wasn't what I'd been expecting at all when I'd first come to the parking lot to take a look at it. Unlike the other vehicles in the parking lot, it wasn't sleek and sporty. It was more like a Jeep or a truck that looked like it could seat about eight people. It had beefy tires, including a spare hanging off the back, and a huge shiny grill on the front that looked a little like bared teeth. It was made more for trips off-road rather than urban driving, which was kind of perfect for the hidden tracks that led to remote beaches back home in Rapid Bay. However, it still looked expensive with a smooth matte black finish and, of course, the Mercedes logo sparkling proudly on the hood. It was most definitely far too excessive for me, but I couldn't deny I liked it.

"What are you girls doing?"

I glanced over my shoulder as Sawyer jogged toward us. He

was dressed casually in jeans and a large sweatshirt. I bet he looked a sight better than his brother this morning.

"Giving Isobel a driving lesson," Anna said. "Her dad just bought her a new car, but she doesn't think she can drive it. I'm going to help her make sure she doesn't let her poor, beautiful G-Class sit all lonely in the parking lot this year."

"You can't drive?" Sawyer gave me a questioning look.

"I can, but historically it doesn't end well."

"Huh." Sawyer looked intrigued "Sounds fun. Can I come?"

"No," I groaned, but Anna quickly replied with an exuberant "Of course!"

I scowled in her direction. "I really don't think I need an audience for this."

Sawyer waved away my concern. "I'm hardly an audience. Think of me as an extra dose of driving wisdom."

"If you're my driving wisdom, then I'm screwed."

Sawyer laughed and shrugged. "So, is this your ride?" Before I could respond, he had already stepped forward and opened one of the back doors.

"This is a bad idea," I murmured to Anna.

She didn't seem the least bit concerned. "It'll be fine. Sawyer loves cars almost as much as I do. He'll be a great addition."

"Will you girls stop chatting and get driving?" Sawyer called out from where he now sat inside the car. "I need to get to town to pick up breakfast burgers to fix my brother's hangover."

"Guess I can't put this off any longer then," I murmured.

"Nope. You really can't." Anna grinned and walked around the car to get into the passenger seat while I slowly made my way toward the driver's side door. There was no way this ended well; I felt sure of it.

I was only more convinced our little adventure was doomed to fail once I sat behind the wheel. All the buttons, switches and dials on the dashboard were enough to over-whelm me before we even got started. Anna spent a while making sure my seat was in the right position and I knew where the lights, wipers, air-conditioner and radio controls were. If she thought I was going to be able to think about all of those things while also watching the road for stray dogs, she was sadly mistaken.

When she thought I was ready, Anna told me to start the car but then laughed at the blank look on my face as I searched for the ignition.

"It's push to start," she chuckled, pointing at one of the buttons on the dash. "Put your foot on the brake."

I did as she instructed, and when I pushed the button, the car rumbled to life. I jumped slightly at the sudden noise of the engine. As if I didn't already seem pathetic enough.

"Okay, let's go," Anna said.

I lifted my hands and cautiously placed them on the wheel. It had been so long since I'd driven a car, so it wasn't a familiar feeling. I wondered if my hands were in the right place, and as I stretched my feet out to touch the pedals, I worried they were too far away. The car was much bigger than any other I'd driven before. Through the front window, the clean black hood of the car seemed to reach out so far in front I wasn't sure I'd even be able to see the road ahead.

I took a deep breath and gently pressed my foot down on the accelerator. The engine hummed, but the car didn't move. Perhaps I was being too gentle. I tried again, pushing a little harder this time, but still the car refused to move. What was I doing wrong?

"Isobel..." Anna's voice was calm next to me. "You forgot to take the handbrake off."

"Ah, right." I shook my head, trying to shake the fog clouding my thoughts and the redness I could feel rushing to my cheeks. I took another breath and released the handbrake. This time, when I tapped the accelerator, the car rolled forward out of the parking space.

"That's it." Anna sounded like she was smiling. "Now, let's head for the exit."

I was too focused to speak, so I just nodded.

"You've got this, Isobel," she added.

It took us an age to get to the school entrance. I drove at a snail's pace as we left the parking lot. The car was so big I felt like there was barely space to move it between the rows of cars, and I was terrified of brushing up against one of them. They were all so shiny and expensive looking. When we finally got to the exit, I was relieved to find the main road outside the school was empty of cars and, with Anna encouraging me, I pulled out.

Once we finally got going on the open road, I felt a little more comfortable. I made sure to keep well below the speed limit so I'd have plenty of time to react should something untoward happen. Much to Sawyer's amusement, cars slowly began to pile up in a line behind me, but I did my best to ignore them.

"See, it's not so bad, is it?" Anna asked, as we came to a stop at a set of traffic lights.

"Yeah, nothing bad can happen when you're moving at ten miles per hour." Sawyer laughed from the back seat.

"Quiet back there, Sawyer," Anna snapped before turning to me. "Don't listen to him. You're doing great."

"Thanks." I nodded. "Maybe I just needed a bit of practice."

I jumped as the car behind us beeped its horn, and I realized the light had turned green. I quickly tried to gather my thoughts and get moving again, but the driver behind was still blasting their horn. I glanced up at the rearview mirror and saw a sports car waiting behind me. The driver was waving his arms through the window in frustration as he banged on the horn again.

"Isobel," Anna said. "Are you okay?"

"Yeah, sorry, I just got distracted."

"Ignore the jackass behind us. Just pull forward and we'll get going before the light changes."

I nodded, took another deep breath and pressed down on

the accelerator. As the car started to move into the intersection though, the sound of the car horn filled my ears once again, and the sports car flashed past my window. The guy was over-taking me at the lights, and as he swerved back into the lane right in front of me, I had to slam on the brakes to avoid a collision.

"What the hell!?" Anna shouted after him, as the car sped off into the distance.

"Yeah, that was not cool," Sawyer added. "He was so close to hitting us."

I was shaking as Anna reached out and touched my arm. "Are you okay?"

"I knew this was a bad idea," I replied. "I'm done."

"But you were doing so well." She protested, but I was already getting out of the car. I hurried around to the passenger side, barely noticing the other cars that were now overtaking us like nothing had happened.

"Isobel, we're right in the middle of the intersection." Anna gasped, as I opened her door.

"Then get in the driver's seat, quick. I'm not driving another inch."

She nodded and clambered across to the driver's seat before I climbed into the car next to her. My heart was still racing as she pulled away. I was never driving again.

Unlike me, Anna had absolutely no fear on the road. Her eyes practically lit up when she got behind the wheel, and I wasn't sure if I felt more traumatized by my driving or hers after she'd raced to the burger joint and back to school in record time.

"I'm shaken. Totally shaken," I said as I jumped out of the car when we finally arrived back at the school parking lot. I couldn't get clear of the vehicle fast enough.

"You weren't that bad," Anna said as she climbed from the front seat.

"She's probably talking about your driving, Anna." Sawyer

looked a little shaken himself as he got out of the car. "Are you sure you're not the one who needs a lesson?"

"What? I can't help that I get my left and my right mixed up sometimes," Anna replied.

"I was thinking more about the way you accelerated toward that yellow light," I recalled. "We nearly took out that old lady."

"I mean, I thought it was a universal rule that everyone went faster when the lights were about to go red."

I shook my head and glanced at Sawyer. "Remind me to never, ever, ever get in a car with Anna again."

Normally I would have expected him to laugh and join in with the joke, but Sawyer looked as pale as I did, and he nodded emphatically. "I'd rather have you driving me, Isobel, and that's saying something."

Anna rolled her eyes. "You're both overreacting."

"Anna, you kept trying to drive on the wrong side of the road!"

"Well, I can't help that we drive on the other side of the road in England."

"But you learned to drive in America."

Anna simply shrugged, and we shook our heads at her. I had no idea why she thought helping me drive was a good idea. She barely knew the road rules herself.

"Maybe get an actual instructor next time, Isobel," Sawyer said. Although I agreed with him, I wasn't sure I'd be brave enough to try again.

Anna let out a long, defeated sigh. "Sorry, Isobel. I thought it would be easy to teach you."

"It's not your fault." I gave her a tight smile and patted her arm. "I told you I'm a terrible driver. But maybe hold off on committing to that career as a driving instructor."

"And maybe question if you should get behind the wheel yourself," Sawyer added. "Seriously, do you always drive that fast?"

Anna lifted her hands in the air. "I said I'm sorry."

"And we forgive you." I shot Sawyer a warning look. "Now, our burgers are probably getting cold. We should go find Wes so we can eat them."

"He'll still be in our room," Sawyer said. "I'll text him and tell him to meet us down by the lake. The sun's finally out, and I want to enjoy it while we can. Who knows how long it will stick around for."

"I'll text Cress," Anna said. "She should be awake by now."

We slowly wandered down to the large lake behind the dormitories, and I relished the feeling of soft earth beneath my feet instead of the pedals of my car. There was a wide-open grass area on this side of the water, and we found a spot to sit close to the water's edge.

My heart was still struggling to return to its normal rhythm after the terror of my driving experience, and I took deep breaths in and out as I tried to relax. The sun was soothing, and it didn't take long before I felt more like myself.

"I can't believe you guys went to get breakfast without me," Cress said as she joined us. Her hair was still damp from her shower, and she wasn't wearing any makeup. It was almost unfair how pretty she looked in the mornings without trying at all.

"You were still snoring when I came by your room," Anna said.

"I don't snore!"

"Don't you?" Anna gave her a wink.

"I don't!"

"I mean, it's really cute, but a snore is still a snore," I joked.

Cress scowled at the two of us. "You guys suck."

I laughed and offered her one of the breakfast burgers. "We're just kidding. You were sound asleep, making no noises at all when we left. And don't stress, we got food for you too."

"I still would have liked to come," Cress grumbled.

I shook my head. "You really didn't miss anything."

"Other than all of our lives flashing before our eyes," Sawyer added.

Cress gave us all a confused look.

"Anna took me for a drive," I explained. "It didn't go well."

Cress groaned. "Oh, man, I could have told you that was a bad idea. Anna always mixes up what side of the road you need to drive on."

Anna flushed. "I really thought it would be fine."

"It wasn't," Sawyer said. "It wasn't even close to fine. I'm going to have nightmares for weeks."

"You're not going to have nightmares," Anna protested.

Sawyer pointed his burger in her direction. "I happen to have a very nervous disposition, and just the slightest thing can set off my nightmares."

Anna rolled her eyes. "Such a drama queen," she muttered.

A low groaning noise came from behind us, and we all turned as Wes finally made an appearance. He looked even worse than he had last night, and he was wearing a heavy set of sunglasses to shade his eyes. He collapsed onto the ground next to me. "Did you guys really have to sit in the seventh circle of hell for breakfast?"

Sawyer grinned. "I don't know what you're talking about, brother."

"I'm talking about the fact you decided this morning was the perfect time for a trip to the sun. It's so damn bright out here."

"Feeling a little hungover, Wes?" Anna asked.

He lowered his glasses for one moment to scowl at her. "Don't revel in my pain, Grant."

She grinned. "I'm just glad it's not me for once."

"It should be," Sawyer said. "We all saw you playing beer pong with Luther and Kaden last night. No one plays them and remembers the rest of the night."

Anna's expression dimmed slightly, and she glanced away. "Well, I guess I'm a first then." I wondered if she was thinking about her mystery kisser. It seemed like she regretted kissing the guy when she'd mentioned it this morning. Perhaps she was wishing she could have forgotten the night altogether. The others continued talking about last night, but I turned to Wes. He hadn't touched his burger yet and was looking a little green in the face. He probably didn't feel much like eating.

"How are you feeling about Sarah this morning?" I said, keeping my voice low so the others wouldn't hear.

He sighed and slowly lowered his sunglasses from his face as he glanced my way. His eyes were red-rimmed and filled with pain. "I feel like she ran me over with a truck last night. When I woke this morning, I hoped it wasn't real, but it is. We're over."

I reached out and gave his hand a squeeze, and he smiled down at the gesture.

"I'm sorry I was such a mess last night," he said.

"I don't blame you. You were hurting."

"That doesn't really excuse how I behaved. Did I really offer to be your rebound?"

I nervously glanced at the others, but they were all too busy chatting to hear what he was saying.

"Uh, sort of." I laughed awkwardly. "But it's okay. I knew it was only because you were drunk. Besides, we also agreed we were better as breakup buddies."

"Breakup buddies?"

"Buddies who help each other through breakups."

He smiled. "We are pretty good at that, aren't we?"

"The best," I agreed.

He exhaled loudly as he leaned back and put his glasses on. "It really is too bright out here."

I laughed and nodded at his burger. "Maybe if you eat something, you'll feel better."

"You think this burger has the power to dial down the sun?"

"Well, it is a pretty good burger."

"True." He took a bite and chewed it cautiously. He normally devoured his food like it was going to disappear if he didn't eat it quickly enough. Today, he was taking it awfully slowly. He must have been in a world of pain.

I considered taking a bite of my burger, but a laugh drew my attention, and I glanced up. A group of people were walking around the edge of the lake, coming back from the direction of the old boathouse. It was a mix of girls and guys. Luther and Kaden were in the group, but Noah held my gaze.

It felt like he was always around. Always there when I wanted nothing more than to escape him. It would make it so much easier to move on if I could. Instead, my heart lurched out of my chest whenever I saw him.

"Isobel?"

I turned to Wes. He hadn't noticed Noah. I doubted he could see anything beyond his burger right now. "Yeah?"

"Promise to remind me to never to fall in love again."

I felt an echoing twinge of pain at his words. I still wasn't over Noah. Not even close. "I will, but you've got to promise me too."

"Done."

"Thanks, breakup buddy." He lifted his burger as though to cheers mine, and I knocked my food against his. "Here's to never falling in love again."

I nodded but couldn't help glancing in Noah's direction once more. As I felt the ache in my chest return, I knew I was more than happy to live by those words.

CHAPTER TEN

O n Sunday morning, we woke to a knock at our door from Lisa, our dorm mom, letting us know she'd called an early house meeting. Everyone in our hall was expected to go—no exceptions.

Cress had been slow to get ready, so most girls were already there when we arrived. They were perched on sofas and sitting on the floor. The one benefit of the meeting was that Lisa had ordered in food, and the smell of fresh coffee and croissants had me salivating.

"This has to be some kind of cruel joke," Cress murmured as we both grabbed a coffee. She took a deep drink and let out a happy sigh before she continued. "No one should be expected to get up before ten on a Sunday."

"Lisa's probably pissed no one listens to curfew," Anna said as she joined us. She picked a croissant off the table and took a quick bite. "What better punishment is there when we've been out too late than making us all get up early?"

Funnily enough, Cress, Anna, and I had stayed in watching movies in the common room last night. We hadn't even been close to breaking curfew. Not that the girls were ever all that worried about breaking the rules. They were both far too skilled at talking their way out of trouble with Lisa.

We took a seat at the back of the room and waited for the meeting to start. Lisa walked in moments later, her usual smile and warm expression completely missing.

She let out a sigh as she went to stand at the front of the room. "Good morning, everyone," she said. "Sorry to drag you out of bed so early on a Sunday morning, but if people can't respect the rules around here, I can't be expected to respect your sleep."

"Told you," Anna whispered with a smile.

"I wanted to bring you all in here to remind you that, with no exceptions, boys are not allowed in your rooms after curfew."

The girls all broke into titters of laughter, and Anna and Cress snorted at my side.

"I wonder who got caught?" Cress murmured.

"Probably Tiffany," Anna replied, nodding at a girl whose cheeks were bright red with embarrassment. "Her boyfriend practically lives in her room."

Lisa cleared her throat and raised her voice as she tried to regain everyone's attention. "If this rule is broken again, I will assign every single one of you to cleaning the bathrooms in the boys' dormitory for a week." The laughter quickly died. "And *I mean* each and every one of you, whether you broke the rules or not. I can't imagine you'll be very interested in sneaking boys into your rooms after that." A small smile curved Lisa's lips like she knew exactly how cruel and effective her threat was.

"So, that's all I wanted to talk about this morning," Lisa continued, her voice suddenly bright like she hadn't just been threatening us. "Please enjoy your coffees and croissants. I look forward to seeing you all together again for family night on Tuesday."

The room broke out into chatter the moment Lisa stopped speaking.

"That's evil, especially for Lisa," Cress murmured. "She's normally so nice."

"Evil but effective," Anna added. "I'll happily chase away any boys who so much as glance at our dorms at the wrong time of night. I am not cleaning the boys' toilets."

"Me neither," I agreed with a shudder. "I think I'd be traumatized for life."

One of the girls standing next to me scoffed, and she rolled her eyes as she caught my gaze. She'd clearly taken issue with something I'd said.

"What?" I asked her as she went to turn away.

"Oh, nothing," she replied, but given the slight smile on her lips and the tone in her voice, it was clear she was hiding something

"Obviously, it's not nothing."

She lifted one eyebrow and folded her arms across her chest as she faced me. "I think we all know there's no way *you* would have to clean the boys' toilets."

"What's that supposed to mean?"

"Just that we can't all be a LaFleur, can we?" She turned and walked off before I could respond, and I stood there gaping after her.

"Did you guys hear that?" I turned to Cress and Anna. They were both glaring at the girl's retreating figure.

"Don't listen to Nat," Anna said. "She's always snarky like that."

"What does that even mean? We can't all be a LaFleur? It's not like I get special treatment..."

"No..." Cress started. "But I'd say that's only because you don't ask for it. Nat's probably right. With your dad being who he is, I'm sure they wouldn't make you clean the boys' toilets if you kicked up a fuss about it."

I frowned at my friends, but Anna was nodding alongside

Cress. "Yeah, we all know the rules are different for certain people in this school."

"Really? Because nothing's changed for me since people found out who my dad is."

"Hasn't it?" Anna asked.

"I mean, I've had a few people try to talk to me who would probably have ignored me completely a week ago, but it's not like I've been treated any differently by the teachers. I definitely haven't had a different set of rules than everyone else."

"I guess we won't know until a teacher tries to make you clean a boy's bathroom," Cress said.

I grimaced at the thought. "Here's hoping that never happens."

"I'll drink to that," Anna said. She downed the rest of her coffee and placed the cup in the bin. We each took another croissant before we started back up the stairs to our rooms.

I wondered how much truth there was to what the girls said. Were the rules here different for me because now people knew who my father was? I didn't want any special treatment, and I hoped they were wrong.

"I'm going straight back to bed," Anna said, munching on the end of her croissant as she spoke.

"Same," Cress agreed. "Lisa could have simply threatened another early Sunday morning wake up, and I would have complied."

"I'll say." Anna nodded. "Not that any of us are sneaking boys into our rooms. *I wish* my dating life was that exciting."

Cress snorted. "Can you imagine Kat's reaction if you tried to bring a boy into your room? She'd avoid you even more than she already does."

"Oh my gosh, she would kill me," Anna replied. "I'd have to sleep with one eye open for the rest of the year."

"One eye?" Cress said. "I think you'd need both."

Anna nodded, and a shudder seemed to go down her back. It

was safe to say the wrath of Anna's roommate was a bigger deterrent for her than cleaning a boy's bathroom ever could be.

We wandered back to our floor before parting ways with Anna as we went back to our separate rooms. Cress immediately threw herself back into bed and cuddled up under the covers while I went to the closet to fish out my running gear. I'd been avoiding running all week for fear of bumping into Noah, but I couldn't give up jogging entirely just because I didn't want to see my ex.

"You're not going back to bed?" Cress asked.

"No, I think I'll go for a run. My coffee has me buzzed."

"Really? I must drink far too much because it barely gives me a kick anymore."

"You practically have a cup glued to your hand twenty-four seven, so you're probably right." I laughed.

"There are worse vices." She let out a big yawn and snuggled farther under her sheets. She looked so cozy I was almost tempted to return to bed myself. But I knew I needed to clear my head, so I changed into my running gear and rushed out the door before I could reconsider.

Thunder rumbled as I emerged outside. It had been storming on and off all week, but it wasn't raining yet, so I was hoping it would hold off a little longer so I wouldn't get drenched on my run. The clouds overhead didn't look promising and were so dark and gloomy I half considered turning back inside and trying again later. I knew I'd only go crazy if I went another day without running to clear my mind, so I started out into the blustering wind.

I headed into the woods. If it was going to rain, at least there might be some protection beneath the trees. On Monday, I'd made the mistake of choosing the path around the lake in an attempt to avoid Noah and had ended up seeing him anyway, so I knew there was little point in choosing my route simply to avoid him. Fate apparently had a twisted sense of humor when it came to the two of us, so it seemed pointless to try to fight it.

Still, I hoped the grim weather would put Noah off running today. I didn't want to see him this morning, especially not after our encounter on Friday night. Hopefully, he was still tucked up in bed like most sane people.

My limbs took a while to warm up, but eventually I fell into a good rhythm as I ran along the winding path. I could feel the breath of winter on the early-morning air, and I knew it wouldn't be long now until the days turned short and cold and any hint of summer was gone for good. I hated the cold and wasn't looking forward to it one bit.

I was glad I'd chosen the woods. Thunder still rumbled across the horizon, and the wind howled as it whipped through the canopy overhead. The weather was turning slightly more apocalyptic than I'd predicted, and I considered heading back. I must have been crazy to head out on a run when a storm was rolling in. What if a tree branch fell on me? Or what if I was struck by lightning? I knew the chances of that happening were practically zero, but it didn't stop the thought from crossing my mind.

The sound of a twig snapping made me glance over my shoulder as a figure appeared on the path behind me. I nearly stumbled over a rock as my gaze collided with Noah's. His green eyes widened with obvious surprise, but I had to wonder if it was faked. Had he followed me here, or was I simply destined to bump into him every time I went for a run? Surely fate wouldn't be so cruel as to throw him into my path once again.

It felt like he was plaguing my existence. When he wasn't physically there, he was in my thoughts. I'd risked life and limb coming out in this storm, simply so I could clear my mind of him, but apparently that wasn't enough to escape him. I couldn't help but feel pissed he'd shown up again, so I slammed to a stop and turned on him.

"What are you doing?" I hissed.

Noah halted and scowled as he folded his arms across his broad chest. "I'm running. Am I not allowed to run?"

I stalked toward him, anger carrying my feet forward. "No, you're following me." I poked him in his stupid chest, but he captured my hand, holding it there.

My breaths had been coming in hard and fast until that moment, but as soon as his skin made contact with mine, I struggled to breathe at all. God, how I hated my reaction to him. How just one touch made me lose control. How my body so easily forgot that he was completely off limits.

"I didn't follow you here," he growled.

I shook my head, unsure if I believed him. "Why can't you just leave me alone?"

He stared at me, confusion and hurt swirling in the bright-green depths of his eyes. Finally, he released a humorless laugh and let go of my hand. "I want nothing to do with you..." He glanced away from me, his mouth forming a hard line as he continued. "And yet I still want everything." He shook his head. "I need to get you out of my head."

"Maybe start by leaving me alone."

"I didn't follow you here," he repeated.

"Fine, fate just has a screwed-up sense of humor then. But you *did* choose to confront me at the party on Friday night."

"Am I supposed to just ignore the fact you already want to move on?"

Now I was the one to laugh, but there was absolutely nothing about this situation that was remotely funny. "You broke up with me, Noah. You dumped me because your grandfather asked you to and because you can't handle who my dad is. What I do now is none of your concern."

I turned to leave, but he grabbed my hand once more, pulling me toward him. I slammed into his chest, and he trapped me in his arms. A million tingles erupted across my skin at the contact. Being this close to him was dangerous. It was heady and addictive. It was not helping me with moving on.

Thunder rumbled overhead, but the sound felt like a mere echo as I stared into Noah's eyes.

"What are you doing?" It took every bit of willpower I possessed to make sure the words didn't come out as a whisper.

I could see Noah was just as tortured as me. "I don't want you rebounding onto somebody else."

"That's not up to you. You dumped me, remember?"

"I know."

"So, let me go, Noah."

"I can't." His arms gripped me tightly, but he seemed to be talking about so much more than just holding me close to him. "I can't let you go," he said. "But I can't be with you either."

I shook my head. "It doesn't work that way."

"I know."

"You made your choice."

"*I know.*" Each word from his lips was pained, and there was a panicked look in his eyes I'd never seen before. "It doesn't stop me from missing you. From wanting you with every breath that I take."

"You can't say that stuff to me, Noah. It's not fair."

"But it's true," he replied. "I just keep thinking that perhaps if I could taste your lips one last time that would be enough. I could stop thinking about them. I could stop thinking about you. Maybe it would take the pain away, even if just for a moment. Maybe I could find some closure."

"You want to kiss me to help you move on?"

"Yes." His voice was rough.

It took a moment to process. "That's really messed up, Noah."

His jaw tightened like he knew it was insane, and yet it didn't change how he felt. "Will you let me kiss you?"

As much as I wanted to pretend I wasn't tempted, I was. I despised this boy for dumping me. I hated him for being an ass to me on Friday night. And yet, my body was acting like it had completely forgotten we were no longer together. I liked to believe I had enough self-respect to refuse him, but all sense went out the window when I was standing in his arms. It took me far longer to respond than it should have, and I stared at him as desire warred with the wiser part of my brain.

"No." I somehow choked out the smart response. My heart clenched tightly in objection. I wanted him just as badly as he seemed to want me, but I couldn't give in. I *shouldn't*.

Somehow, *somehow*, I found the strength to step away from him. To release myself from his grasp. I needed space so I could think. But as soon as I had created it, I knew I didn't want there to be any distance between us at all.

One last kiss. That was all Noah was asking for. And what if he was right? What if one final kiss would help me move on? What if I could finally put him in my past? I was already hurting so much. Would it really be so bad if I took just one moment to forget the pain?

Before I could reconsider, I strode toward him, and he didn't hesitate as he reached for me, dragging me in and crushing me to him. Our lips clashed together as thunder cracked, the storm swirling around us just as violent and passionate as our kiss.

I wasn't even sure if you could call what we were doing a kiss. It was raw and carnal. It was something so much fiercer than any kisses I'd experienced before. It was all heat and need with none of the gentle kindness of Noah's other kisses.

I hated it.

I loved it.

I wanted it to end.

I needed it to last forever.

We kissed with such passion it felt like the whole world quaked in response. His hands were everywhere. His kiss was lips and tongue and teeth. I didn't think he could erase any more of the space between us, but then he lifted me into his arms. My legs wrapped around him, never wanting to let him go. I couldn't think straight. I couldn't think at all. In that moment, all I knew was Noah, and I never wanted to know anything else.

It didn't matter that the thunder was growing louder. That the wind was picking up, tugging at my hair and swirling the leaves around our feet. And when the skies opened and thick rain started to fall upon us, I thought perhaps that didn't matter either. The world could drown, for all I cared.

We were both soaked through in moments and Noah pulled back from our kiss, staring at me through the sheeting rain that fell between us. I didn't need to ask what he was thinking. I already knew. That kiss was it, and we were finished.

I jerked out of his hold and swiped a hand across my lips as I glared at him. That kiss wasn't one that made you forget some- one. It was the kind that imprinted on your soul and left its brand there forever.

"You done?" I growled.

Noah's eyes were wild, his focus still on my lips as he stared at me. I felt like he was trying to control himself. Like he was on edge and could attack me with his lips again at any moment.

"Well?" I prompted, hugging my arms around the drenched clothes that clung to my waist.

He refused to meet my gaze. "I'm done."

"Good." I turned and started running back to school before I could give in to the emotions whirring within me. This was what he wanted. What I wanted. For this thing between us to be over. But if this was what I wanted, then why did I feel like I was going to cry?

Noah would forget me now.

But I was never going to forget that kiss.

CHAPTER ELEVEN

Even the next day, my lips seemed to burn from Noah's kisses. It was like he'd marked himself on them. Like he'd seared his name across every inch of them. They belonged to him, and they ached to return to their owner.

Noah's kiss had done absolutely nothing to help me get over him. If anything, he had only made being apart from him worse. I needed something to help me take my mind off him. And for once, schoolwork just wasn't doing the trick. It certainly didn't help when I had to sit right in front of him during class.

I could feel his presence behind me. The air between us radiated with tension, and I struggled to retain a single thing the teacher said during the business management lesson we shared together.

Lily sat at the desk beside me, and she kept sending strange looks in Noah's direction. I couldn't see why she was looking at him so weirdly, but it didn't make sitting so close to him any easier. I was desperate to turn and look at him, but somehow, I managed to hold myself back.

When the torturous class was finally over and I was out in the corridor, I pulled Lily aside.

"Why did you keep looking at Noah during class?" I asked her.

"He couldn't take his eyes off you." She murmured the words and glanced around nervously like she was wary of being over-heard. "He seemed upset."

"Really?"

"If I had to guess, I'd say he's not over your breakup." She readjusted her bag on her shoulder and looked back at the classroom as Noah emerged. He didn't look our way and strode off in the other direction, so I had no chance to see his expression.

"He should be," I murmured. Especially after demanding one last kiss from me yesterday to help us both move on.

"It's only been a week. I'd be surprised if he was."

I blew out a breath. "Yeah, I guess you're right."

We started to slowly move off down the corridor. It was the end of the day, so it was crowded with students rushing to get out of school.

"How are you feeling about the breakup?" Lily asked.

"I'm getting there." It was a total lie. I wasn't getting anywhere, especially after that kiss. I hadn't been able to get it out of my mind, and even now my heart raced a little faster at the thought of it.

Stupid Noah with his stupid unforgettable lips.

She gave me a small smile. "It's okay if you're not over it too."

"I'm that obvious, huh?"

"Just a little." She laughed. "But I can understand that you don't want to dwell on it."

"Yeah," I agreed. "The sooner I'm over him, the better."

We emerged from the building and out into the afternoon sunshine. As we walked across the courtyard, my phone started buzzing in my pocket.

I pulled it out and saw my mom was calling. "I better take this."

Lily nodded. "Okay, I'll see you later."

I walked over to the nearest bench and sat down as I answered the call. "Mom, how do you get over a boy?"

She chuckled in response. "Hello to you too."

I rolled my eyes but smiled. "Hi, Mom."

"You're still hung up on Noah, huh?"

I'd been doing my best not to burn my mom's ears off complaining about Noah when we'd talked over the last week. I hated the thought of worrying her. I'd been a total mess when my last boyfriend had cheated on me, and I didn't want Mom afraid I was in the same dark place I'd been after Levi. Not when she was so far away. I also didn't want to burden her with my problems when I knew she had issues of her own. She seemed to be dealing with a lot of stress at the café at the moment, and even now she sounded exhausted. She told me she had it all under control, but I wasn't sure I believed her. She tended to change the subject whenever I brought it up.

I exhaled and sank a little lower in the seat. "Yeah, he's kind of hard to forget." Especially when he was staring at me in class and demanding kisses from me in the rain.

"I only spent a short time with him, but I could tell he was special," she agreed. I kind of hated her for saying it, but I wasn't sure I could stomach her despising him either. My feelings for him weren't exactly rational at this point.

"So, any idea how to get over *special*?"

"The best cure for a broken heart is to give it time," she said. "Time usually makes even the worst wounds a little easier to live with."

Sitting and waiting to feel better didn't seem like a very proactive way to get over a guy. The idea of being in pain for any longer also wasn't appealing.

"I don't really have time. I want to get over him now."

Mom chuckled. "Sometimes you sound far older than your years, but then you say something like that, and I remember just how young you are."

"I'm not that young."

"You are to me."

I knew I would never win this argument. I would always be her baby to her. "So, any other ideas for mending a broken heart?"

I heard a sound on the other end of the line, and Mom's voice became muffled like she was covering the end of the phone to talk with someone. I could hear the clatter of pans in the background, so she must have been at work.

"Iz, I have a customer that's asking for me," she said, the line now crystal clear again. "I'll be back in a moment, but Norma will keep you company while I'm gone."

"Okay." I waited as the line went quiet, and then I heard rustling as Norma picked up the phone.

"Isobel, sweetie, how are you?"

I smiled at the sound of her husky voice. She was the person I missed the most from back home—after my mom, of course.

"I'm okay. Working hard at school."

"Your mom says you and that boy you brought home broke up."

I should have known Noah would be the one thing Norma wanted to chat about. When she wasn't making outlandish predictions about the future, she loved nothing more than talking about boys and the heart.

"Yeah, it happened last week."

"I can hardly believe it. He looked totally smitten with you when you were here."

I shrugged. "Guess he wasn't *that* smitten."

"No, he definitely was. But, not to worry, he'll come back to you. Any psychic worth their salt could tell you that."

"I think your psychic powers might be wrong on this one. Besides, I'm trying to get over him."

"Well, if that's what you want, the best way to get over someone is to get under someone else."

"Norma!"

"What?" She sounded genuinely confused by my reaction. "It's true."

"I'm seventeen. I'm not getting under anyone!" My cheeks were so hot right now I felt like I'd walked into a furnace.

"Well, it's still the best advice I have."

"That's terrible advice to give a teenager." I laughed.

"I'm just trying to keep it real."

I shook my head. "Well, any other real breakup advice that is somewhat more age appropriate?"

"Well, my momma always said that you can't heal a heart by dwelling on the past. The only way to make things better is to focus on the present. The heart will take care of the rest."

"So, I need to stop thinking about Noah and the breakup?"

"Yes, and distractions will help. Distractions like finding a cute new boy to get—"

"*Norma!*" She was officially worse than Anna.

She chuckled. "Your mom's back, sweetie, and I better get back to work. I'll talk to you soon."

She was off the phone before I could reprimand her again.

"Why did Norma have a devious grin on her lips when she handed over the phone?" Mom asked as she came back.

"She was giving me breakup advice."

"And..."

"And it wasn't very helpful. I think I'll stick with your advice of giving things time."

"That sounds wise," Mom agreed.

It wasn't exactly easy. Giving things time wasn't the quick fix I was after, but I trusted my mom knew what she was talking about.

A big clatter of plates sounded in the background and Mom swore under her breath. "Our new waitress has butter fingers today," she said. "I better go."

"Okay, talk to you soon."

"Love you."

"Love you more."

I ended the call feeling both better and worse. Speaking with my mom always made me happier, but it was hard not to feel a little disheartened as I was no closer to getting over Noah and her advice was to just wait. It sounded simple enough in theory, but I had a feeling it wouldn't be nearly so easy in practice. Especially not when I constantly saw him at school and time seemed to warp to a standstill whenever I was in his presence. It also didn't help that whenever we were close I felt so drawn to him. No time more so than yesterday in the woods. What we needed were better boundaries—any boundaries at all, really.

The thought gave me clarity and resolve, and my feet moved of their own accord in the direction of the boys' dormitory. I was supposed to be meeting Wes in the library soon so we could work on our economics homework from last week, but I could spare a few minutes. I was probably crazy to think going to see Noah was a good idea, but if I was ever going to get over him, we needed to set some ground rules. I was thinking no kissing and no longing looks would be at the top of the list.

When I got to his room, I banged hard on the door. Noah answered on the second knock, pure surprise lighting his eyes when he found me standing on the other side of the door.

"Can we talk?" I asked before he could say anything.

For a moment, it looked like he was going to refuse me. He glanced past me and looked up and down the corridor. When he saw I was alone, he nodded. Was he that worried about being seen with me?

He stepped back, gesturing for me to enter his room. I clenched my hands as I walked past him, trying my best to ignore the fresh scent of his aftershave. Even now, I still melted a little at the scent of it. He was dressed in his soccer gear, his gym bag slung over his shoulder. He looked like he was on his way out.

"I have to get to practice," he said.

"This won't take long."

He closed the door behind me and indicated for me to continue.

I drew in a deep breath before I spoke, mentally gearing up to put Noah in his place. He interrupted before I got a chance.

"That last class with you was torture," he said.

"What? Why?"

"Because you were sitting right in front of me. I could smell the scent of your vanilla shampoo."

It was the last thing I expected him to say. "You can sit somewhere else, you know."

He shook his head slowly, as though my suggestion was impossible to imagine.

"It's not just your scent that's driving me crazy," he continued. "It's seeing you every day and knowing I can't touch you, knowing I can't smile with you or talk to you. I can't stop thinking about the forest..." His eyes dropped to my lips, and he stepped closer like he was thinking about kissing me again.

"Noah, you said that kiss was it. That we would kiss one last time and move on..."

"One kiss wasn't enough," he murmured, moving closer still.

I backed away from him, jolting as I accidentally knocked into his desk. I'd come here to tell Noah I needed more space, and he was doing the exact opposite. I was already struggling with self-control when it came to him, and the closer he got to me, the more he erased any ability I had to resist. Coming to his room was stupid enough, but giving in to any desire I felt for him could be fatal to my slim hopes of moving on.

"Noah..." I murmured his name in warning. "I came here to tell you that we need to stop this. We need boundaries. The looks you keep giving me, *that kiss* yesterday. You've made it perfectly clear we can't be together, and I can't get over you if you won't let me go."

"Tell me I can kiss you again."

I swallowed, my heart racing as I tried to summon the strength to deny him. His last kiss had shattered me, but another one might destroy me entirely.

"That would be a bad idea." It was all I could manage to say.

"That's not a no."

"It's not…"

He lowered his lips to mine, and I melted into his arms as he kissed me. His kiss yesterday had been raw and filled with hunger, but today's kiss was different. I could almost taste his desperation and sadness on his lips. I could feel he was aching as much as I was in the way he grasped my body tightly in his hands, holding me to him like I might disappear if he let me go.

Everything about this felt so right. But it also felt so, so wrong.

I pulled back from him and gasped for air. "You can't keep kissing me."

"I can't help it," he gritted out. "The only thing stopping us is my grandfather. In the woods, in my room, where no one can see, we can do whatever we want."

His words were so alluring and his lips still so close to mine I almost moved toward them again. But then I saw sense. He was talking about a secret relationship again.

"I'm never going to agree to that, Noah. I'm surprised you keep asking. You hate secrets as much as I do."

"It would be worth it to be with you."

Looking into his eyes, I found it hard to believe he didn't care for me enough to tell his grandfather to go to hell. He was looking at me like he would burn the world down around us just so we could be together. Apparently, those feelings weren't enough.

"Couldn't we just talk with your grandfather?" I whispered. "Maybe if we explained our feelings to him, he'd understand…"

My question seemed to break the moment we'd been sharing, shattering it so thoroughly I had to wonder if I'd perhaps dreamed it. Noah loosened his grip on me and stepped back, his expression turning to ice as he looked away. "He won't understand. His hatred runs too deep."

"If you could just tell me what happened…"

"There's no point." Noah felt so distant now even though he was only a few steps from me. "You think the truth will help. You think if you understand what happened you might be able to find a way around it so we can be together. But this isn't a fairy tale, and there is no happy ending for us."

"I know this isn't fairy tale," I growled.

"Do you? The poor girl who works at a café finds out she's truly a princess and is whisked away to a castle. Sounds like a fairy tale to me. But how are you going to feel when you find out your father is the villain in the story? That you may be a princess, but you're the heir to a throne built on lies and betrayal."

"What are you talking about, Noah? I deserve to know the truth."

"Perhaps." He nodded. "But I won't be the one to shatter your fairy tale."

I was shaking as I stood there. Noah was deliberately keeping things from me, and his excuse was that he didn't want to shatter my fairy tale? He had no right to decide what was best for me. Especially after deciding we couldn't even be in each other's lives.

"This isn't some fairy tale to me," I repeated. "This is my life."

"I'm sorry, Isobel. I shouldn't have kissed you yesterday, and I shouldn't have kissed you just now." My heart felt like it was imploding all over again as he spoke. "You're right; we need boundaries. This won't happen again." I could see from the resolution in his eyes that he meant it.

Seeing him so certain only angered me. He'd been the one demanding more kisses from me. He was the one making things so messy. I'd done nothing wrong, and yet he was acting like this was all my fault.

"You're right. It won't." My eyes were cold as I stared at him, and anger drove my feet toward the door. It had been a mistake coming here. One I wouldn't be making again.

"Isobel..." he called after me, but I walked through the door without looking back, closing it firmly behind me. I didn't want to hear any more of what Noah had to say. I knew he wasn't changing his mind about us.

I was certain there was no way I'd be able to follow my mom's advice. I couldn't wait for things between Noah and I to blow over because my self-control around him was feeble. More time only meant more opportunities to make mistakes. I kept messing up with him, and I hated to think what might transpire if he asked me to kiss him again. I liked to think I'd turn him down, but I clearly had no restraint when it came to his lips. My attempt at setting boundaries had ended disastrously too.

I felt a desperate need to be proactive. To do something, *anything*, to get over him. To give me the strength I needed so I wouldn't be stupid enough to kiss him again. There was only one way I could think to do it, and I was probably going to regret it. But desperate times called for desperate measures. So, I was going to have to give Anna and Norma's advice a go.

CHAPTER TWELVE

I was still riled with anger as I marched from Noah's room and started down the corridor. What I had planned next was the worst kind of idea. But right now, I didn't care. All I wanted was to erase Noah's lips from my own, and no amount of scrubbing them was going to do the trick. No, I needed something stronger. Something drastic. Just like Anna and Norma kept saying, I needed a rebound. And I knew just where to find one.

Within a few moments, I found myself standing at Wes and Sawyer's room. Without a second thought, I knocked on the door. My hands were shaking as I waited for a response, but I couldn't tell if it was because of nerves, irritation, adrenaline, or a combination of all three. This was a terrible idea. Probably the worst I'd ever come up with. I really wasn't sure what I was thinking. Maybe I wasn't thinking at all. There was no way I'd be standing here if I was in the right mind. But maybe that was what I needed. I'd been dwelling on my breakup with Noah for too long, leaving myself vulnerable to falling for him all over again. It was time to stop thinking and start doing something about it.

I sucked in a breath as the door opened to reveal Wes standing on the other side. He was still dressed in his school uniform, but he'd removed his tie, and the top few buttons of his shirt were undone. His brow creased with confusion as he laid eyes on me. "Isobel? I thought we were meeting in the library."

I pushed past him and into the room. "Is Sawyer here?"

Wes shook his head. "He's at soccer practice."

I swore under my breath and started pacing the room. "When do you think he'll be back?"

"He only just left so not for at least another hour."

"Damn," I muttered. I doubted I'd be this riled up in an hour's time, and there was no way I'd have the guts to go through with my crazy plan then. I'd be right back where I started.

I was still pacing around the room as Wes came up and grabbed hold of my arms, forcing me to a standstill. "What's wrong? Why do you need to see my brother so bad?"

I slowly released my breath, a little of my annoyance dissipating as I looked up and into his calming brown eyes. "You're going to think I'm a terrible person."

"Try me."

I let out another slow exhale. "I need to do something to get over Noah. It's too much, and nothing is working. I thought I might take Sawyer up on his offer..."

My voice trailed off and Wes' frown grew deeper.

"What offer?"

"His offer to help me."

"Help...how?"

"By being.... By being my rebound." As I stuttered out my explanation, I felt my cheeks burning with embarrassment. It sounded so silly when I spoke the words out loud.

Wes's eyebrows shot toward the ceiling, and he let out an uncomfortable cough. "You came here to make out with my brother?"

"Yes. No. I don't know." I stumbled over the words. "I told you you'd think I was a terrible person."

"Well, it's just..."

"A terrible idea?" I finished his thought for him.

"The worst," he agreed.

I sighed again, and my shoulders slumped. Wes was still gripping my arms, and it felt like he was stopping me from collapsing in an ashamed heap on the floor.

"I just can't keep doing this," I moaned. "My mind needs something else to think about. My heart needs something else to beat for. Everyone seems to think that kissing someone else will help."

"Do *you* think it will help?"

"I don't know. Probably not."

"And do you *really* want to kiss Sawyer?"

"Gosh no. I'd probably pick up some kind of disease."

Wes chuckled under his breath.

"He's the only guy who's offered though," I said. "And I know he won't think it's something that it's not."

"He's not the only guy who's offered..."

My gaze darted up to meet Wes's once again. Was he talking about himself? Was he offering to kiss me? His eyes were serious as he looked at me, and my mouth turned dry. I was suddenly more aware of his strong hands wrapped around my arms, and the feeling sent tingles to my stomach.

"You were drunk, and you didn't mean it," I whispered. He was standing so close to me, and the room seemed so much warmer.

"Was I..." he whispered.

Wes was incredibly handsome. I'd noticed, of course—you'd be stupid not to. He and his brother looked like they'd stepped out of an Abercrombie campaign. But I'd never thought beyond their good looks before. Sawyer was Sawyer, and Wes had become such a good friend in such a short time I'd never even considered him in a different way. But when he was focused on me so intensely, I didn't know where to look and I couldn't quite remember how to breathe.

The thought of kissing him was tempting. Especially when I was hurting. When I wanted nothing more than to forget. Wes was offering me exactly the distraction I needed and wanted. It was exactly why I'd come to this room in the first place.

I shook my head and gave him a sad smile. "Well, even if you weren't drunk, I'd have to refuse. You're too important to me as a friend, Wes."

He nodded and smiled. "Yeah, your friendship is important to me too. Besides, we're breakup buddies. Not rebound buddies."

I laughed. "And I think breakup buddies is enough responsibility already." I stepped out of his grasp, but my body tensed slightly when I did, as though it was resisting the decision. His arms fell to his side, and the warm smile he'd shown me just a moment ago dropped for a second, but it returned so quickly I wondered if I'd been mistaken.

"A responsibility I take very seriously." He winked at me.

"I feel like an idiot," I replied. "Do you think we can pretend I never came storming in here searching for a rebound?"

"I think I can agree to that." He smiled. "So, it might not be as exciting as making out with your hot friend, but did you still want to go to the library and work on our econ homework?"

I smirked at him. "Definitely not as exciting, but econ homework sounds like a healthier coping mechanism."

"Much healthier," he agreed.

Wes grabbed his bag, and we started toward the door. He stopped me before we left the room though. "Isobel?"

"Yeah."

His expression was serious again, and he looked nervous. "If you ever get desperate for another *coping mechanism* again, please don't make out with Sawyer."

He scratched the back of his neck when he saw the questioning look in my eyes. "This is going to sound weird, but he's my twin, and we're kind of a package deal. Like I said, you're important to me, and Sawyer doesn't have the best track record with girls. If anything bad happened, I wouldn't know whose breakup buddy I was supposed to be."

He looked genuinely worried, and I felt like even more of an idiot. My mind was clear enough now to know just how ridiculous coming here looking for Sawyer had been. There was no way I was going to kiss Sawyer, let alone start and then end a relationship with him. I gave Wes a small nod of understanding.

"Don't worry, I won't," I said. "This little brain fade is well and truly in the past. As long as Sawyer doesn't find out about this, I don't think we'll ever have to talk about it again."

"Well, he certainly won't hear it from me." Wes winked at me again, as we left the room and headed for the library.

IT WAS late by the time I finally made it back to my dorm. I'd missed Cress and Anna at dinner but found them both laid out on Cress's bed doing their nails when I arrived.

"Where have you been all night?" Cress asked as I ditched my bag by the door. "You totally missed girls' night."

I groaned and threw myself onto my bed. "I think I would have preferred girls' night. My life is a disaster."

They both exchanged a look before they focused back on me.

"Spill," Anna demanded.

I hadn't told either of them about the kiss I shared with Noah yesterday or the one we had today. I couldn't keep it to myself any longer, and the words tumbled out as I told them everything that had happened in the last two days.

"You made out with Noah in the woods?" Cress gasped.

"And again today?" Anna's voice was filled with a mixture of disbelief and joy.

"That's not even the most surprising part," I groaned. "I did something even more stupid than that."

"What did you do?" They were both sitting on the edge of Cress's bed desperately waiting for my answer.

"I was so mad at Noah I went straight to the twins' room so I could take Sawyer up on his offer to be my rebound."

"You didn't!" they both cried.

"I did."

"And what happened?" They were going to fall off the bed if they leaned forward any more.

"Well, thankfully, Sawyer wasn't there." I grimaced before I continued. "But Wes was, and he offered to kiss me instead."

"Oh. My. God." I couldn't tell which of them squealed the loudest.

Cress practically leaped off the bed and looked ready to explode as she waited for me to continue. "Did you do it? Did you kiss him?"

I shook my head. "I couldn't. He's my friend, and I really want to keep it that way." Anna and Cress deflated like popped balloons. "I think he felt the same way though," I explained. "We both kind of laughed about it after. Still, he nearly gave me a heart attack when he offered."

"Wow, you really know how to bring the drama to a boring old Monday night." After the initial disappointment at hearing I hadn't kissed Wes, Anna now had an impressed look on her face.

"I feel like I've made a total idiot of myself."

Cress sat down next to me and wrapped an arm around my shoulders. "You're not an idiot at all. You've been having a hard time with the breakup. We all understand that."

"And Noah shouldn't keep kissing you," Anna said. "That's like the worst breakup etiquette ever."

"It's really messing with my head," I agreed. "I swear, the logical part of my brain seems to be on holiday. I can't believe I thought if I started kissing someone else I'd be able to regain some self-control."

"I mean, it's what I would do," Anna agreed.

"But not necessarily the right advice for you, Isobel," Cress added, shooting a look at Anna. "I can chat with Noah, tell him to back off, if you want?"

I shook my head. "No, it's okay. I need to be stronger. I need to learn to deal with breakups myself."

"What you need is to not see Noah every day," Anna said. "If only we could bail on school and go on vacation."

I sat up a little straighter. "Well, it's not a vacation, but we've got that English trip to New York coming up, and my mom said I can stay with you, Cress."

"Yes!" She started clapping her hands together with excitement. "I've already started making a list of everywhere we've got to go. Anna, you're coming, right?"

"Obviously," she said with a wide smile. "It's about time we had a girls' weekend. I'm in desperate need of some new clothes, so this couldn't come at a better time."

For the first time in days, I began to feel a little more hopeful, and I smiled at my two friends. I wasn't all that into shopping, but I'd be happy to do just about anything so long as it took my mind off Noah.

"This is perfect," Anna said. "By the time the weekend's over, you'll have had such a good time you won't even remember Noah's name."

I hoped that meant I'd forget his lips too.

CHAPTER THIRTEEN

Noah seemed determined to keep his word the rest of the week. He didn't bother me once. He didn't so much as look my way. He acted as though I didn't exist at all, and as much as that hurt, it was also somewhat of a relief not having to deal with him constantly staring at me. I was still looking forward to the escape I hoped our field trip would offer though.

"What's this I hear about you girls staying in New York for the weekend after the English trip ends?" Sawyer asked as he and Wes joined us at breakfast on Thursday morning.

The bus was leaving after breakfast, so we were eating quickly to make sure we didn't miss it. The twins were in Anna's English class, so they were coming to watch the play too. We'd been keeping our weekend plans quiet from the boys because Anna was convinced they would try to gate-crash. I had no idea how they'd found out.

"We're having a girls' weekend," Anna replied. "You're not invited."

Sawyer placed a hand against his chest. "Not invited?"

"Here we go," Cress muttered.

"Not invited?" Sawyer's voice had taken on an overly dramatic tone. "How could you girls hurt me so? I happen to be a great addition to girls' trips."

Anna folded her arms. "No, you're a boy. You're not welcome on girls' trips."

"But I love to do all the fluff you girls do."

She shook her head. "The fact you call it fluff shows exactly why you shouldn't come."

Sawyer sank into his chair, a despondent look in his eyes. "I just thought we were all friends," he said. "I thought you'd seen how tough Wes has taken his breakup with Sarah."

"Don't bring me into this," Wes said.

Sawyer wasn't listening though. "I thought you could see how much my poor brother needs cheering up. A weekend in New York would have done wonders for him. Instead, you've all broken his heart even further."

Wes rolled his eyes. "You really haven't."

Sawyer looked at him with pity in his eyes. "See? Poor guy can't even admit when he's in pain."

Anna huffed. "You're not going to let this go, are you, Sawyer?"

He gave her a sly grin. "No, I'll be milking this one for a while."

Anna groaned and then glanced in my direction. "I'll let you decide, Isobel. This is your weekend. We can either invite the twins or listen to Sawyer grumble about it until Christmas. Either way, he'll probably just stay in the city and end up bothering us anyway..."

"Looks like we don't have much choice then." I laughed at Sawyer who was now batting his eyelids at me. "Okay, fine, you guys can come. But no calling girl stuff *fluff*."

"And you're going to have to stay at your own place," Cress added. "I don't want to get stuck explaining to my parents why their front window is broken again."

"That was an accident," Sawyer grumbled. "I blame your

window for not being strong enough to withstand a gentle hit with a soccer ball."

"I'm not willing to take that chance."

"But we wanted to be part of the slumber party..."

"Too bad," Anna said. "Oh, and under absolutely no circumstances are you allowed to moan about the things we have planned. This is a girls' weekend, and you're gate-crashing, so we're in charge."

Sawyer looked between the three of us before he finally grinned and slapped Wes on the back. "Dude, we're going to have the best weekend in New York."

Wes laughed and shook his head at his brother. As annoying as Sawyer was, it was hard not to get caught up in his exuberance sometimes.

The others started chatting about their plans for the weekend, but Wes turned his attention to me. "You really didn't have to let us impose on your plans," he said. "I was going to stay the weekend anyway to spend time with my parents, but I understand if you only want to hang out with Cress and Anna."

"Don't be silly, it will be even better with you guys there too." I shared a smile with him. "I can't wait. I haven't been to New York before."

"You'll love it," Wes said. "What are you looking forward to the most?"

I paused before I answered. Although I was excited about my first trip to New York and all the sights and sounds it had to offer, there was one part of the trip I had been thinking about all week. The way Noah had spoken about my father the last time we talked had left me desperate to speak to Matthew, to question him about everything. He was too busy to see me while I was in New York, so I was considering taking matters into my own hands.

Wes was still waiting for my answer. I hadn't told the girls about my plans, and I didn't want to dampen their excitement for our trip, so I kept my voice low as I spoke to Wes.

"Well, it's not exactly sightseeing," I whispered.

"It's not?" Wes looked intrigued.

"My dad's staying in New York," I explained. "I'm not sure if he's been avoiding me or if he's just too busy with work, but I'm sick of waiting around for him. I have so many questions for him about Noah, the Hastings family, my mother—all of it."

"I can imagine."

"So, I'm planning to track him down and finally get some answers out of him. I just don't know where he lives, and apparently, he's too busy with work to see me."

"Why don't you just go to his office instead?" Wes asked. "He'll surely be there at some point, and The LaFleur Corp's offices are right in the center of town. I could take you there, if you like?"

"Really?"

He smiled. "Yeah, it wouldn't be any problem."

"That would be great. Thanks, Wes."

I felt calmer about the prospect of seeing my father. It felt like I could have the answers I'd been waiting for before the weekend was through.

"Like I said, not a problem," Wes continued. "So, once you've finished tracking down your father and interrogating him, what's next on your list of New York attractions?"

I rolled my eyes as he smirked at me.

"Well, the girls are keen to do some shopping." I sighed. "Lots and lots of shopping actually."

"You don't sound that excited."

"I am. I kind of want to see at least one of the sights while I'm there though."

"I guess we'll have to make that happen then. Anything in particular?"

My cheeks turned red. "You're going to think it's silly."

He leaned in close across the table, and the corner of his

mouth kicked up in a smirk. "Well, if it's anything like our mission to infiltrate The LaFleur Corp, I'm in."

"See, you're already making fun of me." I pouted at him

"Okay, sorry," he laughed. "Seriously, I'm sure it's not silly. I'm intrigued..."

He looked so curious, but I knew he wouldn't push me for an answer if I didn't want to give one. He was the least likely of my friends to think I was a loser though. "Okay, I'll tell you, but no laughing and no making fun of me."

"I promise."

I let out a breath. "Okay, well, I googled things to do in New York, and everything looked incredible, but I saw there's this gorgeous library in the city, and I've started to develop a bit of a thing for beautiful libraries..."

"You must be talking about the New York Public Library," Wes said with a glint in his eye.

"Is it sad that of all the things I want to see in New York a library is the top of my list?"

"It's not even close to sad. It's cute," he said.

I rolled my eyes again. "I said you couldn't make fun of me."

"I'm not, I swear. I mean, I am a little surprised. Most people want to go to the top of the Empire State Building or see the Statue of Liberty..."

"I do want to see those things. It's just, the library looks kind of magical."

"Like I said, it's cute," he replied.

I shook my head and turned to look at the others. They were chatting excitedly and didn't seem the least bit interested in listening to what Wes and I had been discussing. Sawyer was in the middle of an animated argument with Anna about where we should party on Saturday night. There was a buzz in the air, and I was looking forward to the weekend more than ever. This trip was exactly what I needed, and hopefully by the time I returned, I'd have both the space and answers I needed to finally put Noah behind me.

―――――

THE ONE THING I hadn't really considered about going to New York was that Noah was also going to be on the English trip. He might not be staying for the weekend, but he was going to be there for the rest of it. It was just my luck too that we both sat in an aisle seat on the bus, and he somehow ended up sitting diagonally in front of me. I was going to have to look at him the whole way to New York.

He was sitting next to Kaden, who had his head buried in a book. Noah remained focused on his phone and thankfully didn't seem interested in looking my way. A part of me hoped he hadn't realized I was sitting so close, but I knew he must have spotted me when he got on the bus. Besides, if he was anything like me, he had a radar that went off whenever I was near. I knew my senses certainly alerted me to his presence whenever he was around.

"Sawyer knows a guy who can get us into this new nightclub on Saturday night," Anna said. She was sitting next to me while Cress was hanging over the seat in front of us to listen in. "It's supposed to be amazing."

I swore Noah's head tilted in our direction, like he was trying to overhear our conversation.

"Can we get into a club?" I asked. "We're not even close to twenty-one."

Anna shrugged. "Sawyer seems confident. So, what do you guys think?"

Cress had a big grin on her face as she nodded. "You know me. Any excuse to go dancing."

I had to withhold a shudder at the thought. If they wanted to entice me into a club, then telling me it would involve dancing was not the right approach. Anna seemed to realize this and quickly continued.

"Sawyer says there's a great VIP section too. We can just chill on couches, listen to music, and flirt with cute boys."

A loud cough spluttered from farther up the aisle, and I glanced up to see Noah clearing his throat. He was still facing the front of the bus, but he was definitely listening in.

"That sounds great," I replied, shooting a glare at the side of his head—not that he noticed. "Count me in." I said it more for Noah's benefit than my own. I didn't really want to go to a club, but if Noah thought I was taking steps to move on, then hopefully he would too.

New York was several hours away by bus, but the trip went relatively quickly. Anna and Cress chatted constantly, so it was easy to lose myself in conversation with them. I never quite managed to forget Noah was sitting so close to me. He was like a mosquito bite, a dull itch on my skin that wouldn't go away no matter how much I tried to ignore it.

As we drew closer to the city, Anna swapped seats with me so I could stare out the window. I'd never visited a big city before, and I knew I was really exposing my small-town upbringing as I gaped and gasped at the bustling streets and towering skyscrapers that flashed past.

"You're so funny." Anna chuckled, when I started bouncing up and down on my seat. I'd just spotted the Empire State Building for the first time.

"I can't help it. I'm excited!"

The girls laughed. "We know," they said in unison.

"I don't think we've got much choice but to ditch some of the shopping for sightseeing," Cress added. "Seeing you experience New York for the first time is like watching a small kid open presents at Christmas. It's adorable."

I scowled in her direction. "I'm not like a small kid."

"You totally are," Anna agreed with a smile.

"I'd probably be offended if I wasn't so excited by the idea of sightseeing."

The girls laughed again.

Eventually, the bus pulled up outside our hotel. It was an impressive and imposing stately building right across from Central Park. Tall columns flanked the gorgeous stone entrance, and a plush carpet ran down the marble steps leading up to the front doors. Just one look at the hotel made me realize this little excursion must have been costing my father a fortune. There was no way my mom and I could have ever afforded such luxury, and I knew the type of place in our budget would have looked very different.

When we entered the hotel, I was shocked by the grand foyer. A beautiful fountain trickled in the middle of the space, and it was surrounded by large leafy trees that looked like they'd been plucked straight from the park across the street. The soft smell of roses floated across from the floral arrangements that lined the walls, and above it all was a high ceiling with an elaborate golden design. I couldn't help but imagine the many floors that were stacked on top of it, reaching up toward the sky. We were all crowded to one side of the entrance hall as one of the teachers arranged the keys and began calling out our room arrangements. They assigned the girls to share rooms alphabetically, and by some miracle, that meant I'd be sharing with Anna.

"Yes!" she squealed as our names were announced. She darted forward to grab the room key from the teacher and grinned brightly as she came back to me. "This is going to be the best trip ever," she gushed. Cress didn't seem to agree. Her roommate had been revealed just before our names were called. She was rooming with one of Veronica's cronies for the night. Cress was normally able to see the positive side of most things in life, but even she appeared pretty bummed about it.

The teacher finished assigning our rooms before he explained our itinerary for the rest of the day. We were going to spend the rest of the afternoon on a literary walking tour of Central Park. Dinner was going to be at a restaurant close to the theater, and then we'd finish the day by seeing the play.

I was excited about catching a play on Broadway, but I also loved the idea of wandering away the afternoon in Central Park. My friends didn't seem anywhere near as excited as me, but it was a bright and sunny day, so there were no complaints.

The others kept chatting about the day ahead, but I wasn't listening too closely as Noah caught my eye. He was looking at me through the crowd of other students milling around the foyer, but he glanced away the moment our eyes met. I blew out a breath and forced my focus away from him and back on my friends.

This trip to New York was all about getting the closure I needed and the space I wanted so I could finally get over Noah. So far, I hadn't been doing too well with the space part, but now the bus ride was over, I was hoping we could keep our distance for the rest of the trip. I just had to hope fate didn't have other plans for us because it was about time it started working in my favor.

CHAPTER FOURTEEN

The walk through Central Park was wonderful. We applauded the street performers, snapped selfies on picture-perfect bridges, and enjoyed some of the best people-watching you could imagine. We even sort of paid attention when the group stopped to look at a few statues and landmarks and Mr. Wagner tried to lecture us about them. The best part was that it was easy to stay clear of Noah, and I barely noticed him. I was too busy having fun with my friends and admiring the sights.

I didn't see him at dinner either. There were so many students on the trip we sat at a few different tables, and he was nowhere near me. We went to an amazing Asian fusion restaurant Cress told me was one of the best in the city. The servers brought out a wide array of incredible dishes, most of which I'd never even heard of, let alone tried before. Even so, I found myself sampling every dish and wolfing down anything that hit my plate. I loved my mom's cooking at the café, but this was a different world of food altogether.

I was growing tired by the time we made it to the theater. Between the drive to New York and the afternoon exploring Central Park, I was exhausted. I'd also gotten a bit overexcited at dinner, and I was feeling very full. It was a short walk to the theater from the restaurant, but Cress, Anna, and I lagged at the back of the group. When we got to the theater, students were already lining up in front of the entrance where Mr. Wagner was handing out tickets.

We joined the back of the queue and shuffled forward as students filed into the theater and went to find their seats. Anna grinned when she glanced down at her ticket and saw where she was sitting. "Wow, they got us good seats," she said. "We're so close to the front we'll practically be able to feel Romeo spitting his lines."

I looked at her ticket and saw she was in row C. But when I looked at my own, I appeared to be nowhere near her. "You'll have to tell me all about his spit," I said. "I don't think I'll be getting sprayed by it in row MM."

Anna glanced over at my ticket and frowned. "What? Are we really not sitting together?"

"It must be random," Cress said. "I'm in row F."

"Sorry, girls." Mr. Wagner's low voice interrupted our complaints. "Most of the group are in the front rows, but there's too many of us, so some of you will be sitting elsewhere. Don't worry, you won't be the only ones."

"Damn, I can't believe they don't have us sitting together," Anna said as we left Mr. Wagner in the foyer. "I don't want to be sprayed in spit without you guys."

I laughed. "Why do I feel like that's not something people often say?"

"Ha, you may think that, but I bet it is," Anna replied with a smile. She started to frown though as she looked at me. "Shit, and it's your first performance in New York, Isobel. Do you want to swap seats with me?"

I quickly shook my head. "No, I'm fine. I wouldn't want to deprive you of Romeo's spit."

"I'm sure I can live without it. Seriously, let's swap."

"I'm happy to swap too if you like," Cress added. "Though my seat isn't as good as Anna's."

I pulled my ticket in close to my chest. "Nope, like I said, I'm fine." I started toward the stairs that led up to my seat before they could argue. There was a look in Anna's eyes that made me feel like she might try to wrestle the ticket from my hands if I hung around. "I'll catch you guys after the show."

I wandered up the stairs until I found the door I was supposed to enter through. As I entered the auditorium, I could see I was right at the back of the theater. I wasn't just a few rows from my friends. I was a whole other level away from them. The place was packed, but I saw a few other students scattered throughout the seats, so at least I wasn't the only one back here.

I climbed the stairs until I reached my row, which was the very last one in the entire theater. While Anna was being covered in spit from the performers, I'd be lucky to hear them at all. I looked down the row and could just make out an empty seat over the sea of heads. Every seat between me and my destination was taken, so I slowly began to edge my way past the other patrons, keeping my eyes down so I didn't trip and whispering my apologies as I went. I was just about to reach my seat when I looked up and saw who I would be sitting next to. I froze. My blood turned to ice as I locked eyes with Noah. His look of shock must have mirrored mine. I imagined the universe was having a good old laugh right now.

"You've got to be kidding me," I muttered under my breath.

The man I'd stopped in front of cleared his throat, and I quickly jolted back into action. "Sorry." I gave him an empty smile before I slowly continued onward. Every second I delayed was one second less I had to spend at Noah's side.

When I finally reached him, he stood to let me pass. My body buzzed as I lightly brushed past him. He was too big for such a small space, and it was impossible to get by him without touching. I looked at the number on the empty seat next to him, and my heart sank as it was confirmed. I was sitting next to Noah.

I dropped into my seat and pulled out my program, hoping it might distract me from the boy I could feel at my side. There was only so much time you could spend reading about the actors in the play before it became painfully monotonous.

Noah let out a soft laugh, and I couldn't stop myself from glancing up at him. He was watching me, and though he'd laughed, there wasn't a trace of humor on his face.

"What?" I hissed at him.

"It's nothing."

"You laughed. Do you find something funny about this situation?"

He let out a sigh. "Only that no matter how hard I try, I can't seem to get away from you. It seems somewhat ironic given we're seeing a play about fate."

I folded my arms over my chest. "Yes, well, I'm sure the universe will find some other people to mess with once it realizes no matter how many times it tries to throw us together it'll make no difference."

"Perhaps," he agreed.

His response sliced through me. A part of me still wanted him to fight for us. To fight against his grandfather and choose me even though it was the wrong decision. The way he just seemed to surrender to it all only twisted the broken shards of my heart.

I just wished I didn't feel such a strong connection to him. That I could ignore how my body urged me toward him even now.

"How was your afternoon?" he asked, somewhat taking me by surprise.

Apparently, we were making small talk now. It was unusual seeing as he hadn't spoken two words to me all week. "I thought you weren't talking to me."

"I never said I wasn't talking to you."

I kept my arms crossed and stayed as small as I could in my seat. There was barely any space between the seats, and I felt too close to Noah. "Well, you *haven't* been talking to me, and you've been acting as though I don't exist."

He let out a hard breath. "How could I be acting as though you don't exist when you're the only person I can see?"

This boy was more confusing than most of my chemistry lessons—and those were damn near impossible these days. Thankfully, the lights in the theater started to dim, stopping our sad attempts at conversation. I blew out a breath of relief. At least now I wouldn't have to talk with Noah. I could sit here and simply pretend he wasn't there.

It was far easier said than done, and as soon as it grew dark, my body only seemed to become more aware of Noah's presence beside me. His arm was on the armrest between us, only inches away from my own. His legs were close enough that I only had to shuffle slightly to brush against him. The worst part was how clearly I could smell him. His scent wrapped around me, beckoning me to him and tormenting my every breath.

I wondered if he was as plagued by me as I was by him. It practically made me feel sick, and each passing moment only turned my stomach more. I'd always found his presence impossible to ignore, but it had never made me feel quite so nauseated before. Perhaps this was progress. Perhaps I'd gotten to the point in our breakup where he made me feel physically ill.

My stomach clenched, and I lifted a hand to my mouth. Nope. This couldn't be because of Noah. I wasn't just slightly queasy; I was ten days spent on the high seas kind of queasy.

"I'm going to be sick." I jumped from my seat and darted back down the row toward the aisle as quickly as I could. People grumbled as I passed, but I ignored them as I climbed over their outstretched legs and rushed back down the steps and out into the foyer.

Thankfully, there was a women's bathroom just outside the

door, and I ran straight for it. I only just made it to the toilet before I vomited. My eyes watered, and my stomach turned. I hadn't been sick this way in a long time.

I vaguely heard the bathroom door opening and the scuff of feet as someone entered. Whoever it was had a real treat in store because I wasn't sure I could keep quiet. I was too sick to care though.

"Isobel, are you okay?"

Oh, God. *Anyone but him.* Noah had followed me in here, and I officially wanted to die.

I answered him by hurling my guts up again. I heard him swear, and moments later, his hands were brushing against the sides of my face as he pulled my hair back for me. If I wanted to get him to leave me alone by completely repulsing him, I was doing a great job.

When I'd gotten most of the contents of my stomach up, I grabbed some toilet paper from the dispenser and wiped my mouth. I wanted nothing more than to disappear, but that was impossible when I was stuck in a small cubicle with Noah. I slowly turned to him. I felt like hell and probably looked even worse. There wasn't nearly enough space in the small stall for the two of us, and we were both far too close.

"You shouldn't be in here," I said.

Noah ignored my comment. "How are you feeling?"

"I feel like the food at that restaurant isn't nearly as nice the second time tasting it." Especially not the calamari. I was never going to eat seafood again.

"Do you think you're going to throw up again?"

I slowly shook my head.

"Here, let me help you up." He gently took my arm. I felt weak as a kitten as I tried to stand, but Noah did most of the lifting.

"You're missing the play," I said. "And you're in the women's bathroom." Thankfully the play was in full swing, so there was no one else here.

"I'm aware." He didn't seem the least bit bothered by either of those facts. "We should get you back to the hotel."

I groaned and shook my head. "No, we need to see the play."

"You can barely stand, and you're as white as a sheet. I'm taking you back to your room."

"We can't leave the theater. We'll get in trouble."

"Don't worry about the teachers. I'll text Mr. Wagner and let him know you're unwell and I'm taking you back."

"But…"

Noah's eyes turned serious, and I could see there would be no arguing with him. I wanted to protest but felt too exhausted to go through with it.

"Fine," I grumbled. I didn't particularly feel like seeing a play about Romeo and Juliet anyway. Not when things between Noah and me felt like they'd been ripped from its very pages.

Noah went to help me, but I stepped out of his grasp. "I can walk."

He slowly nodded, but he looked like he wanted to object. Instead, he hovered close to me as we left the bathroom. He was acting like he thought I might faint or collapse. If I were honest with myself, I didn't feel that far from it. I couldn't handle the thought of him touching me though.

We were silent as we left the theater, and I tried to keep as much distance between us as possible as we took a cab back to the hotel.

"You really didn't have to escort me back here," I said, as we made our way down the corridor to my room. I still felt really unwell and was grateful Noah had brought me back. I felt terrible he had missed the play though. We had an assignment on *Romeo and Juliet* due in a couple of weeks. And while we didn't need to see the play to complete the work, it definitely would have helped.

"It's no problem." Noah shrugged. "I've seen the play before."

"Really?"

"Yeah, I like watching stage productions. My mom and dad used to take me to the theater a lot when I was a kid."

"Oh." I didn't know that about Noah. I didn't want to know it about him either. I didn't like knowing anything that might endear him more to me when things between us would never work.

"Well, this is me," I said, gesturing to the door when we reached my room.

Noah crossed his arms over his large chest. "You think I'm just going to ditch you at the door and leave you in there alone?"

"I was kind of hoping so, yeah..." My stomach was still rolling uncomfortably, and the last thing I needed was for Noah to see me being sick again.

"That's not going to happen," he said. "I'll stay with you until Anna gets back."

"How did you know I was rooming with..." Noah had always been observant, so of course, he knew I was rooming with Anna. Instead, I nodded. "Fine. But no barging in on me in the bathroom if I'm sick again. I've suffered enough humiliation for one night."

"Deal."

I swiped my key card to open the door to my room. It was a gorgeous space with two large beds and a huge window at the far end that overlooked Central Park. It was dark outside, and the curtains were pulled open so I could see the twinkling lights of the city beyond. I felt far too unwell to really appreciate the view, and I collapsed onto the end of my bed.

Noah disappeared into the bathroom and came out with a glass of water for me. I took the glass but didn't drink from it straightaway. At this point, I wasn't sure if the water was going to help or make me throw up again.

"You need to rehydrate," he said, nodding at the glass.

I let out a sigh and did as I was told, taking small, cautious sips as I waited to see how it went down. Thankfully, I didn't start heaving again.

"I'm going to change," I said. The dress I'd worn to the theater was tight, and it felt like it was suffocating me. I probably would have had a shower too if Noah wasn't here, but the thought of trying to shower with him in the room felt far too intimate.

I quickly rifled through my bag and pulled out my pajamas before disappearing into the bathroom. When I caught a look at myself in the mirror I cringed. My skin was sickly pale, my hair was lank, and my eyes were bloodshot. I would have been mortified by Noah seeing me this way if I felt well enough to care.

I brushed my teeth, washed my face. and pulled my hair back, which all helped me feel slightly more human. When I returned to the room, Noah was sitting on Anna's bed, and he smiled as he caught a look at my pajamas.

"Winnie the Pooh?" he asked, nodding at the print.

I hadn't really thought about the state of my pajamas when I'd put them on, but as Noah's eyes slowly trailed over them, I realized just how short the shorts were and how the top was so old it was almost see-through.

They were the only pajamas I'd brought though. They also happened to be the comfiest thing I owned. I'd snuck into my room and grabbed them when Noah and I had visited my mom a few weeks ago. Of course, Matthew's stylist, who had filled my closet at school, had provided a pair of luxurious silk PJs. But they never felt quite right on me, and I was able to sleep so much more soundly when I was tucked up in something from home. "He was my favorite growing up," I explained.

"Me too," he murmured, but his voice was so quiet I wondered if perhaps I'd imagined him saying it.

His eyes tracked me as I made my way across the room. Under any other circumstance I might have been embarrassed to have him in here with me. To let him see me in my old Winnie the Pooh PJs while I looked like something that had just crawled out of the Upside Down. But I didn't have it in me to care. I pulled back the sheets of my bed and slipped under the covers.

My stomach was still clenching as I curled up under the duvet, and I really hoped it wasn't gearing up for a second date with the toilet bowl. I turned to look at Noah. He was still watching me from the edge of Anna's bed.

"Do you want me to call down to see if the front desk has anything for the nausea?" he asked. "Even some dry crackers might help."

"No, I'll be okay. I just need to rest."

He didn't seem happy with my answer. I got the feeling Noah hated sitting by and doing nothing. He didn't complain and gave me a brief nod before he glanced away. His gaze roamed the rest of the room as though he wasn't sure what to do or where to look.

I rolled over in bed and tried to get comfortable but then immediately rolled back. I squirmed around trying to find a relaxing position, but no matter how I arranged myself, I felt restless. I closed my eyes, hoping it would help, but with my eyes shut, I only noticed more clearly how my head pounded and my mouth tasted like acid.

I let out a sigh and focused on Noah. He was staring at the wall across from him, deep in thought. He seemed different tonight. Less bitter than our recent encounters, and I almost sensed that he was resigned to our fate. He was probably just being nicer to me because I was sick and he felt the need to look after me. I had to admit it was so much easier to be around him when we weren't focused on the painful aftermath of our breakup.

For a moment, I considered pressing him for answers about what happened between our families. I'd had little luck pulling an explanation out of him so far, but something about his attitude tonight made me feel like he might be more open to talking. We certainly had the time if he was going to insist on staying with me. Still, I was nervous to ask. What if he rejected me again?

"Noah?" I asked.

"Mm?"

"Tell me what happened."

His eyes snapped to me.

"Between our families. What happened?"

He sat up a little straighter, and his eyes darkened in response. "We shouldn't be talking about this," he said. "You need to rest."

"I *am* resting," I replied. "And I know you're worried about how I'll react, but that's my decision to make. I want an explanation. I deserve it."

Noah let out a long sigh, and from the way he watched me, I could see he was trying to figure out the best way to put me off.

"Is it really that bad?" I asked.

"It's...complicated."

"You won't tell me because it's complicated?"

"I won't tell you because I don't want to be the one who ruins the relationship you're trying to build with your dad."

I propped myself up on my pillow. "Well, that's only more reason to tell me," I said. "If my father isn't a good person, I don't want to build a relationship with him. But I can't do that if I don't have all the information..."

He still looked hesitant, and I had a feeling my attempt at getting answers out of him was going to be futile yet again.

"Please, Noah..."

I wondered if he could see the desperation in my eyes because he surprised me by nodding. "Fine, I'll tell you what happened," he said. "But it won't change anything. And you can't get angry if you don't like what I have to say."

"I won't," I promised. "So..."

He put his arms on his knees and leaned forward, his head low as he began. "Our families have been business rivals for years. It started back when both our grandfathers set up their pharmaceutical companies. The LaFleurs have always taken issue with us. They would poach our employees or sabotage our research. If they knew my grandfather intended to buy a warehouse, they would buy it before him, or if they knew my grandfather was making a deal with a third party, they'd swoop in and steal the contract. It was constant and petty. They did anything they could to make his life difficult. For years, they buried my grandfather in litigation just to be a pain."

I shook my head, trying to understand. "Why would they do all of that?"

"They're just not good people." He glanced down at his hands, like he couldn't stand to look me in the eyes. "Our grandfathers were once colleagues, but William said your grandfather was always jealous of his success and that's why he targeted us."

My brow scrunched in response. I didn't know how to react to what he'd just said. I'd never met my grandfather, so I could hardly defend him. But Noah still hadn't explained why he thought Matthew was such a villain.

"But you said this was both our grandfathers, right?" I asked. "So, why are you so angry with Matthew?"

"Matthew is just like your grandfather, if not worse," Noah said. There was little emotion in his voice, and I got the feeling he was trying his best to sound calm, so as not to upset me.

"What did Matthew do?"

"A couple of years ago, the patent ended on the main drug my family's company makes. Matthew immediately started manufacturing a generic version of it and practically gave it away. Our sales tanked, and Hastings Laboratories has barely been able to stay afloat since. He knew exactly what he was doing and how it would impact us."

"Oh," I murmured. I'd only just met Matthew, and I didn't know him all that well, but I was surprised he would be so malicious.

"My family's company is in pieces, and my grandfather has

sunk his entire personal fortune into trying to buoy it back to life," Noah continued. "No one knows just how much trouble we're in…"

"That's terrible."

He nodded, but he was still struggling to look at me. Talking about this had to be hard for him, especially if his grandfather's company was struggling as much as it was. I still wasn't sure I understood why my family hated his so much. Why had my father deliberately tried to sabotage them? And had my grandfather really started years of fighting simply because he was jealous? I wouldn't put it past him considering he'd hidden my existence from my father. Still, it seemed remarkably petty.

As I considered Noah's explanation, I felt like I was missing something. If my grandfather had acted out of jealousy, then why did my father hate his family? And why had William and Matthew reacted so strongly when they found out we were in a relationship? I felt like there had to be more to the feud than the business rivalry Noah had described.

"So, is that it then?" I asked.

A flash of emotion crossed Noah's eyes, and I knew he hadn't told me the whole story.

"What aren't you telling me?"

He shook his head. "I think I've said enough for one night."

I sat up in bed. "You can't just give me half the story."

"The rest is… It's personal," Noah muttered. "It goes beyond just business."

He stood and started pacing around the room. There was a deep frown line furrowing his brow, and it was clear he was really struggling with what to say. Whatever was next in the story seemed even harder for him to talk about, so I waited silently to see if he would explain.

"Okay." He held up his hands in defeat. "I've told you this much, I might as well tell you the rest." He finally stopped pacing and sank back onto the bed across from me.

"I don't really know how to tell you this. But my father was having an affair with Matthew's sister, Georgina."

My eyes went wide, and I stared at him for several long seconds as I tried to compute what he'd just said. I definitely hadn't been expecting him to say that and didn't know how to respond.

"My aunt?" I whispered the words almost to myself.

Noah nodded at the shock he saw in my gaze. "I still don't believe it myself some days. It was so unlike my dad, and with everything that's happened between our families... Well, at the time it was unthinkable to imagine a LaFleur and a Hastings getting mixed up like that."

"Are you sure then?" I asked. "That they were having an affair?"

"I'm sure." His eyes were fixed on the ground. "They were together in one of our labs one night." His voice had gone so quiet I could barely hear him as he breathed the words, and my heart ached for him as he spoke. "There was a fire. Some faulty wiring. With all the chemicals in there, the place went up in seconds. Neither of them survived."

My body went cold. All I wanted was to go to him and hold him. I could see how much he was struggling to recount the story, and I felt awful for pushing him to explain. It was no wonder Noah had been avoiding telling me what happened.

"God, Noah, I'm so sorry."

He shook his head. "It's hardly your fault," he said. "It was an accident. But I think a part of me will always wish that my father had never gotten caught up with a LaFleur. That maybe he wouldn't have been at the lab so late that night. That maybe he'd still be alive..."

I couldn't begin to imagine what it was like for Noah to bear that weight on his shoulders. It made sense he couldn't stand my father's family. That his grandfather wanted him away from me and Matthew.

We both sat in silence, the enormity of his confession hanging over us. Matthew had said my aunt died before her time, but I'd had no idea of the circumstances surrounding it. It was tragic and heartbreaking for both Noah and my father. Perhaps this was why Matthew hated the Hastings so much too? Why he had warned me away from Noah in the first place.

"You can't tell anyone what I've told you tonight," Noah said, finally looking my way. "About my father and your aunt, about the financial trouble our company is in. No one knows any of it. Not even Cress."

"They really don't know?" Things had to be pretty bad if Noah hadn't even told his cousin his family was in financial trouble. And I had to wonder how no one knew about his dad and my aunt. Affairs were secretive in nature, but once it had been discovered, I imagined it would have been hard to keep quiet.

"If people knew about the state of the company, it could ruin us completely," he said. "And the affair? My grandfather managed to keep it secret to protect my father's legacy. I don't want him to be remembered for that."

"No, of course," I said. "I won't tell anyone. Not even Cress."

He released a breath and relaxed a little. "I know it's a lot to ask, given everything, but my grandfather would freak if anyone found out."

"I won't say a word," I reassured him.

"Thank you."

We sat there staring silently at one another as I allowed everything he'd told me to sink in. There was a lot to digest, but it meant so much to me that Noah had trusted me enough to share the truth.

"Thank you for telling me," I finally said. "I'm surprised you can even stand to be in the same room as me after all that's happened."

"You're not the problem," Noah said. "You never were. I'd look past all that in a heartbeat for you, but..."

"Your grandfather," I murmured.

"My grandfather." He nodded. "He didn't give me any choice. If I stayed with you, he'd see it as the worst betrayal, and…" His voice trailed off, but I knew what he was going to say.

"You can't lose him too, I get it." Neither of Noah's parents were around anymore, and his grandfather was all he had. If being with Noah meant losing my mom, I would have made the same choice too. "It doesn't make it any easier though."

"No." He shared a sad smile with me. "How do you feel? Now that you know."

"It's a lot to take in," I said. "I can't believe our families have been through so much. I know we can't change the past, but I just wish there was a way we could mend the pain and hurt we've caused each other."

Noah's brow furrowed as he looked at me. "That's impossible."

"But what about your dad and my aunt? If they were together, it means they put the rivalry and the fighting and the history aside. How did that happen if it's impossible? How did *we* happen?"

Noah's frown deepened, but I couldn't tell what he was thinking. He probably thought I was silly for wishing our families could change. They had hated each other since before either of us were born, and hostility like that wasn't easily forgotten.

My phone buzzed, and I glanced at it to see a text from Cress asking how I was. The play was over, and she wanted to know if I needed her to pick anything up on their way back to the hotel.

I sent her a quick text back saying I was fine and didn't need anything before I lifted my eyes to Noah.

"Everyone's coming back now," I said. "You should probably leave. If a teacher catches you in here, we'll both get in trouble."

"I'm not leaving you when you're sick."

"I'm okay," I quickly replied. "I'm feeling much better. I just need to try and get some sleep."

He nodded and started to stand. "If you're sure…"

"I am. Thanks for looking after me."

"It was no problem."

"And thanks for talking to me. I know it can't have been easy." Having everything out in the open felt cathartic. But it also felt like the end of something. Now I knew the truth about why he had to break up with me, what more was there left for us to say? Any slim hope I'd retained that maybe this was all some big misunderstanding had been thoroughly crushed.

He came to the bed and lightly brushed a hand over my hair. The gesture was gentle and surprisingly intimate. He seemed to realize that at the same time as me because he quickly stole his hand away. "Text me if you need me, and I'll be here."

"I know."

He smiled down at me, and it struck something deep in my soul. Noah and I might not be together, but I felt like he would always be there for me despite that.

"How lucky am I to have something that makes saying goodbye so hard," he whispered before he turned and walked from the room.

It was only once the door closed behind him that I realized he'd quoted me *Winnie-the-Pooh*.

CHAPTER FIFTEEN

Our class went to The Met the following morning. I probably should have stayed in my hotel room and continued to rest, but I was far too stubborn and refused to let a slight stomach bug keep me down. I was in New York City, and the last thing I wanted was to let a little food poisoning hold me back.

"It turns out you weren't the only one who got sick from the food last night," Wes said as we walked through the museum together. Mr. Wagner had just told us we could take some free time to explore before meeting back at the entrance in an hour. Cress and Anna had practically sprinted off in excitement. There was a special Alexander McQueen exhibit showing, and they felt like an hour wasn't nearly long enough to take it in. I'd taken one look at their eager faces and told them to run along without me. I was still far too weak to be rushing anywhere and didn't want them to miss out.

"Oh no, really?" I asked.

"Sawyer was up all night sick," he said. "He's still at the hotel recovering now. I heard a few others using the same excuse to stay back too."

"That's not good."

He shook his head in agreement. "So, I'm impressed you're here. You should probably be tucked up in bed as well."

"And waste another second of this trip in my room? I don't think so."

As much as I was enjoying The Met, my mind kept drifting back to my conversation with Noah last night. I'd struggled to sleep after he left and spent way too many hours thinking over everything he had said about the history between our families. Those thoughts continued to plague me today.

Noah had given me answers, yes, but I wasn't sure if I had the full story yet. It felt like there had to be more to it. Surely something had happened to start this whole feud. Considering the hatred and anger between our families, my grandfather's jealously alone just didn't seem like enough.

Matthew's role in the whole thing was also playing on my mind. Why was he continuing his father's vendetta? Was he really the villain Noah made him out to be? I was curious to hear what Matthew had to say, and I wanted to get his side of the story before I decided how to feel about it all.

I let out a sigh as I gazed up at one of the paintings we were passing. The artwork was a beautiful depiction of a ballet class. The painter had really captured the movement of the dancing ballerinas and the controlled chaos of the other girls in the class looking on. It was an impressive piece of work, but just like the rest of our tour of The Met, I wasn't really appreciating it. My head was somewhere else, and this museum just wasn't where I wanted to be right now.

"What's up?" Wes asked. "Are you not feeling well?"

"No, it's not that," I murmured. "I was just thinking about my dad."

"Do you still want to go to his office?"

"Yeah, I'd like to," I admitted. "But I don't know when I'll have time. I'll probably have to wait until after the school trip is over, but then Cress, Anna, and Sawyer are going to have all sorts of stuff planned. I don't want to bail on them." It was hard not to sound disappointed at the idea I might not get the chance to find and talk to my father. After everything Noah had revealed last night, I didn't want to wait until Matthew visited Weybridge to question him.

"Well, we could just sneak off now..." Wes gave me a cheeky smile, and his eyes danced with mischief.

I glanced around nervously, checking there weren't any teachers nearby. When I saw the coast was clear, I whispered, "Won't we get in trouble?"

Wes shrugged. "Your father's building isn't far from here, and it's not like the teachers are keeping close tabs on us."

He looked excited by the prospect of sneaking off, and I slowly started to share his smile. "Okay, but if we get caught, I'm telling them it was your idea."

"Excellent." He grabbed me by the hand and started to guide me from the museum. We didn't bump into any teachers as we wound our way back through the building, and when we neared the entrance, Mr. Wagner was in such a deep conversation with one of the museum staff that he didn't notice us as we passed.

As we stepped outside, I started to laugh. I had no idea how we hadn't been caught. We'd walked right by Mr. Wagner, and he hadn't even glanced our way.

Wes didn't seem nearly as surprised. "I had Mr. Wagner for English last year," he said. "The guy loves nothing more than to hear himself speak. That poor museum curator was such a captive audience I doubt Mr. Wagner would have noticed if the building was on fire."

We hurried down the iconic steps in front of the building, and Wes hailed a taxi. He gave the guy directions, and we took off from the curb, our escape complete.

"How do you know where my dad's office is anyway?" I asked as I stared out the window at the buildings flashing past.

"My father has a hotel across the road," Wes said. "And The LaFleur Corp is kind of hard to miss."

I shot him a questioning look, but he simply smiled in response.

When the cab started to slow, Wes nodded to my window and pointed upward. Curious, I peered out, and as I gazed into the sky, I saw LaFleur printed in bold letters across the top of the building.

"You can see it from practically every high-rise in the city," Wes explained.

"Subtle," I joked, still staring in awe at the building and my father's name proudly displayed as part of the New York skyline. Just when I thought I was starting to understand just how rich and successful he was, I realized there was so much I still didn't know about him.

Wes paid the cab driver, and we got out of the car. I drew in a deep breath as I looked up at my father's building once more. I felt so small and insignificant standing in front of it, and I had to tilt my head back to look to the top. His wealth seemed so vast to me. The differences between us were so impossibly huge.

"So, what are you going to say to your dad?"

I tore my gaze from the building to look at Wes. I'd thought about what I was going to ask my father many times since the White Ball a few weeks ago. After speaking to Noah last night, I had even more questions. Wes didn't know I'd spoken to Noah, and I couldn't give him details because I'd made a promise I wouldn't tell a soul.

"You know how Noah took me home from the theater last night?"

"Yeah..."

"Well, I finally got him to tell me the history of this bitterness between our families." I felt a sudden chill go down my back, and I wrapped my arms around me as I remembered what it had been like to hear Noah's story.

"Shit, really? What did he say?"

"It was a long story," I said, trying to avoid explaining any further. "I just want to ask Matthew for his side of things. I'm sure Noah wasn't trying to be biased, but it's his family so how could he not be?"

"Yeah," Wes agreed. "I guess it would be impossible to be totally impartial."

I let out a sigh and glanced up at Matthew's building again. A wave of nerves rocked through me. What if my father wouldn't see me? Or what if I upset him by bringing up his sister? I didn't want to overstep.

"Do you need backup?" Wes asked "I can wait out front if you like? Or I'm happy to come with you. I..."

His voice trailed off, and I glanced at him. There was a surprised look in his eyes and he was focused on something behind me. I turned to follow his gaze, and I drew in a sharp breath as I saw what had caught Wes's attention. Noah had just walked out of my father's building and onto the sidewalk.

"What's he doing here?" Wes voiced his confusion before I could.

"I don't know." I replied, keeping my eyes locked on Noah.

I couldn't quite believe what I was seeing, but there he was. Through the crowds of people streaming past the building, I was definitely looking at Noah standing at the entrance

He didn't notice us, which wasn't all that surprising given how many people were on the street. He paused briefly as he took out his phone and checked something on the screen before tucking it into his pocket. He took a deep breath and glanced up at the building towering above him. A frown crossed his brow, but it disappeared again as he stepped to the edge of the sidewalk and hailed a cab.

I was still in a state of shock as I watched him climb into the car, and by the time I was able to think clearly again, he was already driving off down the road. Noah had visited my father's building. Was he there for the same reason as me—to visit my father?

I reconsidered our conversation from last night. Noah had given no indication he had any desire to talk with my father. In his eyes, my father was the villain. Even worse than my grandfather. After I had suggested the unlikely idea of one day reconciling the differences between our families, he had balked and said it was impossible. My stomach dipped unpleasantly. If Noah had been in this building, it wasn't for anything good.

I slowly turned to face Wes. "You saw him too, right? Noah was coming out of the building?"

"Yeah, it was him," Wes nodded. "He wasn't at The Met earlier, but I just assumed he was out sick like everyone else who is MIA this morning."

"So, he bailed on The Met to come to my dad's office? Why would he do that?"

"Maybe he was asking your dad for your hand in marriage?" Wes suggested.

I shook my head. I wasn't in the mood to joke about this. "Seriously though, why would Noah come see my dad? They're supposed to be worst enemies..."

"Maybe he wants to bury the hatchet?"

"That's impossible." I echoed Noah's words. "You should have seen the way he spoke about my family last night, especially my father. There's no burying the hatchet between them." I was more confident of that than ever before after speaking to Noah last night and seeing the pain in his eyes when he'd recounted what had happened with my aunt and his dad. Though I didn't repeat that to Wes. "Plus, his grandfather would probably disown him for being within a few hundred feet of this building let alone setting up a meeting to let bygones be bygones. Noah would never go against him."

Wes shrugged. "It could also be a coincidence," he suggested. "There are a few restaurants and some other offices in this building. I guess you'll have to ask Noah or your dad if you want to find out."

"Yeah, I guess."

I jumped as my phone started ringing, and I pulled it from my back pocket. I hadn't realized quite how on edge I was, but my heart rate kicked up another notch when I saw my dad's number lighting up the screen. I flipped the phone around to show Wes.

"This just keeps getting weirder," I said.

"Are you going to answer?"

I nodded and lifted the phone to my ear. "Hello?"

"Hello, Isobel," my father said pleasantly, his deep, English accent making my name sound far posher than it was.

"Hi, Matthew. What's up?" I glanced up at the building as I spoke, wondering if he somehow knew I was out front. Or if perhaps his call had something to do with Noah?

"I know you're in town this week, and I've managed to shuffle my schedule around. I was hoping we could have dinner tonight."

"Tonight?"

"Yes."

I was outside his building right now, but I supposed I could wait until this evening to talk to him. If I went storming into his office, he might not be as receptive to answering my questions. I might be better off letting him do this on his terms.

"Sure, that would be great."

"Perfect. Text me the address for where you're staying, and I'll have a car pick you up and bring you to my apartment tonight."

"Okay."

"I'm just between meetings, so I must rush off, but I look forward to seeing you tonight."

"I'll see you then," I said.

He hung up the phone, and I blew out a breath. "Looks like operation break into my father's office and accost him is off. He wants to have dinner with me tonight."

"That's great." Wes smiled. "And I don't think it's considered breaking in if you're his daughter. I'm sure he would have loved to see you."

"Maybe." That was still something I didn't feel all that confident of though. I hadn't had a proper conversation with him since the ball, and I was quite sure our next discussion wasn't going to be particularly pleasant. Matthew certainly seemed reluctant to talk about his history with the Hastings, and after hearing Noah's side of things I could see why.

I was still in a state of shock over everything Noah had revealed. He had painted Matthew as the bad guy, but I still wasn't sure what to believe. I dreaded to think what further twists Matthew might have to add to the tale.

Either way, this dinner was no longer simply about the rift with the Hastings, it was also about what kind of person my father was. I wanted the truth, but how was I going to feel once I finally had it? And what if Noah was right? What if Matthew was the villain in all of this?

CHAPTER SIXTEEN

W e started making our way back to the museum but not before Wes dragged me to his favorite hot dog stand which was just down the street. He told me it was the best in the city, but I was still feeling too fragile so I watched as he devoured his food.

Once he was done, we jumped in a cab and hurried back to The Met. Our little excursion hadn't taken as long as I'd expected, so we got back in good time. We easily snuck back through the front entrance while Mr. Wagner was talking to another unlucky staff member and returned to wandering the galleries.

While our mission to my father's office hadn't quite turned out as planned, I knew I'd have a chance to get the information I wanted at dinner tonight. I'd also got to spend time hanging out with Wes, which was never a bad thing. Though I was still at a loss as to why Noah was at my father's building.

When it was time to leave the museum, we took the short walk back through Central Park to the hotel. Cress and Anna chatted the whole way about the Alexander McQueen exhibit, while I smiled and nodded as enthusiastically as I could.

I didn't see Noah again until we got back to the hotel. It was late in the afternoon, and all the students and teachers were mingling in the lobby, collecting their luggage and preparing to get back on the bus to Weybridge. I hadn't seen Noah at The Met or on the walk back, so he must have skipped the visit completely.

Maybe Wes was right, and Noah had told the teachers he was too sick to go to the museum. Instead of resting in his room though, he was visiting my father's office. I was dying to pull him aside and ask him what he'd been doing there, but there were too many people around, and I wasn't sure how to ask him without it sounding like we'd been following him. It would be especially embarrassing if I questioned him and he had a simpler reason for why he was there, as Wes suggested. So, I left it, hoping I could come up with an appropriate way to ask him about it at another time.

Cress, Anna, and I said our goodbyes to everyone getting on the bus back to Weybridge before we took a cab to Cress's house. The journey only took a few minutes before the cab stopped in front of a beautiful old brownstone townhouse with tall arched windows that looked out onto the street. It was in a pretty neighborhood with gorgeous tall trees that had truly embraced the golden hues of autumn. Leaves softly fluttered down as we got out of the car, and the sidewalk was covered in a carpet of reds and yellows that crunched pleasantly underfoot as we walked to the front door.

Cress had a big smile on her face as she led us up the front steps. She looked so happy to be home, and I felt a hint of envy. I would have given anything to be walking through the front door of my apartment in Rapid Bay.

I was surprised as I entered the townhouse. I wasn't sure exactly what I expected the interior to look like, but it certainly wasn't something so bohemian. The tiles were all patterned, giving off a Moroccan feel, and large wrought iron lanterns hung from the ceiling dispersing shards of light in pretty patterns. The home was colorful and bright, and the furnishings were completely eclectic. I'd never seen a place quite like it before.

"My parents aren't home," Cress said, as she threw her keys down on the entrance table. "I think they're in Istanbul this weekend."

"They're not here?" I felt sure my mom wouldn't be comfortable with me staying here if she knew there were no adults looking after us. She probably wouldn't force me to head back to school or anything, but I imagined she'd be up all night worrying if she knew.

Cress must have sensed my concern because she waved a hand, dismissing it. "Our housekeeper lives here, so you don't have to worry, we're not *totally* unsupervised."

That didn't make me feel much better, but I guessed that one adult on the premises was better than none. It was probably best I didn't let my mom know all the same. There was no need to freak her out unnecessarily. We were all capable of looking after ourselves.

Cress gave us a tour, starting with the courtyard out back where she introduced us to two massive koi fish she'd named Crabbe and Goyle—because apparently she didn't like fish and she thought they looked a little thuggish. She then quickly flitted past the massive kitchen that housed no less than three ovens, perfect for the many parties her parents apparently threw when they were in town. I barely got a look at the living and dining rooms as Cress only gave them a passing wave as she headed for the stairs.

The place was enormous. I'd spent most of my time in New York gawking at sparkling glass skyscrapers and towering brick apartment buildings. I'd never really imagined the city had such beautiful family homes. I lost count of the number of rooms we passed as we climbed up the floors, and it was only steps from the park. It must have cost a fortune. Cress was so down to earth

I often forgot she came from just as much wealth as everyone else at Weybridge Academy.

When we finally reached the top of the house, Cress waved us into her bedroom. It was completely different from the rest of the home with none of the bold and unconventional furnishings I'd seen in the other rooms. Her walls were painted a subtle shade of pink and plastered in posters of bands and pictures of models plucked from fashion magazines. She had fairy lights twined around the posts of her bed and LED strips along the edges of her ceiling. It was much more suited to Cress than the rest of the place.

Cress put her bag down on her bed and slowly picked up the stuffed bear sitting in the center of the pillows. She frowned as she glanced down at it.

"That's cute," I said.

"My ex gave it to me," she replied, still considering the bear. "I should probably get rid of it." She walked over to her desk and dumped the bear in the trash can.

"Brutal." Anna chuckled.

"What?" Cress shrugged. "It's about time I put him in the past. Fluffy toys and all."

It was time I did the same with Noah. Any lingering hope I might have had that the rift between our families was something that could be repaired had been stamped out when I spoke to him last night. I hoped my conversation with Matthew at dinner would only help me accept that fact.

"Speaking of time, you should probably get ready for dinner with your dad," Cress said as she glanced at her watch.

I checked the time on my phone and was surprised to find she was right. The car would be picking me up here in just twenty minutes.

"I was going to wear this," I said, gesturing at the clothes I'd been in all day. "It's just dinner at his place."

"Oh, I'm sure that's fine then," Cress replied.

"I might run a brush through my hair though," I said. "And maybe clean my teeth." Even now, my mouth still felt gross from being sick at the theater.

Cress gestured toward her door. "There's a bathroom across the hall." I nodded and gathered my things to freshen up. It was hard to concentrate on simple things like brushing my teeth when all I could think about was the difficult conversation I had ahead with my father. It hadn't been easy talking it through with Noah last night, and I felt sure it would be just as hard to hear my dad's side of the story, especially when it came to my aunt. At least I could be thankful I wasn't going into it completely clueless.

When I was done in the bathroom, I came back to Cress's room and found both girls on her bed.

"What are you guys going to do tonight?" I asked.

"The twins want to go for sushi," Anna said.

My eyes widened with surprise. "Sawyer wants to go for sushi? Didn't he have food poisoning too?"

"No one ever said he was smart." Anna shrugged.

"The place is just around the corner from here though," Cress explained. "Give me a call when you're on your way back, and depending on the time, you can meet us at the restaurant, or we can come back home."

"Sounds good."

My phone buzzed, and when I checked the screen, I saw a message letting me know the car had arrived to pick me up.

"That's my ride."

"We'll walk you out," Cress said, jumping from the bed as Anna slowly pushed herself up to follow suit.

We made our way down from the top of the house, descending the many flights of stairs before walking out the front door.

At the bottom of the steps, I could see a large black vehicle with darkened windows waiting by the curb. One of the back doors opened and out stepped my father.

"Matthew?"

He smiled brightly in response. I knew he was sending a car for me, but I didn't expect him to be in it.

"Hello, Isobel," he replied as he climbed the steps toward me. When he reached the top, I wasn't sure what to do. We weren't exactly at the stage in our father-daughter relationship where we hugged in greeting. Instead, we both stood waiting awkwardly.

"I thought I'd be meeting you at your place," I said.

"I managed to get off work a little early so I could come meet you.

"Oh." My cheeks flushed, but I didn't know why. It was nice that he'd gone to the effort, but it wasn't that big a deal. For some reason though, I felt like it was.

"These are my friends, Cress and Anna," I said, hoping to divert his attention away from me.

"It's a pleasure to meet you both." Matthew smiled at them in turn.

"You too, Mr. LaFleur," Anna and Cress responded with polite smiles.

"Please, call me Matthew. How has your trip been so far? Have you enjoyed it?"

"It's been good," I replied.

"Isobel got food poisoning," Anna interrupted.

I shot her a glare.

Matthew faced me. "Are you okay? Do you need a doctor?"

"No, I don't need a doctor," I responded quickly. "I'm fine."

"Are you sure?"

"Certain." I shot Anna another scowl, but she just shrugged like she didn't see the problem. I didn't want Matthew babying me, and I definitely didn't want to see a doctor. I had enough on my plate tonight without my father worrying about me being sick.

"We should probably get going," I said before Anna could add anything else.

"Of course." He stood to the side and gestured for me to go ahead of him, but I raised a hand. "Just give me one second."

He nodded his understanding. "I'll wait by the car. It was lovely to meet you girls." He smiled at Cress and Anna.

"You too, Mr. LaFleur" they chimed in response.

I hovered by my friends as I watched him walk down the steps and over to the waiting SUV.

"Okay, wish me luck," I said to the girls.

"Good luck," Cress replied. "You won't need it though. It's just your dad."

"Your superhot dad," Anna added with a whisper. "Why didn't you tell us he was so dreamy?"

I thumped her in the arm. *Hard.* "You did not just say that."

"What? He is."

I shook my head and did my best to ignore her. I did not want to think about whether my father was good-looking, let alone discuss it with my friends.

"Enjoy the sushi," I called out as I jogged down the steps. "I'll let you know when I'm on my way back."

When I reached the car, Matthew was waiting by an open door, and he stood back to let me in. I gave my friends a brief wave before he closed the door behind me. The driver in the front seat nodded at me in the rearview mirror.

Matthew slid into the seat beside me, and once his seat belt was fastened, the car pulled away from the curb. My fingers fidgeted at the hem of my sweater as I considered launching into one of the many questions I had for my father. I wasn't sure the car was the right place to ask him, especially with his driver in the front seat, but it was hard to wait when it was all I could think about. I'd been wanting answers for weeks.

"I'm sorry to hear you've been unwell. Are you truly feeling better?" Matthew asked.

He sounded so concerned, and I found myself holding back a smile. Noah was convinced my father was a terrible person, and maybe I would have agreed when I'd first met the man. He hadn't given me the best first impression. But the more I got to know him, the harder I found it to believe that was possible. Maybe I was being naïve. Maybe when I finally got a chance to question him, I wouldn't like what I discovered.

"I'm still a bit queasy," I replied. "But I'm not going to be sick or anything."

"Do you feel up to having dinner with me? I can drop you back if you'd rather rest."

"No!" I protested the idea a little too forcefully. "No, I'm okay. I promise."

He slowly nodded. "But if you start to take a turn for the worse, just let me know."

"I will." I highly doubted I would. At least, not before I'd had a chance to talk with him properly.

The traffic was bad as we drove to Matthew's place, and the constant sound of horns and the flashes of brake lights surrounded us. We moved at such a crawling pace I wondered if it might be quicker to walk. I couldn't imagine Matthew walking anywhere though, especially not in the expensive suit and strikingly shiny shoes he wore.

His place wasn't far from Cress's though, and despite the traffic, the car pulled over not long after we'd set out.

"Here we are," Matthew said as the driver got out of the car and came to open my door. I stepped from the car and craned my neck back to look at the building that reached impossibly high into the sky above us. Matthew lived here? I shouldn't have been surprised considering the gorgeous home he'd purchased in Weybridge and the skyscraper that housed the headquarters for his business.

I followed him in through the revolving doors at the front of the building and gasped as I got my first look at the foyer of

Matthew's New York home. The place was incredibly lavish with white marble coating almost every surface and shiny gold finishings on all the doors and light fittings. It was opulent but also light and bright—surprisingly so, considering we were on the ground floor of a high-rise building.

"Good evening, Mr. LaFleur, Miss Grace." An older man in a deep-green suit smiled at us from behind a desk as we entered the foyer. He came around to greet us as we approached.

"Good evening, Edward," Matthew replied. "Have you had a good day?"

"It was very good, thank you, sir. And yourself?"

"Hectic," Matthew admitted with a chagrinned smile.

"I would expect nothing less," Edward replied, smiling back. He walked beside us to the elevator as he spoke.

"Did you catch the game this afternoon?" Matthew asked.

Edward blanched. "Oh yes, it was terrible."

Matthew's eyes widened a fraction with surprise. "Worse than last week?"

"Much worse."

"So I shouldn't bother watching the highlights?"

"I'm afraid I wouldn't recommend it, sir."

"Okay." My father laughed and shook his head. "Thanks for the warning."

When we reached the elevator, Edward pressed the button for us. The doors spread wide immediately, and he held them open as he gestured for us to walk inside.

"Will you be needing anything this evening, sir?" he asked.

"No, nothing tonight. Thank you, Edward."

"Have a lovely evening," the man replied, pressing the button for the top floor.

Once the doors were closed, I turned to my father. "He was nice."

"Yes, Edward's great," my father agreed. "He certainly makes this place feel a little more like home. It's nice to have someone around who I can talk football with. We follow the same team although I think we're both regretting that choice at the moment. They aren't doing very well this year."

"Are you talking about soccer?" I asked. "You like soccer?"

"Well, I call it football, but yes. I don't get much time to watch the games these days, but Edward keeps me up to date."

"Huh." I frowned and faced the elevator doors once more. Every time I thought I had Matthew pegged, he said something or acted in a way that shifted my perception of him. I tried to picture him sitting down with a beer and watching a soccer match, but I just couldn't visualize it.

I was still trying to wrap my mind around the small but altering fact when the doors opened. I expected to see a hallway in front of me, lined with doors to various apartments. Instead, I was greeted by the entrance to an entire apartment. Matthew's home wasn't just on the top floor. It *was* the top floor. The space before us was a vast open-plan space with huge floor-to-ceiling windows. The view beyond truly caught my attention. I could see all of New York from here. It was breathtaking.

"Good evening, sir, Miss Isobel," Caldwell said as we stepped from the elevator and into the apartment. I'd been so busy admiring the view, I hadn't noticed he was there even though he was standing right by the elevator.

"Caldwell," my father replied. "Are there any messages for me?"

"Nothing urgent," Caldwell said. "Dinner will be ready in fifteen minutes. I passed on your instructions regarding Miss Isobel to Jacques."

I wondered who Jacques was and what the instructions could be, but Matthew was already dismissing Caldwell before I got a chance to ask.

"Thank you," Matthew said. "That will be all for now."

Caldwell stepped away, and Matthew gestured for me to follow him into the apartment. "I only bought the place recently," he said, as we moved through the unnecessarily large entrance. "I couldn't resist it when I saw the view."

"I can see why," I whispered. It was incredible, but I couldn't begin to imagine how much the view alone cost.

"Would you like to see the place before we eat?" he asked.

"Sure."

Matthew's tour was much more thorough than Cress's had been. He showed me around the bottom level first, which included the living room, dining area, and kitchen. There was music coming from the kitchen as we approached, and Matthew opened the door to reveal a man cutting vegetables behind a long island bench in the center of the room.

Matthew gave him a smile. "Isobel, this is our chef, Jacques" he said. "He's worked for me for almost ten years now and makes the most incredible desserts you'll ever have the pleasure of eating."

Jacques lifted his eyes and nodded at Matthew before turning to me. I raised a hand to wave, and the chef winked in response before focusing back on the food he was preparing.

Matthew backed from the room, and I got the impression he didn't want to bother the chef too much while he was working. As we continued the tour, he pointed at another door that led to his study but then directed me up the stairs and showed me multiple bedrooms, a library, what looked like another living room, and another study as well as a room totally devoted to a home theater.

I'd lost count of how many bathrooms he'd pointed out, and I was surprised to learn there was a third floor in the apartment, which consisted of two bedrooms separated by a long hallway. His bedroom was to the left, but he directed me to the room on the right.

"This room is yours," he said. His voice quaked a little as he spoke like he was nervous. "You're welcome to stay here whenever you're in the city. I'm hoping you'll be able to visit again soon."

I nodded because the words stuck in my throat. Matthew had organized a room for me here too? I'd been so intent on grilling Matthew about the Hastings family tonight, but as I stood there, I realized this dinner was about so much more than that. I was flooded by thoughts of our conversation at the ball and his admission to me about how much he wanted me in his life. I was really beginning to see that he meant it.

This was just a bedroom, and Matthew clearly had more of them then he knew what to do with, but it meant more to me than he knew.

As he opened the door to show me the room, I wondered if I should backtrack on my previous thought. It wasn't just a bedroom. It was practically its own apartment within the apartment. I had a whole lounge area to myself that was decked out with soft, plush couches and a fireplace against one wall. The bedroom itself was just as gorgeous as the rest of the apartment with sheer curtains draped over the long windows and a bed so large it could have fit three of me.

There was a huge en suite bathroom and a closet filled with clothing for me. The room even had its own balcony. Not that I had any intention of going out there. We were far too high up for my liking.

Just like it had been downstairs, the view outside the window was impossible to ignore. I could see the endless expanse of Central Park below me and the jagged New York skyline surrounding it. I could even see my father's surname lit up on the top of his building, not far from here. I probably could have sat there staring at the view forever. It was hard not to be a little overwhelmed by it all.

I knew Matthew was wealthy, but this was beyond my wildest dreams. A familiar feeling that I'd been experiencing ever since I got to Weybridge came washing over me. I didn't belong here. I'd slowly become accustomed to living at school, but this was a whole other level of extravagance.

"Are you ready for dinner?" Matthew asked.

I'd been standing in silence staring out at the view for slightly too long, and I somehow tore my gaze from it to turn to him. His lips were curved in a half smile like he understood just how easily the view of New York City could suck you in. I gave him a nod, but as I went to follow him, I had to wonder how ready I really was.

This was my chance to hear his side of the story. It was finally time to uncover the reason why the LaFleurs hated the Hastings family so much.

CHAPTER SEVENTEEN

The dining room was just as lavish as the rest of the apartment with a long table that ran alongside one of the huge windows overlooking the city. At the far end of the room, I could also see an outdoor terrace with a swimming pool. It was emitting a warm blue glow as lights shone up from below the surface of the water.

The room felt too big and too grand for a father-daughter dinner. It felt so formal and nothing like my meals back home with my mom. We always sat on stools at the kitchen counter whenever we ate. We didn't have a proper dining table, and I found I was somewhat grateful for that. Matthew's setup didn't feel comforting or homely at all.

We took a seat at the massive table, and waitstaff arrived moments later. I hadn't seen them in the kitchen, so I had to wonder if there were other rooms I'd missed on the tour. It wouldn't have surprised me.

"I know you're not feeling well, so I had Jacques prepare something light to start with," Matthew said. "If you'd like something else, I can have him put it together—"

"This is perfect," I said, interrupting Matthew as a bowl of chicken soup was placed before me along with a freshly baked but plain bread roll. "I'm not sure I could handle much more than this."

He smiled at me before he started on his own bowl of soup. I felt bad he was being subjected to the same bland food as me, but I was glad he hadn't had his staff go to extra effort to accommodate two different meals for us.

I took a small mouthful of the soup and was immediately surprised by how something so basic could taste so good. It made me wish I were feeling better so I could try more of Jacques's cooking. If he could make chicken soup taste this good, I couldn't begin to imagine what else he was capable of.

I lowered my spoon after taking several mouthfuls and considered my father. I knew I needed to ask him about Noah's family, but I wasn't sure where to begin. I also wanted to find out what Noah was doing at his office today, but I didn't know how to bring that up without admitting I'd gone there to ambush him.

"How has school been?" Matthew asked, breaking the silence between us before I had a chance to broach any of the topics on my mind.

"It was fine. Nothing too exciting going on really."

"Have you had a chance to take your car for a spin yet?"

"Uh…" My cheeks reddened as I remembered what a disaster my attempt to drive it had been. "Once. It didn't go well. I'm not a very good driver."

"Your mother said you were still getting comfortable on the road."

I was surprised he'd spoken to my mom about it. Perhaps he'd wanted to get her approval before getting me the car. If that was the case, I'd be even more surprised she didn't tell my father the car was unnecessary. Mom accepted charity even less easily than me.

"That sounds like she was trying to put it nicely," I said. "I'm a terrible driver. I just get so nervous."

He gave me a conciliatory smile. "Would it help if I arranged a driving instructor for you?"

I hesitated.

"They might be able to help you gain a little confidence?"

After my disastrous drive with Anna, I'd been determined not to get behind the wheel again, but perhaps Matthew was right and with an instructor I could build the confidence I needed. "Uh, yeah, that might be a good idea," I agreed. I couldn't be worse than my experience with Anna.

"Okay, I'll have Caldwell set it up."

"Thanks." I smiled.

"Also, Caldwell tells me you haven't used the credit card I got for you."

"Oh, uh, I haven't really needed to yet. They have everything I need at school." I'd completely forgotten I even had the credit card. I felt uncomfortable at the idea of using Matthew's money. It was bad enough he'd paid for my schooling and given me a car.

"Well, it's there to be used."

"Like I said, I don't really need anything."

He chuckled under his breath. "You must be the first teenager that has to be encouraged to use their parent's credit card," he said.

I shrugged. The whole thing made me uneasy. I didn't like spending money unnecessarily, especially his, and I had enough money saved in tips from working at my mom's café to get me by.

He took a sip of his drink before he continued. "I hear you're doing well in all of your classes."

I guessed that meant he'd been checking up on me again. "Yeah, I'm doing okay. I like schoolwork and kind of throw myself into it." Especially when I was trying not to think about a certain boy who'd broken up with me. Not that I was going to admit that to Matthew.

"I was the same at your age," he admitted. "I always had my nose in a book."

"Really?"

He nodded. It wasn't surprising given what a successful businessman he seemed to be. But it felt nice to know we shared that in common.

"Mom never really understood it," I said. "She's always been better at hands-on learning rather than book learning."

Matthew chuckled. "Candice was the same back when we dated. You could show her how to do something once, and she'd be a master in minutes, but there was no way you could get her to learn it out of a book."

It was strange hearing Matthew talk about my mom. My whole life, I'd never heard details of their relationship. I had only ever focused on the fact he'd left and wasn't around. "Mom never really told me much about the two of you dating."

The lightness in Matthew's eyes dimmed somewhat at my words. "I don't blame her. She must have hated me, thinking I'd abandoned the both of you."

I shook my head. "I don't think it was that. I get the feeling she never talked about you because she found it too hard."

"I find it hard to talk about too. It took me a long time to get over your mother," he murmured. "To this day, I haven't met someone as special as her. I can't tell you how many sleepless nights I've experienced since finding out I could have had the both of you in my life all this time."

I slowly stirred my spoon around the bowl as I summoned the courage to ask my next question. With a deep breath, I blurted it out. "What would you have done if you'd got my mom's letter about me?"

My stomach twisted with nerves, and I couldn't look him in the eyes as I waited for his reply. Matthew reached across the table and took my hand in his. Slowly, I peered up at him.

"I would have done whatever it took to keep you both in my

life," he said. "I had a difficult relationship with my father, but I will never forgive him for not telling me about you. I regret that we've missed the last seventeen years together more than anything."

Matthew really wanted me in his life. He truly wanted me. And I could see it now so clearly in his eyes. I gave him a smile as he squeezed my hand. When he released it, he coughed and glanced away, like he was struggling to keep his feelings at bay too. He turned his attention to his food, and I took this as my cue to eat something myself. It was hard sharing emotions with someone when you were still only on the precipice of getting to know one another.

The soup Matthew's chef had prepared was amazing, but I barely seemed to taste it anymore. It was hard to focus on eating when your long-lost father had just told you how much he wanted you in his life.

"I suppose you would like to hear about what happened with the Hastings family," Matthew said.

My eyes lifted in one swift movement to meet his. After everything Matthew had just admitted, I didn't want to put a dampener on our dinner by turning the conversation to a topic that seemed so fraught with pain and anger. I also didn't want to hear what he had to say if it was going to support Noah's claim that Matthew was a bad person. The thought made me a little queasy. It felt like we were finally bonding, and I didn't want to ruin that.

I wasn't sure when I'd have another opportunity to talk with him about this though. And if my father truly had a malicious side, it was better I know that now. I had Noah's side of the story, but I needed my father's too. It was time I had the whole truth.

I slowly nodded. "I just feel like I'm stuck in the middle of something I don't fully understand. You seem to hate them just as much as they hate you. And me... They hate me too just by association."

"I'm sorry you've been made to feel that way. I'll do my best to explain," Matthew started. "There's a history with our families, and it's not very pleasant."

He drew in a breath as if bracing himself for the story he had to tell. "Back when your grandfather and Noah's grandfather were young and just starting out in their careers, they worked together," he said. "James LaFleur and William Hastings were both brilliant and determined scientists, but they also shared a stubborn competitive streak and an inability to compromise or forgive.

"They fell out after a fire started in their lab and destroyed years of hard work," he continued. "To this day, no one could tell you for sure what caused the fire, but they both blamed each other and went their separate ways. That might have been the end of the feud, but William Hastings lodged a patent on the cancer treatment they'd been working on together. A treatment my father believed had been lost in the fire."

"Wait, so you're saying that William stole my grandfather's work?" I asked.

"It was both of their work, but yes," Matthew said. "It only confirmed to my father that William had started the fire to cut him out. It commenced years of backlash and fighting. They were constantly competing or attempting to sabotage one another. My father was in and out of court for almost a decade trying to prove he had a right to his own work."

I swallowed as I considered what Matthew had said. His account of what started the whole feud was far more detailed than Noah's had been. This was the first I'd heard about a fire destroying their work, and that was certainly a more reasonable explanation for my grandfather's hatred than mere jealousy. If William really had started the fire and stolen my grandfather's work, then maybe the LaFleurs' vendetta against the Hastings was justified.

"This isn't just about your father though, is it?"

"No." Matthew let out a sigh. "I've had my own hand in the battle between our families. All my life, I saw my father being torn apart because he couldn't manufacture the treatment he worked so hard to create. And he had to watch as William Hastings grew rich off the back of it. I often wondered if my father would have been a different man, a softer man, if he hadn't been so brutally betrayed."

Matthew seemed to get lost in his thoughts for a moment but then shook his head and continued. "Anyway, a couple of years back, the patent ended on the treatment they'd fought over. So, I started to manufacture a generic version of it. William had been charging extortionate fees for the drug for years, and the price on it was so high that most people couldn't afford it.

"I hated knowing that people who needed my father's treatment couldn't access it, so I decided to sell it as cheaply as possible. I don't make any profit on the drug. Actually, I think we might run at a loss. But, our company is diversified enough that it is not an issue. If one good thing came out of William's betrayal, it was that my father was always striving to be ahead of the game and constantly innovating and developing our products."

"So, William Hastings hates you for selling the same product as him but cheaper?"

"Yes," Matthew replied. "I haven't seen any new developments come out of Hastings Laboratories in years, and they rely too much on this one drug. I think he's suffered a big hit to his bottom line because of it."

If what Noah had told me was true, it sounded like my father's actions were sinking the Hastings' company entirely. Whether Matthew knew that or not, I wasn't sure. Still, I felt a sense of relief at his explanation. I took no joy from the fact that the Hastings' business had suffered due to my dad's actions, but it sounded like Matthew was simply trying to do the right thing.

He was also yet to mention my aunt. Like Noah, Matthew had focused only on the business side of the rivalry. But I now knew it was so much more than that. Maybe my father found it just as difficult to talk about as Noah.

I cautiously continued my questioning. "I understand there's this history of business rivalry," I said. "But I still don't understand what it's got to do with me. Why are you personally so against Noah and I dating? You warned me about him before I even met him."

Matthew swallowed, and his eyes glassed over for a moment. He quickly glanced away before I could see his expression clearly. My question seemed to have hit a nerve. His throat bobbed as he swallowed again and slowly faced me once more.

"There's more to the story." He paused, but I didn't press him as I could see he was going to tell me. He was just steeling himself for whatever it was he had to say. I sat silently, but I leaned forward slightly as I waited.

"My sister, Georgina, went to Hastings Laboratories one night." As Matthew spoke, his eyes fell and his head lowered slightly. "It didn't end well."

I swallowed because this was what I'd wanted to hear more about, but seeing the pain in Matthew's eyes, I quickly decided not to push my father for any more of an explanation.

"You don't have to tell me," I said softly. "I already know about the fire and the affair."

"Affair?" Matthew's eyes snapped to mine.

"Noah told me everything," I explained. "He told me his father and your sister were having an affair. That's why they were at the lab together the night of the fire."

"That's not true." Although Matthew hadn't raised his voice, his words came out so forcefully it was impossible to miss the certainty with which he spoke them.

I shook my head in confusion. "But Noah said..."

"Noah was just repeating what his grandfather told him," Matthew replied. "William Hastings simply assumed my sister was having an affair with his son. He never would have believed what they were really up to."

"So, if they weren't having an affair, what was Georgina doing with Noah's dad?"

Matthew let out a sigh. "It's my fault she was there," he said. "I thought that I could work with Liam Hastings to try and repair the rift between our families. Georgina was helping us. We wanted to put all the toxicity behind us so we could work together once we had more control of the companies. But we had to do it in secret because our parents never would have understood. Their hatred of one another was too ingrained.

"I've regretted trying to work with the Hastings family every day of my life since. All Liam and Georgina wanted was peace, and yet their deaths only drove our families further apart."

He sat up a little straighter in his chair and took a deep breath, regaining his usual calm composure. "So, as you can imagine, this conflict between our families isn't something I take lightly. I hope you can see why I didn't want you anywhere near the Hastings boy. It felt too much like history repeating itself, and I don't think I could endure the pain of losing you too."

"I understand," I said, nodding slowly. Both Noah and Matthew had lost so much because of their families already and were scared to lose any more. I didn't want to be the cause of more pain for either of them.

"Given what you guys were up to, do you think the fire that killed them was an accident?"

"What do you mean?"

"Well, your grandfather thought William started the fire that destroyed his work all those years ago. You don't suspect he started this one?"

Matthew shook his head. "I might not like William Hastings, but I know he would never risk his son that way."

"And your father?" I hated asking the question, but it felt like it needed to be asked.

"I've considered the same thing many times myself, but I always come back to the fact that, despite their faults, neither of our parents would ever want to hurt their own flesh and blood. It was simply a tragic accident."

He sounded so certain, but there was the tiniest flicker of concern in his gaze, and I had to wonder if perhaps my dad still wondered the same thing sometimes.

I glanced at my bowl. There was still some soup left, but I'd lost my appetite after talking about my aunt's death.

"Do you have any pictures of Georgina?" I asked. "I'd love to see her."

"Of course." Matthew smiled and pulled his phone out of his pocket. He flicked through it for a moment before turning it so I could see the screen. The picture on the display was of a young woman, maybe in her twenties. Her eyes were bright with mischief, and she looked a lot like Matthew. They both had the same dark hair and light-blue eyes. Matthew had told me before that I looked like her, and I thought I could see some similarities. We shared the same eyes but also the same smile and small button nose.

"She's beautiful," I said.

"She was," he agreed. "She was always laughing and had a terrible knack for getting herself into trouble. She had an infectious personality that was impossible not to love."

"It sounds like she was a lot of fun."

He smiled but let out a slow breath at the same time. "Certainly more so than me. I think I used to be more fun, but I threw myself into work even more after she died. It feels like it's been so long since I did anything just because I enjoy it. I'm afraid I wouldn't remember how anymore." It was sad hearing Matthew talk about himself that way, but it was understandable knowing he'd lost his sister.

"I'm sure we can figure out a way to remind you," I said, and his eyes lit up. I got the impression that one throwaway comment meant more to him than anything else I'd said tonight.

"Speaking of fun, I've stolen enough of your evening," he said. "I should get you back to your friends."

It felt like we were ending the night too soon, but after everything Matthew had just shared, there wasn't much more to say. I still had so many questions, but I wasn't going to force them on him now. He'd be back in Weybridge soon enough. Hopefully we'd have another chance to talk about everything then.

Matthew joined me in the car when his driver dropped me back at Cress's house. We didn't say much on the drive, and I imagined it was because we were both still reeling from our conversation at dinner.

I glanced at Matthew, watching the city lights flickering across his face as he stared out the window. He looked like his thoughts were a million miles from the car. I couldn't imagine how hard it must have been for him to lose his sister, and he was clearly still torn up about it years later.

I felt like I finally understood why Matthew had warned me to stay away from Noah. It might not be fair that Matthew judged Noah for his family's mistakes and associated him with the danger that getting close to one of them presented, but fear wasn't always rational.

I also understood where Noah was coming from. He too didn't want to lose another family member in his grandfather. But I wasn't so sure Noah's anger toward Matthew was fair. The actions my grandfather had taken seemed justified given everything William did to him. I hadn't wanted to take a side in the fight between our families, but after speaking with Matthew, I felt like I had no choice but to back my father up. He was just trying to do the right thing, and he didn't deserve to be vilified for it.

There was no way to change what had happened. The only thing I could control was what happened next. Noah had chosen to believe my father was the bad guy. If he couldn't understand Matthew wasn't the villain in this situation, there was nothing I could do.

As the car pulled up outside Cress's house, I realized I still had one last question for my father.

"You know," I started. "Noah went missing from our school excursion today. My friend Wes was visiting his dad at the hotel across the road from your office and said he saw Noah leaving your building." It was the only way I could think of broaching the subject without upsetting my father or letting him know I was there too.

Matthew's eyebrows lifted with surprise, but his features quickly returned to neutral

"Why would Noah have been in my building?" he asked calmly.

"I don't know," I replied. "Wes had this crazy theory that he went there to see you."

My father raised his eyebrows slightly once again. "That really is a crazy theory," he said. "If Wes saw him there, I'm sure it was just a coincidence."

I watched him closely, trying to gauge what he was thinking. I couldn't really figure him out.

"Yeah." I laughed awkwardly. "That's what I said too."

In truth, Wes had suggested it was all just a coincidence. I was the one who couldn't stop wondering why Noah was there. I was still questioning it. Despite all of my father's honesty tonight, I had to wonder if he was still keeping things from me.

CHAPTER EIGHTEEN

I couldn't look at the price tags on the clothes the girls were buying. I'd looked at one of them earlier in the day and had nearly fainted when I'd seen the number of zeros. Neither Cress nor Anna seemed bothered they were spending more in a day than I had in my entire life. And the twins were just as bad.

The boys had disappeared into the men's department when we'd arrived at the expensive department store with plans to buy outfits for the night. I hadn't bought anything yet. I couldn't justify it when I knew I had perfectly good clothes packed in my duffel bag back at Cress's place, all of which had been selected by Matthew's stylist in New York.

"How are you getting on?" someone whispered in my ear.

I gasped and spun to find Wes grinning down at me. My hand was pressed against my chest as I scowled at him. "Wes, you scared me. You shouldn't sneak up on people like that."

He chuckled. "I was hardly sneaking. I can't help that your head was in the clouds."

"My head wasn't in the clouds," I responded instinctively, but when I thought about it, he was right. My thoughts had been somewhere else all day. I was still reeling from everything my father had told me the previous night, and no amount of shopping was going to take my mind off that.

"Where was it then?" Wes asked.

"I was trying to figure out if Anna and Cress plan to shop *all* day."

He laughed. "I don't think that's much of a mystery. I'd say the answer to that question is a definite yes."

"Well, that's not the answer I was hoping for." I'd enjoyed shopping for the first couple of hours, but we hadn't even stopped for lunch yet, and I was growing tired quickly. The girls were both in the fitting rooms at the moment and showed no signs of slowing down.

"That's actually why I came to find you," Wes continued. "I was thinking we should make a run for it."

I perked up a little. "Were you just?"

"Uh-huh. Sawyer could be lost in the men's department for hours, and I happen to know that a certain library you were interested in visiting isn't far from here…"

"Really?" I couldn't keep the smile from my face.

"Yep. And now I've seen your eyes light up like that, we haven't got a choice but to go."

I glanced over my shoulder at the fitting rooms. "I should probably tell Cress and Anna we're going."

Wes grabbed my hand and pulled me in the opposite direction. "And let them rope us into more shopping? I don't think so. We can text them once we're out of the store."

Wes didn't let go of my hand as we made our way to the exit. As we approach the wide glass doors, Wes broke out into a jog. "We're almost to freedom," he cried, and I laughed as he pulled me along.

One of the store employees shot us a hard look as we burst out through the front doors, and I gasped for breath amid my laughter as we finally came to a stop.

"I thought you said they wouldn't mind if we left?"

Wes lifted one shoulder. "It was far more fun to leave that way."

I shook my head. "Seriously, do you think the girls will mind?"

"Nah, they'll just buy more clothes to make themselves feel better."

"Yeah, probably." I grinned. "What about Sawyer?"

"I already told him I was done with shopping, and if he sees something I might like, he's going to get it for me."

"And he was cool with that?"

"Totally cool. He secretly loves shopping. He almost likes it as much as Cress and Anna."

"I guess being identical twins means it's easy to shop for you too."

He nodded. "One of the benefits of sharing a face."

Once we'd recovered from our daring escape, we started in the direction of the library. The sidewalk was bustling with people, and I had to keep reminding myself to watch where I was going. It was easy to get distracted as I peered up at the huge buildings that towered high above us. This weekend was the first time I'd encountered skyscrapers in real life before.

"You're spacing out again," Wes said.

I smiled and tore my gaze from the sky to look at him. "Just taking it all in. I love how busy it is here. There are so many cars and people. Growing up, I couldn't walk ten feet through town without seeing someone I knew. Here I feel like you'd be lucky to bump into a single familiar face."

Wes looked around us like he was seeing the city through my eyes. "I think you'd be surprised. It's a big city, but the same people always seem to go to the same places, so it can sometimes feel way too small. Still, I can't really imagine living somewhere you know everyone."

"I could never imagine living somewhere you didn't. But, coming here, I get it. There's a kind of freedom that comes with walking down the street and not knowing a soul you share the sidewalk with."

"Just being one of the masses," Wes agreed. "It is kind of freeing."

"Have you always lived in New York?"

"Always. Though I've spent a lot less time here since starting high school. Still, it's home."

"And you love it?"

"It's a hard place not to love."

I'd only been here a couple of days, and already I was growing to love the hustle and bustle of the city. I loved the way the skyline lit up at night and the fast pace that thrummed through the city like an ever-present heartbeat. It was unashamedly loud and chaotic, and yet I found peace in that. Plus, the bagels didn't hurt. Sawyer and Wes had come to Cress's house far too early this morning and dragged us out of bed to go to their favorite bagel place. I hadn't enjoyed the rude awakening, nor the fact I'd still been wearing my Winne the Pooh pajamas when the twins had arrived, but the bagel had been totally worth it. I'd come all the way to New York just to eat another.

"So, how was dinner with your father," Wes asked.

I didn't know how to answer. Where did I even begin? I'd been given so much new information, and I wasn't sure how much of it I could tell Wes even if I wanted to. I decided to keep my response simple.

"It was good. I feel like we got to know each other a bit better."

"Did you get all the answers you were looking for."

"Yeah, most of them, I think." It was somewhat true. A lot of my questions had been answered, but there was no way to tell if I had heard every part of the story yet.

"What about Noah?" Wes continued. "Did you ask why he was at your dad's office?"

"He just said it must have been a coincidence."

"Yeah, he could have been there for another reason."

"Maybe," I agreed, but I wasn't sure if either of us were completely convinced. I quickly moved to change the subject. "How far is the library?"

"Not far." Wes started smiling. "It's right there."

I followed Wes's gaze across the street to the gorgeous stone building up ahead. It was grand and majestic with tall pillars, graceful arches, and intricate statues carved into the façade. There was even a set of stone lions sitting proudly out front, guarding the entrance.

"Come on." Wes tugged me toward the building, up the stairs, and through the front doors. We were greeted by an impressive foyer with lofty ceilings, sweeping staircases, and elegant chandeliers. The gray stone walls reminded me more of a vast castle than a cozy library. I couldn't even begin to compare it to my local public library back home.

Wes guided us through the building, showing me gorgeous rooms that were filled with so much beauty and history they almost brought tears to my eyes. It was the Rose Main Reading Room that really took my breath away though. Shelves lined with books surrounded the reading space, but the beautiful murals painted on the ceiling and the chandeliers that hung above the room made it truly special. A part of me wished I had brought my laptop so I could spend just a few minutes working in such a special place.

"Come on," Wes murmured. "There's more."

I slowly followed him from the room, disappointed to be leaving it behind so soon.

"What are you showing me now?"

"You'll see."

He led me to a children's section at the back of the building and stopped when he reached a glass case. I frowned at him before I peered inside. I was confused at first but my heart warmed when I saw the original *Winnie-the-Pooh* toys on display.

The toys looked old and worn, but it was clear they were just well loved.

"After catching sight of your Pooh bear pajamas this morning, I thought you might like to see them," he said.

My cheeks warmed at the memory. I'd changed as soon as Wes and Sawyer had arrived at Cress's this morning but not before they'd both seen and commented on my PJs.

"I thought we agreed we weren't going to talk about my pajamas ever again."

"You say that like I can control Sawyer. And the pajamas were cute."

"Maybe for a five-year-old," I grumbled.

"Well, I liked them."

I definitely didn't want Wes continuing to visualize me in my tattered pajamas, so I quickly moved on. "How did you know this display was here?"

"I came here a few times as a kid and I liked visiting the toys," he explained. "My mom would always read us *Winnie-the-Pooh* before bed when I was little. Eeyore was my favorite, and Sawyer was, of course, a Tigger fan. There was a time when he couldn't go a day without saying 'Don't be ridick-orous' or insisting he had a lot of bouncing to do."

It was all too easy to imagine Sawyer bounding around the house like Tigger. "My mom used to read the stories to me too. I always liked Pooh because we both loved honey so much."

Wes laughed, and I turned back to focus on the toys.

"It's kind of nice seeing them in real life, isn't it?" I said. "To be in the presence of something that inspired such beautiful stories and touched so many lives." Wes and I grew up in such different homes, and yet we were connected through the books that had been read to us. Even Noah had recalled a quote from the stories the other night. There was something almost magical in that. I couldn't help but wonder if Noah had come here before and admired the toys too.

"Yeah, it is," Wes agreed. He shared a soft smile with me, and my heart did a small flip in response.

My phone started ringing, interrupting our moment, and I was somewhat glad for the distraction as I pulled it from my pocket.

Cress's name lit up the screen, and I glanced up at Wes. "I think the girls have finally noticed we're gone."

He grinned brightly. "Took them long enough."

I laughed and walked out into the stairwell as I answered the phone.

"Where are you?" Cress asked.

I put her on speakerphone so Wes could hear too. "Wes and I may have called mutiny and abandoned ship."

"Well, that's not cool. I want to get off the ship too. Even I can't keep up with Anna's shopping today."

"*Hey!*" Anna complained in the background.

"Where are you guys?" Cress asked. "We'll come meet you."

"We're at the library."

"The library? What on earth are you doing there?"

"I needed to borrow a book."

"Really?"

"No." I laughed. "I just wanted to see it, and it was close by. We're just about to leave though so we can meet you guys somewhere else."

Wes reached out a hand and beckoned for me to pass him my phone. I handed it over to him.

"I have an idea of what we can do," he said. "Go find my brother, and I'll text you guys where to meet us."

"Okay, catch you soon."

Wes hung up the phone and passed it back to me.

"So, what are we doing then?" I asked.

He gave me a cryptic smile in response. "It's a surprise, but I think you'll like it."

CHAPTER NINETEEN

It wasn't just one surprise. It was a whole afternoon of surprises. Wes played tour guide and took us to all the nearby attractions. We took silly photos in Times Square, ate our body-weight in pizza slices for lunch and went to the top of the Empire State Building. Wes even forced us all to buy matching "I heart NY" T-shirts. We all looked ridiculous in them, but they made everyone laugh as we darted about the city sightseeing. I loved every minute of it.

By the time we arrived back at Cress's place, it was already getting dark, and I was exhausted. We'd walked all over New York today, so I wasn't sure how I was going to handle a night out on top of that.

Anna, Cress, and I collapsed on the bed when we reached Cress's room. The boys had both gone home to change before the evening's activities, so it was just the three of us.

"I'm exhausted," Anna said. "I have shopping stamina that lasts for days but absolutely no endurance when it comes to sightseeing."

I nodded firmly in agreement. "Yeah, my feet are toast."

"It was a fun day though, wasn't it?" Cress said. She was lying on her back staring up at the ceiling.

"It was the best," I agreed. I'd barely stopped grinning all day, but it wasn't the sights that had made me so happy. It was my friends.

"And so sweet of Wes to organize it all," Cress said, glancing in my direction.

"Yeah, super sweet," Anna agreed. "It's almost like he went out of his way for a certain someone who's never been to New York before." She shot me a knowing look. "A certain someone he *really* likes."

"He doesn't like me like that."

"No?" Anna asked. "Because most boys wouldn't go to that much effort unless they liked a girl."

"Definitely not," Cress added.

"We're just friends." I protested, but the girls were right about one thing; it had been really sweet of Wes to be our tour guide today. He knew how much I wanted to see New York. He'd even come to rescue me from shopping earlier and take me to the place I wanted to see most.

"Let's not forget he also offered to kiss you," Anna said.

"Because he's a good friend." Even I didn't think it sounded convincing when I said it out loud.

Anna wasn't listening. "Plus, he's kind, smart, superhot, and finally single. I'm just saying, if you were interested in dating another guy, you really couldn't go wrong with Wes."

I frowned up at the ceiling as I considered it. I wanted to tell her she was wrong, but I couldn't quite bring myself to do it. Wes was a great guy, and I really liked him. But did I like him as more than a friend? I wasn't sure.

The thought of moving past Noah and being with someone else caused my chest to constrict with anxiety. My heart was still resisting the idea of closing that door in my life. As much as I hated it and as much as Noah didn't deserve it, I still had strong feelings for him. We were never going to be together, so perhaps it was time to open a new door. Maybe Anna and Cress were right, and Wes could be something more to me. But it wouldn't be fair to try to move on with him when I was still hung up on Noah. The problem was, I wasn't sure if I was ever going to get over Noah. I shook my head. I was too confused to give voice to my thoughts.

Cress sat up on the bed. "You're thinking about it. Aren't you?"

Anna nodded. "She definitely is."

I looked between the two of them. "I don't know what to think."

"Well, you don't have to think anything for now," Cress said. "You don't need to rush things. Take your time, and I'm sure everything will figure itself out."

I gave her a grateful smile. Cress was right. There wasn't any pressure to rush into a new relationship. Especially not when I was still hurting over my old one.

"Well, I totally think you should rush. It's much more fun that way," Anna said. "But you probably shouldn't listen to me. I have really poor luck with guys."

Cress laughed and nudged her shoulder against Anna's. "That *would* be your advice."

Anna shrugged. "Hey, I'm more a live now, regret it later kind of girl."

"And you're always getting into trouble because of it."

"Always," Anna agreed with a sly smile. "Anyway, who knows, maybe we'll find you another dreamy guy to set your sights on tonight."

"A guy from New York?" I asked.

"Why not? I still think a rebound would do you wonders. It's pretty clear you're still hurting after Noah."

"Is it really that obvious?"

"I guess to us it is," Cress said. "But we're your friends. We wouldn't be very good ones if we couldn't see you're still hurting."

I let out a sigh. "Yeah, I guess I am. Spending the weekend here with you both has really helped take my mind off it though."

"I knew a good distraction would do the trick," Anna said. "Now, let's start getting ready for our next distraction—an epic night out on the town."

Cress clapped her hands together with excitement. "I can't wait to dress up in my new outfit. If we start getting ready now, we can relax until the twins get here."

Cress's prediction was optimistic. There was no time left for relaxing before the twins arrived because the girls used every available minute perfecting their hair and makeup.

They both insisted on helping me, and I had to admit they did a pretty incredible job. Anna had straightened my normally wavy hair and styled it up in a high ponytail so it wouldn't get sweaty while we danced the night away. Meanwhile, Cress had given me a glam makeup look. It was a lot heavier than I normally went for, but I felt much more grown up when I saw myself in the mirror. It was like looking at an older version of myself, and I kind of liked it.

"You guys are beauty wizards," I said, grinning as I turned away from my reflection to look at the two girls. They were finished with their own hair and makeup and already dressed in their clothes for the night. They looked gorgeous. Then again, they always looked incredible.

"Tell me something I don't know," Cress said with a wink.

I laughed and glanced at myself in the mirror again. It was so weird seeing such a different reflection staring back at me, but it gave me a boost of confidence. The face I wore tonight felt like a mask, and the girl behind it could be anyone. I didn't have to be the sad girl who'd had her heart stomped all over by her ex, and the feeling was somewhat empowering.

"Now, go put this on," Anna said, holding out a dress that

looked short enough to be a top. "I want to see the whole look."

I took the dress without complaint and headed into the bathroom across the hall. Anna had taken one look at the outfits I'd packed for the weekend and told me none of them would do. She'd insisted I borrow one of her new items from today's shopping spree, and since I had no idea what *was* appropriate to wear to a club, I hadn't had much leverage when I tried to argue that my own clothes were fine.

I squeezed and shimmied my way into the tight black dress. It was sparkly and short, which highlighted my legs. When paired with stilettos, they looked impossibly long.

"You look hot," Anna said as I stepped out of the bathroom. She was standing by the bedroom door like she'd been waiting for me. "Fair warning, Wes is definitely going to offer to be your rebound again when he sees you like that."

I rolled my eyes. "I'm sure he won't." My heart fluttered a little at the thought.

"He definitely will," Cress said as she appeared in the doorway next to Anna. "Damn, we're good."

"The best," Anna agreed. "I think all our hard work calls for a little champagne." She pulled a bottle out from behind her back and wiggled it in the air.

"Where did you get that?" I asked.

"I raided the Farley wine cellar. There was no lock on the door, so I assumed it was all fair game."

Cress lifted her eyebrows.

"What? It was a champagne emergency!"

Cress laughed and snatched the bottle. "You think everything is a champagne emergency."

"Well, it is!" Anna replied. "Now, you two get in close so I can get a picture. You both look gorgeous."

Cress skipped over to me and wrapped an arm around my shoulders. Anna pointed her phone in our direction before I could object, and Cress and I grinned.

"Cute. But you need to smile like you're having fun."

"We are having fun." I laughed.

"And we'll be having even more fun once this champagne is open," Cress replied. She popped the cork on the champagne, and the bubbles fizzed out the top of the bottle. The two of us squealed as it erupted into the air before we burst into fits of laughter.

"Anna, did you shake the bottle before giving it to us?" Cress asked.

"I swear I didn't." She was grinning widely, so I wasn't sure whether to trust her. She must have seen the uncertainty in my eyes because she continued. "What? I would never. That's like champagne blasphemy. Such a waste."

"Champagne *is* practically her religion." Cress poured the drink into the elegant glass flutes already in the room. I was guessing Anna had helped herself to them too.

"Sure is." Anna wasn't looking at us as she spoke. Instead, she was staring at her phone, her lower lip sucked between her teeth as she concentrated.

"What are you doing?" I asked.

"Just showing the rest of the world what they're missing..." She turned the phone to us, and I could see she'd posted one of the pictures she'd just taken to Instagram. It was the moment the champagne had erupted, and Cress and I were laughing. It was fun and cute, and even I had to admit we both looked amazing in the picture.

She'd captioned the photo *"Girls night with my BFFs,"* and my heart warmed to think she counted me as one of her best friends. I felt like we'd grown close, but it almost had me tearing up to know she felt the same way too.

"Oh, I love it," Cress said.

"Me too," I agreed with a smile. And I loved these two girls. How did I get so lucky?

"Ha! It's already blowing up," Anna said as she checked her

phone again. "Sawyer's posted about a million flame emojis. He also says they're on their way and to stop having fun without them."

Cress laughed. "I bet they were nowhere close to leaving, but now he's gotten FOMO, and they're already in a car."

"Definitely," Anna agreed. "Sawyer gets the worst FOMO."

"What about Wes?" I asked. "Did he comment on the picture?"

Anna smirked at me. "No, but I bet he was leading the charge to get here when he saw you in that dress."

My cheeks flushed as I realized how the question might have looked to Cress and Anna, like I wanted Wes to be just as impressed as Sawyer. "I'm sure that's not true."

"And I'm sure it is," Cress said. "You should have seen the way he was looking at you today while we were out being tourists."

"And how was that?" I asked.

"Like he thought you were adorable."

"I mean, she kind of was," Anna said. "Did you hear her squeal of excitement when we arrived at Times Square? And then how she actually gasped when she saw the view at the top of the Empire State Building? It was like watching a puppy being given a treat."

I poked my tongue out at them. "You guys suck."

They laughed, and Anna raised her glass of champagne above her head. "Here's to a fun night."

We clinked our glasses together before taking a drink. Anna practically downed hers in one gulp while Cress and I only took small savoring sips.

"We should probably head downstairs to meet the boys," Cress said.

"Yeah, we can grab another bottle of champagne too," Anna added. "Your parents have excellent taste." She happily trotted off downstairs, and Cress followed her with a shake of her head.

I went to grab my phone from where I'd tossed it on the bed before I joined them. There was a text message waiting for me, and my stomach tied itself in knots when I saw it was from Noah.

The message had only been sent a minute or so ago, so at least I knew it hadn't been sitting there unread for hours while the girls dolled me up. I was tempted to delete the message without reading it. But I wasn't strong enough. I was far too curious to know what he'd sent. With a mixture of dread and anticipation, I opened the message.

> Noah: I wish things were different. You're so beautiful. It breaks me.

I stared at the text, my heart warming and shattering all at once. Why did he send that? And why now of all times?

I wondered if he'd seen Anna's Instagram post. It was the only explanation I could come up with given the timing. But that didn't make it okay for him to text me. He knew we couldn't be together. He knew I wanted to move on. His message only messed with my head, and I hated him for sending it.

I gritted my teeth and deleted the message, wishing I could wipe it from my brain just as easily. This whole weekend was about forgetting Noah. Why did he have to make it so hard? Every time I felt like I was beginning to make progress, he went and derailed it all with a stolen look or a surprise message.

I hated how much I missed him. I despised how my heart still leaped when I saw his name lighting up my screen. I wished things were different too, but there was no changing the past, and I didn't want to spend another second living in it.

I placed my phone back on the bed where I'd found it, deciding to leave it there for the night. I didn't need any more cryptic messages from Noah, and I refused to let him ruin the rest of my time in New York. I downed the remainder of my champagne in one gulp before making my way downstairs.

Tonight was about having fun and moving on. Noah's message had only made me more determined.

CHAPTER TWENTY

I was somewhat tipsy by the time we arrived at the club. It hadn't looked like a massive venue from the outside, but there was a long line snaking around the block to get in. Thanks to Sawyer, we somehow managed to skip the line and were shown straight inside to the VIP section.

I'd never been to a nightclub before, but I was fairly certain they were supposed to check your ID at the front entrance. Apparently, Sawyer knew the owner, and it wasn't an issue because not one of us was questioned about our age.

The club was loud with a pumping dance floor and dark lighting that flickered and flared around the room. Within minutes of arriving, I decided nightclubs weren't for me. I could barely hear myself think, let alone actually hear what people were saying. We all had to shout at each other to be heard, and I was worried we'd all lose our voices by the end of the night.

I put aside my initial distaste for the place. I was on a mission tonight to have fun and forget Noah.

"This place is great," Anna said, grinning as she looked out over the dance floor. We were sitting in a booth high up on a balcony overlooking the whole club. Our area was cordoned off with its own bar and a server who brought us drinks.

"I told you it would be good," Sawyer said. "It only opened a few weeks ago, but it's supposed to be the best place in town. *Everyone* comes here." He and Wes must have shaken hands with half a dozen people on the way up to our booth. It was crazy to think they recognized one person here, let alone several, but I was guessing their New York friends all went to the same places.

"We should go dance." Anna was almost dancing in her seat as she suggested it. It felt like we'd only just arrived. Our drinks had barely touched down on the table, but Anna had already knocked hers back. I had no idea how anyone ever kept up with her.

"I think I need to finish my drink first," I said.

"Me too," Wes agreed, sharing a smile with me. He hated dancing about as much as I did, so I knew he was eager to avoid it too.

"Fine, but you guys better come join us after a few songs, or I'll come back and force you downstairs," Anna warned. There was a glint of steel in her eyes, and I knew she was being deadly serious.

"Okay, okay, we'll be down in a few songs," I assured her.

"Good." She grinned before dragging Cress and Sawyer down to the dance floor.

I slouched in my seat, somewhat relieved as they disappeared.

"Not in the mood for dancing?" Wes asked.

"It looks pretty crazy down there."

"Yeah, these places aren't really my scene either." He took a sip of his whisky, and I tried not to focus on his lips. It was probably just the alcohol in me, but Wes looked damn hot tonight. He was wearing a dark button-down shirt and dress slacks. He was also sitting very close to me. He must have shifted when the others left because I could have sworn our knees weren't brushing when we first sat down.

It was starting to feel really warm in the club, and I had a feeling Wes's proximity was the cause of all that heat. I'd never really thought of Wes as more than a friend, but since Anna and Cress had put the idea in my mind, I couldn't seem to look at him in the same way.

I was surprised by just how attracted to him I felt and how sitting so close made my skin tingle. A part of me wanted to get closer still, but another, *saner*, part of me wasn't sure it was such a great idea.

I wanted to curse Anna and Cress for suggesting I get together with Wes earlier tonight. There was no way I'd be feeling this way if they hadn't put these thoughts in my head. They'd continuously dropped hints about him liking me when we'd been getting ready, and they'd looked completely victorious when he'd arrived at the apartment tonight and told me I looked gorgeous.

Still, now that the thoughts were there, they were impossible to deny. I was attracted to Wes, but even just thinking that made me want to run away from him and the images that were popping into my head. I picked up my drink and finished it one go.

Wes chuckled as he watched me. "Thirsty?"

"I guess I was," I agreed with an awkward smile. I could barely look Wes in the eyes. I was embarrassed by the thoughts about him filling my head, and I didn't know how to deal with it. "We should probably go dance with the others."

I hadn't even lasted one song alone in the booth with Wes, but he didn't complain as we started down to the dance floor. I wondered if he could sense how nervous I was? If he could tell my mind kept drifting back to his offer to kiss me in his room?

The girls jumped with excitement when we finally found them on the dance floor. "You actually came down!" Anna squealed while Cress grabbed my hand and started dancing with me. "I thought for sure we'd have to come up there and get you guys," she shouted through the music.

I shrugged and gave her a smile. "I guess I finished my drink quicker than I thought I would."

She didn't seem totally convinced that was the only reason, and her gaze teetered between Wes and I. I refused to look at him. It felt like that would only feed her curiosity.

Song after song, we all danced together. The alcohol had loosened me up, so I was moving more than normal. I still had two left feet, so I probably looked like a total idiot, but I couldn't deny it was fun jumping around the dance floor with my friends.

After a while, amid the throbbing crowd of people, I got separated from Sawyer and the girls, and I found myself standing in front of Wes. He gave me a timid smile and held out his hands toward me. I was wary of getting closer to Wes right now, especially given I'd been thinking about him in ways I probably shouldn't. His smile was so genuine though, and there was a hint of hope in his eyes as I took his offered hand.

The music was still moving fast, but he held me close, and we slowly swayed together as though we were listening to a completely different tune. I suddenly couldn't remember why I'd been so cautious. Dancing with him felt like the best decision I'd made all week.

I felt so safe being held by Wes, and his grasp on me was reassuring. I looked up and smiled at him when I realized neither of us had stepped on the other one's feet so far.

"You're not nearly as bad at dancing as I remember," I said. I had to lift onto my toes and bring my mouth close to his ear so he could hear me over the music.

He lowered his head and leaned in close as he responded. "You too," he said with a laugh. "It must be the alcohol."

"Definitely. Although, I thought alcohol would make me a worse dancer."

"Or perhaps it just gave you the confidence to unleash your inner ballerina."

"Well, your inner ballerina is shining tonight too."

"Thanks. I think..." His eyes were bright with amusement. I found it so hard to think straight when he looked at me that way. When he looked at me like I was the only person in the room.

"I never did ask; did you ever find a suitable rebound on Anna's list?"

His question caught me off guard, and I swallowed. Why was he bringing up the list? And why now, when we were dancing so close to one another? When he had to bring his lips so close to my neck whenever he spoke? When I was already being tempted by so many dangerous thoughts about him?

Somehow, I managed to act unaffected, and I rolled my eyes. "I told you I wasn't going to use the list. Besides, the options Anna suggested were terrible."

"Who was on there?" Wes chuckled, but his serious eyes suggested he really wanted to know the answer.

"Practically half the senior class. She even annotated it to tell me which guys she'd kissed herself and how good they were. I think she thought she was doing me a favor."

"She is committed. I'll give her that."

I tilted my head as I stared at him. "Why are you asking about the list?"

His eyes practically glittered as he looked over me, and his gaze tugged on something deep in my gut. "I just hope you know you deserve someone great. Not some random name off a list. Even though you could get any guy on that list without trying, especially looking like you do tonight."

My heart stuttered. It wasn't just the compliment that was making it hard to breathe. It was the way he was looking at me, like perhaps he'd been having dangerous thoughts tonight about me too.

"What about the guys that aren't on the list?" The question was out of my mouth before I could consider it, and Wes's hands tightened on my lower back in response.

He brought his lips in close to my ear. "The guys that aren't on the list too."

A thrill ran down my neck. I wasn't sure what was happening between Wes and I, and I had no idea where it had come from. The only thing I knew was I liked it.

His eyes were heated as he pulled back to look at me. He definitely wasn't looking at me like I was simply his friend, and this felt like more than a little harmless flirting. He started to speak, but then something behind me caught his attention, and his voice drifted off, his eyebrows pulling in a frown.

I glanced over my shoulder and saw he was watching a girl dancing behind me. The girl had waist-length black hair and was practically glued to the guy she was dancing with. When she started to kiss him, I felt Wes tense, and I spun back to face him.

"Who—" I cut myself off when I saw the total devastation in his eyes.

Wes started to back away before he turned and rushed off the dance floor. I quickly raced after him, having to push and shove past people as I tried to keep up. He didn't return to the VIP section. Instead, he made his way to the front of the club. The cool night air hit me as I followed him outside. My ears were still ringing from the deep beat of the music, but the gentle sounds of traffic were a welcome relief.

Wes was already partway down the street, and I hurried after him, my heels echoing through the night air as they hit the concrete. "Wes?" I called out. "Wes, slow down."

He didn't seem to hear me. It wasn't until I finally managed to grab hold of his arm that he stopped. He turned to me with agony thick in his eyes.

I sucked in a breath as I realized there was only one person who could have made him react that way. "That was Sarah back there, wasn't it?"

He slowly nodded, his hands reaching up to grip his hair in

frustration. "I thought she broke up with me because of the distance. I didn't realize there was someone else…"

I hated seeing him this way. Wes was always so sweet and put together, but right now he was a total wreck. I didn't blame him for feeling that way. I'd be the exact same if I were in his shoes.

"Are you sure it was her?" I asked. It had been dark in the club, and all I'd been able to see was the back of the girl's head.

"It was her."

I swallowed, trying to ignore the way his voice broke as he spoke. "Maybe it's not as bad as you think," I murmured. "Just because she kissed someone at a club doesn't mean they're serious. Maybe she's like you and hurting too?"

He wiped a hand down his face as he groaned. "That doesn't make it hurt any less."

"I know." I didn't know what else to say to make him feel better.

I pulled him into a hug, and he grasped me back tightly like I was the only thing holding him together. I could hear his pain in his ragged breath. I could feel it in the way his muscles had seized up.

"I'm sorry, Wes. I'm so, so sorry," I murmured as I held him.

He slowly pulled back to look me in the eyes. "I just want to forget," he said. "I want to forget her, the pain, hell, I'd forget my own name right now if I could. I—"

I didn't wait for him to continue. His every word was a bleeding wound, a deep gash in his chest that I needed to heal. There was only one way I thought I could help him in this moment, and I didn't hesitate as I lifted myself against him and pressed my lips to his.

His breath caught in his throat, and he froze against me. I'd truly taken him by surprise, and his hesitation had me worried I'd made a terrible mistake. It only lasted a moment because suddenly he was pulling me closer. His arms wrapped around me, and his lips moved hungrily against mine.

We might have been standing on a New York sidewalk in the middle of the night, but I lost all sense of the outside world as Wes started kissing me like I was the very oxygen he needed to breathe.

He was the air for me too, and it felt like he was saving me just as much as I was saving him. For the first time in weeks, I felt something other than pain and uncertainty. I felt the blissful ecstasy of a mind clear from churning thoughts.

I was probably going to regret this come morning. But that didn't matter right now. Wes was a really good kisser, and all I could wonder was why I hadn't done this before. Kissing him was like taking a painkiller for a headache, and I was an idiot for enduring the constant dull ache inside of me when there was such a simple and easy fix.

When we finally broke apart, I was nervous to look at him. I wasn't sure how he was going to react, but when I glanced up at him, I was relieved to find he was no longer staring back at me with the same hurt-filled eyes. Instead, he was looking at me in wonder, like he was seeing something amazing for the very first time.

"You kissed me." He finally broke the silence.

"You kissed me back."

He slowly smiled. "Yeah, I did."

He seemed happy, but I wasn't exactly sure what he was thinking. I was still clutching his shirt, and I dropped my hands to my sides. Wes didn't let my hands get far before he caught them up in his own.

"I'm glad you kissed me."

"You are?"

"I've been thinking about it all night," he admitted. "I know I was upset about Sarah, but just so you know, I wanted to kiss you before you jumped on me."

"I didn't jump on you." I blushed

"I didn't say it was a bad thing. In fact, I think I needed it to snap out of my meltdown."

"There were probably other ways."

"Probably," he smiled. "But none I would have liked as much as that. It worked like a charm. Your kisses are kind of magical..." His gaze dipped to my lips, and my heart leaped as I wondered if he was about to kiss me again. I didn't get a chance to find out because his phone started ringing.

I deflated a little as he glanced away, but it was probably for the best. Wes's lips had been kind of magical too, and I wasn't sure I wanted to fall under his spell.

"Sawyer, this better be good," Wes said as he answered the phone. He waited a beat as his brother responded before he spoke again. "Yeah, I saw her too. I'm outside the entrance to the club with Isobel. I don't know if we're going to go back in."

I really hoped we weren't. I didn't think it would do Wes any good to see his ex again, and one night of club dancing was enough to last me a lifetime.

Wes hung up the phone and focused on me once more. "The others are going to come meet us outside. Sawyer said Anna's had a few too many drinks and we should probably get her home anyway."

"Yeah, it feels like time to call it a night," I agreed.

Wes's eyes flicked down to my lips, and my stomach clenched as I pictured kissing him one more time. The last thing I needed right now was for our friends to walk out and find us making out, so I took a step back to remove the temptation. It was the right decision because the others soon joined us.

"You okay, man?" Sawyer asked, clasping Wes on the arm as he came up behind us with Cress and Anna.

"Yeah, I'm fine," Wes said, still smirking at me.

Sawyer frowned in my direction and then looked back at his brother. "I thought you'd be a mess after seeing Sarah."

Wes shrugged. "It was a shock when I first saw her, but I'm feeling better about it now."

"Good, because you deserve so much better than her," Anna said, shaking her head. She didn't seem as drunk as Wes had suggested. "Have you guys been out here long?"

"Long enough that it's starting to get cold," I responded. It wasn't that bad, but I was eager to leave. I didn't want the others beginning to wonder why Wes was miraculously doing so well after seeing his ex kissing someone. And he kept looking at me with that amused look on his face, which wasn't helping.

"I've ordered an Uber," Cress said. "It should be here any minute."

"I'll order one for us too," Sawyer said to his brother.

The girls and Sawyer chattered away as we waited, but Wes and I were both silent. I wondered if he was thinking about our kiss just as much as I was. Given the smiles he kept sending me, he must have been. And he wasn't even being slightly subtle about it.

When our car arrived, Cress and Anna moved quickly toward it. I glanced over my shoulder as I slid into the car after them. Wes was still smiling at me, and I mouthed at him to stop, but that only made his grin wider. It wasn't until I got home and checked my phone that I saw he'd sent me a text message too.

Wes: Thanks for a magical evening.

I shook my head and stuffed my phone under my pillow. Our kiss was a spontaneous, one-time thing, and nothing more.

Still, I couldn't seem to wipe the smile off my lips as I drifted off to sleep.

CHAPTER TWENTY-ONE

"Something totally happened with you and Wes on the weekend, didn't it?" Cress asked as we unpacked our bags on Sunday evening. We'd only just arrived back at school after our trip to New York, and I was already dreading having to return to class tomorrow. The weekend in the city had been a much-needed breath of fresh air for me, and I wasn't ready to face reality. I definitely wasn't ready to see Noah again—especially after I'd kissed someone else.

I hadn't told Cress or Anna about kissing Wes yet, mostly because I didn't quite know how to feel about it. Given the way Cress was looking at me now, I knew I couldn't pretend nothing happened.

"Why would you say that?" I asked.

"Well, for starters, he wouldn't stop staring at you during the car ride back to school. He also didn't seem nearly upset enough about seeing his ex making out with some guy at the club. Something happened, I know it."

Cress was far too observant for my liking, and I still had no idea what to say, so I focused on the clothes I was supposed to be unpacking and continued trying to dodge her question. "Why are you only bringing this up now?"

"Well, I couldn't exactly ask when Wes was around. I'm dying here, Isobel. What happened?"

"Okay, okay." I knew there was no point resisting. "We kissed."

"I knew it." Cress squealed and jumped onto my bed beside me. "Now, dish, I need all the details."

Her enthusiasm was hard to ignore. "Well," I started. "We were getting kind of close while we were dancing in the club, and I thought maybe we were going to kiss. But then Wes saw Sarah, and the moment was ruined. I followed him from the club to make sure he was okay. And when I was trying to comfort him, it just sort of happened."

"I knew he should have been more upset about Sarah," Cress gushed. "This is *huge*."

"It's not that big a deal."

"Of course, it is. Now, tell me more. How was the kiss?"

I started to smile. "Wes is a really good kisser."

She squealed again, making me laugh. "So, are you guys a couple now or what?"

"Gosh, no." I shook my head. "It was just one kiss. I'm not ready to be in a relationship, and he probably isn't either."

A little of her excitement dampened. "Yeah, I get that."

She seemed really pro-Wes, and I wasn't sure what to make of it. Just a few weeks ago she'd been over the moon I was dating Noah. "Isn't this weird for you?" I asked. "I mean, I was dating your cousin—"

"Who's a total idiot," she said, interrupting me. "He was stupid to let you go, so I'm completely on team Isobel-moving-on. I just want you to be happy."

"Thanks." I gave her a warm smile.

"Plus, I think we could come up with a really cute couple name for you guys. I'm thinking either Isley or Wesobel."

I laughed. "Wesobel?"

"What? It's totally cute."

"And it's also totally getting ahead of things. Wes and I don't need a couple name."

"Not yet…"

I rolled my eyes, but it was hard not to be slightly affected by Cress's excitement. I'd enjoyed kissing Wes, but I hadn't really thought about it being something more. If anything, I'd been worried about the kiss driving us apart.

"Do you think things are going to be weird between us now?" I said. "What if this affects my friendship with him?"

"There's only one way to find out."

"And that is…"

"You need to talk to him," she said.

"Anything but that. Talking will only make things more awkward."

"No, it will get things out in the open. You'll find out where you both stand and can go from there."

"But what if I don't know where I stand?"

"Well, you can tell him that too. It's better he knows you're confused rather than thinking you regret the kiss."

"Yeah, I guess you're right." I let out a breath as I looked at the duffel bag on my bed. It was only half unpacked, but now that Cress had me considering talking to Wes, I felt like I had to get it over and done with. I could unpack the rest of my clothes later.

I started toward the door. "I might go chat with him now."

"Probably a good idea. Do you need a breath mint?"

"We're not going to kiss again, Cress."

She rushed over to her drawers, grabbed a tin of breath mints, and offered it to me. "Are you willing to take that risk?" I let out a grunt and took one but only because my mom had told me you should never refuse a breath mint when offered. There was usually a reason people suggested it, and I didn't want to risk chatting to Wes with bad breath.

"I knew it," she said, gleeful as I popped the mint in my mouth.

"You know nothing," I replied, but she was still giving me a smug smile as I left the room.

I didn't share her confidence or her enthusiasm ahead of my conversation with Wes. What if I said the wrong thing and totally messed up our friendship? We hadn't known each other long, but we'd become close in my short time at Weybridge, and I didn't want things to be weird between us. Cress was right though, I needed to talk it out with Wes, so I made my way to his dorm.

THE BOYS' dormitory was lively when I arrived. All the guys were out in the corridors, and the energy was chaotic as though they were making the most of the final weekend hours. There were shouts and laughter as guys tackled each other, and music was blaring from one of the rooms. There were even two idiots throwing a football down the hall, and I froze as the ball came spinning in my direction. Luckily, someone stepped in front of me and snatched it out of the air before it hit me.

I glanced up to find Luther scowling at the guy who'd thrown the ball. "Watch it, Bertram. You nearly hit my favorite new girl," Luther growled before tucking the ball under his arm. "I'm confiscating this."

Bertram looked like he wanted to object, but his friend quickly grabbed him by the arm and ushered him down the hallway.

Luther grinned as he turned to me. "You're just a magnet for trouble, aren't you, newbie?"

I stood a little straighter and shook my head in the direction of the boys. "If those guys are on the school's football team, I can see why they're always losing."

"Yep, they're terrible." He laughed, but his expression quickly sobered. "How are you feeling? I hear your stomach lost a battle with a swanky New York restaurant."

I scrunched my face up. "Noah told you about that?"

"Yeah, poor little dear was a mess on Thursday night. He was messaging me for advice on what he could get to help you. I told him that kisses were the best medicine."

"Luther," I groaned. "Not only are we broken up, but I was throwing up. You did not tell him that."

"No, but I should have." He chuckled. "I think Noah would have done just about anything to make you feel better."

I let out a sigh. "I don't know why you think we're going to get back together. We're over, for good." The sooner everyone accepted that, the better.

"I have faith everything will work out." Luther shrugged.

I rolled my eyes at him. "I'm trying to decide if you're an optimist or just being willfully blind."

"Maybe I'm simply a true romantic," he replied. "Maybe I like to believe love overcomes all obstacles."

"Maybe you like to cause trouble."

"Oh, always that," he said with a grin. The smile slowly dropped from his face as he considered me. "Seriously though, Noah's been irritable and moody ever since you broke up. He's the worst company ever." He let out a sigh. "I was hoping the two of you would have made up by now."

"Like I've been trying to tell you, that's never going to happen."

"Maybe, maybe not," he replied. "Look, just do me a favor, and don't give up on Noah yet."

I stared at him, at a loss for what to say. Did Luther know something I didn't? What could Noah have possibly said to give him the impression there was any hope? I wasn't sure, but the one thing I was certain of was if I didn't give up on Noah now I would never get over him. I couldn't spend my life letting my heart ache for a boy I couldn't be with. It wasn't fair for Luther to expect that of me. "You can't ask me to do that."

"Well, I did." And he didn't look the least bit remorseful about it. "Anyway, I'll catch you around, newbie. Stay safe out there." He went to walk away but paused and handed me the football he'd stolen from the guys. "Here," he said. "A souvenir so you can remember that time I saved your life."

"I don't think my life was in danger…"

"That's not how I remember it," he replied. "And think about what I said. You and Noah belong together."

He turned to leave, waltzing away like he hadn't just tried to blow up my life with the world's most ridiculous request.

"There's nothing to think about," I called after him.

He didn't turn back, and I wasn't sure if it was because he hadn't heard me or because he refused to acknowledge my protest.

Not giving up on Noah? Luther couldn't have asked something more demanding if he tried, especially seeing as Noah was the one to give up on us in the first place. I shook my head and continued down the corridor to Wes's room.

I was relieved when Wes answered the door after only a couple of knocks. I thought he might be surprised to see me, but his face lit with a welcoming smile. A small crease then puckered his brow as he looked down and noticed the ball in my hand. "Trying out for the football team?"

"Trying to avoid the football team, more like." I shook my head when I caught his curious expression. "Don't ask."

"But now I'm all intrigued." He stood back and gestured into his room. "Want to come in? It's kind of mad out there today."

"Just *kind of* mad?" I asked as I followed him inside. Not only was it chaos in the corridors, it was dangerous too. "I swear the boys' dorms have always been so quiet when I've come here before."

"Clearly you've been coming at the wrong time," Wes replied.

"If our dorm parents look the other way for even a minute, the place turns into a jungle."

"Yeah, well, I swear some of the monkeys out there are rabid."

"They should probably put a warning at the entrance," he agreed with a smile. "Enter at your own risk, or something like that."

"Probably." I placed the ball down on his bed and tucked my hands into my jeans as I looked around the room. It was almost like an invisible border ran through the center of the space. One side was a pigsty while the other was spotlessly clean. My eyes landed on the heap of clothes spilling out of a suitcase on Sawyer's bed. It seemed he'd gotten about as far as I had when it came to unpacking.

"Is your brother around?" I asked.

"Nah, Sawyer's out playing a pickup game of soccer. It's just you and me," he said, sitting at the end of his bed.

"Uh-huh." I swallowed down the nerves that suddenly made an appearance in my throat. I didn't want to talk to Wes with Sawyer around, but I was also anxious at the thought of being here alone with him.

"Did you want to sit down?" Wes asked, gesturing to the bed beside him.

"Um, no thanks, I'm good."

He gave me a half smile, like he didn't quite believe me. He stood and approached me slowly as though he was worried I might spook if he moved too fast. "I'm guessing you came to talk about what happened last night?"

I let out a deep exhale and nodded. I had no idea where to begin, and I was glad Wes had been the one to raise the subject. I guessed the best place to start was the one thing I felt sure about. "I don't want things to be weird between us."

"I don't want that either. I really like you, Isobel."

My cheeks felt hot, and my brain went into overdrive. Did he just like me or did he *like me* like me? Because there was a huge difference between the two, and I had no idea which kind of like I wanted him to be feeling.

It didn't help that he looked so cute as he spoke. His warm brown eyes were gentle and filled with hope, and it was hard not to be pulled in by his easygoing smile. Wes was hot and sweet; a girl would have to be absolutely crazy not to want to be with him. Was I crazy for not immediately jumping for joy that he said he liked me? Probably, but I didn't want things moving too quickly. I'd fallen fast for Noah, and that had been a disaster. I couldn't make that mistake again, especially not when it might mean ruining my friendship with Wes.

"I really like you too, Wes," I admitted. "You're one of my closest friends here." Yep, I'd dropped the friend bomb. It was the equivalent of throwing a bucket of cold water on the guy, but it seemed far safer than saying anything else.

Wes didn't seem put off though, and he lifted one eyebrow in response. "Do you kiss all of your friends like that?"

"Uh, only the really good ones."

It was a terrible answer, but he chuckled, and the sound danced down my spine. He wasn't looking at me like a friend right now, and my heart beat quicker as he continued to stare at me.

"I'm just not ready for another relationship right now," I murmured. "And I don't think you are either."

He took a step toward me so we were standing only inches apart and reached up to tuck a stray curl behind my ear. The gesture didn't feel even slightly friendly, and the intense look in his eyes made me feel like he wasn't listening to a word I said.

"So, can we just pretend the kiss didn't happen?" I continued.

"I can't do that," he said. "Kissing you was the only thing that's felt right to me in weeks. Tell me you didn't enjoy kissing me, and I'll forget it ever happened."

My mouth suddenly felt dry. "Wes, it was a one-time thing."

"So, you enjoyed our kiss then." Apparently, he wasn't discouraged.

"Of course, I did, but we're friends. It would be weird. I—"

He didn't wait for me to continue as he lowered his head toward me and brushed his lips against mine. They felt like nothing more than a feather lightly grazing against my skin, and my whole body tingled. He didn't deepen the kiss like I wanted. Instead, he pulled back a few inches, so I could still feel his breath against me.

"Did that feel weird to you?" His voice was slightly deeper and more gravelly than it had been before. It seemed like he was just as affected by my lips as I was by his.

I answered by pulling him back to me and kissing him fully like my body craved. All thought and reason fled from my mind as he wrapped his arms around me, tugging me closer still. I didn't care if we were just friends or something more in that moment. And there was definitely nothing weird about kissing Wes again. If anything, his kisses erased any apprehension I had. Wes was right; this was the first thing that had made sense recently.

The sound of Sawyer groaning interrupted us. "Oh, man, get a room."

Wes and I jumped apart, and my cheeks burned with embarrassment as I turned to see Wes's brother lounging in the doorway.

Wes wasn't nearly as flustered as he answered. "I have a room. I'm using it."

"No, this is *our* room. You could have at least put a sock on the door," Sawyer said, coming inside and closing the door behind him. Now that I took a proper look at him, I could see he was grinning widely. He clearly wasn't as annoyed as his voice portrayed.

"Isobel." He tilted his head at me. "I see you took up my

rebound offer. You got the wrong brother though. That's Wes you're kissing."

Wes shoved a hand against his shoulder. "She doesn't think I'm you, you idiot."

"Are you sure?" Sawyer turned to me again and puckered his lips. "Because I'm ready to rectify the situation…"

I scrunched up my nose. "*Ew*, no."

"Why not?" Sawyer laughed. "Wes and I have never kissed the same girl before. Finally, we can find out who is the better kisser."

"Dude, that's messed up," Wes muttered.

"You need help," I agreed. "I'm not going to kiss you, Sawyer."

"But this feels like a bet I could win…"

Wes took his brother by the shoulders and steered him back toward the door. "You can leave now."

"But it's my room."

"Don't care." Wes pulled the door open and shoved his brother outside.

I couldn't contain my laughter when I saw Sawyer's shocked expression right before Wes slammed the door on him.

"Your brother is ridiculous," I said.

"Ridiculously handsome!" I heard Sawyer shout from the hallway.

Wes banged a fist against the door. "Go away."

Sawyer laughed in response, but the sound soon drifted off as he wandered away down the corridor. It was only after a few moments of silence that Wes seemed to relax. "Sorry about that."

"Sawyer is nothing if not entertaining."

"Yeah, he's a regular clown."

I laughed, but my amusement quickly disappeared as I realized what we'd just done. "Shit," I muttered. "I didn't come here to kiss you."

"But you did." He grinned.

"Stop smiling. That can't happen again. I refuse to ruin our friendship for some rebound kisses. I don't care how good they are."

His smile only grew.

"Why aren't you listening to me? I think we both need to pretend that never happened. Okay?"

"Okay." He nodded. His face was the picture of sincerity, but his eyes danced like he was just playing along and had absolutely no intention of forgetting our kiss.

"You're almost as bad as your brother," I muttered. "I'm going to go now."

I opened the door to leave, and Wes leaned against the door-frame, watching me as I started down the hallway. "I'm glad we *talked*," he called after me.

I shot a scowl over my shoulder at him, making him laugh. I had clearly failed in my attempts to talk with Wes. We'd done a lot more than that. And a small part of me wondered if maybe that wasn't such a bad thing.

CHAPTER TWENTY-TWO

I was running late to PE. I'd left my sneakers in my dorm room this morning and had to rush back to get them before making my way across campus to the school gym. I hadn't had a chance to change yet either. I was almost to the locker room when a hand snaked out and caught hold of me from behind.

"What's the rush?"

I gasped and turned to find Wes grinning down at me. He'd just emerged from the boys' locker room, so I hadn't seen him coming. He was already dressed for our sports lesson and didn't have nearly the same urgency about him that I was feeling.

"I'm running late."

He laughed and looked down at my school uniform. "I can see that."

"And you're not helping. I need to get changed."

His smile simply widened. "You're cute when you're flustered."

"Still not helping." I blushed at the ease with which he called me cute and how it made me feel. He shouldn't be calling me cute. And he shouldn't be standing so close to me. I was trying to forget about the kiss we shared in his room, but it was all I could think about when his body was pressed against mine like this.

"You better get a move on, or you'll be late to class," he murmured.

I scowled at him because I had a feeling he knew exactly the direction my thoughts had been tracking. "That's what I was saying," I complained before turning to dart into the girls' locker room. His soft laughter followed behind me.

I changed in what must have been record time before rushing to the basketball courts. One of my shoelaces was undone, and my hair was a mess from throwing my top over my head, but I didn't care. I could fix it all when I got to class. I just hoped I wouldn't get a detention.

I'd been worried about being late to class, but the teacher hadn't shown up yet either, and most of the students were milling around on the bleachers. I joined Cress and Anna on one of the benches, and as I sat, I noticed Noah scowling at me from the other side of the court. I had no idea what I'd done to piss him off, but I chose to ignore him.

"No Coach August yet?" I asked the girls.

Anna started to respond, but as she did, the teacher walked into view. "We're moving on to squash today, everyone," he said. "So, we're going over to the squash courts."

There were a few groans from the class, but I wasn't sure why. I'd never played squash before, but it looked like fun. I stood with Anna and Cress and was about to follow the rest of the class, but Coach August came over to me.

"Not you, Miss Grace," he said. "You still haven't completed the beep test from the first class of term. You'll be undertaking it today along with one other student. I won't be here to oversee it, so I'm putting a lot of faith in you to be honest with your results. If you score yourself higher than you actually achieve, you'll have no room for improvement this year. You'll only be failing yourself."

"Yes, Coach," I replied, as Cress and Anna both grimaced in my direction. Squash was looking really good right about now.

He turned and joined the rest of the class leaving the gym while Anna and Cress continued to hover at my side.

"This sucks," Cress said. "I thought he'd forgotten about your beep test."

"Me too," I replied. "I guess I better get it over with."

The girls shared sympathetic smiles.

"Maybe we can go to Toddy's after school for milkshakes to make you feel better?" Cress suggested.

"That sounds really great," I replied. "I think I'll need a pick-me-up."

"It's a date then. We'll see you after class." The girls waved and then lightly jogged to catch up with the rest of the class, disappearing from the gym far too quickly.

Once they were out of sight, I turned to search for the cones and the stereo Coach August had left behind for me. Only it wasn't the cones I noticed when I turned. Noah was standing there waiting for me.

"What are you doing? Wait, *you're* the one who's redoing the test?"

"I didn't get the result I was after." Noah shrugged. "Besides, I asked to redo it weeks ago so you wouldn't have to take it alone. It was back when we were…" He didn't need to finish his sentence. I knew he was talking about when we were dating. It was sweet he'd done that, but it made things awkward now.

"Well, I'm sure Coach August will understand if you tell him you don't want to retake it." I was sure the last thing Noah wanted was to spend an entire class alone with me. I certainly wasn't keen given the way things were between us. Everything felt relatively civil, especially after he took care of me last week in New York, but that didn't mean it was easy to be around him.

It hurt to be in his presence. To feel my heart tugging me toward him and know I couldn't act on it. And there was always an underlying tension. Whenever he was near, it was like the air was snapped taut between us, and it didn't matter whether I liked him, hated him, or wanted nothing to do with him, that feeling was always there.

"Who said I don't want to retake it?" he replied.

I let out a sigh. I was trying to give him an easy way out, but apparently Noah was a glutton for pain. "I guess we better get started then."

I walked over to the stereo that had been left on the ground and turned on the recording before walking to the first cone. Noah came and stood right by me. We had the whole court to ourselves; did he really have to stand so close?

The test didn't start right away. There was a monologue at the start of the recording explaining how it all worked. I wasn't sure I heard a single word. I was too focused on Noah. If we were going to be stuck together like this, then I had something I needed to ask him.

"I saw you on Friday," I said as we waited.

He seemed confused by my comment. "That's hardly surprising seeing as we were both on the same field trip."

"Except you weren't on the field trip," I said. "I saw you outside my father's building."

A flicker of surprise shot through Noah's gaze. He quickly covered it with a shrug. "So, we both skipped The Met. Again, not that surprising."

"Given your history with my family, it was kind of surprising. What were you doing there?"

"Certainly not seeing your father, if that's what you're getting at," he said. His features twisted with such distaste I reeled back from him.

I wasn't going to be put off by the irritation in his eyes. "So, what *were* you doing there then?"

"That's really none of your business."

"I guess I'll just have to ask my father then."

Noah huffed in response. "Like I said, my visit had nothing to do with him, so he won't be able to tell you. If you must know, I was there to see my lawyer. He has the great misfortune of sharing an office building with The LaFleur Corporation."

"Oh," I murmured. Wes had mentioned there were other offices in the building. Maybe it was a simple coincidence. I couldn't imagine why a seventeen-year-old needed to see a lawyer, but Noah wasn't your average teen.

"So, is being nosy something we do now?" Noah asked. "Because you looked awfully close with Wes outside the gym just before..."

I shot him a scowl. I didn't need to explain myself to him. Still, I found myself taking the bait. "Wes and I are friends; of course, we're close."

"It looked more than friendly to me."

"Well, you must be seeing things. Maybe you should get your eyes checked out?"

Thankfully the first beep of the test finally sounded, and I started to jog, eager to get away from Noah. He fell in right beside me, his feet slapping against the ground in perfect unison with my own.

"I've heard things too," he said after we'd done several laps between the two cones. Apparently, he wasn't done with our discussion. I definitely was, and I chose to ignore his comment. "Sawyer likes to talk a lot at soccer training."

"He likes to talk a lot period," I muttered. "But I prefer not to talk when I'm running."

I wondered if Noah was trying to hint that he knew Wes and I had kissed. I had a bad feeling that was exactly what he was getting at, and I really didn't want to talk about it with him.

Noah remained silent for several more laps. We were already jogging quite quickly, and my breaths were beginning to come in faster. He barely sounded puffed in comparison, but that was hardly a surprise given how fit he was.

"Are the two of you together?" His voice hitched slightly as he spoke.

I stopped in the middle of the court and turned to him. "Why are you asking me this?" I said between exhausted breaths. "Why do you care?"

He'd stopped barely a foot away from me, his green eyes stormy and filled with pain. "You know I still care. It's just… I didn't think you'd move on from us so fast."

"I can move on however fast I want," I replied. "You broke up with me. You don't get to dictate how I move on."

"You are with him then?"

"Not that it's any of your business, but I'm not. We're friends, just like I told you."

"So, you're kissing your friends now?"

"I'm kissing whoever can make me forget about you for just one moment. You think I'm moving on too fast, but that's just the problem. I can't seem to move on from you at all. You didn't just break my heart when we broke up, you decimated it, and no matter what I do, I can't fit the pieces back together again. So, yeah, I kissed Wes, and maybe I'll do it again. We can't be together, and I'm trying to accept that. Maybe you need to accept that too."

I turned to walk away, but Noah called after me. "You think it's easy for me to accept losing the best thing that's ever happened to me?"

His words were a dagger straight to my heart, and I glanced over my shoulder at him. "If you really felt that way, we never would have broken up."

He opened his mouth and went to say something but quickly closed it again. He looked lost for words, and I shook my head. He was never going to fight for us, and we both knew it.

I spun round and stormed away from him before he could torment me any further.

NOAH'S WORDS haunted me the rest of the day, so I was glad when Wes suggested we study together in the library after dinner. I hated that Noah had gotten in my head, and I jumped at the chance to fill my thoughts with economics homework instead.

Unfortunately, my economics homework didn't want to be in my thoughts. I must have been a terrible study partner. Wes was having to ask me something several times before I registered the question, and even when I heard him, I had no clue what the answer was. My mind was somewhere else entirely, and most of my homework lay unfinished on the desk.

"You seem distracted," Wes said after I'd misheard one of his questions yet again.

"I know. I'm sorry. I..." My voice trailed off as I looked at him. "Wait, you wear glasses?"

I was surprised I hadn't noticed him put them on, especially since they made him look like some kind of hot librarian. They gave off all these sexy nerd vibes, and now that I'd seen them, they were impossible to ignore.

I didn't know he needed glasses. I'd never seen him wearing them before. Maybe he realized he couldn't use them too often because they gave him too much power. He knew he would constantly captivate all the girls at school if he wore them every day.

"You only just noticed? Your head *is* in the clouds tonight." He gave a nervous smile. "But, yeah, I wear glasses for reading some-times. I'm always forgetting them though."

"Uh-huh." Man, even I sounded completely captivated by him right now. I'd only just noticed the glasses, but their power was getting to me already.

He frowned at my response. "You think I look silly."

He went to remove them, but I lifted a hand in complaint. "Don't…"

He paused, lightly grasping the side of the frame between his finger and thumb.

"I like the glasses," I said.

He dropped his hand and tilted his head to the side as he watched me. "I can't tell if you're making fun of me."

"I'm definitely not."

"Sawyer says I look stupid in them."

"I'm sure he's just jealous."

"I don't think so. I'm pretty sure he needs glasses too, but he refuses to get them."

It was probably a good thing Sawyer didn't also have glasses. I couldn't even begin to imagine the kind of damage the twins would inflict on girls' hearts if they both walked around the school looking like young blond versions of Clark Kent.

"Well, I think the glasses look great."

He slowly gave me a smile and shifted slightly closer to me. "Really?"

I nodded, not quite able to find my words now that he was sitting so close. We were at a desk in the main section of the library, and there were enough students around that there was no way Wes was going to kiss me again. It didn't stop my eyes from dropping to his lips though. Ever since I'd told him we were never kissing again, it was all I'd been able to think about, especially when he was around. Things felt so much better when he kissed me, would it really be so bad if I gave in to the temptation again?

I think Wes might have been thinking the same thing because his lips were only inches from mine. I hadn't even seen him move. Or had I been the one that moved? One small kiss in the library wasn't all that bad, was it?

A cough sounded behind us, and we both jerked backward, my cheeks flaming bright red. I turned to find the crotchety, old librarian frowning down at us. "You two. No funny business in the library," she hissed.

I swallowed and quickly nodded. Wes and I responded at the same time, "Yes, Miss Davis."

She lifted an eyebrow, and I quickly turned back to my homework, focusing on it until she moved away. As soon as she was out of earshot, Wes and I burst into hushed laughter, making the whole table next to us turn and shoot us curious looks. I tried my best to ignore them. I'd already overheard them gossiping about Wes and me this evening. People needed to mind their own business.

"That was close," Wes said.

"Was it?" I turned to him. "I had no intention of partaking in any funny business in the library..."

He gave me a smile. "Sure, you didn't."

"I didn't."

"No one would blame you if you did. You do find me irresistible in my glasses, after all."

"I didn't say you were irresistible."

"Your lips might not have, but your eyes did." He gave me a cheeky grin. "And knowing how much you like the glasses, I'm thinking I should be more responsible with my eyesight and wear them more often."

"I mean, if you want girls throwing themselves at you in the corridor, then go right ahead."

"There's only one girl I want throwing herself at me..."

My cheeks flushed as I glanced away. Wes was doing a terrible job at sticking within the friend zone. Ever since we'd kissed, the border of the zone had become blurry, and he'd been dancing right across it far too frequently this week.

The thing was, I didn't hate it when he flirted with me. In fact, I quite liked it. It was easy and fun, and Wes always managed to make me smile. It didn't hurt that he was gorgeous either.

Wes was still grinning when I focused back on him. "We're

really not getting much of our economics homework done, are we?" he said.

"Not really."

"Want to take a walk outside instead? Perhaps we'll focus better if we clear our heads."

I wasn't sure if he was talking in code or not. We'd been so close to kissing before that my mind immediately conjured up thoughts of finding somewhere far more secluded and finishing what we nearly started. He looked genuine enough though, and I was pretty sure I was just wishful thinking. I began to pack my books away. "A walk sounds great."

We went to leave our table, but as I looked up, I found Luther and Kaden seated not far from us. They were watching me closely. Given the matching looks of accusation in their eyes, they must have seen me nearly kiss Wes.

My throat constricted with a feeling of guilt, but I knew I had no reason to feel guilty. I was single and allowed to kiss whomever I wanted. Admittedly, I probably needed to avoid nearly kissing them in the library and with an audience, but I'd done nothing wrong.

"I just need to borrow these books," Wes said, holding up several texts he'd gathered before I met him in the library. "It won't take me more than a few minutes. Can I meet you outside?"

I gave him a tight smile. "Sure."

As he headed over to the librarian, I turned toward Luther and Kaden once more. Their eyes were still on me, and I stormed over to their table. Luther leaned back in his chair as I approached, a disapproving look on his face. Kaden didn't appear nearly so judgmental, but I could see the disappointment in his eyes.

"What's with you and Wes?" Luther demanded.

"That's none of your business."

"Except, I think it is. I told you not to give up on Noah."

"And I told you that was unfair. I never agreed with you."

"So? What? You're with Wesley Montfort now?"

"Like I said, that's not your concern."

He shrugged. "It will be when Noah finds out. And he's going to find out. Every kid in the library has been trying not to throw up from watching the two of you canoodle in here all night."

I glanced around the room, and several people quickly looked away, avoiding my gaze. No matter what I did in this school, it seemed I always had an audience. I didn't want Luther's words to affect me, but they did. My chest tightened, and my heart struggled to remember the way it had been so happily beating only moments ago. I didn't want Noah to hear anything that might upset him, but I also couldn't spend the rest of my life walking on eggshells because I was worried about how he might feel. We were over, and despite Luther's concerns, Wes and I weren't in a relationship. We were just two hurt souls trying to help stitch each other back together.

"We weren't canoodling. Wes and I are just friends," I finally said.

"It didn't look that way to me or anyone else here," Luther replied.

"Noah's going to be really hurt," Kaden added. It was the first thing he'd said in the conversation, and somehow his quiet condemnation hurt just as much as Luther's hard words.

"How is this my fault?" My voice was raised, and several students looked up from their books. I made sure to talk much quieter as I continued. "I know you're both Noah's friends, but he's the one who chose to end our relationship. You can't get pissed at me for accepting that and moving on."

"So, you admit it, you're moving on."

I scowled at Luther. "Of course, I want to move on. Nobody wants to stay miserable."

"I think Noah does." Once again, Kaden's words were calm and thoughtful, and they cut deeper because of it.

"Well, that's his problem. Not mine." I shook my head. "Look,

I'm not going to let you two make me feel guilty about anything I do or don't do. Noah and I are over, and I'm going to keep doing my best to put our relationship behind me. So, stop with your judgmental stares and cryptic advice. It's not helping anyone."

I turned and walked away before either of the boys could respond. I wasn't quite sure what I'd hoped to achieve by talking to Kaden and Luther, but it had only served to make me more annoyed. They were acting like I'd betrayed Noah, but we weren't together anymore, and all I was doing was trying to survive the aftermath of our breakup. Was I really the bad guy for spending time with the one person who helped me forget the pain?

I was still sparking with irritation as I made my way from the library. I was sick of being told how to feel and what to think. And I hated how invested people had become in my love life. It was no one else's business but my own, and yet I constantly seemed to hear other students gossiping about it. I was so sick of it, and I just wanted to take control of the narrative for once. More than anything, I just needed my whirring mind to stop.

Wes was already waiting for me in the corridor. There were other students milling around, but I barely noticed them as he started smiling at me. His expression dimmed when he saw my stormy demeanor.

"What's wrong?" he asked.

I took a breath to try to calm myself. "It's nothing."

"Did something happen?"

"Just Kaden and Luther." I shook my head. "But they're not the real problem. I know they want to protect their friend. It's everyone else that's getting to me. I'm so sick of the gossip in this place. I swear, no matter what I do people are always talking about me. I'm single. I should be able to do whatever I want."

He watched me for a second before he slowly started to smile. "So, you should do what you want then..."

"What—" I started to speak, but my question was cut off as Wes pulled me toward him, my hands landing against his chest as he wrapped his arms about me. His face was so close to mine, and I could sense everyone in the corridor was watching us. His eyes danced with mischief, and my heart raced in response.

"What exactly do you think I want?" I whispered.

"What you wanted in New York. And in my room..."

My eyes went to his mouth as he spoke. "You think I want to kiss you?"

"I mean, it wouldn't be the first time," he said. "And you did nearly partake in 'funny business' with me in the library."

"I did not. I—"

He silenced my protests by pulling me closer and kissing me like we were completely alone in the world. For a few blissful moments, my mind went totally blank, and my body buzzed with a new kind of emotion. Wes's lips worked their magic and somehow rebooted me, so when we drew apart, I no longer felt annoyed or worried.

He grinned, his cheeks turning slightly pink as he looked around at the staring students. "I don't think I've helped you with your gossip problem."

"No," I agreed, my cheeks flushing too. Although if what Kaden and Luther had said was true, the kids who'd been watching Wes and I in the library tonight probably wouldn't be surprised.

"I'm sure they will just blame the glasses. Really, you had no chance of resisting me."

I laughed. "They are kind of irresistible."

"I knew it." He winked. "Remind me again why I shouldn't wear them all the time?"

"Because I have no self-control when you do."

"Now we couldn't have that, could we?"

I swallowed as the more rational part of my brain started to kick in. "We probably shouldn't have done that." There were many reasons why, but I was already concerned about damaging my friendship with Wes. That was only going to intensify now that everyone at school would think we were together.

Wes waved my concern off with one hand. "Don't overthink it. It was just one friend helping another out." It was almost like he could read my mind.

"You're sure it was nothing more?"

"It was nothing more," he agreed. "You ready for our walk?"

"Uh, sure." He was sounding way too calm and collected about all this. Meanwhile, I was internally beginning to freak out.

Wes lightly wrapped an arm over my shoulder and started to guide me away from the library, happily ignoring the whispers and curious looks that trailed us as we went.

I had no idea how he could act so unaffected by the attention. But more so, how he was so convinced that our kiss meant nothing. He was clearly fine with us just being friends. But why was a part of me disappointed?

CHAPTER TWENTY-THREE

L ily collapsed into the chair next to me at breakfast the following morning. She was cradling a cup of coffee to her chest like it was her precious. "I'm so tired," she said, stifling a yawn.

"I can see that. You're looking at your coffee like you wish you could inject it into your veins somehow."

"Oh, that would be the dream," she said before taking a long sip.

"Why are you so tired?"

"My parents surprised me with a trip home over the weekend," she said. "I left straight from New York and took an extra couple of days off. I only got back late last night."

"I was wondering where you've been. But that's so exciting," I said. "I know how much you miss home. How was it?"

"So good." She shared a sleepy smile with me. "I got to see all my friends, and my baby sister is getting so big. She's nearly crawling now." She fished her phone out and showed me a picture of a tiny baby with a big toothless grin. The little girl had chubby cheeks with adorable dimples, and she shared Lily's big brown eyes.

"Aww, she's so cute," I said.

"Abby's pretty sweet," Lily agreed. "But it makes me sad. She's changing so much and so quickly. I feel like I'm missing everything because I'm here at Weybridge."

"That must be hard."

"It's not easy. Though sleep is a whole lot harder to come by back home. Abby wakes up crying at like 3:00 A.M. every morning. I definitely don't miss that here."

"Every morning? Really?"

"Like clockwork. My mom looks like a zombie these days."

"I'd probably look like a zombie too if I was constantly woken up in the middle of the night."

"Tell me about it." She placed her phone back down as she took another sip of her coffee. "So, how was the rest of your weekend in New York?"

"It was fun," I said. "I had dinner with my dad on Friday night, but mostly I hung out with Anna, Cress, and the twins. We shopped and did some sightseeing and ate so much good food. We went to a club on Saturday night, but that was just chaotic and not really my thing."

"I don't think it would be my thing either," she agreed.

"Yeah, I don't recommend it." I focused down on my granola pot. It was mixed with fresh fruit and yogurt and just about the most delicious thing I'd tried for breakfast so far at school. Everyone else raved about the waffles here, but there were only so many mornings a week you could eat them before you were waffled out.

"So, did anything else happen in New York?" Lily asked. "Like maybe you got closer with a certain twin..."

My head jerked up. "You already heard about that?"

Lily's eyes were wide, and I could tell she hadn't been certain if she should believe the rumor. "Amber heard you and Wes were acting all adorable together in the library last night, and then apparently you were seen making out in the corridor."

"Oh, ah, yeah, we did kiss," I said. "But it was just a kiss. We're not dating or anything."

"Really?"

I nodded. "I'm not ready for another boyfriend."

"So, why were you kissing Wes then?"

"Uh..." I didn't exactly have a rational explanation for our kiss. "It seemed like a good idea at the time?"

It had felt like the right thing to do last night, but now I wondered if we'd been a bit hasty. Things between us were getting confusing, and I really didn't want to screw up our friendship. Still, I couldn't bring myself to regret it.

"Wow." She sighed. "I wish I could kiss a hot guy just because I felt like it."

"Why can't you?"

Her cheeks flushed and she quickly shook her head. "I'm not nearly brave enough for that."

"I bet you're braver than you think."

"Nope. I couldn't do it even if one of my book boyfriends showed up at school. And some of them are *perfect*."

I laughed. "Yeah, guys in the real world have a lot to live up to if you read."

"I bet Wes would be pretty close." There was a suggestive look in her eyes. "He's super sweet and very good-looking."

"He is," I agreed. His personality was nothing like Noah's, and for that I was grateful. I was totally done with the whole dark and brooding type.

"And you really don't want to date him?" she asked. "I bet he'd be an amazing boyfriend."

I frowned because she was asking questions I thought I knew the answers to, but I suddenly didn't feel so certain. Lily was right; Wes would make an amazing boyfriend. He was always so kind and generous, and his kisses were incredible. I loved our friendship, but what if a relationship with him was even better?

I did my best to quickly dislodge that line of thinking with a shake of my head. I was in no state to start another relationship. And I didn't want to risk losing Wes as a friend for some short-lived fling. Besides, he'd been clear last night that he didn't see us as anything more than friends.

"I don't want to date him," I finally answered Lily. "He's a really good friend, and that's it."

"If you say so..."

"I do." Although, if I was truly serious, it meant I needed to put a stop to our impulsive kisses, and I didn't know how to feel about that.

I quickly thought of another subject, not wanting to keep talking about Wes. "So, are you reading anything good at the moment?"

Lily's eyes lit up, and she happily launched into conversation about her latest fantasy read. She became animated as she explained the story and the characters. I liked how passionate she was whenever she talked about books. She also spared no detail as she told me about some of the more intimate parts of the book, and I had to wonder how someone so quiet and sweet could enjoy such a spicy read.

I laughed as she described one of the scenes. "It sounds like you're reading some kind of fairy porn."

"Oh, yeah, some parts are a bit like that," she admitted, her cheeks turning pink. "But I like the tension between the characters more."

"I can definitely see why you're not interested in dating the boys at school."

"Are you girls talking about book porn without me?" I looked up as Sawyer joined us at the table. "I need details."

Lily's cheeks instantly went from pink to flaming red, and she sank into her chair to hide herself. "It's nothing you want to hear about," she murmured.

"Clearly, you don't know me," Sawyer replied, leaning forward on the table. His eyes sparkled with excitement. "Tell me everything."

"Maybe later. I have to get to class." Lily practically choked out her response, and she was up and out of her chair before either of us could stop her.

"Class isn't for another twenty minutes," Sawyer called after her, but she was already halfway across the room.

Sawyer leaned back in his chair and sighed. "I miss all the good conversations."

"You wanted to hear about faerie book porn?" I asked.

He grinned. "Why wouldn't I?"

I shook my head and focused on my breakfast.

"Speaking of stimulating content," he continued. "I hear you and my brother put on quite the show last night."

"We just kissed," I muttered, wondering how many more people were going to ask me about Wes today.

"Must have been some kiss. I think he's in love with you."

"That's not true, and you know it."

"Isn't it?" He gave me a devious smile. "Because everyone's talking about what a cute couple you are, and I'm wondering if I should start to call you sis?"

My eyes narrowed on him, but he didn't seem the least bit concerned by my scowl. "Don't call me sis."

"But we're practically family."

"I think I preferred talking about faerie porn with you."

"We can always circle back to that," Sawyer replied.

I stood from the table and collected my empty bowl.

"Where are you going, sis?"

"Class."

"Was it something I said?" He was grinning wickedly at me, and I could see just how much he was enjoying pushing my buttons. I ignored the comment and left the hall, bumping into Cress as I walked out into the corridor.

She caught my arm. "Where are you off to in such a rush?"

"Sawyer's a nightmare."

She laughed. "Tell me something I don't know."

"Well, I'm wondering if he's actually Satan's spawn."

"There's a strong possibility," she agreed. "Speaking of Mont-forts, on the way over here, I happened to hear people talking about a certain kiss between you and Wes."

I let out a sigh. "I guess it was to be expected." I knew people would talk about our kiss outside the library, but I couldn't bring myself to regret it. It had been a great kiss. It just sucked that I couldn't seem to do anything in this school without everyone having an opinion on it. And it was especially hard when I knew my actions might hurt people's feelings—well, one person's feelings. I was trying my best to avoid thinking about how Noah would react. I couldn't imagine he would take it well given our fight in PE the other day.

"Don't let it worry you. I'm sure they'll all be gossiping about someone else before the day is through," Cress replied.

"Want to go make out with someone in the dining hall to take the heat off me?"

She laughed. "I'm a pretty good friend, but I'm not *that* good a friend."

"Maybe I should go back and try to convince Sawyer. I bet he'd do it."

"Probably," she agreed with a smile. "But I don't think anyone would bat an eyelid at Sawyer making a scene, so they'll probably still be more interested in you. You just need to suck it up and get through the day. It will be better tomorrow."

"You promise?"

"I promise."

Despite Cress's reassurance, the whispers didn't let up at all that day and carried over into the next. A few girls asked me about it at breakfast the next morning, and a freshman boy even asked me if I wanted to go to the library with him. He blew me kisses and then ran back to his friends laughing.

I certainly didn't enjoy the attention, but after dating and breaking up with Noah—and the bombshell about my dad—I was growing all too used to it. I might have been able to ignore it entirely, but the more people talked, the more I worried about how Noah would feel. He had to have heard about the kiss by now, and it left me feeling terrible. We might not be able to be together, but I knew he still cared.

I kept waiting to run into him, but he wasn't in any of my classes on Wednesday, and there was no sign of him on Thursday either.

It seemed like too much of a coincidence that he would disappear from school at the same time everyone was gossiping about Wes and me. There had to be another explanation. Noah wasn't the kind of guy who would let mere rumors about a girl he dumped worry him. I wanted to ask Cress if she knew why her cousin wasn't in school, but I didn't want her to know I was thinking about him. So, the question remained unanswered in my mind.

"I hear you've moved on quickly."

I had to smother a dark scowl as Veronica turned to me, a smirk lifting the corner of her mouth. I hated that I was stuck sitting behind her in English. She always had some snide remark for me, and today was no different. She must have cheered the moment she heard I'd kissed Wes. I imagined she felt she was one step closer to finally snagging Noah for herself.

"Aw, Veronica, I didn't know you cared," I replied. I tried to focus on the book I was supposed to be reading, but Veronica didn't want to take the hint.

"Oh, I don't. I'm just pleased to see you've finally proved me right."

She was dangling bait in front of me, and I really shouldn't have taken it, but I couldn't help myself. I lifted my gaze to hers once more. "And how have I done that?"

"It's just clear you never truly cared about Noah. Anyone who did would never be able to forget him so fast. You were obviously just using him."

My hands clenched into fists under the table as I tried to contain my anger. "You don't know anything about how I feel about him."

She shrugged. "I'm not the only one that thinks that."

"I'm sure you are," Cress fired back. "And anyone who couldn't see how much they both meant to each other is clearly blind."

Veronica turned her smug smile on Cress. She didn't seem the least bit bothered by her outburst. "Where is your cousin anyway? No one's seen him at school in days..."

Cress stiffened. "Noah's been sick."

She'd responded so awkwardly that I wondered whether Noah was truly unwell. Either way, Veronica seemed to accept Cress's reasoning, and she placed a hand against her chest in dismay. "Oh, the poor thing. I better go check on him. See if he's okay."

"He's resting. I'm sure he doesn't need or want your help," Cress replied.

"No. If I know Noah, he'll need someone to care for him right now. And I know all the best ways to *care* for him."

My nails dug into the palms of my hands as my fists clenched tighter. I didn't even want to think about what Veronica was insinuating.

She didn't give either of us a chance to respond before she turned to the front of the classroom, lifting a hand in the air. "Mr. Wagner, I need a pass for the school nurse. I have a terrible headache."

The teacher barely opened his mouth to answer her when Veronica gathered her things and started for the front of the room. She looked back in my direction when she reached the door and gave me a knowing smile before disappearing from the room.

"Noah's going to kill me," Cress murmured.

"Is he really sick?"

"Uh, he's actually—"

"You know what, I don't want to know. The less I know about Noah, the better."

I didn't want to think about Noah, but he remained on my mind for the rest of class. I kept wondering if Veronica had found him. If he was letting her look after him like she'd said she would. I knew I shouldn't let her get to me, and I was probably a hypocrite for being hurt he was moving on. But I still cared for him. I just wondered when it was going to stop.

CHAPTER TWENTY-FOUR

"Sawyer has demanded your presence at his soccer game tonight." Wes was standing at my bedroom door, a hopeful expression on his face. "He told me to tell you he, and I quote, 'he will be very disappointed if you miss another of his matches.'"

"Oh no, really?"

"Yep." Wes sounded remarkably positive considering my response.

I'd been avoiding Sawyer's matches for one very good reason. I didn't want to watch Noah play. I'd been trying to purge him from my life, and going to his games seemed an unnecessary torture. I was working on moving on now, so it was probably time I stopped using him as an excuse. Still, it was cold this evening, and the idea of freezing my butt off as I sat in a soccer stadium wasn't that appealing.

"Sawyer won't even know if I'm there or not. Isn't the presence of the rest of the school enough for him?"

"His need for adoration knows no bounds."

I laughed. Sawyer did seem to enjoy soaking up the attention he got during his games. He wasn't even the star player, but he certainly acted like he was.

"Also, he's decided you're his good luck charm. He didn't play very well at his last game, and since you weren't there, he's decided you're to blame."

"He can't be serious. Is he really that superstitious?"

Wes shrugged. "I might be his brother, but not even I understand Sawyer most of the time."

"I'm not going to his game just because he played like crap last week."

"He also promised to stop calling you sis if you come."

"Ugh, he told you about that?"

"Oh yeah. He's already planning our wedding."

I groaned. "Please tell me you're joking."

Wes grinned. "I am, *mostly*. He's very team Wesobel."

"Oh no, not the couple name. Has he been talking to Cress?"

Wes laughed. "Probably. You've got to admit though, Wesobel has kind of a ring to it."

I glared at him, and he held his hands up in surrender.

"Okay, no couple name. But will you come to the game?"

"I don't know. It seems like a lot of pressure to be Sawyer's lucky charm…"

"I'm sure Cress would like you to see her dancing too," Wes added.

I let out a breath, knowing there was no way I could say no now. If Wes wanted me at the game, he probably should have led with that argument. Cress had mentioned she'd like me to be there earlier today, and I was already feeling guilty about letting her down. I couldn't avoid Noah's games forever, so I was just going to have to suck it up and face the cold.

My shoulders slouched. "Okay, fine. You've twisted my arm. I'll come."

Surprise lit Wes's eyes as though he hadn't believed it would be that easy to convince me. "You will?"

"Yeah, I'm not sure I can handle disappointing *both* Sawyer and Cress."

"And don't forget me. I would have been disappointed if you weren't there too."

"Well, we couldn't have that."

I changed quickly and threw on the same outfit I'd worn to the last soccer game, but I added a sweater, jacket, gloves, beanie, and scarf to keep me warm. I looked like the Michelin Man, but I didn't care. I just hoped it was enough to keep me warm. There was nothing worse than being stuck outside in the cold when you weren't wearing enough.

We set off for the stadium, and the moment I was outside, I began to question my decision. It wasn't just cold this evening; it was freezing. Not even the extra layers I'd put on seemed to be helping.

"It's not even winter yet. How is it so cold?" I grumbled as the freezing wind cut through my sweater and lashed against my exposed cheeks. There was nothing I hated more than the cold.

Wes chuckled. "I'm surprised you can feel the cold at all given the way you're bundled up."

"I'm going to turn into an icicle,"

"You'd make a very adorable icicle."

I rolled my eyes. "No one cares if they're adorable or not once they're frozen, Wesley."

He kept smiling at me like my response only made me more adorable to him. I nudged him with my shoulder, hoping to distract him enough that he'd stop looking at me that way.

"Come on," I said. "Let's walk faster so we can get out of the wind."

When we reached the stadium, Anna waved us over to some seats she'd saved. "I can't believe you came," she said as I sat beside her. "Wes told me he was going to talk to you, but I didn't think he'd actually be able to convince you. The weather's foul."

"I guess Wes can be pretty convincing when he wants to be."

"It's a skill," he agreed with a proud smile. His blond hair was sticking out under the sides of his beanie, and his cheeks were pink from the icy wind. I had no idea how he managed to look so good despite the cold. It didn't suit me nearly as much.

I kept sniffing because my nose was runny, and the cold had already permeated my jeans and was chilling my legs. I had expected my gloves to at least keep my hands warm, but my fingers were almost numb. I cupped my hands to my mouth and blew into them, hoping to thaw my fingers out a little, but it was useless.

"You look like you're freezing," Wes said. "Here." He didn't wait for me to respond before he wrapped his arm around me.

I turned rigid as he pulled me in close. I wasn't sure if cuddling up to Wes at a soccer game was really a good idea, but the moment his warmth hit me, all hesitation disappeared. He was practically my own space heater, and I cuddled into him trying to get warmer still. I knew I should have been more cautious, in case this was giving him the wrong idea about us, but I was too cold to care.

The team came out onto the pitch, and I stiffened again slightly in Wes's grasp as I waited to spot Noah. When I didn't see him, I managed to relax. Cress had said he was sick, so maybe he wasn't well enough to play today. I couldn't help but feel a little relieved.

Wes laughed, and I followed his gaze to his brother who was blowing kisses into the crowd. Actually, he was sending them right at us. I scowled at him, but that only made Sawyer smile brighter.

"I think he's happy his lucky charm is here," Wes said.

"I hope he doesn't actually believe that. I'm really not sure I can handle the pressure."

Wes gave me a squeeze, and with his lips close to my ear, he whispered, "Maybe we can tell him you're too busy being my lucky charm instead."

I swallowed, my body tingling as I felt his breath against my neck. "Yeah, maybe that will work." I tried to whisper, but my words seemed to become stuck in my throat.

Anna shot me a curious look, and I smiled back at her as innocently as I could. She shrugged and turned away as the girl next to her said something. I let out a breath. Wes was totally getting under my skin right now in all the good ways, and I hoped it wasn't too obvious.

The game started, and thankfully Wes's attention moved from my neck to the field. The teams seemed better matched tonight than the last game I'd come to, and Weybridge was finding it difficult to score. I wondered if it was because Noah wasn't playing. He was a force to be reckoned with both on and off the field, and our guys seemed to be struggling without him.

Sawyer was playing well, but there was only so much he could do on his own. The rest of the team was lagging, and I had a feeling I wasn't quite as lucky a charm as Sawyer thought.

When the whistle blew for the halftime break, both teams had yet to score. "I was thinking of grabbing a hot chocolate to warm up," Wes said. "Do you girls want one?"

"That sounds great," I said.

"Only if it's spiked with Baileys," Anna replied.

Wes lifted his eyebrows in reply. "I don't think the school canteen spikes hot chocolates with Baileys…"

"I'm joking, obviously." Anna laughed. "Although that would really help warm us up. But yeah, I'll take a regular hot chocolate. Thanks, Wes."

He started off down the bleachers, and I watched him go with a smile on my face. Wes could be really sweet.

"You guys should just date already," Anna said, drawing my attention back to her.

My cheeks flushed. "It's not like that between us."

"It should be, and I bet he thinks it is. He's completely in love with you."

"No, he's still getting over Sarah, and I'm just a distraction."

"He doesn't exactly look like he's crying into his pillow at night over her. They might have been together for ages, but they've barely spent any time together lately. Even over the summer, they didn't see each other. To be honest, I think they've kind of been over for a while."

"We're just friends."

"The whole snuggling into each other as you watch a soccer game isn't exactly giving off the just friends vibe."

"It's only because I'm cold."

"Does he know that?"

I fell silent. Maybe Anna had a point. Things had been changing between Wes and I. We had kissed several times now, and he'd been flirting with me all week. We were definitely straying beyond the friendship zone. It was just a few impulsive kisses though. Did that really mean we automatically needed to be more than friends?

Thankfully, the dance team started their halftime performance and brought an end to our conversation. I didn't have an answer for Anna's questions. The truth was, I didn't really know where I stood with Wes. He'd told me he was happy being just friends, but what if he wanted more? What if I wanted more?

"Did I miss much?" Wes asked, returning with the hot chocolates.

"Thanks," I murmured, taking the drink from him before I shook my head. "Cress and the team only just started."

"Good." He settled into his seat, wrapping his arm around me again. He did it without any hesitation, and Anna's words started rattling around in my head once again. I really liked Wes, and I'd have to be crazy to deny there wasn't something between us. But Noah was still taking up too much space in my heart, loitering there like some kind of unwanted roommate, and it wouldn't be fair to Wes to pretend otherwise.

I cheered loudly with Anna when the dance team finished their routine. Cress was waving up into the crowd as she made her way from the field, and her smile widened when she caught sight of me. I immediately felt bad for missing her other performances in my attempts to avoid seeing Noah and vowed to always come to his games even if I hated his guts just so I could make Cress smile that way.

As the teams returned to the field, Anna nudged me with her elbow.

"What?"

She nodded toward the field, and I saw Noah making his way onto the pitch. My stomach tightened at the sight of him. He looked tired, and he must have still been feeling unwell because there were dark bags under his eyes.

"I didn't think he was playing today," Anna said. "I thought he was sick."

"I guess he's feeling better," I replied.

"Hopefully," Anna added. "Someone needs to turn this game around. It's been too close for my liking so far."

The whistle blew, and the game kicked off again. As the second half got going, it was clear the Eagles were playing far better with Noah on the field. The other team could barely get hold of the ball, and when they did, Noah would be the one to win it back. Whatever illness had kept him from school, it certainly wasn't slowing him down tonight. He was barking orders at his teammates, and they seemed to be responding, as every one of them looked more energetic than they had in the first half.

One of the opposing players became frustrated with the Eagles' sudden dominance. The big, bulky guy with jet-black hair was sprinting around the pitch like a madman, desperately trying to get the ball back. When the ball fell to Noah, I gasped as the guy flew toward him and lunged at him with both feet. Noah didn't flinch. He simply flicked the ball up and over the player, leaving him in a heap on the floor as he dribbled away. The crowd rose to their feet as Noah passed the ball between two defenders and straight into Sawyer's path. It was just him and the goalkeeper, and he calmly curled the ball into the net.

The stadium erupted as the Eagles finally got their first goal, and the players all ran to congratulate Sawyer. Noah remained calm, as though it was no big deal, a focused and determined look still etched on his face. The guy with the jet-black hair wasn't far from him, still on the ground, a furious look in his eyes.

Wes had his fingers in his mouth and was whistling loudly, and I laughed at his enthusiasm. "Stop encouraging Sawyer, or he'll keep scoring, and I'll be his lucky charm for life."

He grinned at me and leaned in close to my ear so I could hear him speak over the cheers in the stadium. "Maybe that's exactly what I want so I can cuddle you at all his games."

I swallowed as he pulled back to look me in the eyes. I'd seen that look before, and it certainly wasn't friendly. I got the feeling he wanted to kiss me again. It was probably a good thing the referee started blowing his whistle loudly and Wes looked away; if we kissed again, the blurry line we'd crossed might disappear entirely.

"Shit," Anna said. "What's he doing?"

I glanced at the field and gasped as I saw two players rolling around on the ground fighting. Everyone on the field was rushing toward them, and when they pulled the two players apart, I realized Noah was one of them.

"That did not just happen." Anna's eyes were wide. "Tell me that didn't just happen!"

"What's going on?" Wes asked, his expression filled with confusion.

"I missed it too," I said. "Why was Noah fighting?"

"I have no idea," Anna said. "But I'm pretty sure number nine started it."

The referee continued to blow his whistle as he tried to calm the players on both sides. Sawyer and some of his teammates had grabbed Noah and were pulling him away from the scene while a group of players on the other team were complaining to the referee. The guy with the jet-black hair was glaring at Noah, a smug grin on his face.

"That's the guy he was fighting?" I asked Anna.

"Yeah," she nodded. "He just ran right up to Noah after the goal, and suddenly they were on the ground throwing punches."

Once things had calmed down, the referee marched up to both Noah and the opposing player and showed them a red card, ordering them off the field.

"Oh no," Wes said. "That's Noah out for the rest of the game."

Noah trudged off the field, and the rest of the Weybridge team shook their heads. Some of them could barely look at him. They'd played so well since he'd arrived, but now they had to go on without him. When Noah reached the edge of the field with his head hung low, it started to rain.

Thankfully our seats were under cover, but the water fell in hard sheets, quickly soaking the players on the field. Noah didn't seem to notice. His wet shirt gripped his skin, and his damp hair flopped against his face.

He finally looked up, but it wasn't to focus on the game as it got back underway. Instead, his eyes went straight to the stands and directly to me. He didn't even need to search for where I was sitting; it was like he could sense exactly where I was.

The agony in his gaze as he looked at me was hard to endure. And it was only once he broke our stare off and disappeared behind the bleachers that I felt like I could breathe again. He'd just been in a fight that got him kicked out of the game, but I couldn't help but feel like there was something else behind the pain I saw in his eyes.

"ARE you sure you don't want to come to Toddy's?" Wes asked as we left the stadium. The Weybridge Eagles had held on to win the game, despite Noah getting sent off, so it seemed my time as Sawyer's lucky charm wasn't over. I'd been secretly hoping the team might lose so he'd fire me from the position.

"I'm sure. I need to have a hot shower to warm up," I said. "Besides, I'm not that hungry."

"You aren't hungry for a Toddy's burger?" Wes placed a hand against my forehead like he was taking my temperature. "Something must be wrong. Are you feeling okay?"

I swatted his hand away. "Very funny."

"Yes, I know, I'm hilarious."

I went to blow warm air into my freezing hands only to realize the reason they were so cold was because I'd left my gloves behind. It probably served me right for taking them off to steal some of Wes's fries.

"Shit, I've left my gloves back at our seats," I said.

"I'll go grab them for you," Wes offered.

"Don't be silly. You've got a date with a Toddy's burger. You can't risk being late."

"It's no problem," he said, but I shooed him onward.

"It's fine. It will take me two minutes to jog back there. I'll catch you tomorrow."

"Okay, if you're sure." He bent down and brushed a kiss against my cheek. "I'll see you in the morning."

As I watched him leave, following the stream of students away from the stadium, I gently touched the place where he'd kissed my skin. He'd done it so naturally, so thoughtlessly. Like giving each other such easy kisses was something we always did. I frowned as I watched him walking away, wondering how I felt about the way things had been changing between us. Our friendship had definitely been developing into something new, and I was trying to decide if I wanted it to change more still.

I walked back to the stadium, passing the few stragglers who were still making their way from the game. It seemed that everyone had left quickly tonight, which was hardly surprising given how cold it was.

I jogged up the stairs to my seat, relieved when I found my gloves waiting for me. I picked them up and put them on before making my way back down the steps. Although everyone had now left the stadium, the floodlights still lit the field. I was just about back to the entrance when I noticed someone alone on the grass, kicking balls into the goal at the far end of the field. It only took me a moment to realize it was Noah, and I stopped to watch him.

He seemed angry as he thumped ball after ball into the net as though he still needed to relieve whatever emotions or aggression had caused him to act out during the game. I hated seeing him like this and wondered if he needed someone to talk to. I stepped onto the field before I could stop myself and started walking across the grass toward him. I was probably the last person he wanted to talk to, but I couldn't just walk away and pretend I hadn't seen him.

Noah didn't notice me as I made my way across the field, but when he struck a ball and it cannoned off the frame of the goal, it bounced back and rolled toward me. He turned to jog after it, but he froze, and his eyes widened with surprise when he saw me.

"You shouldn't be out here, Isobel." He quickly regained his composure as he collected the ball and turned back toward the goal.

I tucked my hands into my pockets and came to a stop just a few meters from him. "I just wanted to check on you."

"Well, you didn't need to bother. I'm fine."

People who were fine didn't get into fights on soccer fields, but I didn't want to say that. Not when he was already so defensive.

"Should you really be out here practicing when you've been out of school sick for days?" I asked.

Noah snorted as he placed the ball on the ground. "If you

consider being pulled out of school by your grandfather sick, then sure."

"Wait, you weren't sick? But Cress said..."

"Cress covered for me. I don't need everyone in this place knowing my business."

I could certainly relate to that. Noah's absence from school was the least of my concerns right now though. "Noah, what happened tonight?" He shook his head, refusing to answer.

"Look, we may not be together anymore, but you know you can talk to me, right?"

He grunted in reply, his eyes focused on the ball as he kicked it toward the goal. He booted it so hard it soared right over the top, disappearing beyond the fence behind the goal. He ran a hand through his hair, pushing it from his face in clear frustration.

As his hair moved, it revealed a red mark on his forehead. I gasped when I realized it was a gash. It must have been from the fight because the area around it was still pink and swollen.

"Shit, Noah," I said, rushing closer. When I reached him, I lifted a hand to his face and pushed his hair aside to get a better look. The cut thankfully looked shallow, but it seemed no one had tended to it because it was still slightly oozing blood.

"What are you doing?" he asked, going completely still under my touch.

I pulled my hand away, aware I might have crossed a line. I also took a step back because I was standing far too close. "That looks like it hurts," I said, nodding at his wound.

He frowned and touched his forehead. He seemed surprised when he pulled his hand back and saw blood on his fingertips.

"Huh," he muttered.

"You're bleeding from your head and 'huh' is all you've got to say?"

He shrugged and wiped his hand on his shorts. "It's just a cut. I hadn't even noticed it."

"*Just* a cut?" I couldn't understand how he could act so blasé about the whole thing. "Noah, why did you fight that guy?"

He huffed out a laugh but didn't answer.

"Noah..."

"He insulted my family," he said. "And he threw the first punch."

"So, what, you just punched him back?"

"Why shouldn't I?" Noah's eyes flicked to mine, and I could see them burning with emotion. "He wanted a fight just as much as I did. I've got my grandfather breathing down my neck, dragging me from school to try and get me in line, and my ex-girlfriend cuddling some other guy in the stands. So, yeah, I punched him. And you know what? I don't regret it. Hell, with how I feel right now, I'd do it again if I could. What I don't need is your sympathy. And I don't need to share my feelings with you. I just need to get this damn ball in the damn goal."

He emphasized his words by turning and thumping another ball toward the goal, only this one went wide of the target, and Noah swore.

"Well, I'm sorry for bothering you." I turned to walk away before he could say anything else. I could feel his eyes on me as I left, but he didn't try to stop me. I didn't want him to.

I walked back to the dorms, trying my best not to think about how my conversation with Noah had left me so much colder than the chill in the air had all night. I should have just agreed to go to Toddy's and forgotten about my gloves.

CHAPTER TWENTY-FIVE

"How was the driving lesson?" Cress asked when I returned to our dorm room on Saturday morning.

I groaned and face-planted on my bed.

"That good, huh?" she said.

I groaned once more before rolling onto my back and pulling a pillow to my chest. "Not as bad as when Anna took me out, but not far off."

"Hey!" Anna complained as she walked out of our bathroom. "I happen to think we made great progress when I took you driving."

"Don't pretend it wasn't a total disaster," I replied. "And today wasn't much better."

"Was the instructor hot at least?" Anna asked as she plopped herself down on the bed beside me.

"If you find a fifty-year-old man who smells like fish hot, then sure."

Anna grimaced. "Yeah, you lost me at smelling like fish."

"But you were cool with the fifty-year-old man part?" Cress asked.

"Well, yeah. He could look like Lucius Malfoy." She fanned a hand against her neck. "I could definitely be with an old dude if he looked like my favorite Death Eater."

I rolled my eyes. "This one looked more like Dumbledore than Lucius."

"Eww." Anna cringed again, making me laugh.

"So, was the lesson really that terrible?" Cress's voice was soft, and I could easily hear her concern.

"It wasn't great. I just get so nervous and overwhelmed when I get behind the wheel that I freeze up. We didn't even get out of the parking lot."

"You'll get the hang of it," Cress said in an unsuccessful attempt to cheer me up.

"Are you going to have another lesson?" Anna asked.

"I think I'm going to have to. I hate driving, but I don't want to give up."

"That's the spirit." Cress gave me a warm smile. "So, I wanted to ask, do you have any plans for today?"

"Just homework," I said.

"You're not spending the day playing tonsil hockey with Wes?" Anna asked.

"Tonsil hockey?" I frowned as Anna and Cress both laughed. Anna really had a way with words sometimes. "No, I'm not playing tonsil hockey with Wes. He's off campus rowing today."

"Oh yeah," Anna said. "I think I remember him mentioning that. Damn, it's a shame the regatta isn't here. I do love me some buff boys in rowing uniforms."

"Of course, you do." Cress giggled.

"If it makes you feel any better, Wes told me the school's hosting a regatta here next weekend," I said. "You'll be able to see plenty of rowing boys then."

"Really?" Anna sat up, and her eyes started to sparkle with excitement. "It's like all my Christmases come at once."

"You have a strange idea of Christmas," I said.

"You say that now, but just wait. It's going to be a hot guy present fest."

"Is the uniform really that good, Cress?"

"It can be." She looked thoughtful as though she was remembering regattas of the past. "It's pretty formfitting, so it depends if the guy has the body to wear it or not."

"And Wes totally has the body." Anna nudged me with her shoulder.

Blood rushed to my cheeks, so I ignored her and continued to focus on Cress. "So, why were you asking about my plans for today?"

Thankfully she chose to answer me rather than point out my glowing red face. "Oh, I was hoping for a favor," she said. "The dance team is painting our booth for the Halloween carnival today, and I thought I could convince you to come give us a hand. Anna's already agreed to help, and there will be good tunes and pizza..."

"You had me at pizza," I replied with a smile.

She beamed in response and clapped her hands. "Thanks, Isobel. You're the best."

"It's no problem at all." It sounded way more enjoyable than being holed up in my room all day doing homework. Plus, I'd been too nervous about my driving lesson to eat breakfast this morning, so I was starved.

"Okay, so, I need to go into town to grab the pizzas, and I want to pop by the shops to get some snacks too. Do you guys want to come?"

"Definitely," Anna said. "It's been forever since I've been to the supermarket, and my deodorant has been spraying nothing but air for about a week now."

"Huh, I thought you smelled more than normal," Cress said.

Anna poked her tongue out.

Cress turned to me. "How about you, Isobel?"

"As long as I don't have to drive, I'm down."

The girls both laughed.

"No, you don't have to drive," Cress said as she grabbed her car keys.

The three of us headed into town and stopped at the supermarket first. Anna insisted she needed to ride in the shopping cart, and Cress and I took turns pushing her around the shop. We loaded the cart up with so many snacks that only Anna's head and arms were poking out from under the mountain of food.

"Don't forget my deodorant," Anna said. "You guys are going to have to choose one for me because I'm buried."

"You were the one who insisted on being in the cart," Cress said.

"Yeah, because that's where all the tasty snacks belong."

Cress and I groaned.

"Do you think she'll ever be less arrogant?" Cress asked.

"Probably not," I replied.

"Guys, I'm right here!" Anna cried, making us both laugh.

Cress added a deodorant to the cart, and we headed to the checkout. The woman at the till had the biggest frown on her face when she saw Anna riding in our cart. Anna had absolutely no shame and grinned widely up at her before asking about her day. She chatted so much that the woman didn't have a chance to tell us off. To be honest, I think she was simply happy to see us leave by the time we were ready to pay.

We stopped by the pizza place and picked up ten massive pizzas before heading back to school. We carried them over to the large shed that had been cleared out so students could work on their booths. There were already some girls and a couple of guys there, all of them painting the booth a bright shade of hot pink.

"I've got pizza," Cress announced.

Cheers of excitement went up from the team. Everyone dropped their paintbrushes and converged on Cress. I was somewhat glad I'd snuck a piece in the car because it was like watching Cress walk into a pack of pizza-eating zombies.

My phone started ringing, and I smiled when I saw it was my mom calling.

"I'm going to take this outside," I said to Anna, somewhat grateful to avoid the horde of hungry dancers. She was carrying some of the pizza boxes herself and looked like she was preparing for the moment when the dance team realized she also had pizza for them.

"Okay, I'll try to save you a slice," she said.

"Thanks."

I went outside and answered my phone.

"Finally," my mom gasped. "You've been missing my calls all week."

"You've been missing mine," I replied with a laugh. "Phone tag is the worst. How are you? How's the café?"

"All good," Mom said. "Frank complimented Norma on her new haircut last night, and Norma's been blushing ever since."

I laughed. "I wish they'd get together already."

"These things take time. How's school going?"

"School is good. I had my driving lesson this morning."

"And…"

"You don't want to know." I pushed down a shiver at the memory. "But, in happier news, I'm spending this afternoon helping Cress paint her dance team's booth for the Halloween carnival in two weeks."

"That sounds like fun."

"Yeah. We just grabbed some pizzas for everyone, and we have so many snacks I'll probably need a trip to the dentist when I'm done. I think it's going to be a good afternoon."

"Well, I won't keep you too long," Mom said.

"No, it's okay. I miss you."

"I miss you too," she replied. "Actually, that's part of the reason

I called. The café's been quiet, so I was thinking of taking a weekend off to come visit you."

"Really?" I could barely contain my excitement. "But you always work weekends."

"Well, that was before you headed off to school. Norma can manage just fine without me. You and me always spend Halloween together."

I let out a joyful squeal, making my mom laugh. These last weeks without her had been hard, and I needed a hug from her now more than ever.

"It's a long drive over, so I'll only be able to make it for one night."

"One night is better than none," I said. "And if you're coming for Halloween, that means you'll be here for the carnival. This is going to be so much fun. I can't wait to see you."

"Me too," Mom said. "And if this goes well, hopefully I can make it up there more often."

"I'd love that." The thought of seeing her more frequently had my heart beating with elation.

"Do you think your father will be in town for Halloween?" Mom asked.

"I'm not sure," I said. "He's been stuck in New York the last few weeks. He was supposed to come this weekend, but something came up, and he had to cancel. He didn't say when he'd be back."

"Oh, okay."

"Why do you ask?"

"No reason." She responded so fast I felt like there definitely was a reason.

"Do you want to see him?" I prompted.

"I mean, it would be nice to catch up with him again after all this time," she said. "But I'm sure we'll cross paths at some stage."

"I could invite him to the carnival if you like?"

"No, you don't have to do that." Her reply came quickly again.

"I was thinking of mentioning it to him anyway..." I hadn't been, but it sounded like my mom wanted to see Matthew. It was understandable given they had a child together and he'd done so much for me lately.

"Oh, well, I'm sure he'd appreciate the invite."

"Yeah, he sounds super busy at the moment though, so I doubt he'll be able to come," I added. I didn't want Mom to get her hopes up.

"I'm sure he'll do his best." She sounded a little relieved, and I didn't know what to make of her reaction. It seemed like she wasn't sure if she wanted to see him again or not.

We spoke about her trip for a few more minutes before she said she had to go deal with something at the café. When I returned to the shed, I had the biggest smile on my face.

"Why do you look like you just won the lottery?" Anna asked as she handed over the slice of pizza she'd saved me.

"Because my mom is coming to visit at Halloween."

"That's so great," Cress said as she joined us. "How long is she coming for?"

"Just the one night. So, we'll have to show her a good time at the carnival."

"I think we can do that." Anna grinned.

"Do you think she'd like to volunteer to be on our kissing booth?" Cress asked.

I spluttered out a laugh. "What?"

"Well, there will be lots of adults at the carnival, so it might appeal to the older demographic."

I was beginning to think she was actually serious. "I mean, I could ask her, but I don't think that's the best idea."

"Why not?" Cress replied. "I've seen pictures of your mom. She's a total babe."

"Yeah, but can you imagine if we have to watch her kiss a teacher or something?" The thought made me want to throw up, and Anna and Cress shuddered.

"You're right, that's a terrible idea," Cress said.

"I bet Coach August would totally line up to kiss her too," Anna added, pretending to gag. "Yuck."

"Okay. Not my best idea," Cress admitted.

"Not even close," I said before taking a bite of my pizza. It was dripping with grease and so cheesy you could barely taste the other toppings, but it was so, so good.

"Well, no one's going to be kissing anyone if we don't get our booth looking right," Cress continued. "We should probably get to work."

I quickly finished my slice before joining everyone to paint the booth. It was a fun afternoon, but most of us got covered in paint when some of the boys decided to start chasing us with their paintbrushes.

Cress, Anna, and I were laughing as we made our way back to the dorms when the booth was finally finished.

"We look like works of art," I said, laughing at the splats of paint covering my clothes and hair. I had no doubt it was probably on my face too.

"Yeah, on reflection, I probably should have warned you guys to wear old clothes," Cress said. "Or organized some coveralls to protect them. Sorry your outfits are ruined."

"Are you kidding?" Anna said. "I think the pink paint adds pizzazz. I want to do this to all my outfits." I couldn't tell if she was joking or not, but she sounded serious. "I'm not so sure about the paint in my hair though."

"Yeah, me neither," I added. I was probably going to have to wash it a million times to get the pink streaks out.

We were almost at our dorm when we ran into Luther, Kaden, and Noah. They were walking toward us, and they struggled to hide their reactions when they caught sight of our paint-covered clothes. Kaden was smiling sweetly while Luther's eyes lit up brightly. I knew he was thinking of all the different ways he could tease us. I couldn't bring myself to look at Noah. Not after Thursday night.

"Evening, ladies," Luther said. "You're all looking fabulous."

"Aren't we?" Anna agreed. "I always thought pink was my color."

"Indeed," he replied. "Now, was there wrestling involved with the paint, or did you all just happily roll around in it?"

"Perhaps there was a bit of both," Anna sassed him.

"I think it's cute," Kaden said. He was looking directly at Cress, and I wasn't sure he'd meant to share his thoughts out loud because the two of them immediately started blushing and refused to make eye contact. Cress definitely had a thing for Kaden, and I think he might have a thing for her too.

As the others talked, I finally risked a glance in Noah's direction. He was staring straight at me. He didn't look nearly as terrible as he had the other night, and the cut on his head seemed to be healing nicely. But his expression was more reserved than normal, and it was impossible to know what he was thinking.

"Can I talk to you, Isobel?" he asked when he caught my gaze.

The others all fell silent, and I slowly started to nod. I wasn't sure I wanted to talk to him. Especially not when I'd had such a good day. But I wasn't sure I knew how to say no to this guy.

"We'll catch you inside," Cress said, as Luther and Kaden also made their excuses to leave.

Within moments, Noah and I were standing alone in the dusky evening light. I waited for him to say something, but he remained quiet as he stared at me.

"You wanted to talk?"

He blew out a breath and nodded. "I wanted to apologize for my behavior earlier this week," he said. "I shouldn't have made you feel bad about trying to move on in PE, and I shouldn't have taken my frustrations out on you at the soccer field. I was out of line, and it was unfair to you, especially when you were only being kind."

"Oh," I murmured. "Don't worry. It's fine."

"It's not," he said. "Not really. I haven't been myself this week. My grandfather dragged me out of school and…" He shook his head. "Sorry, you don't need to hear me complaining."

"I don't mind."

But Noah didn't elaborate. It didn't stop me from wondering what was going on with his grandfather and why he'd taken Noah out of school. He'd mentioned something about his grandfather pressuring him the other night, and I wished I knew what was happening. Did it have anything to do with me or Matthew? Or perhaps it was related to the financial difficulties the Hastings' company was going through. I knew I couldn't ask him though. He clearly didn't want to talk about it with me.

We were both quiet and the seconds between us dragged out. Finally, I broke the silence. "Well, I should probably go inside and get cleaned up before dinner."

I moved to walk past him, but he reached out and lightly touched my arm. It was the smallest brush of his skin against mine, and yet my whole body buzzed from it. "I like the pink," he said, with the softest smile. "Kaden was right. It is cute."

I struggled to swallow as I nodded. He looked like he wanted to say more, but the sound of people walking up behind me made him tear his gaze from mine.

"Have a good night, Isobel," he said before striding away.

I watched him leave and didn't move until he'd disappeared from sight. I wasn't sure what to make of my interaction with Noah, but I appreciated his apology. Maybe it was a sign we were moving in the right direction and one day this would all be behind us.

When I went to bed, my mind kept replaying the small smile he'd given me as he'd looked at the pink paint in my hair.

CHAPTER TWENTY-SIX

Knowing my mom was coming to visit in less than two weeks made it feel like time was standing still. Each day moved by at a painfully slow pace, and not even throwing myself into my schoolwork helped. The only upside was that Noah kept his distance from me. It was so much easier to feel like I was making progress moving on from him when we didn't fight and when we didn't share heated moments.

Anna and Cress took this as a sign that they should make more heavy hints about Wes and I getting together.

"You guys even look perfect together," Cress said as we walked back to Esher Hall after PE on Wednesday. Wes and I had been partners for squash, which must have triggered this latest attempt by the girls to convince me to date him.

"Yeah, like two golden deities walking amongst us," Anna added.

"I don't know where you come up with this stuff, Anna, but we're just friends."

"Friends with sexual tension," Anna said. "I bet if we locked you in a room together you wouldn't be saying the same thing. You guys definitely wouldn't be able to resist one another."

I laughed uncomfortably. "Why are we getting locked in a room together?"

"Uh...there's a pandemic, and you both get exposed to the virus and are thrown into quarantine?" she suggested.

"Pretty sure that's not going to happen." I laughed. "Besides, we spend plenty of time alone together and we manage to resist each other." Most of the time, at least. I was choosing to ignore that time on the sidewalk in New York and that time in Wes's room.

"Aha!" Cress shouted, her voice filled with victory. "So, you admit it. You do have to try and resist him."

I rolled my eyes. "I didn't mean it like that."

"Sure, you didn't."

"I didn't." I let out a sigh. "But if anything changes, you guys will be the first to know."

"We better be," Anna grumbled.

Thankfully, the girls let it drop over lunch. It would have been super awkward otherwise since both Wes and Sawyer sat with us. It didn't stop them from shooting me knowing looks whenever Wes glanced my way. And it really didn't help that he did it frequently, often smiling so sweetly it practically made Anna and Cress explode silently in their seats.

I had economics with Wes after lunch, so we left the room together. We were literally just walking to class together, yet Anna wiggled her eyebrows suggestively at me as we left.

I scoffed as I turned away from her.

"What?" Wes asked.

"You really don't want to know," I said.

"Try me."

"It's embarrassing and stupid."

"Well, now I really want to know." He grinned.

I shook my head, wishing I hadn't said anything at all.

"Come on, I won't make fun of you, I promise," he said.

"Ugh, fine."

His smile only grew. "So..."

"Anna and Cress have been not so subtly hinting that you and I should be more than friends."

"Really?" He didn't sound all that surprised, which made me feel like they'd probably been giving him the same crap they'd been giving me.

"Yeah. Anna thinks there's so much tension between us that if we were ever locked in a room alone together we wouldn't be able to resist each other."

"That sounds like something Anna would say."

"I told you it was stupid."

Wes looked thoughtful.

"What?" I asked him.

"Do you think she's right?"

"Of course, she's not."

"You sure about that?"

"Uh..." The way he was looking at me made me question my resolve. I'd kissed Wes three times now, which probably indicated my ability to resist him wasn't as strong as I thought.

"I say we test it," he said.

"What? Wes..."

He grabbed hold of my hand and started to pull me in the opposite direction of our classroom.

"What are you doing?" I asked.

He was too busy looking up and down the corridor to answer me. Once the coast was clear, he opened the nearest door and pulled me after him into a room. As he closed the door behind us, he spun me round, and my back bumped gently against it. It was pitch-black, so I had no idea where we were. Wes was standing right in front of me, and there was barely room to move. A moment later, the light flicked on.

When my eyes adjusted and I looked around, I couldn't help but laugh. "The janitor's closet. Really, Wes?"

He grinned as he looked down at me. "What better place to test whether you can resist me?"

"Oh, so it's just me that needs to be tested?"

"I already know I can't resist you," he replied. His voice was playful but had a serious edge to it, and I was suddenly very aware of just how small this closet was. Especially with Wes pressed up against me and my back against the door. He was far too big for such a small space. His shoulders practically brushed the stacks of shelves that stood against the walls on either side of him.

"I'm sure that's not true." I tried to swallow down my nerves and did my best not to look directly at him, which was pretty much impossible given that he was everywhere in here. "So, how long do I have to resist you to prove Anna wrong?"

"Hmm, how about until the bell for class rings?"

"That's in like two minutes." I scoffed as I glanced up at him. "You think I can't last two minutes?"

"I'm sure you could," he said. "I guess the question is, do you want to..."

My eyes drifted to his lips and then down to where my hands were pressed against his chest. I didn't remember placing them there and wondered if I was already failing the test.

"What about you?" I whispered. "What do you want?" After I asked the question, I realized just how dangerous it was, because as I peered up and into Wes's eyes, I found his expression had changed. It wasn't hard to guess what he wanted as he looked at me with a hunger I'd never seen in him before.

He leaned in closer, placing his hands against the door behind my head. "I think you know what I want," he said. My heart clashed against my ribs in response, and when I felt his breath against my cheek, my body flushed hot with need.

The bell sounded through the door and I didn't know whether to feel relieved or disappointed. The test was over, but I couldn't seem to relax. I also couldn't seem to bring myself to open the door and leave the room either.

"I guess we proved Anna wrong," I said, my voice sounding far too breathy for someone who was totally in control.

"I guess so," he agreed. He hadn't moved back to give me space, and he hadn't opened the door. Instead, he stayed where he was, his body pressed against me, his lips so close to mine. The tension sparking in the air between us was impossible to ignore.

The longer we stood there, the more the pressure between us seemed to build. It didn't help when he shifted slightly, his leg rubbing against mine, and I struggled to withhold a groan. Yes, I'd proven I could resist Wes, but I was very quickly realizing that wasn't what my body wanted.

At some point, I must have closed my eyes, and when I opened them, Wes was practically devouring me with his gaze. Whatever line I'd tried to draw between us was nowhere to be found. It certainly hadn't entered the closet with us.

"Screw Anna's test." I gripped him by the tie and pulled him to me, wrapping my arms around his neck as our lips met. He pressed me against the door, his kiss filled with desperation and relief. I wanted Wes. I needed him. And in the heat of that moment, I hated myself for even trying to resist him. Our previous kisses had been amazing, but this one was so hot it put them all to shame.

A loud clatter sounded as one of us knocked something off a shelf and onto the floor. We froze and glanced at the door. The sounds of students walking out in the corridor reached my ears. I don't know how I hadn't noticed them before. Luckily, no one seemed to have noticed the noise coming from the closet, and after several seconds passed, Wes and I both managed to breathe again.

I was still wrapped in Wes's arms, but he slowly disentangled them, and I knew the moment was over. He smiled at me , his eyes sparkling in the dimly lit closet.

"So, apparently Anna knows what she's talking about," I said.

He chuckled. "Apparently."

"I feel like we're blurring the lines between..." I trailed off, feeling suddenly worried I was going to sabotage whatever was developing between us by talking too much. I liked Wes's kisses, but I also liked our friendship. Did there have to be a line in the sand between those two things?

"I'm kind of enjoying the blurred lines," he said.

"What does that mean?"

"I'm not sure yet, but I want to find out." His eyes were sincere, and a small smile curved the corner of his lips. His words seemed to touch a part of my heart I was so sure I'd lost.

"I think I do too," I murmured. But then I shook my head, trying to clear the haze that had fogged my brain while looking into Wes's eyes. "But what if this doesn't work? I've been through too much heartbreak recently. So have you. I don't want to lose you as a friend as well."

His gaze turned more serious as he nodded in reply. "You're right, and I feel the same, but I think we could be something amazing."

I rubbed a hand against my face as I tried to process what he was saying. "You're still into Sarah..."

"Not as much as you might think," he said. "It took me some time to realize, but things between us had been over long before she broke up with me. And I know you still have feelings for Noah, but I can see you letting go of him a little more each day."

I started to object but then stopped as I considered what he'd said. Maybe Wes was right. Letting go of Noah had been hard. It was still hard, but I was in a very different place than I had been in the days after the ball. I'd come to accept we were over, but it still didn't stop the small pieces of my fractured heart from leaping whenever he was near.

I think Wes must have realized how confused I was because

he nodded at the door. "We should probably get to class," he said. "Or we're going to be late."

"Yeah, of course."

I wrapped my hand around the handle and cracked open the door to take a look outside. The hallway was clear of students, so I was guessing we were already late. I went to leave, but Wes took hold of my hand, stopping me.

"Just think about it," Wes said. "About us."

"I will."

His smile was so bright and filled with hope it was hard not to just fall into a relationship with him here and now. But Wes was right. I needed to think about this. We both did.

"So, on a scale of one to a thousand, how much do you think Anna will gloat when she hears she was right?" I asked as we made our way to class.

Wes laughed. "It's probably in our best interest she never knows."

"Probably," I agreed, but I had a feeling she'd somehow only need to take one look at me to figure out I made out with Wes in a janitor's closet. She had a sixth sense for these things, and it didn't help that my cheeks flushed just thinking about it.

Anna's reaction was the least of my worries. No, I had a far bigger problem. I somehow had to figure out what the hell I was going to do about the sweet, gorgeous guy beside me. The guy that deserved all of my heart when I only had small fractions left to give.

CHAPTER TWENTY-SEVEN

I was no closer to finding any clarity by the time Saturday morning dawned. The school was hosting its rowing regatta this weekend, which Wes was taking part in. He'd been sharing secretive smiles with me ever since our kiss in the janitor's closet on Wednesday, and I had a feeling he might want to talk more about our relationship-cum-friendship over the weekend. I didn't want to treat him badly, so I knew I needed to try to figure out my head and my heart.

"What am I going to do about Wes?" I asked Cress as we put on our makeup in the bathroom. We were getting ready to go down to the lake and watch the regatta, which would soon be underway.

I'd told her and Anna about kissing Wes in the janitor's closet, and the two of them had screamed before Anna composed herself enough to say "I told you so."

"You're still not sure?" she asked.

"No, and I need a second opinion. What do you think?"

"I can't make up your mind for you."

"I know," I groaned.

"Are you still worried about ruining your friendship?" she asked.

"That, and the fact I can't seem to forget about Noah. Is it fair to start something with Wes when my heart still beats faster every time Noah enters the room?"

"Wes isn't stupid. He understands you're still getting over Noah."

"I know."

"And it's not like anything's going to happen with Noah," she added. "He's never going to go against his grandfather's wishes." She softened her words with a sad smile.

"So, you think I should go for it?"

"I mean, what would you prefer? To continue just being friends or to actually date?"

"Well, kissing without committing to an actual relationship has been pretty great so far," I muttered. "But it's starting to get messy."

"I don't think that's something either of you would want long-term either," Cress said. "Wes isn't the kind of guy that does casual. He's the kind of guy that loves caring for someone and being in a committed relationship. I think you're that kind of girl too…"

I blew out a breath and nodded. "Am I an idiot for even questioning this? The way you described Wes, any girl would be silly to turn him down, right?"

"You're not an idiot," Cress said. "You're just being careful."

"I can't believe I'm even considering another relationship. Not after the last two breakups I've gone through."

"I don't think Wes will break your heart."

"I don't think so either," I agreed. That didn't make this decision any easier. "I thought talking to you would make it clearer in my head. But I'm still a jumbled mess. I don't want to screw things up."

"Sometimes doing nothing screws things up more. I think you need to make a decision."

I knew Cress was right. I couldn't leave Wes hanging. I either had to take a risk and commit to a relationship or let things go back to the way they were before. No more kisses in closets.

"Maybe the universe will give me a sign today," I said.

"You're leaving this up to the universe?" Cress laughed. "That sounds dangerous."

"Well, I don't really trust myself to make decisions like this. I always seem to make the wrong choice. So, I think I'll let the universe take this one…"

Cress shook her head. "Be warned, the universe might be skewed in Wes's favor today. He's going to look pretty hot in his uniform."

"You think I'm going to date him because of a uniform?"

"I mean, it's a very convincing uniform. Why else do you think so many girls are going to the regatta today?"

A small spike of insecurity went through me. Wes was gorgeous, and I didn't like the idea of half the girls at school salivating over him. Then again, they'd all done the exact same thing over Noah. I guessed it came with the territory when you dated a cute boy. The major difference here was that Wes wasn't my boyfriend, and if we went back to being friends, he would be free to entertain any offers that came his way. I didn't like that idea at all.

Cress and I finished getting ready before we headed down to the lake. As we neared the new boathouse that sat proudly on the shoreline, I could see quite a crowd was already gathered. Tents were pitched along one of the banks of the lake with different school logos proudly displayed across the material.

I didn't recognize many of the students walking around the school grounds, and a group of guys nudged each other and grinned as Cress and I passed. One of the cuter ones sent us a wink.

"Anna is going to be drooling over all the fresh meat," Cress said, making me laugh.

"Yeah, she is always complaining about how we always see the same guys at all our parties."

"Not tonight," Cress replied. "There's usually an after-party at Luther's on regatta nights, and some kids from the rival schools come. It can get pretty wild."

"Because Luther's other parties are so tame," I muttered.

"There you guys are!" I glanced over as Anna came rushing toward us with Sawyer slowly trailing behind her. "I was worried you were going to miss all the fun."

"I told her she was being dramatic," Sawyer said. "That there's no way Isobel would miss her sweet Wesley's little regatta."

I chose to ignore him, but unsurprisingly, I was thinking about Wes. "Speaking of Wes, any idea where he is? I'd like to wish him good luck before his race."

"Ha, sure, *luck*," Sawyer replied, his voice dripping with suggestion.

"Sawyer? Where is he?"

He flicked a hand over his shoulder. "He's over by the Weybridge tent."

"Okay, I'll catch you guys back here in a bit." I went in the direction Sawyer had indicated, but he called after me. "Remind Wes to row his little heart out today," he said. "I'd hate for him to lose our bet."

I paused and glanced over my shoulder. Those two boys and their bets. "Another bet? What happens if he loses?"

"If he loses, he has to streak through the after-party tonight."

My eyes widened. "And if he wins?"

"Then I'll be the one who's streaking." Sawyer grinned like he'd be happy either way.

I shook my head. "I guess I better go give him some more motivation to win."

As I got closer to the Weybridge tent, I could see Wes standing in the entrance. My mouth went a little dry when I got a good look at his rowing suit. On a smaller guy, the fitted material would have looked terrible, but Wes filled it out in all the right places. Yep, I could definitely see why the girls were all big rowing fans.

He started smiling as he saw me approach. "You made it."

"Why do you sound so surprised? I told you I'd come."

He shrugged. "Guess I was just worried something else might come up."

It made me a little sad to hear his response. It seemed like he was so used to being canceled on by his ex that he'd come to expect it.

"No way, I wouldn't miss this for anything. Besides, I had to come wish you luck." I reached up and pressed a kiss firmly against his cheek. "Good luck."

His smile grew wider. "You know, I hear that good luck kisses only work if they're on the lips."

"I'm pretty sure that's not a thing."

"I'm pretty sure it is."

"Fine." I laughed and quickly brushed a kiss against his lips. He tried to deepen the kiss, but somehow, I managed to pull myself away. "You're terrible. You know that, right?"

"Terribly handsome?"

"Terribly devious."

"I think I can live with that." He chuckled. "I have to go prep for my race, but come find me after. I'll need to thank my good luck charm…"

I raised an eyebrow. "Don't make me your good luck charm too. Being Sawyer's was already enough pressure."

He winked. "Well, stop being so lucky then."

I shook my head. "Have a good race, and make sure you win. I don't want to see you naked for the first time because you lost a bet with Sawyer."

His eyes lit up, and he smiled devilishly. "You want to see me naked?"

"*Oh, my gosh.* No. I didn't mean it like that."

"I think you did."

"I didn't."

"Then why are you blushing?"

I stammered as I tried to come up with a reply, but he didn't give me a chance to find my words.

"I'll see you after the race, Isobel." He flashed me another wide grin before he turned and walked deeper into the tent.

Stupid cocky boy, I thought as I watched him leave. A part of me hoped he'd lose now, if only to wipe the smug look from his face.

"SO, is my brother going to win?" Sawyer asked when I finally found my friends again. They'd moved from where I'd left them and taken up a spot close to the lake to watch the races.

"He seemed pretty sure of himself," I said.

"Which will only make my victory sweeter." A fevered look entered Sawyer's eyes as he rubbed his hands together like some cartoon villain.

"You guys really need to find a better hobby than placing bets on each other." I shook my head as I faced the girls. "Have I missed much?"

"Only the one race," Cress replied.

"And a group of Bexley boys came to chat with us," Anna added as if that were the more important of the two updates. "They were superhot too."

Sawyer rolled his eyes. "Yeah, if you're into that whole pretty boy look."

"Aw, Sawyer, are you jealous?" Anna crooned.

"Of a guy from Bexley?" Sawyer scoffed. "No chance."

Anna laughed. "You keep telling yourself that."

We watched several races, cheering with the rest of the Weybridge students every time our rowers were on the water. We were pretty evenly matched with the other schools, winning about as many races as we lost. It only made my nerves grow as we waited for Wes to compete. I really wanted him to win.

We all fell silent as an announcement was made over the loudspeaker, and Anna started bouncing up and down on her feet.

"That's Wes's race," she said.

We turned to the end of the lake where the boats were lining up at the start line. It was far enough away that it was difficult to tell which crew was which.

"I've got to admit," Sawyer said as we both watched the start line, "I'm not sure if I want to win or lose this bet."

I snorted. "You actually *want* to streak at the party tonight?"

"Well, everyone else will be all covered up in warm clothes, so it will give me a great excuse to show off my body to all the ladies. I've got to do something to compete with all these damn rowers."

"And streaking is your answer to that?"

"It's also a great icebreaker."

"Because you really struggle to start conversations with girls."

"What can I say? I'm a secret introvert at heart."

"I don't believe that for one second."

He grinned and swung an arm over my shoulder. "That's just because you know me so well, sis."

I groaned and shrugged his arm off me. "Wes told me you'd stop calling me that if I came to your game the other day."

"Oops, I guess I forgot." Given the cheeky glint in his eyes, I knew he hadn't.

The race started and our gazes darted to the end of the lake. The boats were barely larger than specks in the distance, but an announcer's voice was blaring over the speakers as they commentated on the race. Bexley had started strong and was already pulling ahead of the rest of the competitors.

My hands bunched into fists at my side, and my heart raced as I listened to the announcer. Wes's team was pulling up the rear.

I glanced at Sawyer who didn't share any of the tension I felt. He looked the picture of ease as he watched the race, and when he caught my worried expression, he smiled.

"Stop stressing," he said. "Like he does many things in life, when my brother races, he starts out slow but finishes hard and fast."

"Sawyer!" Anna gasped from beside me. "That sounded way too sexual."

He shrugged. "What? I'm just saying it how it is."

I shook my head and focused back on the race, but Anna leaned in close to me. "Sounds like you and Wes should be doing more than just kissing," she murmured, nudging me in the side.

"Anna, get your head out of the gutter. I'm trying to watch the race."

"Okay, okay." She fell silent, but I could still see her smirking at me from the corner of my eye.

My heart leaped as I heard the announcer call out that Weybridge were gaining on Bexley. They were moving up the lake swiftly, and I could see the boats more clearly. Weybridge was easy to pick out in their red uniforms, and they were only just behind their rivals.

The crowd started shouting and cheering as the boats came closer and closer. We were standing right by the finish line, and the two boats were neck and neck as they fought for the lead.

With only meters to go, the Weybridge crew attacked the water with a sudden burst of energy, pulling out in front just as they flew across the finish line. The crowd went wild as our boys came in first, and I found myself jumping up and down as I squealed with Anna and Cress.

When we finally calmed down, I noticed Sawyer didn't look

nearly disappointed enough about losing his bet. In fact, he was grinning brightly like he couldn't be happier.

"And here I thought you'd be disappointed that Wes won the bet."

He winked. "Wes was always going to win."

"So, why make the bet then?"

"Because what is life without a little bit of risk?"

"That's very deep of you Sawyer."

"Like I told you, I'm a secret introvert. I'm really quite profound."

"Sure, you are." I laughed at him. "We should go find Wes to congratulate him."

"And give him the satisfaction of admitting I lost our bet? I don't think so," Sawyer said.

"Anna? Cress?".

"We'll catch up with you," Anna said with a knowing grin.

"Yeah," Cress agreed with a bigger smirk. "We'll be there in a minute. We just want to watch the next race, but you go ahead."

"Fine. I'll see you guys soon."

Their faces were all too smug as I turned to go. I had a feeling they were yet again trying to push their Wesobel agenda on me, but I was too excited to see Wes to let it bother me.

When I caught sight of Wes, he was celebrating with the rest of his team. His whole body radiated excitement, and I loved seeing him so happy. When he saw me, his happy smile morphed into a beaming grin, and he rushed over to me, catching me up in his arms. I squealed as he swung me around before he lowered me to my feet once more.

"Did you see us?" he cried. "We won. We actually won."

I laughed at his exuberance. He was so cute when he was this happy, and my heart was lifted by his brimming enthusiasm.

"You guys were incredible out there."

"I really thought we were done for toward the end there."

"Could have fooled me."

He folded me into his arms once more, and I smiled as I leaned against his chest. It was impossible not to like Wes, especially when he was like this.

When he pulled back, he was still grinning down at me. "Date me, Isobel."

"What?"

"I know I'm supposed to be patient and we're supposed to think this through. But I want this. I want you. Be my girlfriend, for real."

"You're still high on adrenaline from your race."

His expression sobered slightly. "Perhaps I am. But perhaps that adrenaline has also given me clarity. I want you to be my girlfriend."

"Really?"

He nodded, and a hint of uncertainty entered his eyes. He'd probably been slightly high on energy when he'd asked me, but I could see in his gaze that he meant it, and I knew he'd be hurt if I turned him down.

Even as I looked into his eyes, I thought of Noah. My relationship with Noah had been like a starlit sky. It was beautiful and endless, and the darkness had a unique allure all its own. But the dark was also fraught with danger, and there were so many obstacles you couldn't see.

Wes was more like the sunny sky overhead. He was happy, easy, and warm. Being with him wasn't complicated, and his brightness chased away even the gloomiest of shadows. I deserved to be with someone who made me happy. Perhaps this was the nudge I'd been asking for from the universe.

Slowly, I started to nod. "Okay."

"Okay?" A smile tugged at his lips as my nod became more definite.

"Yes, okay."

He laughed and pulled me up into his arms, swinging me around again. When he slowly lowered me to the ground, he sealed our relationship with a kiss. His lips tasted slightly salty, and the intensity with which he kissed me had me feeling light on my feet. I could feel his kiss all the way down in my toes, and I smiled as I heard his team whistling and jeering at us from behind.

Slowly, I pulled away, and when I opened my eyes, he was gazing down at me. He was looking at me like I was the prize he was taking home today rather than the trophy his team had just won.

"I think we just made a bit of a scene," I murmured.

"I think we might have too," he agreed. "Want to make another one?"

I laughed and pushed back from him. "Maybe later."

"I'll hold you to that." He glanced past me to his teammates who had returned to celebrating their win.

"You should get back to them," I said.

"I'd rather stay here with you."

I shook my head. "Go celebrate with your friends. I'll see you at the party later tonight."

He gave me a grin and then swooped down to kiss me on the cheek. "I can't wait." He jogged past me to catch up with his team and head back to the boathouse, and I smiled as I watched him go.

Wes was sweet and fun, and I liked him so much. Things were moving fast between us, but this felt right, and I was glad I'd agreed to be his girlfriend. I knew we were putting our friendship at risk, but I didn't want to let that hold us back. Not when we clearly both wanted to be something more. Sawyer was right; what was life without a little risk.

CHAPTER TWENTY-EIGHT

The party at Luther's was in full swing by the time we arrived. It seemed as though every student at Weybridge was here, and given the number of unfamiliar faces we passed, many kids from the other schools at the regatta had come to the party too.

The sunshine that had felt so warm during the day had disappeared, leaving behind an open night sky and a chill on the breeze. Anna and Cress were wearing short dresses, their skin turning pale from the cool night air. I'd opted for a pair of jeans and a thick woolen jacket, and I'd never been more pleased I ignored my friends' insistence on wearing something more revealing.

"Oh, thank God," Anna said as we arrived at the party. "They've set up a bonfire tonight." She didn't hesitate as she grabbed Cress's hand and pulled her toward the center of the clearing where the large flames crackled.

Despite the fact there were far more people at the party tonight than usual, the atmosphere seemed more relaxed. The music was mellower, and there was no raving dance floor like there had been at the last party I attended. Even the drinks station was a simpler affair with no lavish cocktails or expensive bottles of champagne anywhere to be seen.

I looked at the other side of the clearing, to the slightly elevated rocks where I'd seen Noah hanging out at my first party here. Kaden was sitting there, a group of guys and girls surrounding him, but there was no sign of Luther or Noah.

"There you are." Wes looked handsome as he walked toward me under the warm glow of the fire and fairy lights that lit up the clearing. He was wearing a pair of jeans and a knitted sweater. He had far better taste than I did when it came to clothes, and he wore them all too well. "I just passed Anna and Cress; they looked like they were on a mission."

I smiled. "They kind of tore off toward the fire when they saw it. I barely had a chance to go after them."

He laughed. "Yeah, those two are hopeless at reading a weather forecast."

"And they both really like to wear dresses."

"That too." He smiled before holding out a hand. "You going to come join the rest of the party or hang out at the entrance all night? Either way, I'm in."

I smiled and took his hand. "I think I can handle joining the party."

We walked through the crowded clearing together. It felt right holding hands with Wes. Like I had finally reached a place where I could feel happy again.

"How are you feeling after your big win today?" I asked. I hadn't seen him since we parted ways at the lake, and given the slightly dopey look in his eyes, he'd been celebrating already. Clearly not as hard as some of his other teammates, a few of whom I could see swaying unsteadily on their feet.

"Pretty good," he replied with a sly smile. "I'm not sure I'd call getting you to be my girlfriend a big win, but it definitely feels like one."

I shoved my shoulder against his and laughed. "I wasn't talking about that."

"It's the only win that really matters to me today."

I shook my head but smiled. Wes was far too good for me. I still couldn't understand how Sarah ever could have let him go.

We made our way through the crowd until we found Cress and Anna sitting near the bonfire on a bench seat positioned as close to the flames as possible. They'd be lucky if their boots didn't catch on fire.

"Isobel, Wes, come sit!" Cress called.

The two girls shuffled down, making room for us on the bench. There was barely enough space for one of us to sit, let alone both Wes and I.

Wes placed his hand on my lower back and leaned in close. "I'll go grab us some drinks," he murmured before starting toward the drinks table.

"We turned around when we got to the fire, and you weren't there." Cress wrapped an arm around my shoulders and hugged me as I sat beside her. She'd had a few drinks before coming tonight and was currently in what Anna called Cress's fun and flirty stage of drunkenness. It was probably the best stage Cress had when she was drinking, but Anna far preferred it when she leveled up and entered her "can't stop dancing" stage. I kind of thought Cress rarely stopped dancing even when she hadn't been drinking.

"Kaden's looking hot tonight," Cress continued, letting out a deep sigh. She was gazing over at him, a dreamy look in her eyes. "Then again, he always looks hot."

"Why don't you go chat with him?" I asked.

She blushed and shook her head. "I wouldn't know what to say. He's so smart. Anything I said would sound dumb."

"But he's so nice. I doubt he would ever think you were dumb." Every interaction I'd ever had with Kaden, he'd been sweet and kind. I really couldn't picture him judging someone because they weren't as smart as him. He was so clever, if that were the case, he'd have to look down on absolutely everyone.

"He *is* really nice. Isn't he?" Cress sighed. "And he's pretty to look at."

"You're not just looking," Anna said. "You're practically undressing him with your eyes."

Cress quickly glanced away from Kaden, her cheeks growing pink. "I'm not undressing him. I'm admiring."

"And picturing him naked."

"Oh my gosh, Anna. I'm not!" Cress insisted.

"Well, you probably weren't, but I bet you are now." Anna gave an evil laugh as Cress glared at her.

"I thought you weren't interested in any of the guys from our school," I said.

"I'm not," Cress quickly replied. "I can think Kaden is good-looking without being interested that way. I also think Tom Holland and Liam Black are hot, but that doesn't mean I want to date them."

"Ha, you would totally date Liam Black if you could," Anna said. "You had a picture of him as your phone background for like a year."

"Because I liked his movie, not because I want to date him."

"Liar." Anna grinned. "But we'll let it pass—for now."

Wes returned with two bottles of beer and offered one to me. I took the bottle and thanked him before taking a small sip. I'd barely lowered the bottle from my lips when a cheer went up behind me. I stood and turned to where the laughter, whistles, and shouting was coming from, only for my eyes to meet a very naked Sawyer darting through the crowd.

"Oh my God!" Cress squealed at my side, grabbing hold of my hand.

"Stop covering your goods, and give us a real show!" Anna shouted as she jumped up on the bench to get a better look.

My hand went to cover my mouth as Sawyer lifted his arms

and waved at Anna who started whistling. She was enjoying this far too much while I kind of wanted to poke my eyes out. I must have been the only one who felt that way. Everyone else at the party went wild as they applauded Sawyer.

"I can't believe your brother's actually streaking!" I said.

"Do you even know Sawyer?" he replied through his laughter. "He would have done this even if he hadn't agreed to the bet."

"True." I shook my head and watched as Sawyer's pale butt made its way to the far edge of the clearing and disappeared into the woods.

Anna jumped down from the bench and grinned at Wes. "Please tell me you and your brother are identical in *all ways*," she said, wiggling her eyebrows. "Because, if so, Isobel, you are one lucky girl."

Wes coughed uncomfortably and glanced away. "I should probably go check Sawyer has some clothing," he said before quickly following his brother.

"I'm totally taking that as a yes," Anna called after him.

Cress laughed as Wes disappeared. "I think you scared him off."

"Oh yeah, he looked terrified," Anna happily agreed. "You'd think he'd be proud that he shared his brother's body."

"You're so weird sometimes," I said.

She grinned brightly. "I know. It's great, isn't it?"

"Great. Annoying. Same thing really," Cress replied.

"Hey!" Anna pouted.

Cress laughed. "You know I'm only joking."

Anna folded her arms across her chest. "Ninety percent of jokes are born of truth."

"Lucky for that ten percent then," Cress replied.

"Lucky," Anna muttered.

We sat back on the bench as the excitement of Sawyer streaking through the party dissipated, and the noise levels around us went back to normal.

"I still can't believe you agreed to date Wes," Anna said, changing the subject as she took a swig out of the bottle of champagne she held at her side. I hadn't seen any champagne when I'd looked at the drinks table, but it was no surprise Anna had found a bottle somewhere.

I frowned. "You think it's a bad thing?"

"No, of course not. Wes is great. I just thought you two might stubbornly refuse to see how great you are together for a while longer."

"We weren't being stubborn; we were being careful."

"Well, I'm glad you decided to throw caution to the wind. I hated seeing you so upset after Noah. And no offense Cress, but your cousin was a dick for breaking up with Isobel in the first place."

"None taken." Cress turned to me. "I'm really happy to see the universe wanted you to move on."

"Thanks." I returned her smile, grateful she could be happy for me even if things hadn't worked out with her cousin.

Wes returned to our group several minutes later, looking completely flustered.

"My brother's an idiot." He shook his head.

"What's Sawyer done now?" I asked.

"Take a look yourself…"

I glanced past Wes and laughed when I saw Sawyer parading around in nothing more than a pair of boxers. "What is he doing?"

"Apparently, he wants to make sure all the girls here tonight know he was the one streaking, and he has to be half naked to do so."

"Really?"

"Yep."

I laughed again. "Are you sure you're both related?"

"I ask myself the same thing every day." He chuckled, but then his eyes grew serious as he looked down at the bench Anna,

Cress, and I were squished onto. A flicker of a smile pulled at his lips before he took me by the hands and pulled me up, swiftly maneuvering around me to steal my seat on the bench.

"Hey—" My complaint was barely free of my lips when he snaked his arms around me, guiding me back down and onto his lap. He didn't hesitate to cuddle me close.

"There, that's much better," he said.

I couldn't disagree. Especially not when his hand found its way under my jacket and his thumb drew small circles on the skin just by my hip. Yes, agreeing to date Wes was one of my better ideas, and given the way he was smiling at me, I got the feeling he was thinking the same thing.

"Ugh, you two are so cute together it makes me sick," Anna said.

"Same," Cress complained. "I need a guy to snuggle me by the bonfire."

Anna's eyes flicked across the crowd, and she smiled when her gaze returned to Cress. "I'm pretty sure there are plenty of guys here tonight who would be more than willing to snuggle you, Cress."

"I don't want to settle for just anyone. I'm not you, Anna."

Anna thumped Cress on the arm. "Wow, don't tell me you've bypassed dancing drunk and gone straight to bitchy drunk!"

Cress burst out laughing. "You should see your face. I was kidding."

Anna didn't look impressed. "Ninety percent, Cress. *Ninety percent.*"

"What do you think?" Wes murmured to me. "Is Cress kidding or being honest?"

I glanced between the two girls and laughed. "I think she might be being honest. She's had too many drinks to be joking."

Wes grinned at me. "I like it when you laugh."

"I like it when you smile at me like that."

"I'm beginning to think I liked it better when you weren't

dating," Anna interrupted. She was grinning brightly at us when I looked over. "Seriously, you're making me gag."

We laughed, and Wes hugged me a little tighter.

The three of us spent most of the evening cuddled up on the bench by the fire. I wasn't normally a big fan of parties, but this one was chill and definitely the kind of party I could get behind. I couldn't understand why Luther didn't throw parties like this more often. I could actually hear what my friends were saying, and I wasn't being forced to dance. It was a win-win.

"I'm going to go grab a drink of water. You want anything?" I said to Wes when Cress and Anna started a debate over which school from the regatta had the cutest guys. I was obviously team Weybridge, so I didn't have much to add to the discussion.

"Nah, I'm good," he said. "Want me to come with?"

I smiled and jumped from his lap. "I'm not going far. I've got this."

He gave me big, puppy-dog eyes, like he didn't want to be left in the middle of Anna and Cress's discussion.

"Stay warm by the fire." I laughed. "I'll be back in a minute."

I turned and headed over to the drinks table. There were huge tubs of drinks on the table and under it, but as I searched through them, I couldn't see anything other than alcohol.

"After anything in particular?"

I glanced up and found Luther at my side.

"Water or even just a soda. I'm overheating from being so close to the fire."

"Ah, yes, I'm guessing having an oversized yeti cuddling up to you doesn't help the situation either."

I tilted my head at him. "Wes isn't a yeti."

"I didn't say it was a bad thing." His lips teased a smile. "In fact, if it was snowing, it would probably be a great thing to be snuggled up to."

"Be nice, Luther."

He let out a sigh. "You're right. I'm sorry."

My eyebrows shot up. Was he actually apologizing?

"And I'm also sorry for being so hard on you in the library. I still think you and Noah belong together, but I guess I have no choice but to accept it's not going to happen."

If I thought I was surprised before, it was nothing compared to how I felt now. "Why the sudden change of heart?"

"I guess because you're finally starting to look happy again, and I know you wouldn't be if you were waiting for Noah," he said. "Plus, Noah might have pointed out to me that if he's had to accept it then so should I. I'm not going to stop hoping that somehow you find your way back to each other, but I can stop being a dick about it. Despite everything, we're friends. And friends shouldn't be dicks to each other."

"Thanks, I think."

He gave me a crooked smile and nodded to the drinks table. "I haven't seen any water or soda out here in a while, but there's always some in the storage shed."

"The storage shed?"

"You would have passed it on the way here tonight. It's just behind those trees." He pointed to the edge of the clearing and the path that led back to the house. I remembered seeing the shed and knew it wasn't far.

"You know, I'm pretty sure this is how most horror films begin," I said.

He chuckled. "Do you need an escort? I have a scarily girlish scream, so I can be the sacrificial maiden who gets caught while you escape if you like?"

I laughed. "As much as I'd love to hear this scream, I think I can make it alone."

"Suit yourself," he said. "But if you're not back in five minutes, I'll warn everyone at the party to run."

I laughed again. "Glad you've got your priorities straight."

I made my way to the edge of the clearing and started down the path that led through the forest beyond. The storage shed wasn't far from the party. The flickering glow from the bonfire could still be seen through the trees and the hum of music was only slightly dampened by the distance.

A soft light spilled out the open door as I approached. I walked into the room only to find a couple making out on top of the crates of drinks. The girl's top was open, and the guy's hands were roaming everywhere. I let out a surprised squeak as I darted backward, squeezing my eyes shut as I stumbled back into the night.

"Oh my gosh," I muttered as I tried to erase what I'd just seen from my mind.

A soft chuckle came from the darkness. "I probably should have warned you about them."

I turned to find Noah sitting against a tree opposite the storage shed.

"Noah, what are you doing out here?"

He slowly stood and took a sip of the beer he cradled in his hands. "Getting a bit of fresh air."

"Getting fresh air and listening to a couple of students making out?"

He shrugged again. "I was here first, and it's not like I can hear them over the noise of the party."

"Yeah, I guess you're right." I thankfully couldn't hear whatever was happening in the shed either.

I wondered how long Noah had been out here. I hadn't seen him all night. He appeared tired but not drunk. In fact, there was a clarity to his gaze I hadn't seen in weeks.

"Are you enjoying the party?" he asked.

"Ah, sure." It felt awkward talking to him this way, especially now that I was with Wes.

"You look like you're having fun."

I slowly nodded, not sure what to say. "I should probably head back."

He glanced toward the shed. "You're leaving empty-handed?"

"Oh, right, my water." I'd completely forgotten it, but I suddenly wasn't that thirsty. Not if it meant going back into the shed. "I'm sure I'll survive without it..."

One of the corners of his lips lifted, and he raised a finger, indicating for me to wait. "Give me a sec..." He turned and walked into the shed. "Knock, knock, coming through," he said loudly as he entered. I heard a girly squeal and some muffled voices, and then a moment later, Noah returned with a bottle of water in his hand.

"You didn't have to do that," I said as he passed it to me.

"You're welcome."

This whole conversation was too amicable, but I guessed this was our future now—polite conversations and both of us pretending that we hadn't once meant so much more to each other.

I gave him a tight smile and turned to leave, but Noah reached out and gently touched my elbow. The contact sent sparks across my skin and tugged at my gut. I stopped and turned to him, and he was standing far closer than before. I didn't want to have a reaction to him, but every cell in my body seemed to come alive at his proximity. Apparently, we could pretend all we wanted that we'd moved on, but my body was always going to betray me when he was near.

"Isobel..." he murmured. His eyes stared deeply into mine, making my heart drum wildly against the confines of my chest.

"Don't look at me that way."

"I'm not looking at you any way."

"You are, and you know it." I took a quick step away from him. "I'm with someone else now."

His throat bobbed as he swallowed. "You're right." He ran a hand through his hair, and he squeezed his eyes shut. It was almost like he wanted to pretend this wasn't real. When he opened his eyes again, they were empty of the charged emotions I'd seen moments before. It was almost like looking at a completely different person. I had no idea how he was so good at acting, but it made me wonder if he'd ever used these skills on me before.

"Was there a reason you stopped me?" I asked.

"I just..." He looked away. "I just wanted to say it's good to see you happy again."

I got the feeling he'd wanted to say something else, but I wasn't brave enough to push him for the truth.

"Anyway, I'm sure Wes is wondering where you are," he said.

His words were clearly meant to bring the conversation to an end, so I nodded. "Have a good night, Noah."

"You too, Isobel."

I walked away, but as I moved through the trees, I glanced over my shoulder at him. He was sitting on the ground again, staring up at the stars. Whatever act he'd been putting on when we were talking was gone, and there was a look of pain and longing on his face that reverberated in my chest. We were both supposed to be moving on, but why did I feel like Noah was still living in the past?

CHAPTER TWENTY-NINE

The week leading up to the Halloween carnival was chaotic. All the clubs and sports teams were in charge of different stands, and everyone in school was busy preparing for it. People were skipping classes to work on their booths, and nowhere in the school felt safe as people got in the Halloween spirit. The boys at Weybridge loved nothing more than jumping out from behind things to scare the girls, and I spent most of the week on edge.

The school itself transformed too. There were glowing jack-o'-lanterns in the gardens and spiderwebs dangling in the corridors with huge fake spiders crawling across them. The teachers decorated their classrooms, and some even came to class in costume and handed out sweets. I couldn't believe how much Weybridge Academy embraced Halloween.

"How's everything for your booth going?" I asked Cress as we made our way to lunch on Friday. It was only one more sleep until Halloween, which meant one more sleep until I saw my mom again. I was struggling to contain my excitement.

"Great," she said. "We're pretty much ready. I just have to

finalize the roster so everyone knows when they're manning the booth. Are you sure I can't convince you to volunteer?"

"Yeah, unfortunately not," I replied. "Wes is a pretty understanding boyfriend, but I think there are limits." It was hard to believe we'd only been dating a week. Already, everything about us felt so natural, and it was like we'd been together much longer. I think it was because we'd started out as friends.

"You're probably right," she said. "I can't imagine Wes happily sitting by and watching you kiss other guys. I wouldn't do the booth either if I had a choice. But since I'm the captain of the team I have to set a good example. Anna, on the other hand, can't wait. She was the first one to sign up, and she's not even on the dance team."

"Of course, she was." I laughed.

Someone slung an arm over my shoulder, and I looked up to find Wes grinning down at me. "Hey," he said, planting a kiss on my cheek.

I blushed as I smiled. I liked how comfortable I felt around him and how normal it felt to have him kiss me on the cheek.

"Hey to you too," I said. "Where have you been all morning?"

"I got a pass to skip class," he said. "Had to work on the crew contribution for tomorrow."

"I feel like I should already know this, but what are you guys doing?" Cress asked.

"We're in charge of the haunted house," he said. "It's going to be super spooky this year." He wiggled his free hand in the air to emphasize the point.

"I've never found haunted houses all that scary," I said.

"Well, this one will scare you for sure." Lowering his voice, he said, "Keep this just between us, but we've come up with the most terrifying ending to it. We've roped in Mr. Keech who's going to be telling everyone they failed their chemistry test."

Cress and I laughed.

"That is terrifying," I agreed.

"Yeah, I thought so," he said with a pleased look in his eyes.

"So, have you put any thought into a costume for tomorrow?" I asked.

"Well, Sawyer's pissed at me because I told him I was planning to go as Thor. He wants me to dress as the Goose to his Maverick."

"Of course, Sawyer thinks he's Maverick." I laughed.

"Yeah. He does have a slightly inflated ego."

"Just slightly," I agreed.

"And he loves to play on the fact we're twins when we dress up for Halloween. He thinks it helps him entice girls when we match." Wes rolled his eyes.

"That sounds like Sawyer," Cress said.

"How about the both of you? Got your costumes all planned out?"

"Yep." Cress grinned. "I'm heading down the Marvel path too and going as Black Widow."

"That's great," Wes replied. "You actually look a lot like her."

"Yeah, I thought it would be a good fit."

"How about you, Isobel?"

"My mom and I always dress up as zombie waitresses. She's bringing our costumes." A month ago, I might have been embarrassed to admit I was dressing up as a waitress because my mom and I always did it while working at her café. Especially after Veronica had shared pictures of me in my café uniform around school. I was surprised to find it didn't bother me at all, and not one part of me was ashamed of my background. I might not have grown up in a wealthy home like everyone else at school, but I'd had the best mom in the world, and that was worth more than money ever would be.

"Aw, how fun," Cress replied. "I'm so excited to meet her."

"Yeah, she can't wait to meet everyone too," I said. "I wish she could stay longer than one night, but she said she's going to try and get here more often."

"We're just going to have to make it the best day in Weybridge ever," Cress said.

"Definitely," I agreed.

The rest of the school day was pretty much a write-off. No one was concentrating in class, and the teachers weren't all that focused on schoolwork either.

BEFORE I KNEW IT, it was Saturday. Mom wasn't arriving in town until lunch and Halloween Fest didn't start until the evening, which meant I had no good reason for avoid my driving lesson that morning. I tried to convince Cress I was too sick to go, but she wasn't at all fooled by my pathetic attempts to avoid driving and happily shoved me out the door for my lesson.

I hoped I'd do slightly better this time around, but my lesson was just as pathetic as the last one, if not a little bit worse. The instructor had finally convinced me to pull out of the parking lot onto the open road, but I froze as soon as there were other cars near me. He took over and did most of the driving from then on.

My head was lowered as I returned to my dorm room. It was hard not to feel defeated when most people made driving look so easy. Even my instructor seemed surprised by how slow my progress was. I had a feeling I was the worst student he'd ever had.

I pushed open the door to my dorm room and gasped as my mom jumped out at me.

"Surprise!" she squealed.

All my gloomy driving thoughts completely disappeared as I dashed across the small gap between us and wrapped my arms around her.

"You're here!" I gasped. "I thought you weren't getting in for a couple more hours."

"I made better time than I expected and wanted to surprise you," she said.

"Well, you certainly did that. My heart is beating from my throat." I laughed before pulling out of the hug to look at her. Although she was beaming at me and her face was bright, there were bags under her eyes and she looked tired from her journey. She was wearing her usual long cardigan and fitted jeans, but they hung a little loose on her like she'd lost a bit of weight. I hoped it wasn't anything to do with how hard she was working at the café or how stressed out she was.

Over her shoulder, I could see Cress lingering in the background, a huge smile on her face.

"I see you've met Cress," I said.

Mom grinned as she glanced at my roommate. "Yes, she's been telling me all about her kiss or scare booth," she said. "It sounds like it will be hilarious."

The idea had developed quite a lot since we came up with it. Now, anyone who bought a ticket for the booth would be blindfolded, and they'd either be kissed by whoever was manning the booth or have something strange pressed up against their lips to scare them. The girls had found all kinds of funny things for people to kiss. There was candy floss, cupcakes and other strange feeling foods, but then someone had also managed to commandeer a bunny, some mice, and a pet iguana.

"I hope so," Cress said. "And your mom said she would have been totally keen to volunteer for the booth. Didn't you, Ms. Grace?"

"*Mom*," I groaned, giving her a slight shove.

"What?" she asked. "I like kissing as much as anyone."

"Would you like me to die of embarrassment?"

"I can think of worse ways to go" She shrugged.

I felt like Norma had been a bad influence on my mom while I'd been gone.

"How was your driving lesson?" Cress asked.

"Terrible. I'm this close to quitting." I held up my hand and showed her about a centimeter gap between my fingers.

"Don't give up," my mom said. "I think you'll find it will suddenly click one day and you'll forget it was ever hard in the first place. You just need to keep practicing."

"Well, do you want to come practice with me?"

"I think I'll pass. I love you, Iz, but I don't need that kind of trauma before my morning coffee."

"Fair," I said with a laugh. "I guess you can be glad that at least Matthew's paying someone else to risk their life with me then."

"Yes, of everything he's done for you, that's one of the things I'm most grateful for."

I shook my head. "Have you been to Matthew's place yet?"

I'd told him my mom was visiting and invited him to come to the carnival too. He'd said he couldn't get away from work for the weekend, but he'd insisted Mom stay at his place tonight. She'd been reluctant to accept the offer, but I'd convinced her it would be a waste of money to get a motel when the house was just sitting empty.

"Not yet. I came straight here because I wanted to see you first."

"How about we go there now so you can drop your bags and freshen up. Then we can grab some food and still have time to get ready for the carnival?"

"That sounds great," Mom said. "I could really use a shower. I drove through the night, and I'm feeling a little grimy." She turned and gave Cress a smile. "It was lovely to meet you, Cress."

"You too, Ms. Grace. I'll see you at the carnival tonight."

"I'm looking forward to it."

Mom and I left the dorm and strolled through the school grounds to return to her car.

"I like Cress," Mom said as we walked. "She seems like a good friend for you."

"She is. I'm lucky I ended up with her as my roommate."

"And this school," Mom continued. "I can't believe you attend a place like this. It's incredibly gorgeous."

"Yeah, it's pretty nice," I agreed. "But you know I'd still prefer to be at home with you."

Mom waved my comment away. "That's just crazy talk. I can see how much you like it here. And I love seeing you so happy."

"I mean, I'm just extra happy today because you're here."

"Well, obviously." Mom laughed. "But you seem to have really settled in here. Even before your falling out with your girlfriends back home, they were always making you feel like you weren't good enough, and I can tell the friends you've made here are supportive and kind."

I couldn't argue with that. I was surprised because, when I thought about it, Weybridge was starting to feel like a second home. And as much as I missed my mom, I wasn't homesick for Rapid Bay the way I was when I'd first arrived here.

"So, when do I get to meet Wes?" Mom asked. She looked around like he might magically pop out of the bushes. I'd told her all about us dating earlier in the week. At first, she seemed a bit worried about me moving on from Noah so soon, but I think the fact that Wes had already been such a good friend to me helped win her over. Now she couldn't wait to meet him.

"He'll be at the carnival," I said. "He's over there helping set up this morning; otherwise, he would have been around to meet you."

"Will Sawyer and Anna be there tonight too?"

"Yep, the whole school turns out for this thing. You'll get to meet all my friends then."

"If they're anything like Cress, I'm sure I'm going to love them."

I laughed because Cress was, without a doubt, the most parent-pleasing one of my friends. Although, I bet Wes would be just as charming. Anna and Sawyer, however, were much more unpredictable. "We'll see," I said. "So, how was your drive out here?"

"Long," Mom replied. "It probably would have been easier to take the bus. Perhaps next time I'll consider it."

"So, the drive hasn't put you off coming back?"

"Not at all." Mom smiled.

"And how do you feel about leaving the café with Norma?"

Mom blew out a breath. "I'm not good at handing over control, but it's worth it to spend some time with you."

It meant so much to me she'd made the effort to come visit me. She always went above and beyond for me, even when her work consumed so much of her time. It was no wonder I hadn't grown up wondering where my father was. Mom had been better than two parents ever could be.

"But, let's not talk about Rapid Bay," Mom said as we arrived at her car. It looked completely out of place in the school parking lot, which was filled with high-end, expensive vehicles, but I didn't care one bit. Mom smiled. "This weekend is all about enjoying ourselves and spending time together. I want to get a small peek into your life here."

"Yeah, of course," I said.

"Now, I must admit, I'm starving. Maybe we should grab some lunch before we go to your father's place? Do you know anywhere good?

"You ask that like I haven't been raving about the burgers here ever since I arrived." I laughed. "Come on, I'll direct you where to go."

CHAPTER THIRTY

Just one lunch at Toddy's Burgers was enough to turn my mom into a fan. She normally didn't like burgers that much, but apparently, we'd found the exception to the rule, and the two of us stuffed our faces with so much food that we pretty much rolled our way back to her car.

She also loved the town of Weybridge. She kept gushing over how quaint it was and would let out an "ooh" or an "ahh" whenever we passed one of the cute little shops that lined the main street. It was probably a good thing she needed a shower, or I doubt I could have pulled her away.

When we arrived at Matthew's home, her gushing came to a stop, and she went suspiciously quiet. Her eyes had slowly been growing wider as we'd driven up the long driveway that led to the house, and her lower lip dropped slightly as she parked in front of the mansion. I could tell she was truly surprised by the size of it. It was one thing to know Matthew had money but another thing to see the evidence of it in the flesh.

"I'm not so sure this is a good idea," Mom said as she turned the car engine off.

"What do you mean?"

"I know Matthew insisted I stay here, but it feels weird," she said. "Maybe I'd be better off in a motel tonight."

I glanced up at the huge house towering over us. It was such a world away from our place back home. It felt like stepping into a whole different universe. From the way my mom was staring at the place, she felt exactly like I did when I first came here—like she didn't belong and like she wasn't good enough.

"Do you think I should text him and tell him I'll stay somewhere else?" Mom asked. "He's not here, so it's not like he's expecting us…"

My chest tightened as I glanced at the house once more. "Uh, I wouldn't speak too soon," I said, nodding toward the front door.

Mom looked over and gasped as she saw Matthew emerge from the building.

"He's here?" she squeaked as she finally found her voice. "What is he doing here? He said he wasn't going to be in town."

"I don't know." He hadn't said anything to me either. "He told me he couldn't make it and we'd have the place to ourselves."

Mom grabbed hold of my arm, jerking my attention back to her. "How do I look?"

I let out a soft laugh at the worry in her voice. "Mom, you look beautiful, just like always."

"I haven't showered this morning," she said. "I haven't even brushed my teeth! I knew I should have done it at the gas station on the way here."

She was officially freaking out, and I lightly grasped her hand. "Mom, it's okay. Like I said, you look beautiful. It's just Matthew, there's no need to freak out."

She slowly nodded, but I could see my words weren't exactly helping.

"Why are you so nervous?" I asked.

"Because I haven't seen him in seventeen years…" She glanced out the car window again. "He's still incredibly handsome, isn't he?"

"Ew, Mom."

She laughed, and the sound seemed to shake the fog of anxiety that had been covering her. "I guess we better go say hello."

"Yeah, he's going think something's wrong if we stay in the car much longer."

Mom pulled her keys from the ignition but hesitated before she opened the car door. "One more thing." She turned to me. "Do I smell like a cheeseburger?"

I laughed and leaned over so I could give her a sniff. "No, you smell just like your perfume." She'd been wearing the same one since I was a little girl and always smelled of roses with a hint of vanilla.

"You're not just saying that?"

"Mom, stop worrying. It's going to be fine." I shook my head and opened the door. I had a feeling she'd keep stalling if I let her, and then Matthew really would think something was up.

Mom slowly exited the car after me. She was usually so confident, but right now she was a nervous wreck. I wasn't sure why she was freaking out so much. She'd talked on the phone with Matthew several times over the last few weeks.

"Hey, Matthew," I said as I approached my father. We still weren't at the point where we hugged each other or gave each other kisses in greeting. Seeing as he was usually so formal, I wasn't sure if we'd ever get to that point.

"Isobel, it's lovely to see you," he said. He was smiling, but I thought I could see the corners of his lips twitching slightly like he was nervous too. He turned to look at my mom.

"Candice," he said.

"Matthew," she replied.

The two of them stood there staring at each other for an inappropriately long amount of time. They almost seemed to be drinking each other in. Marking every line and scar that had marred their features in the time they'd been apart.

Matthew was the first to realize he'd been staring too long and jerked his gaze away from her. He gestured into the house. "Won't you come inside?"

"I just have to grab my bags," Mom said, glancing at the car.

Matthew shook his head. "I'll have someone see to that. Please come in."

"Oh, ah, okay," Mom replied.

We followed him into the house, and Mom was still struggling with the surprise of seeing Matthew here. She didn't even seem to notice how ridiculously opulent his home was. I doubted she noticed anything other than my father right now. Seeing him after all these years apart had to be weird for her.

"I thought you said you weren't going to be here this weekend," Mom said as we followed Matthew up the grand entrance staircase.

"I had a meeting cancel on me last minute," he replied. "I didn't intend to crash your girls' weekend, but there were some maintenance issues I needed to oversee here at the house. I'll stay out of your way as much as possible."

I couldn't stop my eyebrows from lifting. Matthew had Caldwell to deal with stuff like that. I doubted my father had ever overseen a maintenance issue in his life. I had a sneaking suspicion he was here because he wanted to see my mom.

"Don't be silly. We don't expect you to stay out of our way," Mom said before slowly glancing at me. "Does that mean you'll be joining us at the Halloween carnival tonight?"

I was surprised my mom had jumped at the opportunity to remind Matthew of our invite. I had asked him earlier in the week but hadn't expected him to be here.

"If that's still okay with you both," Matthew replied, "I would love to."

"Of course," I said. "Though be warned, Mom takes Halloween very seriously. You'll be lucky to escape without some kind of paint on you."

Matthew laughed. The sound was easy and light and so unlike him. "I'm sure I can handle a little paint."

Mom's face lit up with a smile. "Well, it's settled then. We'll go together."

Matthew nodded, returning my mom's smile. He then gestured toward an open door we'd arrived at. "I've had this room prepared for your stay," he said. "If it's not to your liking, I can find you another..."

"I'm sure it's perfect," Mom said.

"It's right next to yours, Isobel," he added. "I've had your room made up so you can stay here tonight as well if you like."

"Oh, that is a nice idea." My mom clapped her hands together. "What do you think, Iz?"

"Yeah, that sounds great. Thanks, Matthew." Neither of them seemed to be listening though. They were staring at each other again. This time, it was my mom who realized the silence had gone on a little too long, and she cleared her throat.

"Yes, thank you so much, Matthew," she said.

"Of course," he replied, shifting slightly awkwardly as he broke eye contact with my mom. "Well, I will leave you to settle in. Caldwell is around, and I'll be in my office if you need anything. I'm sure Isobel can show you the way."

Mom shared a smile with him before he turned to leave. Once he was out of sight, she came to her senses enough to turn and focus on the bedroom.

"Isn't this nice," she said, walking into the room. "There's a view of the gardens. Oh, and it even has its own bathroom."

I gently bumped my shoulder against my mom's. "What was that back there?"

"What was what?" She batted her eyelashes innocently.

"You acting all nervous around Matthew and then checking if he was coming to the carnival."

"I was just being nice," Mom said.

I felt like it had been more than that, and my suspicions must have shown in my eyes.

"What?" Mom asked. "He's your father, and he's being so hospitable to me. It would be rude not to invite him to go with us."

"You couldn't take your eyes off him."

Mom tucked a strand of hair behind her ear. "Only because it's been such a long time since I've seen him. You're reading into things far too much."

"Uh-huh."

She waved me off. "I'm going to take a shower. Hopefully, when I'm done, you'll be over all this silliness."

"If it's just silliness, then why are you blushing so much?"

"I'm not blushing," she said, but she flicked her eyes to the mirror to double-check.

"Sure, you're not."

"I'm just warm. It's a warm day."

It wasn't even close to being a warm day. It was the middle of autumn.

"Why don't you focus less on feeding your imagination and more on thinking up fun activities for our afternoon," Mom said. She disappeared into the bathroom before I had a chance to argue with her.

MATTHEW WAS true to his word and stayed out of our way for the rest of the day, but we spent most of the time in town rather than at the house. Mom loved little trinkets and knick-knacks, so we spent a while trawling through the eclectic antique store, and then we wandered through town taking in the gorgeous Halloween displays in the shop windows. We found a cute café that served incredible hot chocolates and amazing blueberry muffins, and I knew I was going to have to bring Cress and Anna back there soon.

Mostly, I just enjoyed hanging out with my mom. It had been far too long since the two of us had done anything together, and I hadn't realized quite how much I missed it.

We returned to Matthew's place late in the afternoon to start getting ready for the carnival. We dressed up in our bloodied and torn waitress uniforms and were about to start on our zombie makeup when I received a text from Cress.

"Cress is freaking out about her booth," I said to Mom, looking up from my phone. "She needs my help. Do you mind if I meet you at the carnival?"

"Of course, that's no problem," Mom said. "Though you don't look very scary without your makeup…"

I glanced in the mirror and shrugged. "I guess I'll have to be a zombie waitress that only just died."

"I suppose that works." Mom laughed. "Do you need a ride?"

I shook my head. "No, thanks. Cress says she's already sent the cavalry to come pick me up. It's probably Anna."

Mom walked me down to the front entrance. When we stepped outside, I was surprised to find Anna hadn't come to pick me up. Instead, Wes was pulling up the driveway in his Range Rover.

"Looks like you'll get to meet Wes sooner than the carnival," I said, and my mom smiled. My stomach swirled with nerves because I really wanted her to like him.

He parked the car and jumped out when he saw my mom at my side. He was already dressed in his Thor outfit, looking far too tempting to be meeting one of my parents.

"You're the cavalry?" I asked as Wes came around the front of his car.

"Apparently." He smiled brightly before walking straight over to my mom and holding out his hand. "Ms. Grace, it's a pleasure to finally meet you."

"You too, Wes," she said as she took his hand.

"How was your trip?" he asked.

"Long, but it was worth it to be here." She looked his costume up and down as he stepped back from her. "And what are you dressed as?"

"Thor." He grinned. "Really, I just wanted an excuse to walk around with a big hammer."

Mom laughed. "Well, it's very convincing."

"Thanks. I like your costume too, but Isobel mentioned you go all out with your makeup, so I'll reserve judgment until I see you later."

"Just you wait, I'm going to be terrifying," Mom said, making Wes chuckle.

"Well, now I can't wait to see it."

They chatted so easily. I should have known my mom and Wes would get along right away. Wes was so sweet; he was impossible not to like.

"We should get going," I said. "Cress sounded really stressed in her text."

Wes nodded. "I'll see you tonight, Ms. Grace. I'll do my best not to scream when I see you."

Mom beamed in response. "I'd be offended if you didn't."

Wes grinned before he started over to his car while I turned to Mom.

"He seems sweet," she said, lowering her voice so she wouldn't be overheard. "And he's very good-looking. I like him."

"I do too," I whispered with a grin. "Are you going to be okay here on your own?"

"I'll be fine," she said. "Besides, I'm not on my own. Matthew is around. I'll text you when we arrive at the carnival later."

I lifted my eyebrows. "You don't mind going to the carnival with Matthew?"

"You're fussing like a momma duck." She waved my concern away. "Stop your worrying and run along. I'll see you in a bit."

"Okay. I'll see you soon."

I got into Wes's car, and he grinned as my mom waved us off. "I like your mom."

"She seems to like you too."

"I mean, I'm the god of thunder, how could she not?"

I rolled my eyes at him.

"By the way, you're not a very scary zombie waitress," he said as he looked me over.

"That's near-dead zombie waitress to you, and I'm clearly terrifying."

"Clearly." He laughed.

"I didn't have time to do my zombie makeup," I explained. "You're not very scary either, you know."

"That's because my hammer's in the trunk."

"Because a hammer will make all the difference."

"It will!" he insisted.

If I were being honest, I wasn't too concerned about how scary he looked. I was too distracted by how hot he looked wearing the molded silver armor that was strapped to his chest. Wes could have easily been mistaken for a long-lost Hemsworth brother, and the effect was a little overwhelming. He even had a wig to lengthen his hair, and it was impressively realistic.

"What did Sawyer think of your outfit? Is he still pissed you wouldn't be Goose?"

"No, not so much. He came up with a whole other outfit."

"And..."

Wes struggled to withhold a laugh. "Just wait and see. I couldn't possibly ruin the surprise."

"Okay..." I was officially intrigued. "So, any idea what's got Cress so upset? She didn't say much in her text to me."

"I'm not sure. She called me and told me to come get you. She sounded stressed and hung up before I got a chance to ask her what was wrong."

"I hope everything's okay."

"I'm sure it's fine. You know Cress. She's probably worried there aren't enough fairy lights or something."

"Yeah, probably," I agreed.

We arrived at the farm that was hosting Halloween Fest, and my eyes widened as I got my first look at the event. It was insane. We passed a huge hedge maze and some kind of jack-o'-lantern village covered in glowing pumpkins. There was an ice rink splattered in fake blood and a whole field dedicated to zombie laser tag. There were carnival rides and games, but the best part was the huge spooky barn in the center of it all. Wes said that was where they were hosting the haunted house, and it definitely looked the part. It was completely covered in spiderwebs, and given how dilapidated it looked, I wouldn't have been at all surprised if there were rumors of real ghosts inside.

After we parked the car, we headed straight to where the dance team's booth was being set up. Cress was pacing back and forth in front of it. She was already dressed up in her Black Widow costume, the fitted black one-piece suit hugging tightly to her body.

"Finally, you're here," she gasped when she saw us walking up. "It's a disaster."

"What is?"

Cress gestured toward her kiss or scare booth, and I could immediately see what she meant. Someone had sabotaged the booth by painting the word "French" in front of "kiss."

"Oh no. Who would do that?"

"I don't want to name names, but I'm guessing it was the cheerleaders," Cress said. "I've heard a few of them complaining about all the fun changes we've made to the kissing booth this year and how boring their stand is going to be in comparison. Clearly, they're jealous and want us to get shut down, because as soon as a teacher sees this, we're done for. What am I going to do?"

I bit down on my lip as I considered the booth again. "Can't you just paint over it?" I asked.

"Yeah, I was going to, but we've run out of the pink paint we used, and the hardware shop is closed already."

"Well, I think it's a great addition," Anna said, coming out from behind the booth. She was dressed as Jessica Rabbit and wore a long red bustier dress with elbow-length purple gloves and a red wig. She looked incredible. "I reckon we'll double the money we make from that one little addition alone."

"Anna, I can't ask anyone to French kiss strangers," Cress scoffed. "And like I said, the school will lose their shit. This is supposed to be a family-friendly event."

Anna sighed. "Spoilsports."

"So, what should I do?" Cress asked, looking between us.

I had absolutely no clue. Thankfully, Wes seemed more optimistic.

"I have an idea," he said, already backing away. "I just have to go find Sawyer."

"And..." Cress prompted.

"And he should be around; he was helping set up the soccer booth. It shouldn't take me more than five minutes to find him." He turned and started jogging deeper into the fair.

"I meant what happens when you find him!" she called after Wes, but he waved a hand over his shoulder and continued on without a look back. "He couldn't explain what he was thinking before he ran off?" Cress moaned as she watched him run, his red cape flying out behind him.

"I'm sure he'll be back soon," I replied.

That didn't seem to ease Cress's worrying, and she spent every moment Wes was gone fretting. Luckily, he didn't take too long, and five minutes later, he came hurrying back with a bag slung over his shoulder. He was closely followed by a huge man I didn't recognize. As the two of them drew near, I realized the guy in question was Sawyer. I burst out laughing, and Sawyer grinned in response.

"See? That's the kind of reaction I was after," he said, nudging Wes as they came to stand before us. He was wearing checked pajama bottoms, a sweatshirt, bathrobe, and Crocs. He even had a fake belly peeking out of the gap under his shirt. With the long blond wig and scraggily beard, he looked like such a mess it had taken me a moment to realize what he was dressed as. It was the hammer that gave it away. Sawyer hadn't been able to let go of the idea of having a costume that matched his brother's.

"Sawyer, did you dress as fat Thor?" Anna asked, laughing as she finally figured it out.

"Oh my God, Anna. Are you body-shaming me?" Sawyer sounded shocked, but he had a wide grin on his face. "But, yes, I did. And, for your information, I prefer to be referred to as out-of-shape Thor. So, what do you guys think?"

"I'm just wondering why on earth you would dress like that?" Anna asked, still laughing.

"So Wes and I match. It's always a great way to get the ladies."

"You think a beer belly is going to entice the ladies?" Anna asked.

Sawyer looked slightly crestfallen at this. "I just wanted us to match," he grumbled.

"And you didn't think of perhaps dressing up like Loki?" Anna asked. "You would have matched, *and* you would have been the god of mischief."

Sawyer looked like he wanted to throw his hammer across the field. "Damn, I should have thought of that! I was too busy trying to figure out how I could have a hammer too. That would have been brilliant though."

"Yeah, no girl is going to buy a ticket to our kissing booth to kiss you when you've got a beer belly peeking out from under your shirt," Cress agreed, shaking her head. "But, that's the least of our worries right now. What have you got planned?" she said, turning to Wes.

Wes lowered the bag he was holding to the ground to reveal a variety of different colored spray cans. "I know you didn't want to repaint the sign, but if you're up for something different, I was thinking you could do a graffiti sign like the soccer team has done for their booth. Sawyer managed to make theirs look quite good, so I was thinking he could fix yours."

Cress frowned at Sawyer. "You're moonlighting as a graffiti artist now?"

"I did a street art course in London last year."

"Really?" Cress asked. "How did I not know about this?"

"It was just a bit of fun." He struggled to meet her gaze, and I got the feeling it had meant more than that to him. "And you know I take art."

"We figured you either wanted an easy class or were trying to meet girls," Anna said. "We didn't realize you were actually into it."

Cress waved her hands to silence everyone. "That doesn't matter now. Can you fix the sign?"

Sawyer looked up at the booth and nodded. "Yeah, but I'll have to redo the whole thing. You cool with that?"

"As long as it no longer says French kiss, I'm cool with anything."

Sawyer nodded and grabbed the spray cans before he got to work. It was somewhat comical to watch Sawyer painting the sign while dressed in his costume. He looked like some kind of vagrant with his oily hair and baggy clothes. It was probably lucky we were all there watching, or I imagined someone would have tried to stop him and escorted him from the property.

Cress was tapping her hand against her arm, watching on nervously. I could see she was worried Sawyer was going to mess it up, but I had faith he'd do a good job. There was no way Wes would have suggested it otherwise. As he worked, she slowly started to relax, and I could see she was beginning to trust that he knew what he was doing.

In what felt like no time at all, Sawyer had completely transformed the hot pink sign with an edgy street art design.

"Uh, Sawyer, you're like insanely good," Anna said.

"Yeah," I agreed. "You're going to need to show us pictures of the work you did on your course. This is amazing."

"Thank you, thank you, thank you!" Cress said, pulling Sawyer into a hug.

He laughed and tried to shrug her off. "It's no big deal."

"It's a huge deal," Cress replied. "You saved the day."

"I mean, I think it would have been fine to hand out French kisses," Sawyer said. "But I'm happy I could help."

"And just in the nick of time," Wes said, glancing over his shoulder toward the entrance to the carnival. "It looks like we're about to open."

"Shoot, you're right," Cress said. "We better get ready."

"And I better get to the haunted house." Wes turned to me. "I'll catch you later." He planted a kiss against my cheek before running off. I smiled as I watched him go.

Sawyer threw an arm over my shoulder, watching Wes with me. "You're one very lucky girl, sis. My brother's no fat Thor, but he's a total catch."

I rolled my eyes but smiled. "He certainly is."

He lowered his arm from over my shoulder as Wes disappeared from view. "He really likes you," he said, turning to me. "Please don't break his heart."

It was the most serious I'd ever seen Sawyer, and I shook my head. "I don't plan to."

He stared into my eyes, weighing my response, before he finally nodded. "Good. After what happened with Sarah, I just want him to be happy. I'm just a bit worried because you were so into Noah. What if he decides he wants you back?"

"That's never going to happen," I said. "Noah and I are over for good, trust me. And I want Wes to be happy too. I never would have agreed to date him if I wasn't serious about him."

"I'm glad to hear it," Sawyer said. He let out a sigh as people started filtering into the carnival. "I better get back to the soccer booth. Wish me luck."

"What am I wishing you luck for? What is the soccer booth?"

"You'll have to come check it out for yourself," he said with a grin.

As he walked away, I considered what he'd said about Wes. Sawyer was worried for no reason. I really liked Wes, and I couldn't see anything changing that. He definitely didn't need to be worrying about Noah. He would never change his mind about us. And, more importantly, I felt like I was finally done with him too.

CHAPTER THIRTY-ONE

Matthew and my mom were running late. I was waiting at the carnival entrance for them, and when they finally arrived, they were looking far too chummy for my liking. Mom was giggling at something Matthew had said. *Giggling*. And she'd somehow managed to convince him to let her apply a little fake blood to his cheek and to loosen his tie. It was all too weird.

"Isobel, there you are," Mom said, smiling brightly at me. She hadn't applied her usual zombie makeup. Instead, she'd gone light on the face paint and seemed to be aiming for more of a sexy waitress. I had a feeling it was because Matthew was here.

"Hey, you guys. So, we've got a sexy—sorry, I mean—*zombie* waitress..." Mom shot me a scowl, but I happily ignored her. "And a..." I turned to my father, and my mouth puckered as I tried to guess what he was. "Can you give me a clue?"

"Apparently, I'm a zombie businessman," he replied.

He said it so seriously I laughed. "Yeah, I guess I can see that."

Matthew smiled, but his face turned serious again when he caught sight of someone beyond me. "If you will both excuse me for a moment, I see August Montfort. I've been meaning to have a quick word with him."

He must have been talking about Sawyer and Wes's dad. I hadn't told Matthew that Wes and I were dating, but given the way he managed to keep tabs on everything that was happening at school, he'd probably found out somehow. Still, I hoped he was planning to talk to Wes's dad about business or something completely unrelated to me dating his son. I'd already experienced more than enough drama when it came to meeting my boyfriend's family, and I wasn't so keen to repeat it.

"Go ahead," Mom said.

I watched Matthew walk over to a man who was about his age. I could immediately see the similarity he shared with the twins. He had the same blond hair and a similar build to both boys, but he clearly didn't hit the gym as much as they did. Matthew smiled brightly as he shook the man's hand. There definitely wasn't any rift between my father and Wes's family—thank goodness.

"So, did you help Cress avoid her crisis?" Mom asked.

"I really just offered moral support," I said. "It was actually Sawyer who saved the day."

"That's Wes's twin brother, right? The cheeky one."

"That's him." I smiled. Though he hadn't been quite so cheeky when I'd last seen him. He'd been surprisingly thoughtful and honest as he'd questioned me about Wes. Although it was unlike Sawyer, I didn't take offense. If anything, it warmed my heart to know he cared so much for his brother.

When Matthew returned from chatting with Mr. Montfort, I was relieved he didn't come back with any warnings about dating Wes. Perhaps he didn't know we were together. Or maybe he knew and was fine with it. I definitely wasn't going to bring it up voluntarily. Ignorance was bliss, and I didn't want another relationship ruined because of my father's family name.

The carnival was already crowded with people as we entered. Locals from the town, kids from school, and their families and friends had all come out for the occasion. I was impressed by the elaborate costumes everyone wore and surprised to find so many of the parents had dressed up too.

There was something so enchanting about Halloween, and the carnival didn't disappoint with the spooky atmosphere it created. The sound of rides and squeals of delight rang through the air, and when we walked past a fortune-telling tent, I heard a witch-like cackle from within. Everyone had gone to so much effort, and if my mom was only going to attend one school event this year, I was glad it was this one.

We bumped into Lily and her roommate Amber not far from the entrance. The two girls were dressed as hippies, and their outfits looked more appropriate for Coachella than Halloween. Mom gushed over how cute they looked and insisted they join us for food. I was somewhat glad for the company because my mom and Matthew were so busy chatting that, without my friends there, I was sure I'd have felt like a third wheel.

"I hear the haunted house is amazing this year," Lily said as we munched on corndogs Matthew had bought us.

"The haunted house?" Amber scoffed. "It's nothing compared to the soccer team's booth. I'll probably spend most of my night standing there drooling."

"What are they doing?" I asked.

"They have a dunking booth," Amber said. "Which means shirtless soccer players. Need I say more?"

"Probably not." I laughed. "I'm surprised Sawyer hasn't been bragging about it all week. He loves attention, and I imagine he'd love nothing more than to show off his abs."

"I mean, have you seen his abs? I'd want to show them off too if I were him," Amber gushed. "We should go check it out after we finish these corndogs."

I glanced at Mom and Matthew. She was laughing again at something he'd said. The two of them were in their own little world. She'd practically forgotten I was here, but I wasn't annoyed. Mom rarely took time off work to relax or socialize, and I liked seeing her so happy. It was nice to see her getting along so well with Matthew. They were both going to be a part of my life now, and it could only be a good thing if they were on friendly terms.

"Hey, Mom," I said. "I'm going to go visit a few booths with the girls. Do you mind if I catch up with you guys later?" I'd considered asking Mom and Matthew to join us, but after all the girls' talk of checking out shirtless soccer players, I wasn't sure it was an experience I particularly wanted to share with my parents. Besides, they looked so content spending time together, and I wouldn't be gone for long. We had the rest of the evening to explore the carnival together.

Mom smiled and shook her head. "That's totally fine, Iz. You have fun with your friends."

"I will." I flashed her and Matthew a smile before I walked off with Lily and Amber.

"Your mom and dad are so nice," Lily said once we were out of earshot. "I thought you said they hadn't seen each other since before you were born?"

"They haven't," I replied. "But they do seem pretty relaxed around each other."

"Definitely," Lily agreed. "I never would have guessed they weren't a couple or at the very least close friends."

"And they look so cute together," Amber added. "Are you thinking of trying to parent trap them?"

"That's the last thing on my mind. They're very different people with very different lives. I don't think they'd work out, even if they were interested in each other that way."

"That's a shame," Lily said.

I shrugged as though I didn't care either way, but that wasn't really true. Until now, I hadn't really thought much about my parents' relationship and what it would be like when they saw each other again. Now that they were reunited, it was clear there was something between them. The slight glow of an ember from a fire that burned out long ago. I wondered if they had noticed it too. Even if they had, there was no denying I was right about them being different people from different worlds. Surely it couldn't work, could it?

"Oh, is that the kissing booth?" Amber asked, saving me from my thoughts. I looked up as we rounded a corner and saw Cress's booth up ahead. It looked amazing, and Sawyer's sign was even more impressive when it was lit up at night.

"Yep, that's it. Though they've called it a kiss or scare booth," I said. "It's pretty much a game of chance. You don't know if you're getting a kiss or something else."

"Oh, sounds fun," Amber replied. "We should give it a go, Lil."

"Maybe later," Lily said, refusing to meet Amber's gaze. I didn't blame her for being hesitant. Lots of people were standing around watching, and they burst into cheers and laughter when the blindfolded contestant spun the wheel and it landed on scare.

Cress was manning the booth, and she grinned as she pulled a guinea pig from a cage behind her and offered it out to the poor unsuspecting victim to kiss. The guy leaned forward and then flinched away when his lips brushed against fur. He pulled the blindfold off and burst out laughing when he saw what Cress was holding.

"Oh my gosh, is that Kaden?" Amber said. "Surely, he doesn't need a kissing booth to get a girl to kiss him?"

Amber was right. I hadn't recognized Kaden with the blindfold on. I smiled as I watched him talking with Cress. They were laughing nervously as Cress returned the guinea pig to its cage and Kaden pulled out another ticket. As he handed it to Cress, I swear I could see his hand shaking slightly, and her cheeks flushed prettily in response. She nodded toward the blindfold, but Kaden shook his head. Instead, he reached over and took her hand, placing a gentle kiss across the back of it. Cress almost fainted.

Kaden gave her one last smile before he got up from his seat and left the booth. Cress was frozen, her mouth hanging slightly open in shock as she watched Kaden walk away. Then she shook her head and got up from her seat before the next person in line could sit down. She beckoned to Anna to take her spot, and Anna happily obliged.

Cress was pacing back and forth at the side of the booth as we walked over to her.

"Oh my gosh, Isobel, did you see that?" she said as we approached. "Kaden just kissed my hand. He kissed it!"

She usually tried her best to act like she didn't have a crush on Kaden, but she was totally failing right now.

"Yeah, we saw," I said with a grin.

"And he's asked me to meet him at the Ferris wheel," she said. "I think I'm going to faint."

"You're not going to faint." I laughed. "But you should probably take a few deep breaths."

She nodded and slowly dragged a breath in before easing it back out.

"Better?" I asked.

"Not even close."

"When are you meeting him?"

"In, like, five minutes."

"You should probably get going then."

She nodded but didn't move. I think she was still in shock.

"Do you want us to walk you there?" Lily asked.

"No, I'm good." Cress shook her head. "I guess I better head over there. Wish me luck."

"Good luck." I gave her arm a squeeze, and she smiled at me before heading off in the direction of the Ferris wheel.

The sound of raised voices caused me to turn back to the kiss or scare booth. Anna was standing behind her seat with her arms crossed over her chest. She was glaring at Luther, who sat opposite her.

"You can't buy all the tickets, Luther," she complained. "That's not how it works."

"I'm just doing my part to help the fundraiser," he said, grinning at her. "Just like you're doing yours."

"You don't actually want to kiss me. Let alone twenty times or however many tickets you just bought," Anna said. "You're just doing this to mess with me, and it's not very funny."

"I would never," he said.

"Fine. Put the blindfold on, and get ready for a scare because you better believe I'm going to find a toad for you to kiss."

"I'm not afraid to kiss a few toads." Luther smirked and lowered the blindfold over his eyes. He spun the wheel, and Anna breathed a visible sigh of relief when it landed on scare. Despite her promise to make him kiss a toad, Anna reached down into a box at her side and produced a bunny for him to kiss. Luther spun the wheel once more, and when it landed on scare again, Anna made him kiss a snakeskin handbag. By some miracle, Luther's third spin also landed on scare, and Anna held a chocolate doughnut to his lips.

Luther didn't complain once and simply smiled brightly after every unexpected kiss he experienced. He was actually enjoying it. "Mmm, fluffy," he said after kissing the rabbit, and after the doughnut, I heard him moan dramatically, "Anna, your lips are so soft and sweet."

Luther's enthusiasm was only frustrating Anna more and more with each turn. She looked like she was ready to get the toad out if Luther spun the wheel and landed on scare for a fourth time.

However, on Luther's fourth spin, the wheel finally landed on kiss. Anna scrunched her face up with disgust. She glanced around like she was searching for a way out, but she must have realized there was no escape. After one last grimace, she leaned over to Luther and gave him the quickest peck on the lips I'd ever seen. If there was a contest for speed kissing, she'd just won it.

"That was hardly a kiss," Luther said, pulling the blindfold up to look at her.

"Well, you can take that up with management because I'm done." Anna lifted her arms before storming away. She headed straight over to us, her cheeks flaming red.

"Oh my gosh, you guys saw that?" she said.

"It was hard not to," I replied. "You two weren't exactly subtle."

"Ugh, because Luther is so ridiculous. Can you believe him? He bought every ticket for my shift at the kissing booth."

I laughed.

"Shut up. It's not funny," she said. "I'm so embarrassed."

"There's nothing to be embarrassed about."

"Isn't there? Because him buying all the tickets wasn't even the worst part. Did you see the way he was dressed?"

I slowly shook my head. I'd been so caught up in their argument I hadn't noticed what he was wearing. "No, how is he dressed?"

"He's dressed as Draco Malfoy," she said. Her eyes were wide, and I could see she was fighting some kind of internal battle. "And you know how I feel about Draco..."

"Like you want him to *slither-in?*" Amber guessed.

"Ha, that's a good one, and exactly," Anna said. "Man, my head is so messed up with all this. How did he even know I'm obsessed with Malfoy? I swear, he dressed up that way because he knew it would get me all confused."

"So, you're feeling confused about Luther?" I asked.

"No!" She shuddered. "Please let's just pretend this conversation never happened. I'm planning to wipe this entire night from my mind."

"Okay, from now on, this conversation never happened," I agreed.

"Good." She drew in a deep breath, which seemed to calm her.

"Why couldn't Luther have just kissed my hand instead?"

"I thought you didn't want to talk about him," I said.

"I don't," Anna gasped. "I need to get away from here. What are you guys up to?"

"We were just on our way to see the highlight of the carnival," Amber said. "The soccer team's dunking booth. That should help take your mind off the kissing booth."

"Perfect," Anna said. "Lead the way."

A large crowd had already formed around the dunking booth by the time we got there. Most of them were girls. Amber wasn't the only one with the bright idea of standing around watching shirtless soccer players waiting to get dunked.

"They should really charge to watch," Anna said. "They'd make a killing."

"I know," Amber agreed. "I'd probably pay."

I laughed because the two girls were hopeless. But, when I saw Noah sitting on the collapsing seat, waiting to be dunked, I didn't find it all so funny. Somehow, I'd forgotten just how gorgeous he was, but it was impossible to deny when he was sitting there in all his shirtless glory.

The crowd was wolf whistling him and cheering as people took turns throwing a ball at the target. A direct hit would plunge Noah into the water. As he sat there, watching balls fly at the target, he was smiling along with everyone else. It felt like such a long time since I'd seen him smile that way. It might have been as long ago as the beach in Rapid Bay, when he flew me home to see my mom. Or maybe as we danced at the White Ball.

"I can't believe you've kissed him." I turned to find Veronica walking past us. She was with one of her friends, who was talking far too loudly to her. "Noah is so hot."

Veronica's eyes narrowed on the girl. "Sylvie, you're staring...."

Sylvie stopped talking and looked a little embarrassed, but Veronica didn't notice because her focus was also on Noah as she gave him a small wave.

"Did Veronica come dressed as Paris Hilton?" Amber asked. I was guessing she'd heard Sylvie's comment about Noah too.

"Looks like it," I said. Veronica was dressed in a pink Juicy Couture velour tracksuit with a long blonde wig. She even had a small, yapping dog in the purse she wore over her shoulder.

"If she was going to use a dog as an accessory, I would have thought she'd come as Cruella de Vil," Anna said, making us laugh.

A huge cheer erupted from the crowd, and we turned back to the booth just in time to see Noah dropping into the tank of water. The guy who had struck the target bowed with pride, and the applause increased, especially from the girls in the front row, when Noah emerged from the water dripping wet.

Veronica was the first one over to him, and she offered him a towel. It was harder to watch than I thought it would be. Noah had told me before he wasn't interested in her, but I wasn't sure if that was true when I saw him thank her and they shared a smile.

"Well, I think I've had enough shirtless fun for one evening. I'm going to go find my mom," I said to the girls. "I'll catch you all later."

I didn't stick around to see what else Noah and Veronica might share.

CHAPTER THIRTY-TWO

I wandered the carnival, checking out the different stands as I waited for my mom to text me back. It took her a while, and when she finally got back to me, it was to say that she and Matthew were just finishing up ice-skating. They were planning to go to the jack-o'-lantern village next, and she suggested I meet them there.

My eyebrows lifted, and I scanned the text message again to check I'd read it correctly. Ice-skating and a candlelit pumpkin village? It almost sounded like they were on a date. A date I was totally going to gate-crash if I met up with them like I had planned. I might have considered leaving them alone, but I did want to spend some time with my mom tonight.

I'd seen the jack-o-lantern village when I'd first arrived at the carnival. It was positioned at the edge of the forest on the other side of the makeshift parking lot that had been set up in one of the fields. There was a path that followed alongside the driveway to reach it, but cutting through the parking lot would take half the time, so that's the route I took.

It seemed so much quieter among the cars as the sounds of the carnival became muted in the distance. I wasn't sure why they'd set up the pumpkin carvings so far from the rest of the event, but I was guessing it was to create a spooky atmosphere. The carnival was so loud and bright it would probably ruin the creepy glow of the candlelit pumpkins.

I was almost to the other end of the parking lot and could see the entrance to the village of jack-o'-lanterns up ahead when a man came around the side of one of the cars. He'd appeared out of nowhere, and we almost collided.

"Sorry!" I gasped as I stumbled back to avoid plowing into him.

The man grunted in response, and as I lifted my eyes to look at his face, I froze. I was looking into the cruel green eyes of Noah's grandfather.

"Watch where you're going," he barked. My heart was in my throat as he looked down at me. He didn't seem to recognize me at first, but then something in his eyes flared. His expression turned dark, and his upper lip seemed to curl as he eyed my waitress costume.

"Ah, Matthew LaFleur's bastard daughter," he said.

The blood drained from my face at his words. "Excuse me?" I choked out. I couldn't believe he'd called me that. Who the hell did this guy think he was?

"I was hoping never to see your face again," he continued. "But now that I've had the misfortune of running into you, I've got a message for your father."

He was either oblivious to the fact he'd insulted me or, more likely, he simply did not care. I was still too stunned to move or speak.

"Tell LaFleur to back down. If he thinks I'm going to sit back and do nothing while he throws another lawsuit at me, he's got another thing coming."

"I—I don't know what you're talking about."

"Of course, you don't." He pointed a finger at me and stepped closer, towering over me. "Just tell your father. Make sure he understands that he isn't the only one with the power to make other people's lives difficult. You tell him that if he continues to try and take me down with legal action, I will make your life at Weybridge Academy extremely unpleasant."

I took a step back from him, giving myself a bit of space to breathe, and managed to stammer out a response. "Are you threatening me?"

"It's just a friendly warning." A slow, hateful smile formed on his lips. "You'll know when I'm threatening you, girl."

"Grandfather!"

I turned as Noah stormed up behind me. His hair was still wet from being dunked in the tank at the soccer team's booth, and he pushed the damp strands that hung across his face aside as he came to stand between his grandfather and me.

"What are you doing?" Noah growled at his grandfather. He hadn't so much as looked my way, but it was clear he'd overheard William's threats. "Is this why you wanted me to meet you out here? So, I could watch you threaten Isobel?"

His body was practically shaking in anger, and it seemed like William had finally pushed his grandson too far. Was Noah actually going to fight for me? For us?

William's eyes narrowed as he looked between Noah and me. A vein seemed to pulse in his forehead as his gaze eventually settled on his grandson. "How could you still have a soft spot for this LaFleur girl after everything that we've been through because of them?"

My heart was racing as I looked at Noah. I wasn't sure what would be worse—if Noah declared his love for me or said I didn't matter to him at all. William was clearly trying to elicit an emotional response from him, and Noah looked torn as he returned his grandfather's hard stare.

Only a handful of seconds passed, but they stretched out painfully long as I waited for Noah to say something—anything.

When he finally released a breath, all the fight seemed to leave his body with it.

"I don't," he muttered.

It was the right thing for Noah to say. We were over, and it wasn't worth messing up his relationship with his grandfather because of me. It still hurt. I stupidly thought he'd finally grown strong enough to stand up to William.

"You told me you were over her," William replied, clearly not satisfied with Noah's answer. "Were you lying to me?"

Noah straightened as he stared his grandfather down. "I wasn't lying."

"I. Don't. Believe. You."

I wanted to disappear into the mud beneath my feet. I wanted to be anywhere but here. Not only had Noah's grandfather threatened me, but he was now grilling my ex-boyfriend about his feelings for me.

As if this moment couldn't get any worse, I spotted my father at the other end of the parking lot. He must have sensed my eyes on him because he looked at me and smiled. But when he saw who I was with, his expression turned, and he started stalking toward us. Thankfully, I couldn't see my mom anywhere.

"What's going on? Isobel, are you okay?" Matthew demanded as he approached. Concern lit his features, and he reached out and gripped my arm. He was standing far closer than normal, and from the way he positioned his body between William, Noah, and me, I could tell he was trying to be protective.

He only let go of me when I nodded. "I'm fine."

"Are you sure?"

"Yes, I'm sure." I sent Noah's grandfather a sharp look. "William was just letting me know what can happen when you get on the wrong side of a Hastings."

Ever so slowly, Matthew's eyes hardened, and he squared his shoulders as he faced William Hastings. Even without the fake blood splattered on his face, my father would have looked fierce as he glared at the man who had caused our family so much pain.

"Threatening my daughter in a darkened parking lot, William? And I thought you could sink no lower." I had no idea how Matthew managed to keep his voice so calm but also sound so powerful. His tone only carried a hint of his tightly coiled rage, and the worry that had been evident in his words just moments ago was nowhere to be seen.

"I was simply reminding her to keep her distance from my grandson. They both appear to have forgotten..."

"We haven't forgotten," Noah said.

"We broke up just like you all wanted," I added, anger pulsing through my veins. "Isn't that enough?"

"No, it's not." William spat. "I wouldn't be satisfied if you were in a school on the other side of the world. And even that wouldn't be far enough."

"Watch your tone with my daughter," Matthew ordered.

"Why? So she thinks I'll just stand by while she ensnares my grandson the same way your sister did my son?"

Don't you dare mention my sister."

The tension and anger between them was almost unbearable, and as I glanced at Noah, I could see he was struggling with it just as much as I was. This all needed to stop.

"Can't we just put the past behind us?" I shouted over them.

Matthew and William both turned to face me.

"Seriously." I focused mostly on my father. "You said you tried to work things out with Noah's dad before. Maybe we can try again now?"

A flicker of concern shot through Matthew's eyes, and he glanced at Noah. For a second, they shared a look, but I had no idea what they communicated in that fleeting moment.

"What's she talking about?" William's voice was low and filled with so much ice it rivaled the chill in the air.

My father's expression turned just as cold as he faced Noah's grandfather. "I've got no idea. She must be confused because I would never try to mend things with a Hastings. Especially not Liam."

"What do you mean by that?" Noah asked. He'd gone completely rigid, and I gave Matthew a worried look. Why was he pretending he hadn't tried to fix the feud? Surely, he knew to tread lightly where Noah's father was concerned?

Matthew seemed completely oblivious to the fact Noah had gone lethally still.

"I mean that your father was the worst of you. He was a liar, a fraud and a cheater who got my sister and himself killed—" Matthew didn't get a chance to finish as Noah's fist came swinging through the air.

"Noah!" I screamed. But my alarm did nothing to stop him.

Matthew's head cracked back as Noah's fist connected with his cheek. He stumbled away, his hand clinging to his face as he stared at Noah in horror.

I ran to my father's side, grabbing hold of him as I turned to glare at Noah. "What the hell is wrong with you?" I yelled before turning to my dad. "Matthew, are you okay?"

He slowly nodded, but he had to be in pain. His cheek was turning red, and I had no doubt it was going to bruise. What on earth had Noah been thinking? And why had Matthew felt the need to taunt him about his dad? Matthew was clearly on edge after finding me alone out here with William and Noah, but I'd never seen him lose his cool that way before.

Matthew gave Noah a tight smile. "You'll be hearing from my lawyer. Come on, Isobel."

Matthew placed a hand on my lower back, and I let him lead me away. I was too shocked to put up any complaint. I couldn't believe what had just happened. I'd thought Noah and I were in a more civil place, that maybe we could rise above the conflict between our families, even if we weren't going to be together. Any hope I'd harbored that we could both somehow stay out of it had been completely torn apart the moment his fist had come flying toward my father.

I glanced over my shoulder at Noah and his grandfather. Noah was still brimming with barely leashed anger as he stared after us. His eyes were hard, and his mouth formed an unforgiving line. I could tell he was still livid about the way Matthew had insulted his father. But that didn't excuse his actions, and I found I had no sympathy for him.

William's demeanor couldn't have been more different. There was a pleased look in his eyes as he watched us leave. Somehow, it felt like he had just won. And I hated him a little more for that.

"Oh my gosh, Matthew!" Mom cried out as we neared the candle-lit pumpkins.

She was waiting by the entrance to the jack-o'-lantern village, and she rushed over to us when she caught sight of Matthew cradling his cheek, his eyes scrunched in pain. The bright red mark was looking worse. He was probably lucky it wasn't bleeding.

Mom hurried toward us. She reached out a hand to Matthew's cheek but quickly dropped her arm to her side. "That's not fake, is it?"

"No," he grunted. "I wish."

"I go to the bathroom for two minutes, and you get in a fight?" Her eyes were wide with confusion. "What happened?"

Matthew glanced at me as both of us hesitated. I didn't want to explain what had happened with Noah. It hurt my heart too much. I'd known he was on his grandfather's side in all this. I'd been well aware that he would always choose the Hastings over me. But when I saw him punch my dad to defend his family, I finally realized I'd never even had a chance with him. Not in a relationship. Not as a friend. He would always choose them.

"Somebody better tell me what happened..." Mom said.

I knew there was no way she was going to let this go, so I

answered as briefly as possible. "Let's just say Noah and I will never be getting back together."

"Noah did this?" Mom gasped.

She looked like she had a million more questions, so I headed them off before she got a chance to start firing them at me. "Can we talk about it later?" I said. "Maybe when there aren't so many other people around? I think we just need to get Matthew some ice for his face."

Mom looked around, finally realizing she wasn't the only one who'd noticed Matthew cradling his cheek. There were several other students and their parents giving him strange looks.

"Okay, we'll talk about it later," she said as she turned her attention back to us. There was a sense of promise in her tone, and I knew she'd be wanting every detail. "Now, I'm sure we can get some ice from around here somewhere."

"I think I'd just like to go home," Matthew said.

"You're right, maybe we should call it a night," Mom replied.

It was still so early, and the thought of missing the rest of the carnival made me sad. I couldn't imagine staying though. Not after what had just happened. There had been way too much drama for one night for my liking, and I didn't want to risk sticking around and potentially seeing Noah or his grandfather again.

"Yeah, I think I'm ready to go," I agreed.

"Give me your keys, Matt, I'll go get your car," Mom said.

He pulled them from his pocket without complaint and handed them to my mom. I imagined he didn't feel up to driving right now.

"You two wait here for me," she said. "I'll be right back."

Mom hated feeling powerless in situations like this, and I had no doubt that getting the car as quickly as possible was her way of feeling useful.

As soon as she was out of earshot, Matthew turned to me.

"I'm sorry about what just happened," he said. "I didn't mean to upset Noah."

"I mean, you probably shouldn't have said those things about his dad, but if anyone should be apologizing, it's him," I replied. "I can't believe he hit you."

"I deserved it for bringing up his father that way. I was really just angry at William. He shouldn't have threatened you."

"I was okay," I murmured. "And you didn't deserve to get hit. Violence is never the answer." I glanced up at his cheek and caught him wincing as he went to touch it. "Does it hurt much?"

"It's not too bad," he admitted. "I'm sure it will feel much better once I've iced it."

"I hope so."

We waited in silence for my mom to return. The car mustn't have been parked too far because she pulled up and ushered us into the vehicle after only a few minutes.

As she drove us back to Matthew's mansion, I couldn't stop looking at the mark on his cheek. The bruise was such a small thing. Within a few days, it would fade and the pain would be forgotten. But it felt so much bigger than that. It was yet another painful scar etched into the history of my family and Noah's family. A mark that would only fester and grow worse as the years went by.

Deep down, I guess I'd always known there was no fixing the rift between us. It felt like our families were inextricably pulled together and yet doomed to always fall apart. We were caught in some never-ending spiral of pain and hurt. And when Noah had thrown that punch, he hadn't just shattered whatever tenuous harmony there was between us. He'd cemented that rage in my own heart. I wasn't just angry with him. I hated him. And I didn't think it was possible to ever come back from that.

EPILOGUE

Noah

It was well after midnight as I slowly drove my car down Matthew LaFleur's tree-lined driveway. I was probably crazy for coming here tonight, but I couldn't sleep after what had happened this evening. The ache across my knuckles was a constant reminder of the punch I'd thrown, and I had to make sure everything was okay.

The hurt in Isobel's eyes as she stared at me was going to haunt me long after the pain in my hand went away. I wasn't sure she'd ever be able to understand my reasoning. And I was quite certain she would never forgive me for hurting her father that way.

My grandfather couldn't have been more pleased though. All night, he had been patting me across the shoulders and commenting on how my father would have been proud. Clearly, William didn't know my father at all because I knew he would have been disappointed at the idea of me punching anyone.

I parked under the shadow of a tree a short walk from the mansion and snuck around the back to enter the house through the kitchens. It was so risky to be here, and if I was caught, everything would be ruined. But the house was asleep, and I'd been told it would be safe.

The back door to the kitchen opened as I approached.

"I thought you'd get here sooner."

My heart froze, only to relax again as the dim light of the kitchen flicked on to reveal Matthew LaFleur.

"Sorry," I murmured. "I got away as quickly as I could."

Matthew stood back and gestured for me to enter the house, and as I passed him, I saw he was holding an ice pack. I glanced up at his cheek and grimaced.

"Sorry about that." I nodded to the bruise that was still forming.

Matthew waved my apology away. "It was necessary." He drew in a breath. "And I'm sorry for what I said about your father. You know I didn't mean any of it, right?"

"I know. Still, I wish it hadn't come to that. I panicked when Isobel started talking about how you, my dad, and your sister and tried to fix things. How did she know about that?"

"That was my fault." Matthew shook his head. "I shouldn't have told Isobel about them. Especially with what we're trying to do... I just didn't think it would cause any harm to let her know."

"No, you couldn't have known she'd bring it up in front of my grandfather." I sighed. Tonight had been a disaster, but at least it hadn't been completely pointless. "One positive thing has come from punching you. William's confident I'm on his side."

"Good."

"He's still not convinced I don't have feelings for Isobel though." I'd been stupid to rush to her defense tonight. But when I first saw her standing before my grandfather and heard him throwing thinly veiled threats her way, I hadn't been able to stop myself. I'd acted without thinking, and now Isobel wasn't just a weapon he could use against Matthew. She was one he could use against me too.

"So, convince him," Matthew replied.

I let out a laugh. "Yeah, because that's so easy."

"I didn't say it will be easy," Matthew said. "But it is necessary. He can't suspect you have any sympathy for my family. And if it comes to it, you know he'll try to use her against you."

"I know," I growled. "But what do I do?"

"You suck it up and act like she's the enemy your grandfather thinks she is," Matthew said.

"If we could just tell her what's going on..."

Matthew shook his head. "It could put her in more danger. I don't trust William Hastings, and the less Isobel knows, the better. We saw that firsthand tonight."

I nodded. If keeping Isobel in the dark afforded her even a small amount of protection from my grandfather, I would do it. It didn't make any of this any easier though.

"She's moving on," I murmured. "She might never forgive me."

Matthew gave me a sad smile. "It's a risk you have to take. If you ever want to be with her, this is the only way."

"I know." It still pained me to admit it out loud. "I should go. I just wanted to check we were on the same page after everything that happened. Sorry again for hitting you."

"You did well to think so quickly on your feet, and besides, I look like a badass now."

I chuckled under my breath. I'd never heard someone sound so posh while saying the word badass before. It totally defeated the purpose. "Totally badass," I agreed.

We both went silent as the sound of creaking floorboards echoed from above.

"Go," Matthew hissed, reaching for the door to let me out. "Isobel and her mother are staying here tonight. They can't know you were here."

I rushed out the door, but Matthew kept it open a crack as he went to close it. "Just keep to the plan we talked about at my office," Matthew whispered. "It's all going to work out, I promise."

"I know."

He gave me a tight smile before he closed the door and quickly turned to face whoever had entered the room.

"Matthew?" The sound of Isobel's voice struck my heart, and I quickly darted down behind the kitchen window so I couldn't be seen through the glass kitchen door. Matthew was right; she couldn't know I was here.

"Is everything all right?" she asked.

"Fine," he said. "I couldn't sleep, so I'm just getting some more ice for my face."

I slowly edged myself up to catch a glimpse of Isobel, and I smiled when I saw she was in the cute Winnie the Pooh pajamas she'd worn in New York. Her curly hair was piled in a bun on her head, and she wasn't wearing any makeup. I had no idea how someone could look so beautiful, and it killed me that I couldn't walk in there and say as much to her.

"I couldn't sleep either," she said, her voice soft.

I wanted to stay and find out why she couldn't sleep. I didn't get to hear her voice nearly enough anymore. I couldn't risk getting caught at Matthew's house though. Not when everything we had planned hinged on no one knowing we were working together.

With a sigh, I started back to my car. I had a tough road ahead of me. Not only did I have to keep my feelings for Isobel a secret, I somehow had to convince my grandfather they didn't exist at all. William Hastings wouldn't be satisfied with simple indifference though. No, I was going to have to go further than that. I was going to have to convince him I hated her.

Matthew and I had a solid plan, and I felt confident everything was going to work. But I had a bad feeling I would hate myself by the end of this. I was going to move heaven and earth for Isobel, but I was afraid by the time I had it would already be too late.

The story concludes in book 3: Sweet Ruin

ABOUT THE AUTHOR

Alexandra Moody is an Australian author who writes romance novels for young adults. She lives in Adelaide with her husband, son and their naughty dog. When she's not busy writing, you'll find her reading or spending time with her family. She loves to travel, is addicted to caffeine and has a love/hate relationship with the gym.

For more information, visit: www.alexandramoody.com or follow Alexandra on Instagram or TikTok: @amoodyauthor

ALSO BY ALEXANDRA MOODY

Weybridge Academy

Sweet Heartbreak

Sweet Temptation

Sweet Ruin

The Wrong Match Series

The Wrong Bachelor

The Wrong Costar

The Wrong Prom Date

Stand-alone books

I Hate You More

Stuck with You

Christmas Magic Series

Christmas Magic

Christmas Chaos

Christmas Curse

The Liftsal Guardians Series

The Liftsal Guardians

The Brakys' Lair

The Oblivion Stone

The Rift War

Made in the USA
Middletown, DE
25 September 2023

39368319R00220